Ralph Beamer holds a Master of Science in chemistry from Texas A&M University and worked in the petroleum industry for more than thirty years. He has a keen interest in alternate energy solutions and spends several hours a week scanning articles and technical papers for ideas. He grew up in the mid-west, has lived in seven different states, and currently resides in north-central Georgia.

The Nelson Project

Ralph Beamer

The Nelson Project

Vanguard Press

Vanguard Press is an imprint of
Pegasus Elliot Mackenzie Publishers Ltd.
www.pegasuspublishers.com

First Published in 2024

Vanguard Press
Sheraton House Castle Park
Cambridge England

Printed & Bound in Great Britain

Prologue

The snow had stopped when the plane touched down. Outside, temperatures were falling, and a sharp wind swept across the runway. As it turned to taxi, Melvin Richards exhaled in resignation. *Thank God! It's about time.* He'd spent most of the ninety-minute flight searching for a comfortable position. *I hate window seats.*

"Welcome to Billings," said the flight attendant. "The local time is twelve minutes past three, and the temperature is a balmy eight degrees below zero. Please remain seated until the plane is parked at the gate and the pilot has turned off the 'Fasten Seat Belt' sign."

Melvin relaxed as best he could and switched on his cell phone. Seconds later, it was vibrating— the first message was about work, and the second was from Sharon.

He opened the first.
Melvin:

Text me when you land, things have changed. Don't come to the office trailer, meet me at Lucky's instead. Don't stop anywhere—just come straight to Lucky's.
Dan

Why Lucky's? His eyes narrowed. Everything's going so well. The plant is up and running ahead of schedule. Nugent is happy...

Through his window, he saw the jetway roll up to the door. The operator was dressed for the weather, but his breath was clearly visible in the frigid air.

Oh well, at least I'll get a good lunch. Robin makes a mean bison burger!

The second message brought a smile to his face:

Hi Mel,

I hope the trip goes well. I am truly bummed that you have to be gone tonight. I miss you.

And by the way, thanks for the roses. You know I love them—they are so beautiful! What a nice surprise! Check it out…

Fingers crossed for the promotion.

Love ya,

Sharon

She included a selfie with the flowers, so he zoomed in for a better look.

Wow, they look great!

He responded:

Hi babe,

I miss you too.

I had a hunch you might like them.

Love the pic. I'll see you tomorrow night.

Gotta run now, more later.

Love ya,

Mel

He glanced at his watch and responded to the other text:

Dan:

I just landed. A bit on the mysterious side. What's changed?

I'll be at Lucky's at about 4:30. See you there.

Melvin

He angled his body out of the seat and ducked to stand. *Ugh! I wish I could fly first class. These seats were not built for people like me.* He retrieved his backpack from the overhead bin, inserted his laptop, and proceeded down the jetway. When he reached the rental car desk, the agent was standing with her back to the counter.

"Reservation for Richards," he said.

At the sound of his voice, the agent straightened up, smoothed her uniform jacket, and turned with a beaming smile. "Ah, Mr. Richards, we've missed you. Planning to stay the week, as usual?"

His face brightened. "Hi Meagan, it's been a while. Are you doing okay?" He placed his credit card and driver's license on the counter.

"I'm fine, thanks. How long has it been, Melvin? It seems like months." He was at least a foot taller, so she had to tilt her head back to see his face.

"We've been working on a new project in South Dakota."

"Does that mean you won't be coming to Billings any more?" She frowned, and her eyes dropped a bit.

"Not as much, I guess, but I'll be back once in a while. You know, to check on things."

Her smile returned. "That's good to know, I'm glad..." She scanned his license and credit card, returned them, and then selected an envelope from her left.

"Well, anyway, I have your portfolio ready. It's a red Malibu this time, Spot 112."

He took the envelope and read the tag on the key bob. "Chevy Malibu? What happened to my SUV?"

"Sorry, it's all we have at the moment."

"But I reserved an SUV. What do you mean, 'it's all you have'?"

"I know, I know... you need the headroom." She glanced up at his wavy hair. "But we just don't have any this afternoon."

He looked again at the key bob and shook his head.

"We have three due back in a couple of hours if you'd like to wait."

He considered that for a moment... "No, I can't. I have to get out to Broadview. The Malibu will be okay, I guess."

She lowered her head slightly, "I'm really sorry, Melvin."

"It's okay, forget it. Besides, it's not that far, and it's only for one day." He picked up his backpack and turned to leave. "Thanks. I'll see you in the morning."

She rose to her tiptoes and leaned over the counter as he walked away. "Okay, then, until tomorrow..."

A few minutes later, he was in the Malibu, driving out of the airport. At the roundabout, he turned west on Route 3, a scenic drive along The Rims, some five hundred feet above the city.

He looked forward to this part of the trip. The view could be amazing, and people would often park at the overlooks to take pictures.

But there were no lookers on that day. More than a foot of new snow had fallen, and the guardrails along the cliff were all but buried. He turned his attention back to the road, selected a country-western playlist, and settled in for the ride.

After Zimmerman Park, the road curved north, and the wind was stronger—a steady stream of dry powder blew across the highway. But it was dry, so he set the cruise control at sixty-two miles per hour.

About twenty minutes later, he passed the 'Welcome to Broadview' sign. He tapped the brakes, slowed down, and turned into 'Lucky's Bar & Grill'. The gravel lot was covered with a thick layer of packed snow, and his tires made a muffled crunching sound as they rolled to a stop.

As he stepped out, a swirling gust greeted him. It was icy on his neck, so he pulled his collar tight, grabbed his laptop, and jogged to the door. Once inside, he stomped his feet a couple of times to knock off the snow—Robin James was tending the bar.

"Well, as I live and breathe, if it isn't Mr. Melvin Richards! How the hell are ya?"

"Hi Robin, I'm doing fine. And you?"

"Oh, you know, just working along. I understand we got a little snow today."

"Oh really? I hadn't noticed." He unzipped his jacket.

"So, what's your poison this fine afternoon?" she said.

"I think maybe a light beer and a bison burger."

"Coming right up!"

"Have you seen Dan? He was supposed to meet me."

"Not today, sweetie. Not yet, anyway."

She swept her hand toward the dining area. "Grab a table, and I'll fetch ya that beer."

Melvin walked toward the back and sat near the slot machines. Robin was right behind him.

"Your burger will be out in a few minutes, Hon, just the way ya like it, extra onions and no tomato."

He nodded. "Thanks, Robin, and maybe a little cheddar cheese?"

"You got it."

It was the best place to eat in Broadview, and for him, it was like a second home—he'd spent a lot of time there during construction. The walls were polished knotty pine, the ceiling was white tile, and the floor was painted concrete. Across from the bar were a jukebox and two slot machines. He especially liked the framed picture of Lake Zurich that Robin snapped during her last trip to Europe.

She walked up and smiled. "Here's your burger, Hon. If ya want anything else, just let me know. It's really nice to see ya again." She touched his shoulder and then walked back to the bar.

***

Fifteen minutes later, the burger was history, and his beer was nearly gone. He was about to order another when the front door opened, and Dan Turner stepped through.

Dan was the Broadview Plant Manager. He was about five feet eight inches tall and built like a wrestler. He wore a green camouflage parka with a fur-lined hood and matching winter boots. His face, barely visible inside the oversized hood, sported a toothy grin and a bushy red mustache. He stepped to the bar, said something to Robin, and then turned toward Melvin.

"Hey, Melvin!" He raised his left hand.

"Hey. Want a beer?"

"Thanks, but not right now."

He pulled out a chair on the other side of the table and sat down.

"I'm glad you made it. I see you had your lunch already—you really love those burgers. Was the trip okay?"

"Oh, you know, like any other, just fine. At least until I got to the rental car desk."

Dan said nothing.

"There were no SUVs in the lot, so they stuck me with a dinky Malibu."

"That red one in the parking lot? I'm surprised you could even get into that thing."

"Yeah, that's for sure. My head scrapes the ceiling, and there's no legroom," he said. "But it'll do for one night. My flight home leaves at noon tomorrow."

He took a sip of beer and paused for a moment. "So, what's all the mystery? How come you wanted to meet here instead of in your office?"

"No mystery," he smiled. "We don't need drawings this time, so I thought this might be more comfortable. And yes, we decided to cancel the wrap-up meeting."

"Okay, I'm confused. Why am I here, exactly? Your text said things have changed?"

"We'll get to that. But first things first," he said. "Do you have the Broadview Report?"

Melvin booted up his laptop and turned it so Dan could see the screen.

He scanned the report and scrolled through several pages. This looks just fine. "How about the backup?"

Melvin fished in his pocket and retrieved a thumb drive. "Here you go. Everything is there—equipment specifications, drawings, and all correspondence."

"Perfect." Dan looked up. "You know Melvin, you've done great work on this project. Really, first-class."

"I just did my job, like everyone else."

"No, you've done so much more. And Dr. Nugent and I would like to show our gratitude."

Melvin studied his face. "Gratitude?"

"Yes," he said. "We would like to give you a substantial raise and promote you to Senior Engineer."

"Really?"

"Yes. In fact, we already have. You should see the increase in your next paycheck."

Melvin's face went blank, and he sat motionless for a couple of seconds. "Really."

Dan nodded his head. "Really. So, what do you think?"

"Well, I'm not sure. I'm a bit surprised. I thought we were going to discuss the report and then move on to the Rapid City project. But I guess I would start by saying thank you, this is great news. And thank Dr. Nugent for me, too."

He straightened up in his chair and leaned forward. "But just for interest's sake, what do you mean when you say 'substantial'? I only ask because Sharon and I are thinking of getting married, and a little extra money would come in pretty handy."

Dan smiled. "Well, with the promotion and your excellent performance, we decided the raise should be about eighteen percent. That will put you about mid-way through the next pay bracket."

Melvin was stunned. "Eighteen percent? That's very generous." He lifted his mug and drained it. "She'll be thrilled."

"Did you say you're planning to get married?"

Melvin nodded.

"Congratulations," he said. "Have you set a date?"

"No, I haven't exactly asked her yet—I was planning to pop the question this weekend. But now, I might just move things up and do it tomorrow night."

He looked at his empty mug. "I need a refill."

Dan reached over and touched his arm. "You won't have time for a refill. You'll be leaving in a few minutes—that's the other thing that's changed."

"But I just got here!"

"I'm afraid you'll have to postpone your date with Sharon, too—we need you in Rapid City in the morning."

"Tomorrow morning?"

"I'm sorry. Really, I am. But Dr. Nugent has moved up the schedule and it has to be tomorrow. You fly out this evening."

"There are no more flights to Rapid City today. I know the schedule."

"That's not a problem. A jet will be waiting at the airport."

"A company jet?"

"Yes, a company jet. Nugent wants you there in the morning."

"Well, okay then, I guess. But still, I was supposed to be back in Denver tomorrow night... Come on, Dan. Can't we put it off until next week? A couple of days won't matter. You know that."

He leaned forward and put his elbows on the table. "Is there a problem, Mr. Richards?"

He was quiet for a moment. "No, I guess not." He paused. "There's no problem. I'll just text Sharon and let her know. I'm sure she'll understand." He reached for his phone.

"I'm afraid you can't use this phone. I need to keep it with me."

"What?"

"You know how Nugent is about security. There will be a new one waiting for you in Rapid City."

"But."

"You can call Sharon from the airport. I'm sorry." He picked up the phone. "The jet will be there in about two hours, but if you leave now, you'll have plenty of time. Park the Malibu at the general aviation terminal and leave the keys under the floormat—I'll have someone return it in the morning."

He put the thumb drive and cell phone in his breast pocket and pulled the zipper closed. "So, what are you waiting for, Senior Engineer? Get moving." He nodded his head and looked at the door. "Don't just sit there…"

Melvin glanced around and checked his watch. He reached for his wallet.

"Don't worry about the check. I'll take care of it."

"Well, okay then, I guess. Thanks again." He reached over and shook his hand. "I'll call you from Rapid City."

On the way out, he stopped briefly at the bar. "Thanks, Robin. It was great, as always."

"You are very welcome, Hon, and thanks for stopping in. You're missed around here, you know."

"I miss you too. But it might be a while before I can get back. Dan's sending me to South Dakota."

She frowned a little. "Well, I'm sorry to hear that, but safe travels. And just so you know, I did manage to catch a bit of your conversation."

Melvin looked at her expectantly. "Oh, yeah?"

She glanced briefly toward Dan and then turned back with a smile, "Congrats on the promotion!"

***

Outside is was bitterly cold, but Melvin barely noticed. And for some reason, the Malibu seemed almost roomy. He turned south on Route 3 and started for the airport…

Sharon will be so excited—a promotion, a raise, a new project. There are so many things to consider…

A thousand details began to flash through his mind…

Where should we go to pop the question? Somewhere romantic, with a view of the Rockies, maybe. Or should it be elegant? Like the Rose Trellis, perhaps—candlelight, white table cloths, flowers… And where should we get married? Will we stay in Denver? Maybe we'll move to Rapid City…

Before he knew it, he had passed Zimmerman Park and was through the roundabout.

The view from The Rims was spectacular. The sun was just setting, and the western sky was a brilliant tableau of crimson and pink.

It will be dark soon. The air's so clear!

To his left, a plane was lifting off. He watched it climb for a few seconds. Its landing gear retracted as it gained altitude.

Suddenly, there was a pop, like a shotgun in the distance. And then, from nowhere, a massive farm tractor appeared in front of him. It was just sitting there—right in the middle of the road!

He snapped out of his trance. *Where in the hell did that come from?* He stomped the brake pedal, but nothing happened. And for some reason, the pavement was covered with ice.

Ice! There shouldn't be any ice… I'm going to hit it! Is there enough room on the right?—I'll swerve into the overlook.

He cranked the wheel to the right to miss the tractor, and then there were three more pops. His front tire was shredded, his accelerator was jammed to the floor, and a small tear appeared in the bottom of his fuel tank.

The car sped up, and the missing tire caused it to lurch further to the right. Melvin tried to correct, but momentum was in control. And like the road, the overlook too was a glaze of ice.

Why is it so icy? It was dry as a bone all the way down. The overlook is loose gravel—it should help me slow down. If I can glance off the berm, I'll be back on the pavement.

He cranked hard to the left, but the drag from the damaged wheel pulled him toward the cliff. He put both feet on the brake pedal and pulled on the emergency brake—nothing. It was hopeless. Finally, the car plowed through the snow berm and shattered the guardrail. The car was going fifty miles per hour when it reached the edge.

Once airborne, the front of the car dropped quickly and began rotating end over end. Inside, Melvin's seat belt kept his body in place and he braced against the ceiling and dashboard—but there could be only one result.

Did I just drive off a cliff? How did that happen? It was perfectly dry! And what were those popping sounds? Gunshots? No, more like firecrackers...

Oh my God, I'm going to crash—

In an instant, his mind was back at the university, and he was sitting in a physics class. The professor was drawing arcs on the chalkboard while discussing ballistic trajectories, velocity, altitude, and gravitational acceleration...

I wonder how long I'll be in the air...

Sharon. My darling Sharon, I wish—

In five and a half seconds, the Chevy Malibu flew more than four hundred feet from the edge of the cliff. It arced downward and crashed, upside down, at a bone-crushing speed of one hundred thirty-two miles per hour. The effect was catastrophic.

Melvin was killed instantly, and the car was reduced to thirty-one hundred pounds of twisted scrap metal. On impact, the fuel tank split wide open, and a large pool of gasoline formed beneath the wreckage.

Fifteen seconds later, there was a fifth pop. The resulting fireball reached hundreds of feet in the air, and a thick column of black smoke rose high above the cliff.

***

Up on the road, the farm tractor pulled slowly into the overlook and stopped. The driver leaned out and peered down at the wreckage. He chuckled softly as heat from the flames warmed his face. "Good job," he said to himself. "Excellent!"

Then without further expression, he removed his right glove and composed a short text message:

MR complete.

Chapter 1

The cell phone vibrated incessantly, and the glass tabletop magnified the sound. Two feet way, Jack Nelson stirred. He had been out late, and his body was in no mood to respond. But the humming and rattling persisted.

Mercifully, after several moments, it stopped. He relaxed and settled back to his sleeping position. Then, seconds later, it started again.

What is that? Make it stop! He groaned and rolled toward the source. *Who in the hell can be calling at this hour?*

He picked up the phone and swiped the answer button. "Yeah, what do you want?"

"Hey, boss, thank God. I thought you'd never answer. I need your help."

"Huh? Who is this?"

"Wake up, Jack. We've got a real problem out here."

The clock read five minutes past four. He snapped on the light and tried to concentrate. "Luis, is that you? Do you know it's four o'clock in the morning?"

"Yeah, I know, Jack. I'm sorry. But you have to get out here."

"Whatever it is, I trust you. Just go ahead and fix it—we can talk about it later. Besides, I had a very late night…"

"No, Jack. I wouldn't call if it wasn't important."

He threw back the cover, swung his legs out, and sat up. "Okay, slow down. Can you give me a hint?" He shook his head and tried to concentrate.

"Well, it's hard to explain exactly. It's the crude. It's changing. It's getting really thick."

"I don't understand. Just slow the pump down a little. It will be fine."

"This isn't my first day, Jack. I already tried that, and it's not working. It's getting worse. Come as soon as you can."

He paused for a moment. *Luis never calls…*

He took another look at the clock, dropped his head, and exhaled. "Okay, Luis, you win. Grab me a couple of samples, and I'll be right out. It'll be about thirty minutes."

***

It was nearly five before Jack got to the loading rack. As he stepped out of his pickup, he was struck by the utter silence. A dense fog hung in the air, and the tanker truck parked under the canopy was barely visible. Its engine was shut down, and the loading pump was not running.

A light was visible in the operator's shack, so he headed in that direction—Luis' radio was playing quietly. He stepped over a loading hose and entered the shack.

He was sitting at his desk with his feet propped up on a five-gallon bucket. He turned down the music as Jack entered.

"What's going on? Why are you just sitting there? Why is everything shut down?"

"There was nothing I could do. I had to shut down. I thought you'd be here sooner." He pointed at two samples next to the door. "Take a look at those."

Jack bent down, picked up one of the bottles, and held it to the light. "It is almost black," he said.

"Give it a shake," said Luis.

He shook the bottle, but the fluid inside did not move, "Strange," he said. He pointed at the desk. "Hand me a pencil."

Luis retrieved one from the top drawer and gave it to him. Jack unscrewed the cap, and sniffed its contents. "It smells funky," he said. He stuck the pencil inside to probe the contents. "It is very thick, almost solid."

"Right, just like I said. It happened about five minutes after we hung up. The flow got slower and slower, and then it stopped altogether. I tried a restart, but the pump was completely seized. I've never seen anything like it." He paused for a moment and then looked directly at Jack. "What should we do?"

"I'm not sure. Is it all like this?"

"Yep, all of it," he said. "The pump has seized, and the whole system is locked up. The oil in the truck is solid too, and so is the oil in the tank."

"The tank too?" Jack set the bottle back on the floor and headed out. "Grab your flashlight and the gauge tape. I need to see this."

Outside, he gave the loading hose a kick with his foot—it felt like concrete. They spent a few minutes checking things over and then walked out to the tank. When they reached the top, Luis opened the hatch.

"Take a look. You won't believe it."

Jack took the gauge tape from Luis and dropped the weighted end into the tank. Expecting a slight splash and ripple as it sank into the oil, he was rewarded instead with a dull thud. He took the flashlight from Luis, dropped to his knees, and peered inside. "The gauge weight is lying sideways on top of the oil," he said. "How is that possible?"

Luis just stood there.

"What about the other tank? Did you check it?"

"I took a look before you got here. Whatever happened, it started in this tank and then got pumped into the system."

"Well, it's a good thing you took samples while it was still liquid."

"Yeah, I guess so," he said. "What are we going to do with them?"

Jack thought for a moment. "I'm not sure. I'm just not sure..." He looked into the tank again. "But I think we're going to need help."

Luis was standing next to him on the platform. "Tylor York?"

"Yeah, Tylor," he said. "I'll give him a call when I get back to the office. Maybe he can make some sense of it."

He rose from his crouched position and started down the stairs. "Pack up one of those samples, and I'll text you the address."

"No problem, I'll get it ready."

"Good," he said. "And while you're at it, grab one from 102 for reference... And get some photos."

"I'll get on it," said Luis. "What do you want to do about the truck? It is really messed up. It'll take weeks to get it back in operation."

"We'll deal with that later," he said. "For now, let's concentrate on getting the samples packed up. I'll go back to the office and make the call."

His watch read twenty minutes past six. "He should be awake soon." *What time is it in Georgia, anyway? And where did I put that cell phone number?*

***

19

A short time later, near Mowata, Louisiana, the sun was hot, and Sam Wilson was in the middle of his morning run. It was already eighty-five degrees, and the humidity was stifling. He was about to turn north on Hundley Road when James pulled up beside him.

"Hey, buddy, what's up?" His shirt was soaked with sweat, and he flapped it to get some air inside.

"Boy, am I glad I found you. I've been looking all over the place."

"I'm just out running. You know my route." He continued his pace and glanced at his brother.

"That doesn't matter right now. Just stop for a minute and listen." James applied his brakes, and Sam turned toward the truck.

He spoke rapidly, "I was just out at the patch. I can't believe it." His breathing was short and labored.

"Calm down. What's going on?"

"Well, it's all wrong. That's what it is. It's all wrong."

Sam wiped a bead of sweat from his forehead and stepped a little closer.

"The whole patch, Sam, it's all brown," he said. "All ten acres of it— completely dead."

He stood perfectly still for a moment and stared at the tread on the truck's left front tire. "What are you talking about? I was out there yesterday."

"I know. It looked fine yesterday, but today it's all dead. Get in."

The test patch was located along Gum Point Road, about three miles away—they were there in less than five minutes. James parked a few feet off the pavement, and they got out to inspect the damage.

Notched from a larger field, the test patch contained nearly one hundred thousand stalks of experimental sugarcane. It was a new drought and disease-resistant hybrid called W201 and was expected to revolutionize their rotation. They stepped in to take a closer look.

The plants were brown and desiccated from the ground up. The stalks were brittle, and the leaves crumbled at their touch. But the surrounding field looked perfectly normal—green, strong, and healthy.

"This can't be real. Yesterday, everything was great. W201 is supposed to be disease resistant. How could this happen in one day?"

"This was no disease, Sam. Look around you." He pivoted to survey the rest of the field and swept his hand from left to right as he turned. "A disease would have killed all of it."

"And the pattern is unmistakable. The damage follows a straight line around the perimeter of the patch, a perfect rectangle. Somebody wanted to kill the hybrid."

"But why? And for that matter, how could anybody even do this? Did they walk through the field in the middle of the night and spray? Even if you had a dozen people, it would take hours to do this," said Sam. "Ten acres is a lot of space if you're on foot."

"I don't know how it was done," he said. "But somebody sure as hell did it."

"But what can we do about it? We need this hybrid. Can we replant? This is going to set us back at least a year."

They continued to survey the damage.

"I wonder if the soil is damaged too. *Can* we even replant? Does that lab have enough hybrid on hand?"

"All good questions, my brother, and I don't have any answers at the moment. So, I guess the first thing we should do is give the sheriff a call. And then I think we need to get in touch with Karen. Maybe she'll have some ideas." He started for the truck. "Let's get going."

"Hold on a minute." Sam bent over and pulled up several dead stalks. "Let's ship her a few of these. It may help if she can see them first hand."

Chapter 2

Tylor York grew up in Two Harbors, Minnesota, a small town located along the north shore of Lake Superior. His father, Thomas, was a large-framed man with jet-black hair, and Tylor inherited both of those traits. His mother, Elizabeth, an attractive woman of petite stature, contributed her beautiful green eyes, straight white teeth, and gentle smile. They were no-nonsense, God-fearing parents who did their best to show the importance of honesty, integrity, and hard work.

Those principles were reinforced when he was in high school through employment in his father's company. He worked first as a laborer on building sites and later as an office assistant. He learned a lot about the construction business in those years.

Next was college at Minnesota State University, where he studied chemistry and engineering. After that, he got a job with an oil company. Soon, he was promoted and asked to move to the West Coast.

But like his father, he wanted to be on his own, so he turned down the promotion and started a consulting firm instead. Of course, he considered moving back to Two Harbors but opted for warmer location instead—namely, lakefront property east of Atlanta.

Tylor was sipping his morning coffee when the phone rang. The caller ID read 'Nelson Oil.' He paused for a moment and then picked up the handset. Out on the lake, his neighbor was sailing downwind—propelled by a stiff northly breeze.

"Good morning Jack," he said. "It's been a while. How are things in Oklahoma?" He looked at his watch. "You're getting an early start today."

"Hi, Tylor. Yeah, I guess it is pretty early. Sorry about that. How's the weather in Georgia?"

"Well, you know, it's springtime here, warm sunshine, pink azaleas… But I doubt if you really care," he said. "What's on your mind?"

"No, you're right. I don't care about the weather in Georgia. But just so you know, it's crappy here—overcast, cold, and damp."

"Okay, okay. So how can I help you? What's going on?"

"Well, I'm not sure really—we're still trying to figure it out," he said. "Something extraordinary happened in the middle of the night, and we've been up since four trying to wrap our heads around it. I think we're going to need your help."

Tylor watched as the maroon and white sailboat swung to port and began a windward tack.

"Extraordinary, you say." He grabbed a pad and pen. "That's a word I don't hear every day. Tell me more."

He and Jack spent the next thirty minutes discussing the events of the morning. And by the end, he was more puzzled than when they started. It seemed impossible.

"Well, Jack, you were certainly right to call it extraordinary. I've never heard anything like it."

"Do you have any ideas?"

"Not just yet, but the samples will help. Go ahead and send them to Denver. I'll fly out this afternoon and be there when they arrive. Mo and I will take a look and get back to you. I have no idea what we'll find, but he's the best."

"Great. We'll send them out this afternoon, and I'll talk with you tomorrow. In the meantime, Luis and I have to come up with some way to load trucks. The whole system is locked up." He paused for a second and shook his head. "What a mess, what a goddamn mess."

"I know it looks bad, Jack, but keep the faith. Mo and I will get to the bottom of it."

"Thanks, Tylor."

Chapter 3

"Fort Collins Research, Christi Snow speaking. How can I help you?"

"Good morning, Christi, Sam Wilson here. Is Karen available?"

"Sam! Good morning. How are you?"

"I'm fine, thanks. But we have something of a situation here. Is Karen around?"

"No, I'm sorry. She's out running errands today and won't be back until tomorrow. Is there something I can do?"

"Oh, okay, I guess tomorrow will do. Can you take a message? Please ask her to call the minute she comes in."

"Sure, no problem. But maybe you could tell me what's going on so I can include a note with the message."

"It's the W201, Christi. It's all dead."

Christi Snow had been Karen Well's research technician for the past five years and was intimately familiar with the hybrid.

"I don't understand, Sam," she said. "How could it be dead?" She sat down and pulled out a pad.

"We don't know, but it is. It's all brown and dried out, all ten acres of it. Some kind of herbicide, we think."

She swept her blonde hair to the side and began writing. "Go on, Sam."

"James took me out there this morning—it's all dead..."

Christi listened quietly as he explained the condition of the test patch.

"Okay, I think I've got it," she said. "And yes, from your description, it does sound like a herbicide."

"Any suggestions?"

"Not yet. But we'll know for sure after we take a look. I'll bring Karen up to speed when she comes in, and she'll call you first thing. If you send the samples for early delivery, they might get here before she arrives."

"Okay, I'll do that. Thanks, Christi."

***

Early Tuesday, Tylor arrived at 'Avenue 38 Labs' and stopped in the visitor's parking lot—the morning air was crisp. He stepped out of his rental car and walked to the front door. The receptionist put down her donut as he entered.

"Good morning, Pat. How are you this morning? Is Mo in yet?"

"I am fine. Nice to see you again, Mr. York. And yes, he's expecting you. The samples arrived a few minutes ago." She glanced at the laboratory door. "But before you go in, would you like a donut? I bought a dozen this morning."

"What kind?"

"Bear claws." She opened the lid so he could see.

"Hmm, tempting," he said. "Maybe later."

"Fine. They will be right here on my desk. I have fresh coffee too." She smiled.

"Thanks, it sounds great," he said. "I will definitely be back." He smiled and walked toward the lab. "But I'm afraid, first things must come first."

Mordechai (Mo) Finkelman was in his mid-fifties, five foot eight inches tall, two hundred pounds, with thinning gray hair. He wore thick black-rimmed glasses, dark slacks, black tennis shoes, and a white lab coat—complete with a pocket protector.

"Good morning, Tylor. How was the trip?"

"Not bad. The plane was actually on time for a change."

"That's great."

"Is that the package from Jack?"

"Yes. I was waiting to open it."

"Okay, great," he said. "Let's take a look."

Mo rotated the box on the table, pulled off the packing tape, and opened the flaps. Inside were two, one-pint plastic bottles, labeled T101 and T102. He placed them in a fume hood. "They are quite different. Aren't they?" he said.

Sample T101 was thick and black, almost solid. He turned it upside down, and it stuck to the bottom like dried peanut butter.

Sample T102 was thin, like gasoline. It sloshed freely from side to side when he shook it.

"And these are supposed to be the same crude?"

"That's what he said," replied Mo. "T102 looks normal, T101 is strange, indeed."

He held it up to the light with his right hand and turned it back and forth. The plastic bottle gave slightly when he squeezed it. "Amazing, it's a thick gel, I guess. Most curious." Using a box cutter, he sliced the top from the bottle and dumped its contents into a large glass beaker. It slid out as a lump. He scraped it with a stainless steel spatula. "Hmm, a bit grainy," he mused. "Like graphite, or sand, maybe. Fascinating."

***

The Fort Collins Research Laboratory was in a small business park on the south end of town. It was owned by North States Renewables and had been in operation for ten years. Surrounding it was a retention pond with pine trees to the west, a parking lot to the south, a truck-access driveway to the east, and a greenhouse nursery to the north. Inside were a suite offices, a large shop area, and a laboratory. It was a state-of-the-art facility for bioengineering and plant genetics, and Dr. Karen Wells was the director.

Karen was born in Sandusky, Ohio. As a high school student, she was one of the popular girls. Her accolades included junior prom queen, Miss Sandusky South, and senior class president. She spent her undergraduate years at the University of Toledo and earned a Ph.D. in biochemistry at Colorado State University. She was thirty-three years old, weighed one hundred twenty pounds, and was five feet six inches tall in her bare feet. She had long black hair, deep blue eyes, and a creamy complexion. Had she not chosen science—she could have been a fashion model.

Christi was standing at the office door when she entered. "Good morning," she said.

"Good morning. How are things? Is there any coffee?"

"I'll bring you some," she said. "But before you get started, you should check out the note on your desk." She gestured toward a sheet of yellow paper. "There, next to your phone. Sam called yesterday. They have a problem."

Karen picked it up, and then looked at Christi.

"Apparently, somebody sprayed their hybrid with herbicide and killed the whole patch."

"Really? Why would anyone do that?"

"I have no idea, but he wants us to check it out."

Karen looked at the note more carefully.

"Give it a read, and then call him. He is probably waiting by the phone. He sent samples too." She pointed at a long narrow box on her credenza.

"Okay, thanks. I'll call him in a few minutes. How about that coffee?"

"Coming right up." She moved away from Karen's door and walked toward the break room. "I'll be back in a sec."

Moments later, she picked up her desk phone and called Sam's number. He answered on the second ring.

"Hi, Karen, thanks for calling back."

"Morning, Sam," she said. "When are you coming to see me? It's been too long."

"I know. I miss you too. How are things?"

"Oh, I'm fine, I guess. But this winter weather seems to go on forever. I'll be happy when spring gets here."

"It's already hot down here—eighty-five yesterday."

"Sounds good to me."

"Maybe we could arrange a visit? Sometime soon?"

"That would be nice."

"Say, did my samples arrive? I sent them for early delivery."

"Yeah, they're here on my desk. Hang on while I open the box." She picked up a utility knife, sliced through the packing tape, and peeked inside. "These look terrible. What happened?" She peeled back part of the plastic wrapping.

"I don't know," he said. "I was hoping you might have a clue. Everything looked perfect a couple of days ago, and then yesterday, James found them like that. The entire patch is dead."

"Hmm." She squeezed one of the stalks with her left hand. "Brown and brittle, completely dried out. Did you say this happened overnight?"

"Right. In less than twenty-four hours, we think."

"Amazing."

"So, any initial impressions?"

Christi returned with the coffee and handed it to Karen. It smelled delightful.

"Thank you," she whispered. "You're a lifesaver."

She smiled and backed out of Karen's office.

"Well," she said. "There is no way the whole patch died on its own. It had to be some kind of herbicide. And a fast-acting one, by the looks of things." She squeezed the stalk again—it crumbled in her hand. "We'll get right on it. We should have a pretty good idea in a couple of days, and then we'll work on replacing it."

"That would be great," he said. He paused for a moment and then continued, "I really would like to see you. Maybe we could turn this into a little opportunity."

"I like how you think. Could you come out for a couple of days?"

"Yeah, I think so," he said, glancing at his calendar. "We could talk about the samples, say on Friday afternoon, and then do something fun over the weekend."

"Sounds great. But I don't think we'll be ready by Friday afternoon. Can we make it Saturday morning instead? We could go back to that new Italian restaurant."

"Yeah, sure. Saturday morning will be fine. I'll meet you at the lab at around ten o'clock. And yes, I would love to go back to Antonio's! Their ravioli is fantastic," he said.

"Okay, terrific. I'll make the reservations."

"Later, then."

"Okay, bye for now."

Christi was standing outside the office door and stepped in when she hung up.

"I gather that Sam may be coming for the weekend?" she said with a smile. "You are so lucky."

"Yeah, it looks that way. It will be great to see him again. But to get back on topic." She picked up the samples, carried them into the lab, and sat them on the benchtop. "Let's dig into these and see if we can figure out what happened. We have a decent inventory in the nursery, so we could send a shipment in a week or so."

"Okay, no problem," said Christi. "I'll get started." She picked up the box and carried it to her workstation. When she was alone, she pulled out her cell phone and composed a quick message:

W201 replacement is planned for the end of next week. Should we talk?

Chapter 4

On the street, anyone who met Dr. Amil Nugent would automatically peg him as the meek, nerdy, professor type. He was five feet four inches tall, sixty-two years old, and wore black slacks—his tweed jacket even had elbow patches. But first impressions were deceiving.

In social settings, people were drawn to him—especially women. Despite his graying hair and average appearance, they found him personable, polite, and charming.

In the business world, he was the president of North State Renewables, Inc. A five-hundred-million-dollar company with plants in three states. His peers respected his business acumen, and his employees appreciated his no-nonsense management style. He paid well, detested waste, and had little patience for laziness or stupidity.

He was in his Broadview office when the telephone rang—the caller ID read 'Louis Jicard.' He picked up the receiver and barked, "It's about time you called. You are eight minutes late."

"Good morning, sir. I'm sorry for being late."

"Good morning, my ass. What the hell is going on down there? According to your report, you are two full months behind schedule."

Louis Jicard was six feet tall, weighed 187 pounds, and ran five miles every day before breakfast. He kept his dark hair cut short and had a small scar on the left side of his chin—a souvenir from an old knife fight, he claimed. His polished boots always had a mirror finish, and he typically wore camo fatigues with a navy-blue beret.

"I'm not sure what you mean, sir," he said. "Could you be more specific?"

"Wow. Where do I start?" He leaned forward in his chair. "It's been over two months since Mr. Richards, ah, departed, and the project in Rapid City remains at a standstill. Your billet deliveries are below target, and I have seen no progress at all on the farnesene project. And on top of that, your monthly expenditures are twice what we agreed. I am beginning to think we made a mistake with you."

He rose from his office chair, placed his left hand on top of his mahogany desk, and held the handset with his right fist. "Do you have any idea how much is on the line? What kind of circus are you running?"

Jicard was silent.

His grip tightened until his knuckles turned white, and his voice grew louder, "Well, what do you have to say for yourself?"

"Yessir, of course, I know what's on the line," he said. "And I am sorry, sir. It is simply taking longer than we anticipated. We are working on it. If you can give me a few minutes, I would be happy to explain."

"I'm not interested in excuses, Jicard. We hired you for results, and that is what I expect."

"Yes, sir."

"Your top priority should be the engineer. I need him in Rapid City, now."

He paused for a moment and then continued, "And concerning the other items. I had better see some improvement soon."

"Yes, sir. You can depend on me, sir. I will address the schedule issues, and you will have a new engineer by the middle of next week. We will redouble our efforts to get back on track."

"You damn well better. I will give you two weeks. If you can't deliver, I'll find someone who can." He slammed down the receiver.

***

Jicard paced back and forth in his office. His back was straight, his fists were clenched, and the veins in his neck were pulsing. *Nugent! That pencil-necked prissy, wimp-ass nerd, I've taken about all I'm going to take. I'll snap him in two. Who does he think he is? Nobody talks to me like that. I'll rip his head off.*

After a few laps around his desk, he stopped at his credenza and picked up a bottle of Macallan. He poured a full glass and drank it in one swallow. Then, he poured a second.

Half way through the second glass, he started to calm down. *No, I won't kill him, not yet. Other things need to be dealt with first.*

Feeling more in control, he put the drink on his desk, lowered himself into his chair, and punched a number into his cell phone.

"Dan," he said. "This is Jicard."

"Good morning."

"Say, do you remember that guy we were talking about last week? Betson, I think you called him."

"Yeah, Paul Betson. What about him?"

"I just talked with Nugent, and he's all hot about getting someone over to Rapid City as soon as possible. Do you think he can handle it?"

"Yes, I'm sure he can."

"Can we control him? We don't want another boy scout."

"Yeah, he's up to his neck in it. I'm sure he'll toe the line."

"How much will it cost us?"

"About thirty grand, I would guess."

"Okay, thirty will be fine. Tell Betson we'll pay off his tab and then get him over to Rapid City next week. Be sure he's completely on board, and then let Nugent know."

"You got it."

"Make it Tuesday morning. That should make him happy. Are you sure he's solid?"

"Yes, he's a top-notch engineer. He just can't seem to stay out of trouble."

"Well, he needs to understand our zero-tolerance policy on gambling. There will be absolutely none of that while he's working for us."

"I will make it very clear, and he'll be on the job Tuesday morning."

"Good."

"Also, reach out to BJ in Denver and get him started. We need to bring Wells inside as soon as possible."

"He's going to need time for the setup."

"I understand. We'll give him two days to prepare. But it must be finished Friday night. And tell him we need a thorough job on this one— budget is not an issue. I will call Wells later today, so everything should fall into place."

"Consider it done."

"Excellent. Now, tell me about Dusty Fork."

"The job went perfectly," said Dan. "He spiked the tank at about two o'clock while their operator was loading trucks."

"Did anyone see him?"

"No chance. It was foggy, and he's one of our best men."

"And?"

"As I said, it worked perfectly. The stuff started working almost immediately, and by four-thirty, the whole system was clogged up. The pump was smoking before he could shut it down."

"Only two and a half hours, that's better than we expected," said Jicard. "Thanks, good job. We'll talk soon."

***

He took another sip and then punched in a second number. The phone rang three times before she picked up.

"Morning, Jicard, what can I do for you?"

"Good morning, Christi," he said. "Is everything good in Fort Collins?"

"Things are fine here, I guess. But I am a little concerned about the W201."

"I got your text, and you were right to be concerned. We certainly cannot allow a replacement shipment."

"That's what I thought you'd say."

"I talked with Nugent this morning, and he is really hot about farnesene and our billet deliveries. I think we need to bring Karen inside as soon as possible. We are planning for Friday."

"This week?"

"Yes."

"That may not work. Sam is coming for the weekend, and I'm not sure she'll bite that soon."

"Don't worry. I'm going to make an offer she can't refuse. She'll bite, all right."

"If you say so," Christi said. "Well, she's out at the moment, but I expect her back anytime. Wait for about twenty minutes and then call her office number. She should be at her desk by then."

"Will do," he said. "It will be nice to have you back inside."

"Yeah, I'm looking forward to it," she said. "Who will be doing the job?"

"BJ."

"Oh, BJ, okay, he's an excellent choice. I'll send him a text to see if he needs anything. And don't worry, I'll manage this end."

"Thanks. But wait a couple of hours, Dan needs to call him first."

"Check."

***

His last number was Timond Forgue in Baton Rouge. He drained his glass and then made the call.

"Hey Jicard, what's going on?"

"Good morning, Forgue. How's the weather down there?"

"Hotter than it should be, for this time of the year. It's been in the nineties for the past week or so."

"I actually wouldn't mind a little heat," he said. "We still have snow up here."

"Get to the point, Jicard."

"Okay, Forgue. I need your report, and I know you're not going to send one. So, tell me how it went."

Timond Forgue was a powerfully built man, six feet two inches tall, with shoulder-length stringy blond hair and a receding hairline. He preferred blue jeans and black tee-shirts, seldom shaved, and bathed only when absolutely necessary.

"It went fine, precisely as we planned. The drones worked perfectly. They did the whole patch in about twenty minutes, and the weed killer was very effective," he said. "The next morning, I drove by to check it out, and the whole patch was dead. It was a big brown rectangle in the middle of the field. The cane outside the patch was still green, completely untouched."

"Good. That's good to hear. What did the Wilsons do when they discovered it?" Jicard leaned forward in his chair and held the handset close to his ear.

"James noticed it first. Then, he went to find Sam and brought him back in his truck. They spent about fifteen minutes in the patch, walking around, bending over to look at the stalks, and pointing in different directions. I was too far away to hear what they said."

"I see," said Jicard. "Anything else?"

"Well, from their body language," he continued. "I could tell they were not happy. James was very agitated, that's for sure, but Sam seemed less so. He was almost calm. He took it more in stride, I guess you'd say. Then they walked back to the truck, tossed a few dead stalks in the back, and left—samples, I guess. I don't know what they did with them."

A wide grin spread across Jicard's face, and he nearly dropped the handset. "Thanks, Forgue, that's all I needed to hear. The funds will be wired to your account this afternoon." He paused, "And go ahead and start planning for the next one. Schedule it for Sunday night."

Chapter 5

"Two years?" said Karen. "That's not possible. My mother just moved out here last summer. She needs me, and we spend a lot of time together. No, I couldn't possibly be away that long."

Karen's mother was fifty-four years old and worked as a secretary at Loveland High School. She lived on the west side of town in a small two-bedroom house.

"We'll take good care of your mother—you needn't worry," said Jicard. "We will write her a letter explaining everything, and Christi will deliver it personally. Also, we will pay off her mortgage and cover all of her expenses for the duration of your assignment, one hundred percent."

They'd been talking for nearly thirty minutes, and she had two pages of notes. She shifted position in her chair and continued.

"And the compensation?"

"As I said, you will be promoted to Manager of Research with an annual salary of $175,000. And since the unit is self-contained, the company will provide everything you need: food, lodging, clothing, medical, everything."

She wrote the number and underlined it several times. *Wow! How much is that per month? Over fourteen thousand, no, fourteen thousand five hundred! I've never seen that much money!*

"It's a generous offer, Mr. Jicard."

"Well, the job is critical to the success of our research, and we believe you're the right person to fill it. Also, we know the team will work more efficiently if you are onsite."

She shifted positions again.

"And what about Sam Wilson? We are working on his hybrid problem, and we have a meeting scheduled for Saturday morning."

"Christi can handle the meeting. She'll be running the lab while you're gone, anyway. So, she may as well get used to it."

"Yeah, I guess she could handle it all right. But I want to see him. I can't just up and leave. "I need to talk to him before I go," said Karen.

"I am sorry. But if you want the job, you must agree to complete secrecy, starting right now. You may discuss this with no one, not even your mother. The work will be extremely sensitive, and nobody can know about it, not even by accident. It is top secret."

"I understand."

"So, can we count on you?"

"Hang on for a moment."

She looked around her office and then walked to the door. *I'm going to miss this place a lot, and I'll miss Christi... She'll explain it to Sam. I'll be on a special assignment. And I'll get a message to him somehow. The work sounds so exciting, and it is a lot of money... They're going to take care of mom's mortgage... How can I refuse?*

She returned to her desk. "Okay, Mr. Jicard, I accept. I'll take the job."

"Excellent," he said. "Take the rest of today and tomorrow to tie up loose ends. Pack your laptop and a warm jacket, but don't bother with clothing—everything you need will be provided. We will send a Limo tomorrow evening—about six o'clock, and a company jet will be waiting at Loveland Field."

"A limo. Really? And a company jet?"

Wow, they're sending a limousine!

She smiled, "Thanks, Mr. Jicard. I'll be ready."

"Great. And welcome aboard."

Chapter 6

"Nugent speaking. How can I help you?" He leaned back in his chair and swiveled toward the window.

"Dr. Amil Nugent?"

"Yes, this is Dr. Amil Nugent. With whom am I speaking?"

"Thank you for taking my call. This is Sharon Wagoner, Melvin Richard's girlfriend."

Sharon was five feet six inches tall, twenty-eight years old, with blonde hair, blue eyes, and flawless skin. She had dimples on both cheeks, especially when she smiled, and her teeth were brilliant white. She met Melvin two years earlier during a dental checkup—she was his hygienist. And six months later they were living together—she was calling from their apartment in Denver.

"I see. Well, how can I be of assistance, Miss Wagoner?"

"I am looking for Melvin. Have you seen him recently? And please, call me Sharon."

"Okay, Sharon. But no, I haven't seen him. Why would you think I might?"

"Well, he works for you. And he was on his way to your plant the last time I saw him. That was the fifteenth of January."

She had called everyone she knew, all of his friends, the airlines, every hospital within a hundred miles, and even the Montana State Police. Nobody had seen him.

"Well, Sharon, he doesn't actually work for me any more."

"Of course he does! What do you mean he doesn't work for you? Did you fire him?"

"Please, Miss Wagoner, let me continue," he rolled his eyes. "As I understand it, he didn't come to the plant that day. Instead, I believe he met with Dan Turner in Broadview—at Lucky's, I think he said. I haven't seen Melvin myself since our last progress meeting back in December. I have no idea where he is. I only know he was supposed to go to Rapid City, but he never showed up."

"That's the same story I got from Dan," she said. "He said he met with Melvin at Lucky's to close out the Broadview project and then he sent him on to Rapid City."

"Well, then, there you go. I don't know what else I can tell you."

"But Melvin isn't like that. He would never do that. He loves his work."

"I was surprised too," said Nugent. "Melvin was always reliable. But I have to say, I am pretty upset about it."

"So, you have no idea where he is?"

"No. I wish I did. He gave us no warning at all before leaving. He just didn't show up. And since then, we have lost weeks and weeks of time and a great deal of money. We are still searching for a replacement."

"Unbelievable. You money-grubbing bastard! You're complaining because you lost a little money? Melvin is the love of my life, and he's missing. We are planning to get married. I would give everything I have to get him back. I need you to help me find him, and instead, you're trying to replace him!"

"It wasn't a little money, Miss Wagoner. It was millions. We've had employees quit in the past, but they usually give us some notice. We have no reason to think anything untoward has happened. He simply didn't show up, that's all. We don't spend our time searching for ex-employees. We have a business to run. And yes, we are trying to replace him. We need to move ahead with our projects."

"Ex-employee? You fired him, then."

"No, we didn't fire him. In fact, we promoted him to Senior Engineer, and we gave him a generous raise."

"Now, I am truly confused. You think enough of him to promote him, but you don't bother to look for him when he doesn't show up?"

"We did look for him. We repeatedly tried to reach him by telephone and by email, but he never responded. And after several weeks with no success, we had to move on."

"You mean, you gave up. We'll I haven't. And you and Dan seem to be the only people who might be able to help. I need your help. Something must have happened to him. Maybe he was kidnapped or is lying somewhere in a coma. You have to help me!"

"I understand that you're upset, Miss Wagoner. I certainly do. But I simply cannot help you. I am very sorry. Maybe you should call Dan again. He was much closer to him than I."

Her face flushed red. She held her breath and almost threw the phone at the wall.

Another dead end, I am getting nowhere. All I ever get from these people is the runaround. Somebody somewhere must know something. People don't just disappear. But since nobody seems to care, I guess I'll have to go there and find him myself.

"Thank you for your time, Dr. Nugent. I am sorry that I disturbed you. I guess I'll have to figure this one out for myself."

"Not at all, Miss Wagoner. Have a nice day. And good luck to you. I do hope you find him."

***

After they hung up, Dr. Nugent sent a text to Dan Turner:

I just got off the phone with Sharon Wagoner, she wants us to help her find Richards. I told her there was nothing we could do. Just a heads-up, she might try to contact you again.

Chapter 7

Molly Greene and Linda Johnson were huddled together under a pile of dirty blankets. Outside, the temperature was near zero, and the frost on their slats grew thicker with every breath. Their packing crate was located under a freeway on the south side of Denver. The concrete structure did a great job of protecting them from rain, but was no help at all against the cold.

"Are you doing okay?" asked Molly in a quiet voice. "The Sterno is nearly gone."

"Yeah, I think so," said Linda. "My feet are pretty cold, but it's not too bad." She nestled closer.

"We still have that leftover chicken sandwich from yesterday. Are you hungry?"

"Not right now. Let's save it for later."

"Wait, what's that?" She held up her hand, "It's a car."

Outside, a skinny black man got out of a black SUV, stepped up to the crate, and knocked on the frame.

"Molly? Linda? Are you in there? It's BJ."

For a couple of moments, they said nothing. *BJ again? What does he want this time?*

"Molly, can you hear me?"

"Yeah, yeah, we hear you. What do you want?"

"Oh, good, you're here." He paused a moment. "Good morning Molly, good morning, Linda. Sorry to disturb you."

"What do you want, BJ? We're sort of, you know, busy in here."

"Yeah, sure, of course," he said. "But if you could give me a couple of minutes of your time, I have a little news."

A gust of wind shook the crate, and BJ pulled his coat tight around his body. *Man! How do they survive out here?*

"Okay, you have two minutes. Spill."

"Do you remember that job I told you about? Well, it looks like it's going to happen. They told me you can start tomorrow. If you're still interested, that is."

"Yeah, sure we can," said Linda. "What kind of scam are you working this time? Huh? What's the scam?"

"No scam, honest," he said. "If you let me, I'll tell you all about it."

"We've heard that one before. I think we'll stay right where we are. Hit the road, BJ!"

"Honest, I'm not kidding. I have the money with me."

"You have the money?" said Linda. "I doubt that. You just want us out, so you can take our crate."

"No, really." He stuck a fist full of bills inside.

Linda looked at the wad of cash. "That doesn't look like enough. You said it would be a thousand each."

Molly chimed in, "Right, it was supposed to be two thousand dollars."

"I know what I said, and you're right. I only have five hundred at the moment. But when the job is done, I'll get you more. How about fifteen hundred apiece?"

Linda turned to Molly and whispered, "Three thousand dollars is a lot of money. And my feet aren't getting any warmer..."

Molly nodded and said, "Okay, you convinced us. We're coming out."

They wasted no time getting into the warm SUV. The engine was running, and the heat was exquisite.

BJ shivered as he climbed behind the wheel. "It's frigid out there."

"We've seen worse."

"I have no doubt." He turned and gave them each five hundred dollars. "Here is your down payment. You'll get the rest when the job is done," he said. "I'm happy to have you aboard."

"Fifteen hundred each?"

"Right, five hundred now and a fifteen hundred more when the job is done. I Promise."

"Okay, that will be fine... and thanks, BJ," said Molly—Linda nodded.

He reached over to the passenger seat and grabbed two duffel bags. "Here," he said. "I got you a few odds and ends that may be useful." He passed them back. "Just some essentials, like, you know, a change of clothes, shower soap, shampoo, basic cosmetics..."

They peeked inside their bags, smiled, and looked up. "So," said Molly. "Where are you taking us?"

"Well, first, to a nice motel room, so you can get warmed up and rest a bit. Then we'll go to lunch and get ready for the job."

"Motel room? What's the game?" she said. "And what about our crate? They'll steal everything."

"It will be fine, Molly, I promise," he said. "The job is legit, and I'll have someone keep an eye on your stuff."

She exchanged glances with Linda. "Well, then, I guess it's a deal," she said slowly. "What is this job, exactly?"

"You're going to be extras in a movie. Molly, you will be playing a scientist, and Linda will be a waitress in a restaurant," he said.

"Movie extras? Why us?" asked Molly. "We are not exactly Hollywood material."

"Trust me. You'll be fine. I know the director. He's a great guy, and he likes to help folks out when he can."

Twenty minutes later, BJ checked them into the Mountain Valley West Motel and then left to run some errands. The place was a dump, but to the girls, it was like heaven. The room was clean and warm, the water was hot, and the beds were soft. They dipped into their duffels and proceeded to take full advantage of the amenities.

When he returned at noon, he was amazed. "You two look fantastic," he said. "I had no idea you were such foxes under all those layers. May I escort you to lunch?"

"Let's go someplace fun," offered Molly. "Maybe a sports bar with music and big screen TVs."

"Okay, by me," he said. "I know just the place."

They spent the next two hours enjoying lunch and talking about their jobs. When they were done, he took them back to the motel.

"Okay, ladies," he said. "For the rest of the day, you're on your own. I have a few more things to arrange, but I'll be back to pick you up in the morning—about eight-thirty."

"Thanks, BJ. We'll be ready."

Chapter 8

Jack climbed into his pickup truck and checked his phone. He scanned a waiting message and then hit the call button.

Tylor answered, "Hi, Jack. How are things going?"

"I just saw your text. Sorry for the delay."

"No problem, have you made any progress? I have Mo here with me, and you're on speakerphone."

"We've been scrambling out here, that's for sure. Luis and I strung about two hundred feet of hose from Tank 102, and I found a temporary pump to use. So, we can load trucks again, sort of. But Tank 101 is still dead, and the piping and the pump are still plugged solid. I hope you have some good news."

"Well, we do have some news, but I am not sure how good it is."

Jack's shoulders slumped. "Okay, give it to me."

"We've been doing a lot of tests, and we think we know what the stuff is."

"Yea?"

"You tell him, Mo. You know more about it than I do."

"High Jack, it's Mo."

"Well, good afternoon, Mor-de-cai. How are you doing, Morty?"

"You never miss a chance, do you?"

"I don't know what you mean."

"I have told you a thousand times. I had no input when my parents named me."

"I'm sorry, you know I'm just kidding. What do you have?"

"Well," he said. "We think the stuff in Sample 101 is a supramolecular polymer gel—a very thick, very stable gel. We believe someone spiked the tank with a polymer-based organogelator. Then, when Luis started loading, the mixture flowed through the pipe and into the truck. In a couple of hours, the reaction finished, and the gel formed."

"A supra what? You lost me. What in the hell is a gelator?"

"I'm sorry, Jack," he said. "We've been talking about this for two days straight, and I forgot that it would be new to you." He paused. "Okay, think about making a gelatin dessert in the kitchen. You dissolve the gelatin in warm water and then put it in the refrigerator. When it cools, it turns the water into a thick gel."

"Okay…"

"So, it's like that, but the stuff we're talking about works in oil. It takes only a tiny amount to get started, and once it's introduced, it molecularly self-assembles. You don't have to heat it or chill it, and the resulting gel is much stronger. It's like a cross-linked cage of carbon atoms that surrounds and entraps the crude oil molecules—quite remarkable, from a chemistry perspective. We believe it was specifically developed to work in crude oil."

"Why would anyone do that?"

Tylor answered, "Well, there have been significant advances in the use of organogelators in oil-spill cleanup applications, but this one goes far beyond that. We think it could be used as a weapon."

"Wow, you think so? You think a terrorist did this?"

"We don't know, maybe, it's just a theory for now," said Tylor.

"So why didn't they hit both tanks?"

"Again, we're not sure. But we think it may be experimental, and they just wanted to test it."

"Lucky me, why my tank?"

"We have no idea. Can you think of anyone who might have a grudge against you?"

"No, of course not," he answered. "And now you have me officially worried." He considered the information for a moment. "But in the meantime, how do we fix it? How do we get rid of the stuff?"

"We haven't figured that out yet. I'm sorry to say. But we're working on it."

"I see," said Jack. "So, where do we go from here?"

"Well, Mo has a few ideas that he wants to explore, and if it's okay with you, I would like to visit the tank farm and take a closer look."

"Fine with me. When can you come?"

"How about Monday morning?"

"That works for me."

Chapter 9

At five-fifty-nine on Thursday afternoon, a black stretch limousine pulled up to Karen's front door. She had been watching from her living room window.

This is crazy. I am leaving for a two-year assignment, and all I have with me is a laptop and an overnight bag. Unreal!

She set her bag outside and locked the door. As she turned to leave, a man appeared on the sidewalk, "Good afternoon, Dr. Wells, my name is Darren. I will be your driver today."

"Hi Darren, thanks for picking me up."

"It is my pleasure, ma'am. Let me help you with that."

He picked up her bag and gestured toward her laptop.

"No, thanks. I'll carry the laptop."

"As you wish," he said.

They walked to the limousine, and he opened the rear door on the passenger side. "If you please, ma'am."

"Thank you, Darren," she said as she stepped in.

She had never experienced such luxury. There was seating for six, a lighted bar along the right side, and a sliding glass window behind the driver—it was open as they pulled from the curb.

"Are you comfortable, Dr. Wells? Should I turn up the heat?"

"No. I am quite comfortable. Thank you."

"Okay, we are all set. Just sit back and relax. And Dr. Wells, what would you like for dinner?"

"Dinner?"

"Yeah. Since you won't have a chance to eat, we need to pick up some fast food to snack on during the flight."

"Oh, I see." She thought for a moment. "Well, my favorite place is Roberts Barbecue on Trilby—that would be great. Travis is such a nice guy."

"Travis? Is he the owner?"

"Oh no, he just works behind the counter. We always chat when I go in. I think he likes me a little."

Darren studied her face in the rearview mirror, smiled, and then continued, "Do they have a take-out window?"

"Sure, you can drive right through. I go there a lot."

"Sounds good," he said. "We'll stop there first."

"Okay."

Karen settled in to enjoy the ride. The leather seats were deep burgundy and buttery soft, and the skylights were framed with recessed lighting.

"You'll find champagne and glasses in the bar if you are so inclined."

"No, thanks. I would rather stay alert."

"There are also soft drinks, or water, if you prefer."

"Okay. Maybe some water." She twisted the cap off a small bottle and took a sip."

When they arrived at Roberts Barbecue, Karen scanned the menu and selected a pulled pork sandwich with coleslaw. Darren paid for it and set the bag on the front passenger seat. Moments later, they were back on the street.

"Okay, we are all set. We should be there in about fifteen minutes."

Wow. If the next two years are like this...

She sat back and looked out the left window. The sun was dropping behind the snow-caps, and the sky was a burst of color. *So majestic. I'm really going to miss this.*

A few minutes later, they entered the airport and proceeded toward general aviation. Ahead, she could see a medium-sized hanger with three large letters painted on the side, 'NSR', and a Learjet was parked nearby. Darren drove straight for the hangar and stopped next to the jet.

"Okay, Dr. Wells, we're here." He tilted his head. "Your plane over there."

A Learjet? For me?

"That was a quick fifteen minutes," she said. "But I enjoyed it. Thanks for the ride."

Darren helped her out and gave her the take-out. When they reached the plane, he handed her overnight bag to the pilot and then bowed slightly at the waist, "It was a pleasure driving you this afternoon. I hope you enjoy your flight."

She smiled, nodded slightly, and then climbed four steps to the cabin. Her eyes went wide as she scanned the interior. *Incredible!*

Inside were six over-stuffed passenger seats—she selected one next to the door and sat down. The sidewalls were plush leather, light taupe at the top, and darker at the bottom. The ceiling panels were white, with indirect lighting, and the carpet was a soft russet. She smiled and drew her fingers lightly across the leather upholstery. *I had no idea! It's so beautiful.*

The pilot poked his head inside, "Welcome aboard, Dr. Wells. I see you have dinner with you, that's good. Also, the mini-fridge is fully stocked with beer, wine, and soft drinks, you name it. Feel free to help yourself. And if you're still hungry, there are some snacks in the cabinet. You have two or three minutes before we start taxing, so grab a drink and relax. We should be there in about an hour."

"Where are we going, exactly?"

"Billings, Montana, Ma'am."

Well, at least I will still have the mountains to look at. That's something. I wish Jicard had shared more about the facility. I wonder what he meant by tight security?

She reached for a bottle of water and settled in as the pilot closed the door. The engines spooled up, she fastened her seat belt, and a moment later, they were on their way.

Back in the limo, Darren picked up his cell phone and sent a joint text to Christi and BJ:

They are taking off now—seven p.m.

The restaurant is Roberts Barbecue on Trilby.

The guy at the restaurant is Travis.

Chapter 10

Christi was at her desk when Darren's message came in. She jotted down the information and then grabbed one of Karen's menus. *This should do the trick.*

As she looked up from her computer, she noticed a red light flashing on the alarm system. One of the truck bay doors was opening. The clock on her computer screen read 7:14. "Right on time," she murmured.

She closed out her computer and walked into the shop area. The north access door was open, and a man dressed in black was waiting.

"Hi Christi, we're here to clear out the nursery."

"Right, I've been expecting you," she said. "The gate is on the north side of the building."

"Okay. We'll get to it."

"Remember, you have to be finished by morning."

He nodded, "I understand." He started toward the north side and motioned to the rest crew. "This way," he said.

Christi walked back into the lab and plugged a portable hard drive into the network server. She then opened the system maintenance screen and clicked 'Full Backup'. When the blue LED on the drive started blinking, she returned to her office.

***

The Learjet 45 landed in Billings ten minutes after eight and taxied toward the airport's west end—a black SUV was waiting near the NSR hangar. As the plane rolled to a stop, the driver approached and helped her descend the stair.

"Welcome to Billings, Dr. Wells," he said. "My name is Torrence. I will be your driver this evening." He gestured toward the SUV.

"Thank you," she said. "It's good to be here. Is the research facility very far?"

"No, ma'am, not far at all."

Torrence took her bag from the pilot and opened the rear passenger door. As she sat down, he reached behind her head and injected one milliliter of a clear yellow fluid into the base of her neck. She was unconscious in seconds. He then reclined her seat, made sure that her seat belt was fastened, and closed her door. As he turned the key to start the engine, he repeated, "No, ma'am, it's not far at all. We should be there in about an hour and a half."

Soon, they were on Interstate 90 headed west. At Exit 434, they turned south and continued on Route 212, also known as Beartooth Highway. They passed through Red Lodge an hour later, and fifteen minutes after that, they turned left onto a steep gravel road. It dropped quickly below the pavement and was nearly invisible from the highway. The road wound its way through the pine trees and around several rocky outcrops before ending at the base of a granite cliff. Torrence leaned forward and touched a remote-control unit mounted on the dashboard.

Seconds later, a crack appeared, and a massive rectangular slab moved to the right. Behind it, was a dark opening. The SUV rolled inside, and the slab slid back in place. Ceiling lights came on automatically to illuminate a long narrow tunnel. They drove through and parked in a large circular cavern.

Chapter 11

At eight-thirty Friday morning, BJ picked up Molly and Linda and took them to breakfast. While they enjoyed ate, he went over their itinerary.

"Linda, your shoot has been delayed until late this afternoon. So, I'll take you back to the motel and have a friend pick you up at about three. And Molly, yours begins at about one o'clock, so we'll head over there right away."

The girls nodded in expectation.

"Would you like anything more to eat," he asked.

They shook their heads.

"Okay, then," he said. "Let's get started."

Ten minutes later, they dropped Linda off at the motel. She hopped out and then poked her head back inside. "Have fun, Molly, and break a leg, girl. I'll see you tonight." She gave BJ a big hug and said, "Thanks a bunch. I'll be ready at three."

BJ and Molly drove off, and Linda strolled back to her motel room. The air was bitter cold, so she walked quickly. When she closed the door, something sharp pricked the back of her neck—her vision blurred, her knees buckled, and then there was nothing.

The man with the needle caught her as she fell and laid her unconscious body gently on the bed. He then stripped her naked, redressed her in street clothes, and wrapped her in a plastic drop cloth. To finish, he cleaned the room thoroughly, wiped down all surfaces, and used a pair of long tweezers to remove hair from the shower drain. Finally, he put everything in a large trash bag and deposited it in a dumpster outside. He place Linda in the back of his SUV.

The drive back to her crate took about twenty minutes. He checked for witnesses when they arrived and then quickly transferred her body the packing crate. The Sterno flame was out, so he set it aside to make room. He then removed the drop cloth and positioned her body strategically inside. Finally, he removed her gloves and scarf and unbuttoned her coat. When he left, he made sure the side of the crate was cracked open.

The frigid temperatures did the rest. Within two hours, Linda was dead.

***

Headed north on Interstate 25, BJ and Molly were making good time.

"Why are we headed out of the city?"

"I'm sorry, I meant to tell you. A message arrived while we were at the motel—they want us to go to Fort Collins instead. On the way, we'll stop in Loveland for makeup and costume."

"Fort Collins? Loveland?" she said. "Will we get back to the motel tonight? What about Linda?"

"No, you'll stay in Fort Collins tonight," he said. "A friend of mine will collect Linda and make sure she gets where she needs to be."

"Good," she said. "I'm a little worried, you know. She is my best friend in the world."

She turned in her seat and looked directly at him. "And we are so grateful for what you're doing. We talked about it last night. We think you're a great guy, and we hope you are getting something out of this too."

"You're both very welcome. And yes, I'll make out fine on the deal."

An hour later, they stopped at a health and beauty spa on the south side of Loveland. *Eleven-thirty, right on time.*

As they entered, the receptionist looked up and smiled.

"Good morning, BJ," she said. "Is this the actress you were telling me about?"

"Yes," he said. "This is our Molly. Take good care of her."

He handed her several photos of Karen Wells. "And this is the star, do your best."

"Wow, she is stunning. And the payment?"

He reached into his pocket, retrieved a white envelope, and handed it to her.

After peeking inside, she smiled and stuffed it in her desk drawer. "Thank you, sir. You will not be disappointed."

In the back room, a small army of technicians was waiting to tackle the project. The receptionist extended her hand, "Come with me, my dear. This way."

Molly smiled and followed her into the salon.

"We have a full schedule for you today, so just relax and let us do our thing. We will have you looking like a star in no time." She checked her list and continued, "Your services today will include a deep tissue massage, a facial, a little hair treatment to get the color right, and some styling. Then we'll finish up with a mani-pedi." She paused for a moment. "And after that, we will do your makeup and fit your costume. We're going to have so much fun."

She glanced back at BJ, who was still standing in the reception area, "We'll take it from here. She should be ready in about four and a half hours."

He looked at his watch and nodded. "Okay, thanks. I'll see you later."

Back in the SUV, he sent a short text message to Christi:

I received the overnight envelope this morning. Thanks.

We are at the spa and on schedule. Send the menu when available.

***

Christi was at her computer when his text arrived. She scanned the menu into the system and replied:

The menu is attached. Good luck. The lab is ready, and the hard drive will be erased. I will be leaving soon.

After sending the message, she unplugged the backup drive from the server and opened the maintenance screen. She located the 'Format Hard Drive' option and clicked 'Enable'. Several warning screens appeared, but eventually, the computer went to work.

As a final step, she programmed the telephone system to forward calls to her cell phone. *That's it. Everything's ready.*

THE CAVE

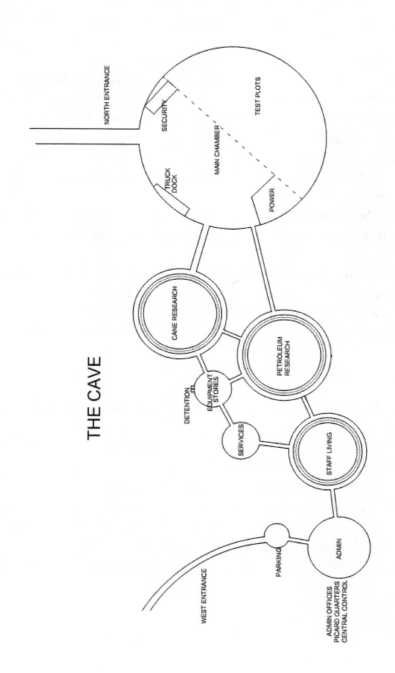

NORTH ENTRANCE

SECURITY

TRUCK DOCK

MAIN CHAMBER

TEST PLOTS

POWER

CANE RESEARCH

PETROLEUM RESEARCH

DETENTION

EQUIPMENT STORES

SERVICES

STAFF LIVING

WEST ENTRANCE

PARKING

ADMIN

ADMIN OFFICES
PICARD QUARTERS
CENTRAL CONTROL

Chapter 12

Karen awoke feeling alert and well-rested—the bed was very comfortable. She rolled to her left to look at a digital alarm clock—it read 8:30 a.m. *Eight-thirty? Have I overslept? Where am I?* She reached for the reading lamp, and switched it on—a warm glow flooded the room. *How did I get here?*

It was unlike any hotel room she had ever seen. It was ultramodern with a high ceiling and light gray walls. It was accented with sharp vertical detail and smoked glass sconces. The furniture was black and gray with chrome lines. The artwork was abstract, depicting strong geometrical shapes in primary colors. The floor was hardwood with strategically placed area rugs, and a soft indirect lighting shown from beneath the floating bed frame. *Beautiful. Just beautiful. I wonder what hotel this is? I must've slept like a rock, and I don't remember checking in. I'm famished, maybe some room service.*

She picked up the phone next to the bed and dialed zero.

"Good morning Dr. Wells," said the voice. "How can I be of assistance?"

"I would like to order some breakfast."

"Oh, I'm sorry, we don't do room service. But if you're ready, we will escort you to breakfast. The valet picked up your things from yesterday, but you will find fresh clothes in the wardrobe."

"An escort? Fresh clothing? What are you talking about? What hotel is this? I don't remember checking in."

"You are in the North States Renewables Research Center, Dr. Wells. You arrived somewhat disheveled last night, and Mr. Jicard appreciates a crisp appearance. Please help yourself to the wardrobe. Your escort will arrive in thirty minutes." The voice hung up.

For the first time, Karen noticed that she was not in her pajamas. Instead, she was wearing a white silken nightgown with a low-cut neckline and delicate lace trim. *This is not my nightgown! How can I be wearing it? Where am I? What in the hell is going on?*

She got out of bed and peeked out the door—it was quiet. The hallway was bare concrete with some generic artwork hanging every ten feet or so. Wall sconces provided illumination.

She closed the door and crossed to the wardrobe. Inside, she found a rack full of new clothing and her overnight bag and. She opened it and was relieved to find everything just as she had packed it; pajamas, toiletries, a pair of shoes, and a change of clothes. She looked up and saw her laptop sitting on the desk. *Well, that's a little better.*

She removed her clothes from the bag and started to lay them out on the bed when the phone rang. "Dr. Wells here. Who is this?"

The voice replied, "I'm sorry I was short with you earlier. You must be feeling a bit disoriented."

"That would be a fair statement," she said. "What exactly is going on? Where did all these clothes come from."

"Most new arrivals feel this way. Please do not worry," said the voice. "The clothes are part of your allotment. They should fit perfectly. The dresser, chest, and bathroom should also be stocked."

"Hold on a minute." Karen sat down the phone and opened a couple of drawers. They were filled with undergarments, socks, sweaters, and sportswear—all in her size. On top of the dresser was a small jewelry box filled with earrings, necklaces, and bracelets. She picked the phone back up, "They are," she said.

"Excellent. We have done our best to fill your immediate requirement, but if there is something else you desire, please let us know."

"Okay… But who, exactly are you?"

"Relax, Dr. Wells. Everything will be fine. It is part of the process," said the voice. "You will be having breakfast with Mr. Jicard this morning, so please be ready in thirty minutes. Max will escort you."

"Escort? Why do I need an escort?"

"It's a bit complicated, but trust me, it will be easier with an escort. Max will be there in thirty minutes."

"Okay. Thank you, I guess."

***

56

Karen was ready when Max arrived. He knocked three times, and she opened the door. "Good morning, Dr. Wells, my name is Max." His voice was low and concise. His body filled the doorway, and he ducked to enter the room.

At three hundred pounds and nearly seven feet tall, Max was an imposing figure, to be sure. He had a serious-looking square jaw, cold dark eyes, a jagged scar on his left cheek, and a shaved head. He wore black fatigues and military-style boots.

"I will escort you to breakfast. Jicard said you would be ready."

"Good morning, Max. Thanks for coming to escort me," she said. "But first, I have a couple of questions."

Max fixed his eyes but said nothing.

"The last thing I remember was getting into the SUV at the airport, but nothing after that, until I woke up this morning. How did that happen? And for that matter, how did I wake up in a silk nightgown?"

"Jicard said that you would be ready," he repeated.

"Are you going to answer me?

No response.

"Okay, you win," she said. "Let's go. Maybe Mr. Jicard can fill me in."

It was chilly in the hallway and the air felt damp. She walked with her arms folded to keep from shivering.

When they arrived, Max knocked on the door three times. "Come," was the response.

As they entered, Karen was immediately impressed by the sheer size of the office. It was huge. It had a high ceiling with suspended lighting and a thick carpet. There were lighting panels on the walls but no windows. *Why are there no windows?*

The back of the room was dominated by a large executive desk and matching credenza. And in the center was a small round table with two chairs—it was set for breakfast.

"Please come in, Dr. Wells." Jicard was smiling. "It is a pleasure to finally meet you."

Karen walked further into the room. Max entered quietly, stepped to the left, and stood next to the door.

"It's a pleasure to meet you, as well, Mr. Jicard," she said. "And please, call me Karen." She shifted her weight to her left foot. "But before we get started, I have a couple of questions."

"I am sure you do." His smile broadened.

"Well, the trip was just fine until I landed in Billings. After that, my memory is a little sparse. Can you explain that? And how did it happen that I woke up wearing a silk nightgown?"

"Good questions," he said. "Very reasonable."

"Well?"

"It is part of our security protocol. You see, this facility's location is secret, only a handful of people know where it is. And to keep it that way, we sedate all new arrivals before transport."

"You drugged me? I don't think I'm okay with that."

"Yes, we did," he said. "Torrence injected you with a sedative when you sat down in the SUV. And when you arrived at the facility, he carried you to your room. One of our female associates got you ready for bed."

"Incredible. You drugged me. Surely I can be trusted with the facility location."

"I am sorry, Karen, but we keep that secret very close. It's been our policy from the beginning, and it works well for us." He paused a moment. "And until now, there have been no ill effects. Are you feeling all right? Are you experiencing any pain or discomfort?"

"No, I feel fine. But I think it's an extreme measure."

"That may be," he said. He moved toward the table. "Anyway, I'm glad you're okay, and I'm happy to share breakfast with you." He pulled out a chair for her. "Please have a seat. You must be starving. Maurice has everything prepared."

"We have a nice selection of brunch items to choose from this morning." He waved his hand toward a server against the far wall. "To start, we have coffee or juice with assorted fruit and Danish. Then, we have a lovely quiche Lorraine, some hash browns, and a choice of bacon or sausage, if you desire. Or, if you prefer something else, my chef will prepare anything you want. Maurice is Cordon Bleu-trained and has worked for the best restaurants in Europe." He lifted his eyes toward the door, and like magic, his chef appeared.

Maurice Duval was about five feet eight inches tall, one hundred and eighty pounds, with a deep-receding hairline. His appearance was impeccable. He wore black pants, black shoes, and a double-breasted white chef's jacket with two rows of black buttons. His name was embroidered in the script above his left breast pocket, and his collar was detailed with three French stripes; blue, white, and red.

"Good morning, madam. I am Maurice. What can I get for you?" He bowed at the waist. "Perhaps some coffee to start?"

He stepped closer, nodded to Jicard, and then turned to Karen.

"We have a fine Turkish blend, or maybe you'd prefer decaf?"

The aroma was overwhelming, and Karen was indeed hungry. "Okay, I guess, some coffee and maybe a strawberry Danish."

"My pleasure." Maurice stepped to the server, selected the items, and delivered them with another bow. He then cut a slice of quiche, dished up some sliced kiwi, and poured a glass of orange juice for Jicard.

"Now, this is more like it," said Jicard. He took a spoonful of kiwi and washed it down with a sip of juice. "Please, enjoy. We have only the best, I promise."

Karen tasted the coffee, it was warm and smooth, without a hint of bitterness, and the Danish was equally delicious. "It's marvelous, Mr. Jicard."

"Just Jicard, please."

"Okay, Jicard," she said. "The breakfast is lovely, thank you." She bowed her head and then squared her shoulders. "But could you share a bit more about the facility? What little I've seen has been extraordinary. For instance, there don't seem to be any windows. Why is that?"

"There are no windows because we are underground," he began. "Or, to be correct, under a mountain." He took another sip of orange juice. "The mountain is mostly granite and is situated on the east edge of the Bear Tooth Plateau, just north of the Wyoming border. The facility, which we call the Cave, was built during the cold war to augment NORAD but was never commissioned. Over the decades, it was written off and abandoned.

"Then, about twenty years ago, one of our founding partners learned of it while visiting with an elderly gentleman suffering from Alzheimer's. The old man drifted in and out of clarity but seemed to have no difficulty remembering his youth. And as the story goes, he was part of the initial tunneling crew.

"Of course, nobody believed him. He was simply a dying man with diminished capacity, and the stories were part of his progression." He took a bite of his quiche and continued.

"Our partner, however, was intrigued and started a quiet investigation. Within a couple of months, he was able to verify the stories and eventually found a way to acquire the facility, a ninety-nine-year lease, as I understand it. Since then, the company has invested millions in upgrades and modifications to meet our specifications. Today, it's a state-of-the-art bioengineering research facility."

"Hmm," said Karen. She took a sip of coffee.

"The mountain above our heads is solid rock, almost two thousand feet thick, and we are virtually invisible to the public."

"Invisible?"

"Well, almost," he said. "The entrances are well hidden and camouflaged."

"If nobody knows we're here, then how do we get fuel and supplies?"

"We have our own fleet of trucks, and the drivers are sworn to secrecy. Regarding fuel and supplies, we are self-sufficient for power and have stored provisions for more than five years."

"How many people work here?"

"Currently, we have two hundred and three researchers on staff. You will make it two hundred and four. Ninety-three people are dedicated to sugar cane research—the rest are working on several petroleum-related projects. We would like you to manage the sugarcane group."

She raised her eyebrows, "You want me to manage a staff of ninety-three? I am not sure that's a good idea. I have no experience in management."

"We disagree. We have great confidence in your ability. Much of our research is based on your work, and we can think of no one better to bring it to fruition."

He took another bite of his quiche and smiled. "Let's finish our breakfast, and then we will have a little tour. You will be impressed. I promise."

***

Jicard drove a four-place golf cart with Karen on the passenger side and Max in the back. He steered north through a short tunnel to enter a large cavern. It looked like it had been carved from one massive chunk of granite. High-intensity light fixtures were hanging from the domed ceiling, and a second tunnel was visible in the opposite wall. He circled to the left and stopped.

"We will begin here," he said. "Feel free to ask questions as we go."

She nodded.

"Okay then, the Cave comprises a system of eight interconnected chambers, or caverns, with a total area of five hundred sixty-six thousand square feet, about thirteen acres. This is one of the smallest, we call it the west chamber or the parking chamber, and as you can see, it has space for ten vehicles. The largest chamber has a diameter of six hundred feet, with an area fifteen times larger than this one. One of the system's two entrance tunnels is connected to this chamber." He pointed toward the opposite wall. "We use it for passenger vehicles, only. The other is at the north end of the system for commercial vehicles and delivery trucks."

Karen twisted her body to see the incoming tunnel and then craned her neck around. There was nothing else in the chamber—it was a parking garage. And at that moment, only three vehicles were present—a Mercedes sedan, which she assumed belonged to Jicard, a red Ford pickup truck, and a black SUV.

"That looks like the SUV from the airport," she said.

"It is," said Jicard. "Torrence used it last night to pick you up."

"Hmm."

"To continue," he said. "You should know that access to this chamber is restricted to authorized personnel only. From a security point of view, it's one of the most important chambers in the Cave, and it is monitored continuously." He swept his hand in a circle to point out four security cameras. "And there are three more cameras in the tunnel."

Karen held her right index finger in the air. "Excuse me. Authorized personnel?"

Jicard nodded. "Security and transportation personnel only. Nobody else is allowed."

"So, I am not authorized?"

"No, not without an escort. You will seldom require access to this chamber."

She started to object but thought better of it. *This place must be mammoth.*

Jicard switched the golf cart on and steered back the way they'd come. When they re-entered the tunnel, he activated a remote control unit, and a six-inch steel door closed behind them. It moved silently like a bank vault door, then latched securely with a resounding thunk.

The tunnel walls were also carved granite, and the floor was concrete. It was about twelve feet wide and fifty feet long, with a single row of light fixtures mounted on the ceiling. They were through it in seconds.

"This chamber, of course, is where we started. It is larger than the parking chamber. We use it for administrative offices and upper management living quarters, including yours."

Karen nodded.

"It also houses the central control room." He pulled into a small parking area. One of the four spaces was occupied by a dark-blue cart bearing a sign, 'Cave Security'. Directly ahead was a steel door, with a sign reading, 'Central Control, Authorized Personnel Only'. "Let's stop in here for a few minutes."

She was stunned when they entered. The room was huge, at least forty feet square, with a raised white-tiled floor, an acoustic ceiling, and low indirect lighting. The temperature was comfortable, and there was soft music playing in the background. In the middle of the room were two security stations arranged back-to-back, each with a dozen or more flat-screen monitors showing images from different parts of the Cave. The operators were busy taking notes as the screens cycled from camera to camera. As they approached, the operator nearest to the door rose to greet them. Jicard raised his hand, and he returned to his station.

"In this room, we collect data and monitor all activity. Currently, we are recording signals from nine hundred forty-five motion-activated cameras inside the Cave. In addition, we monitor sixty-three cameras mounted outside the Cave. They are located along the access roads and at various points around the mountain. It is impossible to approach the Cave without being detected. About ten percent of the cameras have two-way audio communication, and few have closed-circuit monitors for two-way video."

"Don't the people complain about all of the surveillance?"

"Some do, initially. But they get used to it."

"What about personal privacy?"

"Yes, good question. We do not monitor bedrooms or bathrooms."

Karen's eyebrows rose, and her mouth opened slightly. "That's something, I suppose."

They moved beyond the security stations and entered a smaller room in the back. It was packed with racks of video recording equipment and computer servers.

***

Christopher (Chip) Woodsen, one of the security operators, leaned over and whispered, "Hey Pedro, who was that?"

"I have no idea," he said. "A new tech, I guess. Pretty good looking, though."

"'Good looking'? Are your blind, man? She's a goddess!"

***

"I like to think of this room as the heart of the system. The computers in here store data and control heating, ventilation, and lighting for the Cave. It took quite a while to optimize the programming."

"Really?"

"Yes," he said. "The natural temperature in the Cave is about forty-eight degrees. So, we need heat twenty-four-seven."

The room was stuffed with electronic equipment and hundreds of colored lights— they were everywhere.

"In the beginning, we assumed that a temperature of seventy-two degrees would be ideal, and we had the lights on continuously. That worked for a while, but we soon noticed a reduction in worker enthusiasm and a general drop in morale, so we started experimenting. For several months we varied temperatures and light cycles throughout the day while tracking productivity. In the end, we found that people responded best to a standard twenty-four-hour cycle, fifteen hours of daytime, and nine hours of nighttime. And they seemed to appreciate corresponding temperature changes.

So now we control ambient conditions throughout the twenty-four-hour cycle, from seventy-two degrees and full light during daytime hours to sixty-one degrees and ten percent light at night. Of course, we never allow the lighting to drop to zero. It gets very dark in here when the lights are completely off." He paced around for a few more seconds and then said, "Okay, let's continue."

They left the control room and resumed their trek eastward through the tunnels. The next chamber was larger still, three hundred feet in diameter, with a ninety-foot ceiling. In the middle stood a four-story apartment module, with a track around the perimeter.

"How many laps to the mile?" asked Karen.

"Eight," he said. "Eight laps equal one mile on this track; seven on the other two."

"There are three running tracks?"

"That's right. "

"Are they open to everyone?"

"Of course. I run five miles here every morning," he said. "But to move on… In this chamber, we have living space for two hundred people—maintenance and service personnel mainly. Right now, it's about two-thirds full."

The next chamber was 'Petroleum Research'. It was slightly larger but similar in configuration, with a four-story module in the center and a running track around the perimeter. But instead of apartments on the ground floor, there were suites of laboratories. The upper three levels housed one-hundred-fifty people.

"You mentioned the petroleum group during breakfast," she said. "What sort of projects are they working on?"

He paused for a moment, hesitated, and then decided to answer. "They are working on several things, like gasoline additives to improve mileage while reducing emissions and petroleum additives to reduce friction in pipelines. But my favorite is our new gelation compound for oil spill applications."

"Really, a gelation compound? How does that work?"

"Well," he said. "It is a very exciting product." He turned toward her in his seat. "We dispense it from a helicopter or a customized drone." He held both hands over his head with his fingers pointing down and then wiggled them. "We sprinkle it onto the spill so it can mingle with the oil and the seawater. When it reacts, it forms a self-assembling gel that selectively traps oil molecules and repels water." He lowered his hands. "When the reaction is complete, the gel floats on the water like a giant orange sponge until it can be scooped up. It's amazing stuff."

"It sounds fascinating," said Karen. "Can we stop and take a look?"

"We don't have time today, but I'll arrange a tour for you tomorrow afternoon."

"Great." *This place is fantastic!*

They drove around the track clockwise and found three exit tunnels; one to equipment stores, a second to cane research, and a third to main receiving—they chose the third.

Wow! Her mouth dropped open, and her eyes grew wide as they entered.

It was massive. And like the others, it was a near-perfect circle. Its size was unbelievable, and the ceiling, at one hundred and twenty feet, seemed impossibly high. The chamber was illuminated by hundreds of lighting fixtures suspended on long steel rods. The combined effect was like natural sunlight. It was brilliant.

Most of the floor space, about five acres, was used for sugarcane test plots; some had new stalks, three to six feet high, while others had mature plants at twenty feet or more. The rest was dedicated to operations.

There was a receiving dock where three semi-trucks were parked, a large, fenced area for power generation, and a two-story barracks module on the opposite wall, designated 'Security'. Leading out of the chamber were two more tunnels, one about thirty feet wide, labeled 'Exit', and a smaller one, labeled 'Cane Research'.

"I have to admit," she said. "This is incredible. I have never seen anything like it."

"Few have," he said. "But I think you'll like the next chamber even more." They continued northwest via the smaller tunnel to the cane research chamber. As they entered, he turned to Karen, "Welcome home, Dr. Wells. This is where you'll spend most of your time."

It was essentially the same as the petroleum research chamber. The housing module had laboratories on the ground floor and living quarters above. But in addition to the labs, there were six environmental units for cane hybrid development.

"Wow, it must cost a fortune to operate this place. Where does the money come from? Do you rely on donations?"

"That information, Dr. Wells, is above your pay grade." He stopped the cart and gestured toward a middle-aged man next to the entrance. "Bud! Thanks for coming out to meet us."

"My pleasure, sir," he said as he walked closer. "And this must be Dr. Wells." He extended his hand. "I have been looking forward to meeting her."

Jicard turned in his seat. "Dr. Wells, this is Bud, or rather Dr. Xavier Thomas. He heads up the genetics group."

She used a firm grip to shake his hand, "It's good to meet you, Dr. Thomas, and please call me Karen."

"The same here, and Bud will do just fine."

She smiled. "Okay, it's good to meet you, Bud."

"Max and I are headed back to the office for the rest of the afternoon. Let me know if you need anything."

"But aren't there eight chambers? What about the other two?"

"You'll see them in time."

Bud stepped closer to help her out. "Come with me. We have a lot to talk about."

Chapter 13

BJ returned to the spa just after four o'clock and strolled inside. Molly was waiting.

"Wow, you look fantastic!" he said. "They did a great job. You're the right height, have the same blue eyes, and the long brown hair looks super. Girl, you could be her twin."

"I know. Right?" said Molly. "They showed me Karen's pictures, and I can't believe how much she looks like me. Even the white lab coat matches."

"And here is the finishing touch." He reached into his pocket and pulled out a ring. "Put this on. She always wears a pinky ring on her right hand."

She slipped the ring on her little finger. "It's a nice ring, BJ. Can I keep it when this is all over?"

"Absolutely," he said. He stepped back a few feet. "You look perfect."

He bowed at the waist and smiled. "Your car is waiting, my lady. We should be on our way." He held the door, and they walked out to the parking lot. At the SUV, he helped her in first and then walked around to the driver's side. Minutes later, they were back on the street and headed for Fort Collins.

"BJ, I don't know how to thank you. I haven't felt or looked this good in years! Even if this job turns out to be a bust, I'll never forget what you did for me today. Linda and I are going to use the money to find new jobs and move into an apartment. We don't want to go back to the street."

"That's great. I'm happy to help."

"So, is she getting the same sort of… preparation? I doubt she'll need as much work. She was a real beauty before we lost our jobs. We used to work together at Snow Cap Realty—she was our receptionist."

"Yeah, she told me that once. She said you used to be a broker." He glanced at the clock on the dashboard, "By this time, she should be on her way to a spa on the west side. Her shoot is later this evening, in a restaurant downtown."

"You get to know someone pretty well when you live with them on the street, and we've been together for almost two years. We are both so grateful."

"Well, you're both very welcome. And neither of you needs much 'work' as you put it. You are both beautiful. I'm just happy that I was able to do this."

"Okay, so what happens next?"

To start, we need to know how much you look like Karen. So, we'll visit one of her favorite restaurants in Fort Collins. The server has seen her many times, so we're golden if you get past him. Now your voice doesn't sound much like hers, so we want you to pretend to have a sore throat when you order. Would that be okay?"

"Yeah, sure, I can do that. It sounds like fun."

"Great. We'll be there shortly."

***

They pulled into the Roberts Barbecue parking lot at half-past five. Molly got out and walked into the restaurant alone. As she approached the counter, a man called out to her, "Hey Karen, great to see you. How's it going? Your usual, I assume…" His name nametag read 'Travis.'

"That would be great," responded Molly in a gravelly voice.

"Wow," he said. "That sounds pretty bad. Are you feeling all right?"

"I have a bit of a sore throat today, that's all," she said. "Sorry."

"No problem. Grab a seat, and I'll give you curb service."

She chose one near the door and checked out the room. It was pretty much empty. *I guess it's still a bit early for the dinner crowd.* The walls looked like the inside of a log cabin, and an old plow was hanging from the ceiling. But the aroma was delightful, and five minutes later, he arrived with her order.

"That was quick," she said.

"Jiffy service for one of my best customers," he said. "Besides, it's a little slow right now, so no sweat."

She smiled. "Thank you."

"Can I get you anything else?" he said.

"No, I'm good."

Travis lingered for a few more seconds. He loved her long brown hair. "I'm surprised to see you so early. You don't usually come in 'till about seven."

"I know. I thought I would leave a little early today, you know, sore throat and all."

"I see. Well, enjoy your dinner and take care of yourself. I have to get back." He moved slowly away, stealing glances every couple of steps.

Molly enjoyed the pork sandwich and coleslaw and then washed it down with a lite beer. *Karen sure knows her barbecue. This place is excellent.* Ten minutes later, she was back in the car.

"So, how did it go?" said BJ.

"Just great," she said. "I am sure he thought I was Karen. I got the feeling that he likes her quite a bit."

"Yeah, that's what I understand," he said. "Okay, then, we can check this box and get on with the rest of the evening. Let's go straight over to the lab and get you set up."

"Okay, I'm ready."

It took less than ten minutes to drive to the lab. Karen's car was in the lot when they arrived, the lights were on, and the front door was unlocked.

"The place looks deserted," said Molly. "Are you sure this is the right address?"

"Absolutely. Let's go inside and get ready. The camera crew will be here any minute."

He helped her out, escorted her into the building, and moved directly into the laboratory area.

"Okay, this is where you'll be doing the first scene," he said. "Let's practice one of the shots. Okay?"

"Sure."

"So, in this scene, they will ask you to put your hands on the bench, lean forward a little, and gaze out the window."

"Really?"

"Yes. Let's try it."

When her back was turned, he pulled a heavy steel rod from his back pocket and struck the back of her head. She dropped like a rag doll.

Two feet away, a cylinder of carbon dioxide was strapped to the lab bench. He released its tether and rolled it closer to Molly. Then, with great care, he tipped it over and dropped the one-hundred-seventy-pound cylinder directly on her face.

Her cheekbones splintered audibly, like the sound of a dozen eggs being crushed at the same time. Several shards of razor-sharp bone were driven deep into her brain. He lifted the cylinder and then dropped it several more times, just to be sure.

Then he opened the cylinder valve to flood the room, it made a loud hissing sound. Had Molly still been alive, she would have suffocated in seconds. It took several minutes for the cylinder to empty.

During that time, he went into the shop area to prepare for the next step. He took two one-gallon cans of methanol from a shelving unit and filled several large Erlenmeyer flasks. When he could no longer hear the gas escaping, he grabbed the flasks and returned to the laboratory area.

The floor was covered with a thick layer of carbon dioxide, like fog in a horror movie. An electric fan was sitting on the bench, so he turned it on to clear the room. And after a couple of minutes, he stepped closer.

Molly's body was lying about two feet from the bench, so he dropped the flasks in the space between. When they shattered, the thin flammable liquid spread rapidly. It formed a large puddle under the bench and soaked into the hem of her lab coat.

Finally, he lit a Bunsen burner and dropped it. Flames rushed across the floor, and within seconds, the room was fully engulfed.

BJ ran outside, and by the time he reached his SUV, the entire building was ablaze.

As the fire took hold, he heard cans of solvent exploding, one by one, in the shop area. He drove slowly out of the parking lot and stopped a few blocks away.

From his parking space, he watched with satisfaction as a billowing cloud of smoke rose from the building. Firetrucks sped toward the scene, but they could do nothing. The fire would be a total loss, and by morning, there would be nothing left.

He pulled out his phone and composed a couple of short messages; the first was to his friend in Denver:

Any problems with the packing crate?

The response:

No problems; everything went as planned.

He answered:

Understood.

The second was to Dan Turner:

Fort Collins complete.

Dan responded:

Understood. Next project: pipeline, Sunday Night.

BJ responded:

Will do.

Chapter 14

"Excuse me, ma'am? My name is Sam Wilson. I'm here to see Dr. Karen Wells. What's happened?" He stood motionless behind the police tape that surrounded what was left of the laboratory building. A middle-aged woman dressed in a blue uniform walked toward him. Her jacket had 'Coroner' printed above the breast pocket.

"Mr. Wilson, did you say?"

Sam nodded, "That's right, Sam Wilson. I have a meeting with her this morning. Is she around?"

"No, I am afraid not, and as you can see, there's been a fire," she said. "I am sorry to tell you that Dr. Wells did not survive."

"Did not survive? What are you talking about? Who are you anyway?"

"My name is Nora Peterson, with the coroner's office. I'm investigating the accident." She adjusted her glasses and pulled out a notepad.

"Accident?" Sam was dumbfounded. "How can that be? When? How?"

"As far as we know, the fire started a little before seven last evening. Apparently, she was alone in the building at the time. Her car is still here." She gestured toward the parking lot. "Did you know her?"

"She is, or rather, was," he paused for a second. "A consultant for my company."

"And which company would that be, sir?" She opened her pad and began taking notes.

"Riverside Sugar, we're located in Mowata, Louisiana. She was doing some work for us... I can't believe this."

"How well did you know her?"

Sam stared at the burned-out building. He ran his right hand through his hair and turned away. "This can't be real," he said in a whisper. "It can't be."

"Mr. Wilson? Sir? Are you all right?"

"What?" He turned back to the investigator. "Oh, yes, I'm okay. It's just the shock of it, I guess. What were you saying?"

"How well did you know the deceased?"

"Fairly well, I'd say, I was in love with her. We've been seeing each other pretty steady for the past year or so. I came out for the weekend." He turned his head away and took several shallow breaths. "What about Christi? Is she okay?"

"Do you mean Christi Snow?"

"Yes, Dr. Wells' assistant."

"She's fine. We talked with her early this morning and then sent her home. She had already left for the day when the fire started."

"Oh, good, I'm glad she's safe," he said. "And what about Karen's mother? Has anybody called her? She lives on the west side of town." Sam continued to stare at the ruins.

"Yes, we sent an officer to see her last night."

He pursed his lips and shook his head. "No, this won't do. I need to go to her right now. She must be devasted." He started to walk away.

"Hold on a moment, Mr. Wilson. How can we get in touch with you?"

"I'll be staying at the Horsetooth Mountain Inn. You can reach me there," he said. "I have to go."

***

It was a red-brick house, forty years old, with white trim and light-gray asphalt shingles. Decorative white shutters flanked its windows.

Sam walked up the front walk and knocked on the door. There was no response. He leaned to the right, peeked in one of the side windows, and then knocked again. "Mrs. Wells?" he called out. "Susan, It's Sam Wilson. Are you okay?"

A few seconds later, the door opened a crack. "Sam? Is it really you? How can you be here? Please come in."

He followed her into the living room and sat next to her on the couch. The room was dark, and the curtains were drawn. The only light was from a small table lamp in the hallway.

"How are you doing?" he said. "I was just at the lab. I can't believe it."

She was still wearing her nightgown and robe, and her hair was a mess. "Not so good. How in the world did you get here so quickly?"

"I was on the early flight this morning. I came for the weekend. We had reservations at Antonio's for dinner." He moved closer. "Oh, Susan, I am so sorry. What can I do? Have you had anything to eat? Can I get you something?"

There could be no doubt that Karen was her mother's daughter. The resemblance was striking. They had the same soft brown hair and the same deep blue eyes. People often mistook them for sisters. They were two of the most gentle and caring women he had ever known. He loved them both.

"It's been pretty rough," she said. "It is just so unbelievable. When the officer came last night, I told him he must have the wrong address. And after he left, I started to cry and couldn't stop. I cried most of the night. Karen was always so careful, so meticulous. How could this happen?"

"I wish I knew." He shook his head. "I wish I knew. I talked with the investigator, a Mrs. Peterson. She's looking into it." Susan leaned forward on the couch, head down, hands together, with her elbows on her knees. He put his arm around her shoulders. "Say, can I get you some coffee? I could make us a couple of omelets."

"Thanks, sweetie, maybe later. I don't think I could eat anything right now." She patted his hand and continued to stare at the coffee table. "But there is one thing you could do for me."

"Just name it."

"Well, last night, when the officer was here, he asked if I could go downtown and identify her body. Would you mind coming with me? I am not sure I can handle it on my own."

"Of course, I'll go," he said. "We'll do it this afternoon."

***

At the morgue, an attendant took their names and escorted them to the identification area. The room was small, chilly, and all-white. It had a white tile floor, white masonry walls, and a white acoustic tile ceiling. The overhead fluorescent lights were harsh, and there was a distinct smell of disinfectant in the air. The room's only feature was a large plate glass window with an intercom pad on the left side.

Curtains on the other side of the glass had been opened for viewing, and Molly's body was lying on a gurney, covered with a white sheet. A pathologist stood nearby with the top corner of the sheet grasped firmly in his left hand. He spoke into the intercom.

"Mrs. Wells? I am Dr. Simons. Thank you for coming down this afternoon. I am very sorry that you have to make this identification. And in this particular case, I must warn you. It will not be pretty. During the accident, she was struck by something heavy, and it caused a lot of damage. So, if you want to wait and do this another time, I will understand." He looked directly into her eyes.

She covered her mouth with her hand, glanced at Sam, and then turned back to the pathologist. "Thank you, Dr. Simons, but no. I need to do this now," she said. She grabbed Sam's right hand with both of hers. "Please go ahead."

The pathologist nodded, turned toward the body, and drew the sheet back. Mrs. Wells took one look, gasped, and turned away, "Oh my God, it's horrible." She tightened her grip on Sam's hand. It felt like someone had punched her in the stomach.

Sam put his left hand gently on her back and said, "We don't have to do this right now. We can come back another time."

She moved her head slowly from side to side, and after several moments, turned back. "No, it won't be any easier, later. I need to do this now." He nodded and continued to hold her hand as she turned to the window.

The pathologist said, "I am very sorry, Mrs. Wells."

Molly's face had been completely crushed. It was unrecognizable.

"Well, I'm not sure," she said. Her breath was shallow. "It looks like her, but…"

"Take your time Mrs. Wells. There is no hurry."

"It looks like her hair. She had it cut last week… and the shape of her face…" she said. "I just don't know." She stepped back and looked at Sam—her eyes were glazed.

"Was she wearing a ring?" she asked the pathologist.

"Yes, she had a gold ring on the little finger of her right hand."

Mrs. Wells leaned closer to the intercom, "Did it have an inscription?"

The pathologist said, "Yes, I think it did, just a moment." He picked up an evidence bag and looked at the inside of the ring. "Yes, it reads 'From Mom, Congratulations'."

Her neck and face flushed red, and her eyes filled with tears, "Yes, that's my Karen. I gave it to her the day she graduated." Her body shook.

"I am very sorry, Mrs. Wells, but we need you to state her full name, for the record."

"Okay," she said. "Yes, that is Dr. Karen Wells."

"Thank you, Mrs. Wells." The pathologist put the sheet back in place. "And thank you again for coming in."

Sam caught her as her knees buckled. She buried her face and his chest. "Oh, Sam," she sobbed. "My sweet darling Karen is gone. What am I going to do?"

He held her close. "I'm not sure, Susan. But you won't be alone," he said. "James can handle things at the farm for a while."

***

Later that day: "Hello, Nora Peterson, speaking, how can I help you?"

"Good afternoon Nora, this is Jicard."

"Yes, Mr. Jicard." She held her breath.

"I am calling to make sure you remember the deal we made—two years' tuition for a quiet resolution of this case."

"Yeah, about that, I'm not sure I can…"

"We are ready to transfer the funds today, it's the University of Texas, and your daughter's name is Michelle Peterson. Is that correct?"

"Yes, the University of Texas, but I am still not sure…"

"Nora, don't forget, we know where your daughter is."

"Oh my God, you wouldn't hurt her. Would you?"

"Of course not. We only want to pay her tuition, that's all. Why do you think we might hurt her?"

"Okay, okay, I will do what you ask."

"Thank you, Mrs. Peterson. We will transfer the funds within the hour."

Chapter 15

Nelson Oil had seven oil fields. The one attacked the previous week was their smallest, with eight wells and two storage tanks. And because of its remote location, tank trucks were required to collect the crude oil. Their largest field, with sixty-three wells and eight storage tanks, produced enough crude to justify pipeline access. And on this occasion, the pipeline was the target of choice.

It was three o'clock in the morning when BJ arrived at the tank farm. He had two men with him, and he was nervous. He hated depending on other people.

To him, more people meant more chances for mistakes. But this job required three, so he brought Tiny along for muscle and Junior to work on the control systems. Tiny was a large-framed, powerfully built man with a bald head—Junior was much smaller, almost skinny. He wore thick, black-rimmed glasses.

They cruised slowly past the main gate until they were well out of camera range and stopped behind one of the tanks. When they stepped from the SUV, the sky was clear, and the air felt crisp. There was no moon, so they used their flashlights.

They walked down a short embankment until they reached the eight-foot perimeter fence, and Tiny got right to it. He knelt in the frost-covered grass, retrieved a pair of cable cutters from his backpack, and went to work on the heavy gauge wire. BJ was in charge of the injection canister, and Junior stood to watch. It was dead quiet, and each clip of the cutter echoed on the tank wall like a plucked guitar string. It took more than fifteen minutes to create an opening big enough to crawl through.

The grass was about a foot high inside the fence and made a rusting sound as they went. They crept through the tank farm for about two hundred yards and stopped within sight of the pumphouse. Four pole-mounted floodlights surrounded the area. It was like daylight.

"Crap. I didn't know about the lights. Keep your hoods up and your eyes down." Tiny and Junior nodded. "Okay, let's move."

They dashed across the driveway and then stood close to the pumphouse wall. BJ reached for the handle door handle and pulled. *A padlock! Shit! Why do they need a padlock out here? We're miles from nowhere. Who's going to break into a pumphouse?*

"Shit," said BJ. "They padlocked the damn door." He looked at Tiny. "Break it down."

"You're kidding. Right? The door is steel, and the pumphouse is cinderblock. Do you happen to have a sledgehammer with you? Because I don't."

"Junior, can you pick it?"

He studied it for a moment. "Nope, not this one—there's no keyway. It must be one of those magnetic locks."

"But we have to get inside. Are you sure you can't break it down?" Tiny scanned the area—a chunk of iron, a prybar, a length of pipe… "I don't see anything we can use," he said. "It looks like we're screwed."

BJ glared at him in disbelief. *You were supposed to be the muscle.*

"Okay then, if you can't break down the door, then cut the lock off."

"You said the door would be open. You didn't tell me about no damn padlock!"

"Cut the lock off the door, Tiny."

"Okay, I'll give it a shot. But it's going to take a while." He retrieved a small pair of bolt cutters from his pack. "I brought these along in case the fence wire was too heavy, not for a damn padlock."

He went to work, and after a couple of minutes, BJ checked his watch. "Hurry up, man, we're exposed out here."

"I'm doing the best I can," he grunted. "The shackle is hardened steel." Sweat dripped from his forehead as he pulled hard on the handles. "And these damned cutters… they aren't big enough." He grunted again and nipped away at the shackle. It was almost ten minutes before it cut through. "There you go, BJ," he said. "The damn padlock is open. Nothin' to it." He wiped the sweat from his bald head and adjusted his hood. "And by the way, you're welcome."

BJ pushed past him to turn on the lights. Junior followed and opened the pump control panel. "It's a piece of cake," he said. "Just hook the canister up that drain port." He pointed to a valve in the pump suction line. "It shouldn't take long to pump it in."

He connected a hose to the drain port and opened the canister while Junior started the pump. Ten seconds later, it was finished. "Okay, that's it, the canister is empty. Put everything back the way you found it and pick up your stuff. Let's get the hell out of here. And for God's sake, keep your heads down."

Tiny led the way, across the driveway, past the tanks, and through the opening in the fence. BJ was close behind, and Junior brought up the rear. Five minutes later, they were in the SUV headed away from the tank farm. BJ was driving, Tiny was in the passenger seat, and Junior was alone in the back.

Junior relaxed and put his hand on the armrest. It felt cold to the touch. He rubbed his hands together to warm them. "My gloves," he muttered. "Where are my damned gloves?" He clenched his fists. "Damn it!"

"Did you say something, Junior?" said BJ. "There's a lot of road noise."

He thought for a couple of seconds and then replied, "No. It's nothing. Never mind." He turned his head to the left and gazed out the window.

Chapter 16

Tylor stepped out of his rental car, and a yellow pickup truck with 'NOC' stenciled on the door stopped beside him. Jack Nelson was behind the wheel, and the passenger window was open.

"Good morning, Jack," said Tylor through the window. "I just got here."

Jack nodded. "Yeah, I know. I saw you pull in. We got hit again last night, and it isn't good. Hop in. We can talk on the way."

Tylor grabbed his notebook and climbed into the truck. They pulled out of the lot and headed south.

"Where are we going? The tank farm is the other way."

"They hit No. 4 this time—the pipeline. It handles sixty percent of our production. Without it, we're seriously screwed. We have a lot of families to support, mortgages, car payments, and college tuition. The last thing I want to do is lay people off."

"The pipeline," said Tylor.

"Tank 401 was full this morning, and we were getting ready to pump it out. But when Luis tried to start the pump, it wouldn't run. He checked the drain ports, and nothing came out. It looks like they pumped the stuff in while the pump was running. So, now it's inside the pipe… what a mess."

"When did it happen?"

"We pumped Tank 402 yesterday, so it must have happened last night."

"Were the security cameras working?"

"Fortunately, yes. The sheriff is out there now."

"Really?"

He nodded. "I called him after we talked last week, and he came out to look at No. 1 field. So, when this happened, I called him again."

"When did he arrive?"

"About an hour ago—Luis let him in," he said. "I flat out can't afford this, Tylor. If I get hit again, I'll be out of business. I need to hire a security firm and get some guards out here."

When they arrived at No. 4 field, a patrol car was parked at the pumphouse, and the sheriff was standing behind it. The car, a forest green sedan, had a light bar on the roof and a gold star on the door, with 'Warren County Sheriff' printed beneath. The sheriff was wearing a khaki uniform with a black stripe down the pant leg, a star above his breast pocket, a black leather belt with a holster, and polished cowboy boots. His white Stetson glowed in the morning sun as he approached.

"Hi, Henry," said Jack as he climbed out of the truck. "How are you this morning?

"I'm fine—it's good to see you again. And yes, we have made a little progress," he said. "Who's this?"

"Oh, I'm sorry. Sheriff, please meet Tylor York. He's the guy I told you about. And Tylor, this is my old friend Henry Mason, Sheriff of Warren County."

"Right, I remember. He's the one who's been helping you out." He turned to Tylor. "So, you're from Georgia, I understand."

Tylor shook his hand. "Good morning, Sheriff," he said. "It's nice to meet you. And yes, I'm from Georgia, well, at least for the last few years, anyway. I'm originally from Minnesota, Two Harbors, Minnesota."

"I don't know much about Minnesota. Is that near Minneapolis?

"No, it's way up north, on Lake Superior, about seventy miles south of the Canadian border."

"Ooh, so you're no stranger to cold weather, then."

"Yeah, I know all about cold weather. That's why I live in Georgia."

The sheriff smiled and turned toward the pumphouse. "Luis showed us the pair of gloves they left behind. I guess you already know about them."

Jack nodded. "Yes, we talked earlier."

The sheriff went on, "Right. Well, they seem to be ordinary leather work gloves, nothing exceptional. But we did find some partials on the control panel."

Jack looked expectantly. "Fingerprints?"

He shook his head. "Just partials, I'm afraid. And most of them are badly smudged. I doubt they'll be of much use unless we find some to compare them with."

"And nothing special about the gloves?" said Tylor.

"Not really, they're just ordinary leather work gloves. You could get them almost anywhere."

"That's disappointing," said Jack. "When Luis told me about them, I thought they might help you find the guy."

"Well, about that," he said. "It wasn't a guy. It was a team of three guys."

"How do you know that?"

"We have them on tape," he said. "We downloaded the security footage for the pumphouse area." He stepped inside and hit play on his laptop. "Take a look."

When the playback started, they could see three men run from the tank farm, across the driveway toward the pumphouse, and then huddle against the wall. They wore dark hoods and kept their faces turned away from the camera.

"I can't see their faces."

"Yeah, they were pretty careful, but we did get their footprints," he said. "And take a look at this part. It seems they had one hell of a time getting in. They worked on that padlock for a long time. And the big guy was sweating a lot, so we might find some DNA."

"Look at the one in the middle, the skinny black guy," said Jack. "Something is hanging from his shoulder... it looks like a scuba tank."

"Yeah, we thought so too. But we can't figure out why they would need compressed air. And from the way it cut into his shoulder, it must have been heavy."

Tylor thought for a moment. "You know, Jack, that might be how they transport the gelator."

"The what?" said the sheriff.

"The gelator..." Tylor paused. "Never mind, it's a long story. Please, keep going."

"Okay..." The sheriff zoomed in on the cylinder for a few seconds so they could take a close look and then fast-forwarded about ten minutes.

"This is where they gained entry." He pointed at the screen. "Watch. Two of them go in, and the big guy waits outside. Then about three minutes later." He fast-forwarded again. "They all run out." He hit the pause key. "And check out the last guy—his hands are bare. We figure the gloves must have been his."

"Any other footage?"

"A little bit. We checked the video from the main gate cameras and found this." He selected another file, fast-forwarded about three hours, and then pressed play. "We caught a glimpse of their vehicle as it passed by. Look close—it enters the frame from the left."

On the screen, an SUV with three people inside rolled slowly past the gate entrance. But it was too far away to make out their faces.

"Can you see the numbers on the plate?"

"Unfortunately, no. The angle is wrong. But it looks like a Montana Plate. They have that blue background with a white outline," said the sheriff.

"They could have done us a favor and turned into the gate," said Tylor. "That would have been nice."

"Yeah, it's not very clear. But at least we know it was a black SUV, there were three guys inside, it might be from Montana, and it was moving south at three o'clock this morning."

"Anything else?"

"Nope, that's pretty much it. We'll take everything back to the office and get to work."

"Can I get copies of the video files?" asked Tylor.

The sheriff looked at Jack and received a nod in reply.

"It's okay with me, Sheriff. I've known Tylor for a long time. We can trust him."

"Okay, then, sure. I don't see why not. I have an empty thumb drive in here, somewhere. Hang on a minute." He found one in the bottom of his bag and plugged it into the laptop.

"How about last week? Did you find anything at Tank 101?" asked Tylor.

"Not very much. There weren't any cameras out there, and the guy who did the job was a pro. He left no trace at the tank. But," he held up his finger.

"Next to the road, we did find a couple of tire tracks. And there were several footprints near the fence. We made castings."

"Do you think he was one of these guys?"

"Can't say for sure, just yet," answered the sheriff. "But the tire tracks look like a match. So, it was probably the same van."

"Well, that's something."

"Yeah, maybe we'll get lucky. We'll verify the match when we get back to the office. And then we'll get started on the footprints."

He continued, "So at this point, it looks like they used the same vehicle for both attacks, and if the first guy did come back as one of the team…" He pointed at the laptop. "I'd bet he's the one carrying the cylinder."

The video files finished copying, and the sheriff handed the thumb drive to Tylor. "Here you go, friend. Take a good close look, and let me know if you find anything. We appreciate the help."

Chapter 17

"What do you mean, cameras? They have you on video?"

"No, I don't think so. We kept our heads down. It just took a lot longer than it was supposed to."

"But you got it done. Right?"

"For sure. We injected it while the pump was running. It's in the pipeline. That's for sure."

"Okay, then. Get your ass back to Denver as soon as you can. And remember, if anything comes of this screw up…"

"Yes, sir. I am aware…"

"You hesitated. Is there something else?"

"Just one thing, boss."

"Yes?"

"I heard they plan to hire a security firm. They will have armed guards in every field."

"It doesn't matter. We proved the formula. We'll soon be on to bigger things."

"Right."

"So, get back to Denver and team up with Christi. We need to arrange an accident for someone."

"We're planning to drive all night. So, we should be there in the morning."

***

"Hey, boss, Forgue here."

"Go ahead."

"We did not deploy last night."

"Say again."

"James Wilson was in the area, and we couldn't risk it. We had eight drones programmed, loaded, and ready, but we had to abort."

"And you're just telling me this now? That was fourteen hours ago, Forgue! Why didn't you call last night?"

"No excuse, sir. Circumstances did not permit."

"Well, set it up again for next Sunday night. And this time, make sure it happens."

"Yes, sir."

"I don't care who might be in the area. Get it done."

"Yes, sir."

Chapter 18

"West Side Express," said the agent. "How can I help you?"

"I need a ride to the airport tomorrow," said Sharon. "My flight leaves at one-forty-five in the afternoon."

"May I have your name, flight number, and destination, please?"

"My name is Sharon Wagoner, and the flight will be on Colorado West Airlines, 4023, to Billings, Montana."

"Thank you, Miss. And where should we pick you up?"

"I live at 485 Clinton Street, in Aurora, apartment 3A. The Telcorn Apartments."

"One moment, please," he said as the dispatching system processed the information. "Okay, Miss, we recommend an eleven-thirty pickup to catch that flight."

"That would be fine."

"Will you be traveling alone?"

"Yes. It's just me."

"Thank you, Miss... Your driver should be there about five minutes early, at eleven-twenty-five. His name will be Christian, and please be at the curb."

"Thank you."

"Have a nice day, and thank you for calling West Side Express."

A few moments later, the dispatcher composed a short message to Jicard.

SW is flying to Billings.

Tomorrow: CWA 4023; it lands at 3:15 p.m.

***

Sharon traveled about once every three years and had never been to Billings. So, when she entered the terminal, she was anxious.

Which way should I go? I'm no detective, and this is not a movie. I shouldn't even be here.

She entered the gate area and followed the overhead sign: 'Baggage Claim and Ground Transportation'. She turned left and proceeded down the concourse.

Melvin was here two months ago. He was right here, maybe walking in this very spot. I have to find him... Calm down, Sharon, and think! Get a grip! Where would he have gone first?

She rode the escalator down to the baggage claim—the carousels were on the right, and the rental car desks were on the left. She hoped one of the rental agents might remember him, but there were eight of them. *I have no idea which rental car company he used. Where do I start?* She paused and composed herself, *left to right, I guess.* She approached the first agent.

"Yes, Miss. Do you have a reservation?"

"No, I'm sorry, I don't. I was hoping you might be able to help. I'm looking for a friend. Would you help me, please?"

"I will if I can, Miss. What do you need?" said the agent.

She relaxed a little. The agent seemed nice. She pulled a photograph from her purse and placed it on the countertop. "Have you ever seen this man before? His name is Melvin Richards, he is twenty-nine years old, and he was here on the fifteenth of January."

"January 15th? That was over two months ago, Miss. I don't know. I see a lot of people."

"I know it was a long time ago, but please, look closely. He traveled to Billings often. Last year, he was here almost every week."

"I see—every week, you say." The agent picked the photo up and studied Melvin's face. "No, Miss. I'm sorry. He doesn't look familiar. I don't think I've ever seen him before."

Her face dropped. "Oh, okay, then. Well, thank you just the same." She retrieved a business card from her purse. "Please take my card. My name is Sharon Wagoner, and that is my cell phone number on the bottom edge," she said. "If you think of anything, please call me."

"I will, Miss. And again, I am sorry. I hope you find him."

She took the photograph back from the agent and moved to the next desk. "Excuse me, could you help me find someone? I need your help."

She moved from desk to desk, but nobody remembered his face. And after the fourth rejection, she turned to look at the baggage carousel for her flight. It had stopped, and there was the only bag on the belt. She shuffled over and picked it up. *You've come this far, Sharon. You can't give up now.*

She pulled the handle up on her roller bag and towed it back to the rental car area. There was an elderly gentleman at the fifth desk; his name tag read 'Tony'. He smiled as she approached.

"Good afternoon, Miss. You look a little lost. How can I help? I've been watching you go from desk to desk. Are you looking for something?"

"Yessir, I am. I'm looking for my friend. He seems to have disappeared."

"Disappeared, you say? Hmm. Do you have a picture of your friend?"

She handed him the photograph. "His name is Melvin Richards, and he was here on January 15th."

"What time of the day would that have been? Any idea?"

"About now, I guess. His flight landed about three in the afternoon."

"I see. Well, I didn't work afternoons during January—that would have been Meagan. Ah, Meagan Murillo."

"Meagan? Is she around?"

"No, I am sorry, she doesn't work here any more."

"Do you know where she went?"

"I'm not sure. She left sometime in February, as I recall... yes, early February. I think she found another job."

"Oh, okay then, thanks anyway. She probably wouldn't remember anyway." She stared down at the photo and gave him one of her cards. "But I do appreciate your time, and if you think of anything else, please contact me. My cell phone number is on the bottom of the card."

She then visited the last three desks, but nobody recognized his picture.

Disheartened, she shuffled back to the elderly gentleman.

"Excuse me, Tony. It's me again."

"Any luck?"

"No, not really. Nobody seems to recognize him. It's very frustrating."

He pursed his lips and nodded slowly. "I understand, and I'm sorry I couldn't help."

"Oh, that's all right. I thank you for your concern, but I'll figure it out somehow."

He nodded his head. "I'm sure you will."

"Anyway, I have a couple of places to visit tomorrow, so I'm going to need a rental car," she said. "Do you have any available?"

He smiled. "Of course, let me check." He punched a few keys on his computer and then looked up. "According to the system, we have several SUVs on the lot."

"Anything will be fine. Do you have a local map?"

"No problem." He gave her one from under the counter. "May I see your driver's license?"

She opened her billfold and placed it on the countertop.

"Thanks. This will only take a couple of minutes."

He finished the transaction and wished her good luck. As she made her way to the exit, he picked up his cell phone and sent a message to Jicard:

SW was here. She has left the terminal.

Jicard responded:

What did you tell her?

Tony typed:

Nothing.

***

The following morning, She drove up to Broadview and found Lucky's Bar & Grill. She pulled into the lot, parked, and went inside. Three people were having breakfast, and a middle-aged lady was standing behind the bar—her name tag read 'Robin James'.

Robin perked up when she walked in. "Welcome to Lucky's. We're serving breakfast at the moment. Would you like a table?"

"No, thank you. I already had breakfast."

"I see. Then, is there something else I can help you with?"

Sharon hesitated, shifted her weight from foot to foot, and then took a seat at the bar. She fidgeted with her purse.

Robin could see that she was upset and said, "Can I get you some coffee?"

"No, thank you." Sharon held up her hand. "But if you could spare a moment…"

"Okay, go ahead."

She looked closely at the name tag and said," Thank you, Mrs. James."

"Actually, it's Miss. I never married."

"Oh, sorry, I just assumed."

"No worries. You were saying?"

"Oh yeah, well, my name is Sharon Wagoner, and I am looking for a friend. He's been missing since the fifteenth of January." She placed his photo on the bar. "His name is Melvin Richards, and I was hoping you might know him."

Robin was stunned. She staggered back a step and grabbed the edge of the bar for support. "Melvin is missing? I can't believe it."

"You know him, then."

"Of course, I know him. He is a great guy," she said. "What do you mean he's missing?"

Sharon's heart started beating again. "I'm so glad you know him. I haven't heard from him since January, and I've been worried sick. Nobody knows where he is. People I've talked to said they either didn't know him or that I was just imagining things. I called everyone I could think of and got nowhere. So finally, I decided to come here and search for him myself."

Robin thought for a couple of minutes. "Then you must be Sharon, his girlfriend. Right?"

She nodded. "Yes, we are planning to get married."

"He never stopped talking about you. I've never seen someone more in love," said Robin. "He told me you were beautiful, and he wasn't kidding."

"Thank you for that." Her neck and cheeks flushed red.

"We all love him. He was here almost every night while they were building the ethanol plant." She pointed at the back corner. "He used to sit right over there and work on his laptop. Yep, he and that laptop were inseparable."

Sharon looked at the table. "When did you see him last?"

"Let me see... I'm not certain of the date. But I remember it was late afternoon when he arrived. He had just flown in from Denver, I think. It was snowing hard that day. Did you say the fifteenth? Yeah, it could have been the fifteenth."

"When he left, did he say where he was going?"

"He did. He stopped to chat on his way out and said he was headed for Rapid City. I remember because I was upset that he was leaving. He was in good spirits, though. They had just given him a nice raise, and they were sending him by corporate jet."

"How do you mean? He would have called if he had good news."

"Well, he couldn't call you," she said. "Not on his cell phone anyway. He gave it to Dan before he left. I think he was planning to call you from the airport."

"How do you know all of this?"

She pointed toward a table in the back of the room. "He and Dan were talking at his table. And well, this place isn't exactly soundproof, you know." She leaned closer to Sharon. "I overheard their whole conversation."

Sharon turned to look at the people eating breakfast and then spoke in a low voice, "I think I would like to talk with you for a while if it's okay. And maybe I'll take you up on that cup of coffee."

Robin smiled. "I'd love to. Let's find a table."

They talked for the rest of the morning. Sharon told her all about Melvin, how they met, and their plans for the future. Robin talked about the times they spent at the restaurant and how she grew to care for him. And as the conversation drifted, they also covered other subjects like families, movies, vacations, and Sharon's career as a dental hygienist.

By the time they were finished, they both felt better. And Sharon, in particular, felt re-energized. They stood by the door to say goodbye.

"Robin," she said. "Thank you so much for this. I feel a lot better."

"It was my pleasure, sweetie." She put her right hand on her shoulder. "So, what will you do next?"

"Well, this afternoon, I am going to the plant to see if I can get some time with Dan Turner. Thanks to you, I now have more information, and I might be able to pry a few details out of him. And then, depending on what I learn, I may decide to hop over to Rapid City. Maybe, someone there will remember him."

"Let's hope so. And please, let me know if there is anything I can do."

Chapter 19

From Lucky's, Sharon drove a mile north on Route 3 and turned left on Kesterman Road. She was amazed at what she saw. Hundreds of acres of tall, bright-green plants stretching to the horizon.

It is so green. I love the way it waves back and forth in the breeze. It looks like bamboo, but it can't be. Is it sugarcane? It looks like sugarcane, but this is Montana! Is that possible?

She followed a curve to the right and found more green fields. *This is amazing!* A sign on the right side of the driveway read 'North States Renewables—Broadview Operations'. She pulled in and stopped in the visitors' lot.

A large two-story building with a high roof was in the center, with storage tanks on the east side. On the west were several enormous piles of sugarcane and a railroad siding. A warm sensation spread through her chest as she stepped onto the pavement. *Melvin built this place!*

She opened the office door, walked inside, and stopped at the receptionist's desk. "Excuse me, but I have to ask. Is that sugarcane out there?"

"Yes, Miss, it is. We use it to make ethanol. This is an ethanol plant."

"Really? I thought sugarcane only grew in the south."

"We use a special hybrid designed to grow in colder climates," said the receptionist. "Did you want something?"

"Oh yes, sorry, my name is Sharon Wagoner, and I would like to see Dan Turner if he's available."

"Do you have an appointment?"

"No. I just happened to be in town and thought I would drop by. Is he here today?"

"Let me check." The receptionist rang Dan Turner's office.

***

"Yes?"

"There's a lady here to see Mr. Turner. Is he available?"

"He's in a meeting at the moment. Is it important?"

"I don't know."

"What's her name?"

"Sharon Wagoner."

"I'll hand him a note. Do you want to hang on, or should I call you back?"

"Give me a ring, and let me know."

"Fine. I'll call you in a few minutes."

"Thanks." She hung up and looked at Sharon.

***

"His secretary will call back in a few minutes. Please have a seat." She motioned to a group of black-covered chairs by the front window. "It shouldn't be long."

Sharon opted to explore a little instead.

The room was efficiently sized. The receptionist's desk and the waiting area were on the left, and a door with a keypad entry was in the back. On the right was a long wall with four framed pictures. She walked over to check them out.

The first three were aerial views of the plant at different times during construction. And the fourth was a photograph of the ribbon-cutting ceremony. She stepped closer and saw Melvin standing next to an older gentleman in black slacks and a tweed jacket. Behind them were three other men.

"Was this the ribbon-cutting ceremony to open the plant?"

"Yes, that's right," answered the receptionist. "Boy, that was some party."

"Really. I'm sorry I missed it," said Sharon. "Who are these men in the photo? The older gentleman in the tweed jacket looks interesting."

"Oh, that's Dr. Nugent, president of the company. He does look a little odd. Doesn't he? But actually, he's quite charming." She stepped from behind her desk and continued, "The younger man on his left was our engineer, Melvin Richards. And the three behind him are Governor Olsen, Mayor Dellinger from Billings, and Mr. Fu, a wealthy businessman from Helena."

"You said Melvin Richards *was* your engineer. Why the past tense?"

"Oh, Melvin left us back in January. Everyone was so surprised. We miss him a lot."

"Did you know him well?"

"Not really," she paused. "You see, I used to work in Ellendale. That's where the original offices were. I didn't transfer down here until last fall. And by that time, the construction was nearly complete. So, I only got to meet him a couple of times... you know, toward the end of the project."

"I see."

"But I really liked him. He was very smart, and he didn't act like it. He always took the time to talk with me. He was so handsome."

"Do you know why he left?"

"I haven't a clue," said the receptionist. "He was supposed to come up for a meeting one day and never did. I heard he quit. Imagine that. He just up and quit. Who does that? We were all stunned, you know, the secretaries and me."

"I understand. Really, I do. I'm his fiancée."

"Fiancée? No, you can't be. Her name was... Sharon, I think... oh, you're *that* Sharon!"

"Right. I'm that Sharon."

"Well, glory be. It is really nice to meet you. I'm Millie Carson. He talked about you all the time. You are one lucky girl!"

Sharon smiled but said nothing.

"But why did you pretend like you didn't know him?"

"Because, Millie. He's missing, and I am trying to find him."

"Missing?"

"Yes, missing. You know that day he didn't show up? Well, that was January 15, and I haven't heard from him since."

"Oh, my God. "

"Right," continued Sharon. "That's why I want to see Dan Turner. He was the last person to talk with Melvin before he disappeared."

The telephone rang, and Millie picked it up.

"Hi Tammy, what did Dan have to say?"

There was a pause.

"I see." She shook her head at Sharon. "Are you sure?

Another pause.

"Okay then, I guess that's it. Thanks."

She listened for another couple of seconds.

"I'll tell you about it later."

She hung up and turned to Sharon. "Mr. Turner's secretary says he doesn't have time to meet with you. He'll be tied up all day."

"Really? All day? He can't spare ten minutes?"

"It appears not." She stepped closer. "I am really sorry, Miss Wagoner, ah, Sharon... But that's what he said."

"I understand. He's been avoiding me for weeks. I just thought if I showed up in person, he might... you know, give me a few minutes."

"Again, I am sorry, very sorry. I wish there were something I could do."

"Thanks, Millie."

***

On the way back to Billings, her cell phone started to vibrate. She pulled off the road to check the message.

This is Tony from the rental car desk.

Please call.

She selected the voice function on her cell phone and called his number. He picked up on the second ring.

"Tony here. Good afternoon."

"Hi, Tony. You wanted me to call? This is Sharon Wagoner."

"Yes. I didn't want to use text because someone might see it someday. And I'm not supposed to contact you."

"Why not? Who would care?"

He hesitated. "Nobody would care, exactly... What I meant was, I am not supposed to contact customers. It's company policy."

"Really? That seems strange, but all right, I guess. What did you want?"

"Oh, yeah. I remembered about Meagan Murillo."

"You remembered where she went?"

"Yes. I believe she's working as a waitress at the Happy Omelet downtown."

"What is that, a breakfast place?"

"Yes, I've been there a few times— it's amazing. But they're only open for breakfast and lunch, so she's probably gone by now."

"That's okay. I've had enough frustration for one day. I'll check it out tomorrow."

"Good, I hope you find her. Well, that's it then, I guess. Good luck to you."

"Thanks, Tony, and thanks for this."

"Bye."

Sharon smiled. *Finally, a little break, and I love omelets.*

***

At seven-thirty the next morning, she arrived at the restaurant. The lime-green dining area was long and narrow, with booths along each wall and a row of smaller tables down the center. The wall along the street was plate glass, and the opposite had framed art and colorful sconces. It was bright and cheery and about two-thirds full. As she entered, she was greeted by the delightful aroma of fresh-baked bread.

The sign at the door said 'Seat Yourself', so she selected a booth close to the door. *It smells wonderful. I guess I'm hungrier than I thought.*

Soon, a waitress approached, carrying a coffee pot and a menu. She wore blue jeans, white sneakers, and a bright yellow tee shirt. A laughing omelet with red lipstick and big white teeth was on the front of the shirt. It was doing a high kick with black shoes, a cane, and a shiny top hat.

The waitress handed Sharon the menu. "Welcome to the Happy Omelet," she said. "Can I pour you some coffee?"

"Please." She pushed her mug to the edge of the table.

As she poured, a delicate wisp of steam rose from the mug. The aroma was incredible. "Can you do a mushroom and cheddar omelet?"

"Of course. We have a build-it-yourself section on page two." She leaned over and pointed to the menu. "It would normally be served with roasted tomatoes, wheat toast, and a side of fresh fruit."

"That sounds fabulous."

The waitress wrote down the order and turned to leave. "It should be about ten minutes."

"Wait a minute, Miss, if you would."

"Sure. Would you like something more?"

"No, the order is fine. But if you don't mind, could I ask your name?"

"It's Meagan, Meagan Murillo," she said. "I forgot to wear my name tag today, sorry." She stepped closer. "Is there something I can help you with?"

"Oh, yes," Sharon said with relief. "I was hoping to find you—Tony said you might be working here. Please, could you sit for a couple of minutes?" She raised her eyebrows and motioned toward the opposite side of the table.

Meagan glanced at the kitchen door. "Well, maybe just a minute. I'm not supposed to." She slid in across from her. "You've been searching for me? Why? Are you talking about Tony at the airport?"

"Yes," said Sharon. She fished Melvin's picture from her purse and placed it on the table between them. "Please tell me. Have you ever seen this man before?"

Meagan glanced at the photo and then hesitated. "Wait a minute. Who are you, and why do you want to know?" She sat back and crossed her arms.

"I am trying to find him."

"Why? I don't know who you are, and he's a good friend of mine. I'm not sure I should even be talking to you."

"Really? You know him? That is so good to hear. Where did you see him last?"

"Who are you?"

"My name is Sharon Wagoner, and he is my fiancé." She pulled a business card from her purse. "We're planning to get married."

Meagan looked at the card and thought for a moment. "Okay," she said. "If you're his fiancée, where did he go to college?"

"University of Texas," she replied. "And their mascot was called Bevo."

She relaxed. "Correct." She smiled and extended her hand. "It's nice to meet you, Sharon. He brags about you all the time. What do you mean 'you're trying to find him'?"

"Just that," she said. "The last time I saw him was on January 15 when he left for his trip. He texted me when he landed, and I haven't heard from him since."

"How odd." She put her hands on the table and closed her eyes. "Well, let's see… the last time I saw him was at the Billings airport. I guess Tony told you, I used to work out there. Melvin was one of my regulars." She sat back and gazed out the window. "He was always so nice to me. And quite frankly, he's a hunk. I had a serious crush on him. All the girls did."

Sharon squinted her eyes a bit.

She continued, "He usually arrived on an afternoon flight and always rented an SUV—he liked the extra headroom."

"Was there anything special about that day?"

"Well, now that you mention it, yes. I remember because we were out of SUVs, and I had to give him a Malibu instead—he was not happy about it."

Sharon smiled a little and nodded her head. "Was it a red Malibu?"

"Yes, it was. How did you know that?"

"It was just a guess. It doesn't matter… Can you remember anything else?"

"It's funny you should ask," she said. "He was supposed to return the car the next day, but he never showed up. I watched for him all morning." She leaned closer to the table. "And it was weird because when I checked the inventory, the car was listed as 'Returned'."

Sharon listened intently.

"So, it seems that Melvin drove up to Broadview, turned around, and then drove straight back to the airport—all in the same afternoon."

"Huh."

"He never did that before, so weird. Right? And oh yeah, there was one other thing."

"What was that?"

"Well, I never saw the red Malibu again."

"Never?"

"Nope, never. The following day, a customer wanted to rent a Malibu, and when I checked the system, it was gone. I guess someone rented it one way and drove it out of the state."

They heard voices coming from the kitchen, and Meagan turned to look. "But in any case," she continued. "I never saw it again. It was bizarre."

The kitchen door swung open, and she saw the manager watching them. His arms were crossed. "I think I need to get back to work now." She tilted her head toward the kitchen. "I'll put your order in right away."

Sharon reached over and touched her arm. "Thank you, Meagan. Thank you so much for talking with me."

She smiled. "Not at all. If Melvin's in trouble, I'm happy to help. When you find him, tell him I said hi."

"I'll be sure to do that."

So, he did return the car. I guess I'm going to Rapid City.

Chapter 20

Thirteen acres was proving more extensive than she'd imagined, and there was little time to explore. But in a few days, she had a fair idea of the general layout.

There were two main routes between her apartment and her laboratory. One followed the path Jicard took on the initial tour, and the other passed through the two chambers he skipped, namely the 'Services' and 'Equipment Stores'—she preferred the latter.

The services chamber housed the dining hall, medical/dental offices, and other personal services. Equipment stores had row upon row of shelving units jammed with equipment, tools, spare parts, and countless other items. And in the north wall of the chamber were two small detention cells—holdovers from the original construction plan.

Karen found the cells irresistible, so on her third day, she stopped to take a look. Cell 'A' appeared to be in better condition, so she checked it out first.

The door was solid steel, except for a barred viewport, and its rusty hinges squeaked as it swung open. Inside, it was small, barely ten feet square. The ceiling was low with a single lighting fixture, the walls were of rough-hewn granite, and the furniture was sparse—one table, one chair, and one small bed—on the opposite wall were a stainless steel toilet and a sink. Every surface was covered with a thick layer of grit. It was dark and chilly, and the air smelled foul.

Revolted, she shuddered and stepped quickly outside. *I think I've seen enough! I'm sure glad they don't use these any more—leftovers from the old days, I guess.*

Otherwise, her daily routine was beginning to take shape. She rose early, was at work by seven, and took her exercise in the afternoon. There was a fitness center in the services chamber with machines and free weights, but she preferred jogging. So most days, she found herself on the running tracks. And for variety, she used a different track each day. It was a Tuesday, so she was in the petroleum research chamber. She was halfway through her fourth mile when Jicard showed up.

He wore camouflaged pants, an army-green tee shirt, and running shoes. "Good afternoon, Dr. Wells. How is it going?"

"Mr. Jicard! I'm surprised to see you. I thought you ran before breakfast."

"I decided to change things up a bit. Besides, I didn't really feel like it this morning."

Karen nodded. "Yeah, I get that." They were running counterclockwise around the track.

"So, it's been six days since you joined us. Are you finding everything you need?"

"So far, so good, I guess. The work is interesting, and the staff is remarkable," she said. "The people you recruited are some of the best in the country."

"I'm glad you think so. We are constantly looking for new talent."

He dropped back a few paces to watch her run. Her powder-blue tank top and running shorts had white piping, and the lightweight stretch fabric accented every curve. Her ponytail flipped back and forth with each stride.

"But I think the most challenging aspect is the administrative role. Overnight I went from one assistant to a team of ninety-three—it's is quite an adjustment."

"It may be difficult for a while, but I'm confident you'll succeed. And if you have a real problem, Bud will be happy to help."

"Bud is truly amazing. He's an expert in his field, he's great with people, and he's been here long enough to know where everything is. I'm thankful to have him."

They passed the tunnel to staff living quarters and came to a black steel door embedded in the south wall.

"I've been meaning to ask," she said. "Where does that door lead? I see it every time I run here."

"Oh, that door?" he said. "It's an unfinished chamber. The original design called for nine chambers, but they ran out of money near the end and decided to stop at eight."

"I see."

"Access is restricted to security personnel—life support systems are not operational."

Interesting. An unfinished chamber…

"Thanks," she said. "I was just curious."

"That's okay. I am happy to answer any questions you have."

"Okay, here's another."

He increased his pace to run beside her. "Okay, shoot."

"Does Dr. Nugent ever visit the Cave?"

"Occasionally. Why?"

"I would like to set up a meeting next week, if possible," she said. "I have several questions concerning farnesene and the oil cane hybrid that I would like to discuss with him."

"Would a video conference suffice?"

"No, not really. I would like to meet him in person. A hands-on session in the lab is what we really need."

"A hands-on session. Hmm. Okay," he said. "I don't know his schedule, but I'm due to call him in the morning. I'll see if he can manage it."

"Thanks, that would be great." She slowed down and stopped at the tunnel leading to the staff living quarters. "That's it for me," she said. "It is time to hit the showers. Enjoy the rest of your run."

She jogged through the tunnel, around the staff apartments, and into the administration tunnel.

Hmm, an unfinished chamber. That might be fun.

***

The following day, she was sitting at her desk when Bud came in. "Good morning, Dr. Thomas. What's up?"

He smiled. "Not much, Dr. Wells. How about you?" He smiled and sat down across from her.

"Well, since you asked, I have been thinking about that locked door in petroleum research. Have you ever been inside?"

"Nope, and I don't care to."

"Why not? Jicard said it's an unfinished chamber. It might be interesting."

"Did he also say it's restricted access only?"

"Yes. That's what makes it interesting."

"I think not. There was a chemist here last summer who said he was going to explore it, and he never came back."

"What do you mean?"

"I mean, one afternoon Dr. Gilford was here, and the next morning he wasn't. They cleaned out his apartment the following day."

"But people don't just disappear, Bud."

"They told us he was reassigned to another facility, but that's bullshit, Karen. This is the top research facility in the country. Where else would he go?"

Karen hesitated. "I don't know. Maybe they have other facilities. I didn't know about this place before I got here."

"In any case, I have no interest in poking at it. I'll take a pass on the secret door."

Chapter 21

It was after nine o'clock when Sharon landed in Rapid City. There were no non-stops from Billings, so she was forced to fly through Denver. By the time she arrived, she was tired and frustrated.

Her first stop was the baggage claim area to pick up her roller bag, and her second was the rental car area. She talked with each rental car agent, but no one recalled seeing Melvin.

Damn it! Nobody seems to know him. More wasted time!

The next morning, she drove to the job site to find out if Melvin ever arrived. It was located in Owanka, a small community forty-five minutes east of town. When she got there, it was deserted.

Did I make a wrong turn somewhere? This is a ghost town.

There were no people and no cars. The streets, what was left of them, were cracked and overgrown with prairie grass. The few buildings still standing were weather-worn and dilapidated—roofs were collapsed or completely gone, and siding boards were missing everywhere.

I suppose it used to be a town, but there's nothing left. Why would they pick a place like this to build a plant?

She turned left across the tracks and found an entrance marked with a small sign, 'North States Renewables—Owanka Operations'. She parked next to the construction trailer and turned off her engine. The only other vehicle was a dirty pickup truck.

I hope this is the right place. It's creepy out here!

Moments later, the trailer door opened, and a man stepped out. He was in his mid-thirties, about six feet tall, and thick around the middle. He wore blue jeans, work boots, and a blue denim shirt. The sun was behind him, so it was difficult to see his face.

He hopped down from the small porch and moved toward her car. As he approached, she saw short brown hair and an unshaven beard. He was not a handsome man.

Maybe I should just start the engine and drive back to the airport...
Come on, Sharon! Buck up!

She pushed the door open, got out, and stood by the front fender. The breeze felt cold on her cheek.

"Good morning," he said as he approached. "I'm Paul Betson. I wasn't expecting visitors today." He had a friendly smile.

"Good morning," she said, extending her hand. "My name is Sharon Wagoner. I don't have an appointment. But I was hoping you might give me a few minutes."

He shook her hand. "Sure, I have some time. In fact, I would welcome the distraction. It can get pretty lonely out here."

She glanced around. *I guess it would, and maybe I should leave right now.*

"Thank you," she said. "Could we go inside? It's a bit chilly."

"Of course, right this way." They walked toward the trailer. "So, are you with the press? I could tell you a little bit about our project. We are building an oilcane processing plant. We have thousands of acres already planted." He opened the door, and she stepped through.

The trailer had a very functional layout. The lighting was fluorescent, and cheap plywood paneling covered the walls. Paul's desk sat to the right, with a computer and a bookshelf, and there was a second desk at the far end. The center was occupied by a long, slanted table piled high with three-ring binders and drawings. The vinyl floor was missing a few tiles, and there were muddy footprints everywhere.

"No, sorry. I'm not a reporter. Did you say oilcane?"

"Yes, it's a sugarcane hybrid engineered to produce oil in addition to sugar. Check it out." He pointed out the window.

She stepped close to see better. Behind the trailer was a large field of green sugarcane, waving in the breeze.

"Wow, that's impressive. I guess North State Renewables is heavy into sugarcane. I saw a similar field in Broadview."

"Yeah, but this is a different hybrid. They just look the same from a distance. But you said you weren't a reporter..."

She turned as he closed the door. "No, I'm not. I have a different reason for coming. Do you work here, all alone?"

"Yeah, but only for another week or so. The contractor will be onsite soon." He pointed to a metal folding chair by his desk. "Please, have a seat. I don't have much to offer, but the coffee's not bad."

"I would love a cup, thanks. Just black, please. It smells delicious."

He grabbed a mug from the top of the bookshelf and poured it full. "Here you go. But be careful. It's hot."

"Thanks," she said. *Maybe this won't be so bad. He seems nice enough.*

He poured one for himself and sat down at his desk. "So, what are you doing way out here? I don't get many visitors. There's nothing for miles in every direction."

Sharon had unbuttoned her coat and was sitting with her legs crossed— her long delicate fingers wrapped around the coffee mug. For Paul, it was a truly unusual experience, quite surreal. He couldn't look away.

She brushed a blonde hair from her forehead and began, "It's kind of a long story, I'm afraid. Are you sure you have the time?"

"I have nothing scheduled this morning." He took a sip of coffee and admired the dimples that formed when she smiled. "Please, regale me."

"Okay. So, I've been looking for a friend of mine." She took Melvin's picture from her purse and placed it on his desk. "Have you ever seen this man before?"

Paul picked it up and studied it carefully. After a few moments, he tilted his head to the left and glanced at his computer. "Possibly, he does look a little familiar... Yes, I think I've seen him." He paused. "Maybe in a meeting somewhere, or... no, at a conference, I think. Could his name be Mark, or maybe Thomas?"

Confused, she shook her head, "No. I mean recently, in the last two months or so. His name is Melvin, Melvin Richards. He is twenty-nine years old and lives in Denver."

"No, not recently. This is my first week on the job anyway. No, it was some time ago. I'm not quite sure." He hesitated. "Hang on for a quick minute." He opened the contact list on his computer and typed in Melvin Richards. "Yes, I thought I remembered him."

She stood up and looked over his shoulder.

"I met him at an engineering conference two years ago." He pointed at the screen. "He lives in Denver, specializes in fermentation, and wait a minute. He works for North States Renewables." He spun his chair. "I don't understand. He works for NSR?"

She nodded her head. "Yes, that's right."

He rocked back in his chair. "Maybe you should start from the beginning."

She sat back down, took another sip of coffee, and began. They talked for the next hour and a half. She did most of the talking, and Paul mostly listened. She told him how they met, about their life together, and about their plans to get married. She described how much he loved his job and how well he was doing with North States Renewables. And finally, she shared everything she had been able to learn about his disappearance.

"So," he said. "Nobody has seen him since he left Lucky's. Is that right?"

She nodded. "That's right."

"When NSR hired me, they were in a panic. They told me their engineer had left them in the lurch—they said he just up and quit. They never told me his name, but he must have been your Melvin."

She tipped her mug for a sip, but it was empty. "Could I have a little bit more, maybe half full this time?"

He rose from his chair and refilled her mug. "Here you go."

"Thank you so much, Paul. It's been great talking to someone about all this." She downed the coffee and stood to leave. "But I've taken up enough of your time. I should be on my way."

"Well, wait just a minute, don't be in a hurry. I have an idea forming," he said. "But first, tell me a little more about the red Malibu and its disappearance."

She sat down again. "Are you sure? I don't see how it can help."

"Please, tell me about the Malibu."

"Well, all right then, if you really want me to," she said. "According to what Meagan told me, the car must have been returned on the fifteenth. Because when she checked the next morning, it was listed as 'Returned'. And then on the seventeenth, it was gone—she never saw it again."

"I see. Then maybe the car was never there at all, and the computer entry was faked."

"Could they do that?"

"I should think so, and they wouldn't have to be a nerd like me." He smiled. "Anyone with access to the system could have done it."

"I guess it could have been faked. That possibility never occurred to me. But why would anyone do that?"

"I have no idea," he said. "But it might be worth looking into." He took another sip from his mug and thought for a moment.

"You know, I have a friend from my college days who used to love this stuff." He studied her face for a moment. "And I think your story might be right up his alley. Let's call and see if he would like to help."

"You would do that?"

"Sure. Why not? Your story is intriguing, and parts of it sound a bit fishy. Yeah, I think Tylor would find it irresistible." A grin formed on his face. "He'll jump at it."

He looked up a number on his contact list and punched it into his cell phone. Tylor answered on the fourth ring.

"Paul? Is that you?"

"Hey man, how is it going?"

"I can hardly believe it. Where the hell are you these days?"

"I took a job with North States Renewables in South Dakota."

"South Dakota? There is nothing out there but prairie dogs."

"Yeah, you're right. There's not much to look at."

"North States Renewables? I think I know that company. Sure, they do alternate fuels. Right? Biofuels and ethanol, I think. But I didn't know they had anything in South Dakota."

"That's NSR, okay, and you're right. They don't have anything in South Dakota, not yet. This is new construction." He paused. "But that's not the reason I called. I have a favor to ask."

"Oh yeah? What's up?"

"Well, I have a lady here who has quite a story to tell, and I think you might find it interesting."

"What kind of story?"

"It's a missing person story, actually. Do you remember that guy we met at the engineering conference a couple of years ago? His name was Melvin Richards, a young engineer specializing in fermentation design."

"Melvin Richards, huh, let me think a minute."

Paul and Sharon exchanged glances. A smile formed on her face.

"Yeah, I think so. He was a big, tall guy with boots and a cowboy hat."

"Yep, that's him," said Paul. "Apparently, he went missing in January, and his girlfriend has been trying to find him. She's with me now. Would you like to hear her story?"

"Sure, I have some time to spare. Why don't you put me on speakerphone, so I can talk with her directly?"

"Okay, just a sec." Paul pressed the speakerphone button on his phone and placed it on his desk. "Okay, that should do it. Tylor, can you hear me?"

"Loud and clear."

"Good, then allow me to make the introductions. Tylor, please meet Miss Sharon Wagoner, Melvin's girlfriend."

"Hi, Sharon."

"And Sharon, this is Tylor York, an extraordinary engineer and one of my oldest friends."

"Good morning, Tylor. It's great to meet you."

"Okay, then," continued Tylor. "As Paul said, he and I go way back. And if he thinks I can help, then I am happy to listen. So please tell me the whole story, right from the beginning. I have plenty of time, so feel free to start when you're ready."

Her dimples were deeper than ever.

Chapter 22

"Sam, there is something wrong! Come look at this." Susan was in the living room, crying. She was holding Karen's keepsake box from the funeral.

He walked in from the kitchen, "I know, I know, I miss her too," he said. "But it has only been four days. It will get easier."

"No, it's not that," she said. "I was looking at her ring. It's not right." She stopped crying extended her hand.

He sat down beside her. "What do you mean? 'It's not right'," he said in a low voice. "How is it not right? It's a beautiful ring."

"It's the font. Look at the inscription."

Sam took the ring and looked closely at the inside— "From Mom, Congratulations," he read. "Simple but meaningful, I think it's quite lovely."

She pointed at the ring. "Look closer."

"What do you want me to look at, Susan? It looks fine to me. What's wrong with it? How is it wrong?"

"It's not the words, Sam, it's the font. It should be more… scripty," she said. "I don't think it's the same ring."

"What?"

"No," she said. "I am one hundred percent sure this is not the ring that I gave to Karen."

"But how could that be, Susan?" he said. "It must be her ring. She was wearing it when they found her."

"I know. I don't understand it, either. But the ring that I gave her had a prettier font. I remember it distinctly."

"Well, if you say so, then I believe you." He turned the ring slowly in his hand so the light could enhance the engraving. "But I don't understand how it could be true." He gave it back to her. "Maybe we should call the funeral home and check into it."

"Yes, let's do that. Let's call right now."

***

Sam turned the box over and found an engraved label showing the name of the funeral home, a date, and a phone number. He took out his cell phone and entered the number.

"Eternal Rest Funeral Home, how can I help you?"

"This is Sam Wilson calling for Susan Wells. You handled her daughter's funeral this week."

"Yes, I remember. It was lovely. How can I help you?"

"Well, we were looking through her effects in the keepsake box, and there seems to be something amiss."

"The keepsake box? Something is missing?"

"No, not missing exactly. Could we come in and speak with the director? We would like to resolve this as soon as possible."

"She is meeting with another client at the moment. Would three o'clock be satisfactory?"

He looked at Susan. "How about three o'clock?"

She nodded. "Yes. The sooner, the better."

"That works for us. We'll be there."

"Fine, she'll see you then. And thank you for calling."

***

"Welcome, Mrs. Wells, Mr. Wilson. Can I get you something to drink?"

There was a pitcher of ice water on the conference table.

"No. Thanks, I'm fine."

"How about you?"

Sam shook his head. "I'm good."

"Okay, then, please, have a seat."

Susan and Sam sat together, and the director took a chair opposite them.

"Good afternoon, and thank you for coming in," she began. "My name is Eunice Forester. I am the director of the funeral home."

112

"Thank you for meeting with us, Mrs. Forester," said Sam. "We are very concerned about the ring."

"Please, Mr. Wilson, it's Ms., not Mrs."

"My apologies, Ms. Forester."

"It's all right, really. It happens all the time," she said. "But back to the purpose of your visit." She consulted a small piece of paper on the table. "Ah, Kim said you found something wrong with your daughter's keepsake box? I am deeply sorry if we made an error. What can I do to make it right?"

"No, the box is lovely. There is nothing wrong with the box. It's the ring."

"The ring, Mrs. Wells? I don't understand."

"It is not the ring I gave to my daughter on her graduation day. The font is wrong."

"What do you mean, it's wrong?"

"The inscription is in the wrong font. The ring I gave her had a prettier script. Someone switched rings."

"I assure you, we did nothing of the kind. We would never tamper with a client's effects."

"I am not accusing you, Ms. Forester. But the ring is different. It is not the ring that I gave to Karen. How could that happen?"

"Well, it couldn't happen. Not here, at least. There is just no way anyone on my staff would do that."

"Again, I am not accusing you. But someone must know what happened. The ring didn't just materialize out of nowhere."

"You are probably mistaken, Mrs. Wells. It is quite common for people to see things differently when they are grieving."

"I'm telling you, it is not the same ring." She pounded her fist on the table. "Karen was the most precious thing in my life, and I took special care when I ordered the ring. I will never forget it." She rose from her chair and glared at Ms. Forester. "It is not the same ring!"

"Calm down, Mrs. Wells. I am not disagreeing with you," she said. "If you are that sure, then I think we should call the morgue and check with them. Maybe they can shed some light on the situation."

She leaned toward the table and continued, "And since the ring is not the right ring, then maybe it wasn't Karen on that gurney. Her face was so badly damaged—I really couldn't be sure. It was when the pathologist read the inscription, that's when I knew. It was the inscription that convinced me." She calmed down, and her breathing became more measured. "I don't think it was her body. I think Karen is still alive!"

Ms. Forester thought for a moment, then looked at Susan. "It seems there may be room for doubt, Mrs. Wells. And if you're right, we need to get this straightened out as soon as possible." She picked up the phone and punched the fourth number on her speed dial.

***

"City Morgue, how may I direct your call?"

"I would like to speak with Dr. Simons, please."

A few seconds later, he was on the line. "This is Dr. Simons. With whom am I speaking?"

"Good afternoon, Dr. Simons. This Eunice Forester."

"Oh, hi Eunice, what can I do for you?"

"Well, there seems to be a problem with the Wells case. I think the deceased may not be Karen Wells. It looks like someone may have switched bodies on us."

"I doubt it. Her mother made the identification."

"I know, but she came in this afternoon with the keepsake ring, and she claims it's not her daughter's ring. Someone must have substituted it for the original."

"Eunice, it was the ring from the evidence bag. It was on her finger when we found her."

"Yes, that's the point, Parker. We think the body may not be that of Karen Wells."

"I see."

"Did you take fingerprints or DNA from the body? Is there any way we can prove it was Karen?"

"Sure, I guess so. We routinely take fingerprints, and I am sure they're in the file," he said. "If her mother could bring something in with her prints on it, we would be happy to make a comparison."

"I am sure she could do that. I will explain things to Mrs. Wells, and she'll be down directly."

"Okay. I have quite a bit of work on my desk, and I was planning to stay late anyway. So, tell her I'll be here until eight o'clock this evening."

"Thank you, Dr. Simons."

***

Sam and Susan wasted no time. They went directly to Karen's apartment and collected a telephone handset, a water glass from her bathroom, and a TV remote from the living room. They placed the items in a plastic bag and drove straight to the morgue. They were in Dr. Simon's lab by four-thirty.

"Thanks for coming down," he said. "We should be able to clear this up very quickly."

Sam handed him the plastic bag.

"These should do fine," said the pathologist. "I will dust them all and scan them into the computer. We'll use the best examples for the comparison."

Ten minutes later, the system was checking Karen's prints against the set on the file.

"Well, would you look at that," he said. "It appears you were quite correct to be suspicious. The prints do not match." He motioned for them to take a look at the monitor. "You see, the prints you supplied on the left side of the screen all match each other, but those from the deceased are different." He turned to look at Susan. "Mrs. Wells, the person in that grave is not your daughter."

She nearly collapsed with joy. "Thank you, Dr. Simons. Thank you so much!" She put her arms around his neck and hugged him tightly. "This is such a relief."

"I am sure it is, Mrs. Wells." He grabbed her arms and pulled them away from his neck. "I am happy to do it."

She calmed down a little and looked at Sam. "But if Karen isn't dead, then where is she? And who is that unfortunate girl in her grave?"

"Those are two excellent questions, Mrs. Wells, and we'll get started on them as soon as possible," he said. "Tomorrow morning, a criminal case will be opened, and the detectives will start looking for Karen. Also, we will have the body exhumed to start figuring out whose it really is. DNA analysis may help."

"Is there anything we can do?" said Sam.

"Not right now," said the pathologist. "If the detectives need anything, I am sure they'll get in touch. They do this sort of thing all the time." He paused. "But for now, I would like to apologize sincerely for this unbelievable situation. I can only imagine what you've been going through."

"It has been pretty rough, that's for sure," said Susan. "But now we have something positive to look forward to. We'll start looking for Karen, and we won't stop until we find her."

***

On the way home, Sam asked, "Do you remember where you bought the ring?"

"Sure, I do," she said. "It was Omega Jewelers, back in Sandusky."

"Oh, I guess that won't be much help, then," he said. "I thought maybe they got the substitute from the same place."

"Not very likely, I'm afraid."

"No, I guess not."

"But how would anyone even know there was an inscription? Karen never took it off."

"She must have shown it to someone at some point," he said.

"Not just someone," said Susan. "It must have been a friend, someone she trusted. Why would she show it to a stranger?"

"She wouldn't."

"No, she wouldn't."

"So, who are her closest friends here in town?"

"She actually doesn't have a lot of friends. She spends so much time at work... I guess her closest friend would be Christi, her lab assistant. But she loves Karen. She would never do anything to hurt her."

"You're probably right, but she seems to have disappeared," he said. "The investigator said she talked with her that morning and then sent her home." He slowed down to make a turn. "And when I went to her apartment the next day, she wasn't home. She is not answering her phone, and she wasn't at the funeral."

"You're right. She wasn't."

"I wonder where she is."

Chapter 23

BJ was on his third vodka when Christi walked in. He called out to her. "Hey there, Miss Snow," he said. "You are looking hot today! Get your sweet ass over here."

He was sitting at a table near the back of the room. His jacket was hanging on the back of a chair, and his beard was heavier than usual.

She sat down across from him. "It's Sunday afternoon, and you're drunk, BJ."

"Not yet," he said. "But I'm working on it." He raised his hand to summon the waitress. "Hey babe, over here. Set me up again."

"How much have you had to drink?"

"Not enough. That's for sure. Waitress! Hurry up with that refill." His cheeks were flushed, and his half-closed eyes were swollen and bloodshot.

"I think you should slow down a bit," she said. "We have work to do."

"Screw that," he said. "I'm doing just fine."

"Jicard said you'd be here."

"Screw Jicard. He's a bastard. He doesn't appreciate my skills."

"What are you talking about?"

"He sent me on that job in Dusty Fork. He knows I work alone, and he sent me anyway."

"So?"

"So, I had to take Tiny and Junior with me—the morons. They almost blew the whole gig. Junior left a pair of gloves behind, and Tiny, well, he's just stupid. He took forever getting into the shack, and there were cameras everywhere. The stupid ass."

Christi looked around the room and then back at BJ. "Keep your voice down, you idiot."

"I don't care. I have a reputation to protect, and Jicard is an asshole."

She reached over and touched his left arm. "BJ! Shut the hell up. Someone might hear you."

His head bobbed to one side.

"To hell with this. I'm not your babysitter," she said. "When you sober up, let me know."

"Huh?"

"Send me a text when you're sober." She got up and walked out of the bar.

***

Later that night, Christi was in her hotel room when his text message arrived:

Meet me at the coffee shop on 4th Avenue first thing in the morning. We need to plan for LW.

That's it? No apology? Idiot! Fine, I don't need his bullshit excuses.

Christi responded:

8:30 am. Be on time!

***

It was four o'clock in the morning in Mowata, and Forgue was fuming.

"What do you mean you lost it?" He was livid. "You had eight drones, and now you have seven? How is that possible? Did you search the entire field?"

The person on the other end spoke rapidly. "We looked everywhere, sir—it must have lost a rotor or something."

"Bullshit! You get your lazy ass back out there and find it, and I mean today! Or there'll be hell to pay." He slammed down the receiver.

***

At eight-fifteen, Christi walked into the coffee shop on 4th Avenue. It was a popular spot for the college crowd, and nearly every table was occupied. It was laid out with windows on the right and the serving counter on the left. The room's back wall was covered with floor-to-ceiling shelving units displaying all manner of coffee-related items—mugs, coffee makers, hand towels, keychains, and countless bags of coffee. The hanging lights were stained dark brown and shaped to resemble coffee beans.

She found BJ at a four-top next to the windows. He nodded as she approached.

"Hey, Christi. Nice to see you." He was clean-shaven and wearing his standard outfit—black jeans, a black tee shirt, and a black leather jacket.

She took a chair, scanned the room, and then sat down. "Are you sure you want to meet here?"

"Absolutely, I come here all the time. The pastries are excellent, and the college kids are completely oblivious. They're too absorbed in their social media nonsense to care about us." He retrieved a cardboard box from one of the open chairs. "I got you a large dark roast and a cream cheese Danish. I think you'll like it."

"Thanks, it sounds good," she said. "Now, let's get to it."

"Okay, fine. Did Jicard give you any guidelines?"

"Yes. He wants her to back off from her crusade to find Melvin Richards. We can rough her up if necessary, but he doesn't want her dead."

"Melvin Richards?" he said. "We took care of him back in January."

"I know, but she thinks he's still alive and just missing. From her point of view, he seems to have disappeared."

"Really? I guess we did a better job than I thought."

"Yeah, she's been running around asking a lot of questions. She was in Billings last week, and she even went to Rapid City."

"It won't make any difference. She's wasting her time. I can assure you there is nothing to find. We did a first-class job on him. It was one hell of a crash."

"I'm sure, but she's becoming a distraction, and Jicard is concerned that she may attract the wrong kind of attention."

"Maybe we should just tell her he's dead."

"Jicard says no," she replied. "He thinks that would start a whole new investigation, and he definitely doesn't want that."

"Okay then, we'll take care of it," he said. "All we need to do is corner her in an alley somewhere and discuss the situation. We'll give her a taste of the real world... It shouldn't take much—a punch to the gut, a knife to the throat, a sprained wrist. I don't like punching women, but a little pain can go a long way when a person has no training."

"Fine. We'll work on the approach." She took a bite from her Danish and then turned back to BJ. "I understand she got back from Rapid City yesterday, so she's probably working today."

"Great," he said. "We'll follow her for a while until we find just the right spot for our... discussion."

"Here, this is her address." She passed him a three-by-five index card.

"485 Clinton Street, Aurora," he read aloud. "No problem."

"Okay, then. And remember, we need to get the message across without drawing a lot of attention to ourselves."

They spent the next hour planning the surveillance and working out logistics.

Their exchange at the bar was never mentioned.

Chapter 24

They started mid-morning and were in the shopping center when Williamsford's opened. Susan stepped out of the car, and Sam joined her. "You know," he said. "This could take all day. There are fourteen jewelry stores in town."

"I don't care if it takes all week. We need to find out where the ring came from and who bought it."

Williamsford's was a typical jewelry store; the suspended ceiling was bristling with can lights, the walls were impeccably decorated, and the carpeting was aqua-blue. Polished-glass display cases lined both sides of the room, filled with neatly arranged trays of rings and bracelets and sparkling baubles of every description.

A salesperson was waiting as they entered. "Good morning," she said. "How can I be of service?"

Susan approached the counter and set her purse on the spotless glass case. "Good morning, my name is Susan Wilson, and I wonder if you can help me."

"Of course, Mrs. Wilson, I would be happy to help you," she continued. "Can I show you some bracelets? This week we have a forty-percent sale on white gold."

Susan looked at the salesperson's name tag and said, "Thank you, Polly. I am sure they're beautiful, but maybe another time. What I need today is some information."

Polly's exuberant smile was replaced with closed lips and a vacant stare. "Information?" she said. "What sort of information?"

She opened her purse, removed the ring from its plastic bag, and placed it on the glass case. "Please take a look at this ring. We found it last week, and we're trying to return it to its owner. Does it look familiar? Do you think they may have purchased it here?"

Polly picked up the ring and placed it under a lighted magnifying glass. "It's stunning," she said. "A beautiful design. But no, it's not one of ours."

"There's an inscription inside. Do you recognize it?

"Yes, I see the inscription. But it doesn't seem familiar. I'm sorry, ma'am." She called the manager over to take a look, but she didn't recognize it either. "I'm very sorry. I wish we could be more help."

"That's okay," said Susan. "Thanks for your time." She picked the ring up from the counter, placed it back in its bag, and returned it to her purse.

"You know," continued Polly. "It looks like something Wheeler's might carry. You might inquire with them."

"Thanks. We may do that."

***

Back in the car, Sam and Susan pulled out of the parking lot. "Susan Wilson?"

"Well, I didn't want to reveal my real name. You never know who might be listening."

"I guess so," he said. "Maybe we'll have better luck at Wheeler's."

As they turned north, Sam's cell phone started to vibrate. He pulled it from his pocket, saw his brother's name on the screen, and touched the 'Answer' button.

"Hey, James. How is it going?"

"Not so good, I'm afraid. Not good at all. Do you have a minute?"

"Sure, but hold on, I'm in traffic." He looked at Susan. "It's James. He wants to talk. I need to pull over."

Susan nodded. "Of course. Fine with me."

***

They slowed down and pulled to the curb. "Okay, James, we're stopped now. What's going on? What's happened?"

"We got hit again, Sam. It happened sometime last night."

"Really? I can't believe it. Where *this* time?"

"Along the west side of McCain Road. The entire field is gone. Why is this happening? What did we do? Nobody else around here is getting hit. Why us?"

"I have no idea, but it all seems to be connected somehow—the hybrid patch, Karen's lab, her fake death, and now her disappearance. Susan and I are working on the origin of the bogus ring, so maybe we'll have an idea soon."

"I'm sorry, Sam, I forgot what you're going through out there."

"That's okay. We need all the information we can get."

"Right."

"But for now, I suggest you give the sheriff a call. Maybe he'll find something that'll help us understand all this."

***

Sam ended the call and brought Susan up to speed.

"That's horrible," she said. "Who would do that?"

"Your guess is as good as mine," he said. "But let's keep pushing. If we figure out what happened with the ring, maybe it will help us figure out the rest of it."

A few minutes later, they arrived at Wheeler's Jewelry Emporium, but no luck. Nobody there recognized the ring either. They spent the rest of the day going from jeweler to jeweler, nine stores in all, until they walked into a store called Jenna's Jewels and Accessories.

"Oh sure," said Jenna Bosner, the owner. "It was a big seller last Christmas. It's an elegant design. But I'm afraid it's a catalog item—we don't keep it in the store. It comes from Goldstein's, down in Denver—they do the engraving too."

"I see," said Susan. "But we would like to get this one back to its owner. So, is there any way you can tell us who bought it?"

"I should think so. We always record inscriptions, so we can check them when the order comes in. Give me a minute." She opened a form on her computer and entered the inscription text. "Here it is," she said. "A Miss Karen Wells purchased the ring on the seventh of March. And according to the note, it seems she lost the original and bought this one to replace it."

Susan looked at Sam and then turned back to Jenna. "Are you sure Karen Wells purchased it?"

"Yes, ma'am, I am very sure. In fact, I seem to recall the day… it was in the afternoon, raining, I believe. I remember how stunning she looked, with her long brown wavy hair. Very pretty."

"Oh, okay. Can you tell if she financed the ring or if she used a credit card?"

"It was a credit card," she said as she studied the computer screen. "It was a company card, Denver City Productions, 1531 Larimer Street, Suite 2A, Denver, Colorado."

"Ah, Denver City Productions. Thanks for that."

"Is that significant?"

"It could be. And it might help answer a few other questions, as well." Sharon scribbled the information on a small notepad and then put it and the ring back in her purse. "Thank you so much, Jenna. You have no idea how much you've helped."

"Oh, you're very welcome. Please come again."

***

"I am confused," said Susan. "According to Jenna's computer, Karen ordered the replacement ring herself. If that's true, then maybe she really is dead, and we're just fooling ourselves. I think we should call Dr. Simons."

"Hold on a minute," said Sam. "Dr. Simons told us the fingerprints don't match, and we looked at the prints ourselves. So that means the body in the grave absolutely cannot be Karen's." He took his eyes off the road for a moment to glance at Susan. "No. There must be some other explanation."

"But if she bought the ring, then the reason I was upset was never true," she said. "It was the wrong font, but that was because she replaced the ring and wasn't able to find a perfect match. I don't know what to think any more."

"Well, try this on for size. What if the person who took Karen planned to do it all along and simply wore a wig when she bought the ring? Jenna would never know the difference."

"Who on earth would ever do that?"

"Maybe Christi was involved."

"Christi?" she said. "There is no way she would have done this. She loves Karen."

"Maybe. But whoever did it must have known her intimately. After all, the ring was duplicated to the last detail, and the inscription was almost perfect."

Susan turned to Sam. "But the ring was purchased on the seventh of March, which means it was planned long before that. She and I and Karen have been to lunch several times, and she was always around when I visited the lab. She's a wonderful person."

"I know Christi too. I've always liked her. And I agree it's hard to imagine. But who else could have done it?"

***

Later that afternoon, Jicard was in his office when the phone rang. He checked the caller ID and then picked up the handset.

"Talk to me, Forgue."

"We hit the eighty-acre field last night. We checked this morning, and the whole field is dead."

"Any problems? How long did it take?"

"We used eight drones, and they were done in ninety minutes. No problems. It was a complete success."

"Good. The funds will be transferred today. We'll be in touch."

Chapter 25

Tylor was in the 'The Patio' on twenty-eighth-floor of the Forsyth Grande Hotel. The lounge area, decorated with black leather chairs and polished stone tables, was surrounded by sliding glass panels on three sides. The view was stunning with the Denver skyline to the north and the Rockies Mountains to the west. From six-thirty to ten every morning, it was the hotel breakfast area. But at night, it was a trendy destination for high-end dining and fancy cocktails.

The table Tylor selected was on the west side of the lounge facing the mountains. In front of him were a chocolate croissant, a steaming cup of French roast coffee, and his open laptop. He was concentrating, once again, on the security footage from the pipeline attack. It had become a part of his morning ritual; breakfast, coffee, video footage, breakfast, coffee, video footage, morning after morning for the past week. It was in his head all the time; when he was eating and while he was driving… he even dreamt about it.

And once again, for the umpteenth time, he watched the team of saboteurs dash across the driveway and huddle against the pumphouse wall. The skinny black guy was making gestures at the big guy while he hacked away at the padlock, and… *Wait a minute! What was that?*

Tylor stopped the playback, backed it up a few seconds, and then hit 'Slow Motion' to view the video frame by frame. At 3:23:43.4 on the clock, the big guy turned to say something and looked directly at the camera! *Wow! How did I not see this before? I have to send it to Henry.*

He took a screenshot and attached it to a group text message.

Henry and Jack:

I found something in the security footage that may be helpful. I've watched it a hundred times, but this morning I caught a glimpse of something I missed.

Fast-forward to time stamp 3:23:43.4, and watch the big guy next to the pumphouse. He looks directly at the camera! Maybe you can send it through your facial recognition software.

Let me know if anything turns up.

I attached a screenshot for your reference.

Tylor

***

Later that morning, he went to Mordecai Finkelman's lab to see how he was doing with the samples.

"The gelator in the pipeline seems to have worked better than the one in the tank farm," said Mo.

"Why do you say that?"

He pulled a sample of each gel from a nearby shelf and set them both on the benchtop. "Watch this," he said. He picked up a stainless steel spatula and probed them in turn.

The one from the tank farm attack crumbled like a hardpacked snowball. But the one from the pipeline was much harder, more like a chunk of ice.

"What did the analysis show?"

"They seem to be identical, except for the elemental analysis," he said. "The pipeline sample has trace amounts of Tellurium."

"As a catalyst, I suppose."

"Perhaps… We're not sure yet."

"Interesting. But have you made any progress toward getting rid of it?"

"A little," said MO. "It seems to be somewhat soluble in hot dimethyl sulfoxide, DMSO."

"Really? So, we can just pump some into the pipeline to clear it out?"

"Maybe, but I doubt it. If experience is any guide, it probably won't be that easy."

"It never is," he said.

"And even if it were, we would still need an effective delivery system."

"Okay. So, do you have any idea how long it might take?"

"Maybe another week or so, perhaps two."

***

Tylor's cell phone began to vibrate on the way back to the hotel. He picked it up, and a text message from Sharon appeared:

Tylor, are we still on for this evening?

He responded:

Absolutely. Dinner at The Patio, seven-thirty.

Sharon:

Okay. I'll see you then.

Chapter 26

BJ was parked on Clinton Street when she pulled out It was six forty-five p.m. He picked up his phone and sent a quick text:

She is leaving now. I will follow.

He angled away from the curb and accelerated to catch up. When they reached Colfax, she turned west and proceeded toward downtown. The stoplights were interminable, but eventually, they entered the Voorhies Memorial curve and exited to the northwest on Fifteenth Street. *Where in the hell is she going?*

He stayed close as she made two more turns and then slowed to enter a parking garage. He couldn't believe his luck. *A parking garage will do nicely.* She stopped briefly to grab a ticket from the machine and then proceeded up the ramp. BJ followed.

The garage was positioned strategically between three high-rise hotels. It was eight levels high and could hold up to sixteen hundred cars when full. The access ramp spiraled up the south side.

When they reached the fourth level, Sharon drove to the far end of the structure and pulled into a spot marked 'Forsyth Grande Parking Only'. He proceeded past her and found a place about halfway to the door. He donned his ski mask, got out, and took up a position behind a support column.

It was seven twenty-five on Tuesday evening, and except for a small cluster of cars at the hotel entrance, the garage was empty. Outside, the sun had already dropped behind the mountains.

Sharon turned off her engine and checked her cell phone for messages. Finding none, she stole a quick glance in the mirror, grabbed her purse, and started toward the hotel entrance. It was cool in the garage, and the sound of her high heels echoed in the cavernous space.

BJ pressed his back, tight, against the concrete column and waited. "One quick punch should do it," he said to himself.

***

Upstairs, Tylor had snagged a choice table in the northwest corner of the lounge; the sunset had been a sight to behold. He took a sip of scotch and checked his watch. "I wonder where she is," he muttered. "It's almost seven-thirty."

***

When she reached the column, BJ wasted no time. He stepped out and struck her solar plexus with the palm of his right hand. The air left her lungs immediately, her diaphragm spasmed, and she dropped to her knees. He then slipped a black hood over her head, cinched it with a drawstring, and struck her face with his left fist. She dropped to the floor, and he jumped on top.

"Good evening, Miss Wagoner," he said. "I've been asked to give you a message."

Sharon gasped for air.

"If you can hear me, please nod your head."

She did so with a jerking motion.

"Okay then, here it is, and I will say this only once." He was on his knees, straddling her body. He held her shoulders down with his hands. "You have been sticking your nose where it doesn't belong. Melvin Richards is not coming back. So, just leave it alone. He is gone."

Sharon kicked her legs and tried to say something, but there was still no air in her lungs. Then, he took out a knife and held it to her throat—she stopped thrashing.

"I am sure you can feel this against your throat," he said. "One quick slice is all it would take…"

Inside the hood, her eyes went wide. She tried to scream, but no sound came out.

He paused for a moment and then pulled the knife back. "No, I won't kill you, at least not tonight. I'll just break a couple of fingers. I guess it would be tough to do your job if your right hand was in a cast. What do you think?"

130

Sharon stiffened her body and tried to push him off, but he was too strong. He struck her again, this time with his right fist. Her head lolled back, and he grabbed her hand. His grip was like a vise.

"And if you'd like, I could arrange to meet with the other ladies in your office. Think about them when you hear your fingers snap."

He held her right hand under his left knee and began to rock his weight forward. "This is going to hurt a lot, so I suggest you grit your teeth." He adjusted his weight a bit. "But if you scream, I might change my mind and just kill you. It would be easy enough."

As she started to scream, a shadow swept over her body. BJ turned to see what was causing it, and a massive fist struck him full in the face. He rolled to the side, nearly passed out, and then tried to stand.

A large man stepped across Sharon's body, grabbed BJ's upper arms, and threw them against the concrete column. His head hit hard, and he slumped to the floor. "You know, sir, where I come from, we take a dim view of men who beat up on women."

He moved closer. "And you're even wearing a mask, you lousy coward. Let's see what you look like." He stepped in, ripped the mask off, and grabbed his throat. "Tell me your name, you skinny little bastard. Who in the hell are you?"

BJ squirmed and tried to break his grip. "Piss off, asshole. This is none of your business."

"I'm making it my business." He pulled him upright, stood him against the column, and struck him hard with his left fist. "Didn't your mother teach you how to behave around young ladies? I'd bet she did, and you were just too stupid to pay attention." He pinned him firmly against the column and took a deep breath. "Well, I think it's time for a little refresher course." He punched him twice in the stomach.

They weren't perfect punches, but they were powerful. The first drove most of the air from his lungs, and the second felt like a sharp knife in his side.

He doubled over in pain. *Where did this guy come from? I have to get out of here.*

"Did you like those?" said the man. "Good, I'll give you another." He threw an uppercut to his chin, BJ's knees buckled, and he nearly passed out again. He dragged him back to his feet. "Stand up, you slimy, lowlife piece of shit."

Behind them on the floor, Sharon was regaining her breath. She turned on her side, pulled her legs up to a fetal position, and managed to make a low groaning sound. The man heard it and turned to look.

BJ took his chance—he brought his hands up sharply between the man's arms and broke his grip. He staggered away. "You were lucky this time, you bitch," he said. "But remember what I told you. Leave it alone, or the next time I won't be so nice." He stumbled to his SUV, climbed in, and drove away.

The large man knelt next to Sharon, "I'm sorry I didn't get here a little sooner, Miss. Are you okay?" He pulled the hood off, and her blonde hair spilled out on the concrete. Her cheeks were puffy, her eyes were wet with tears, and blood was dripping from the corner of her mouth. "Can you sit? I don't think that scum will be back any time soon."

She tried to push herself up but couldn't. Her chest was on fire.

"We need to hurry, Miss," He reached down, scooped her up, and carried her toward the hotel entrance. The attendant saw him approach and opened the door.

"What happened?" he said.

"Call 911, man. This little lady needs a doctor."

***

Tylor was concerned. Sharon was more than a half-hour late. *Something must have happened.*

As he reached for his phone to send a text, it began vibrating, and the caller ID read, 'Sharon Wagoner'. He touched the 'Answer' key.

"Hello, Sharon. I'm so glad you called. I was starting to worry," he said. "Is everything okay?"

"Is this Tylor York?" It was a man's voice.

He hesitated. "Yeah, this is Tylor York. Who are you, and how did you get Sharon's phone?"

"She asked me to call."

"I don't understand. Where is she?"

"Well, that's why I'm calling. She's in the hospital. She won't be able to meet with you this evening."

"Hospital? How? Why?" he said. "Who are you?"

"She was attacked in the parking garage at your hotel. I happened to be there at the time and managed to run the guy off. We called 911, and I came with her to the hospital."

"Attacked? Why?"

"I have no idea, sir. I'm just glad that I happened to be there."

"Yes, of course. And thank you for that. But who are you?"

"My name is Sam Wilson," he said. "We're at Northside Memorial. You might want to come."

Chapter 27

It was eight-thirty when Tylor arrived at the hospital; he took the elevator to the sixth floor and stopped at the nurse's station. A middle-aged woman wearing a light-blue uniform and a white hat was standing behind the service counter.

"Excuse me, ma'am. I am looking for Miss Sharon Wagoner, and I believe she's on this floor."

She checked her computer screen and then looked up. "Yes, sir. She's in room six-fourteen." She gestured to her right. "It's the next-to-the-last room."

Tylor checked her name tag and smiled. "Thank you, Nurse Combs. It was a pleasure to meet you." He nodded his head and smiled.

"You are most welcome, sir." She followed him with her eyes as he made his way down the hall.

When he reached the room, the door was open, so he stepped inside. "Sharon? Are you in here?"

It was a double room, but the second bed was empty. Sharon's was against the end wall, next to the window, and a man was with her. He rose as Tylor entered.

"You must be Tylor," he said. "I'm Sam Wilson. I called you earlier."

"Yes, I'm Tylor," he said. "It's good to meet you, and thank you for calling." He shook hands with Sam and then looked at Sharon. "So, how are you doing? I didn't expect to meet like this."

She was lying on her back with her head propped up. There were cold packs on her cheeks, a bandage on her right wrist, and an IV drip in her left arm. She smiled weakly. "Yeah, me either. I was hoping to make a better impression."

"I think we can let that slide under the circumstances." He continued to smile and touched her right hand.

She reached out with her left. "Thank you for coming. You didn't have to."

"Be careful! The IV."

She glanced at her arm and put it back on the bed. "I guess they tubed me up, pretty good."

Tylor reached over and touched her left. "No worries," he said. "It's nice to meet you in person... I am very sorry about all of this."

"It wasn't your fault."

He paused for a second. "So, ah, what did the doctor say?"

"He thinks I'm fortunate that Sam came along when he did. It could have been much worse."

He glanced at Sam. He was about an inch shorter than Tylor, but in much better shape. He had broad shoulders, wavy brown hair, and hazel eyes. His face was tight with concern.

"The doc says there'll be some bruising on my cheeks, and I'll have a couple of black eyes in the morning, and I guess my ribs might be sore for a while. But other than that, I'll be fine. He hooked me up with some good pain medication." She lifted her left arm. "He wants me to stay overnight for observation."

"What about your wrist?" He pointed at the bandage.

"It hurts quite a bit," she said. "The son of bitch had his knee on my right hand when Sam showed up. He was in the process of breaking my fingers."

She looked at Sam. "I don't know how I'll ever thank you."

Tylor stared at the bandage and tried to imagine the scene.

"But the doc says it will be fine, no permanent damage."

"Did you call the police?" he asked.

Sam stepped in. "Yes, of course, we did. They've been here and gone already. I'm surprised you didn't see them on your way up."

Tylor shook his head. "I didn't see anyone. Maybe they took the other elevator."

"I guess so."

"Do you feel up to talking about it?"

Sharon looked at Sam. "You tell him. I wasn't able to see much at the time."

He nodded and turned to Tylor. "I was getting out of my car in the hotel garage. I'm in town for a couple of days on business," he paused. "And then I heard a scuffling sound that didn't seem right. It sounded like someone was scraping their shoes on the concrete. Anyway, I walked over to see what it was."

"Where were they?"

"I found them on the floor next to one of the support columns. She was on her back with a black hood over her head, and he was sitting on top, just pounding away." He leaned forward in his chair. "Down in Louisiana, we don't take kindly to that sort of thing."

Tylor nodded.

"So, I knocked the skinny bastard off her and went after him. I held him up against the column and proceeded to beat the shit out of him, but he squirmed away before I could finish."

"Too bad…"

"Yes," he said. "But while we were fighting, I did manage to rip off his ski mask. I don't think I'll ever forget that face."

"So, then, you were able to describe him for the police." It was not a question.

"You bet," he said. "I gave them a detailed description, right down to the scar on his left cheek. I hope it helps them find the bastard."

"I'm sure glad you showed up when you did. I was just sitting up in the lounge, watching the sunset," he said. "I'm sorry I wasn't there to help."

"Don't feel guilty. There is no way you could have known," he said.

"Well, thank you anyway."

Sam looked a Sharon. "So, how do you two know each other anyway? It seems like this is the first time you've met. I'm a bit confused."

Tylor answered, "Well, we don't know each other, not exactly." He glanced at Sharon. "It's a bit of a story."

"Well, I told you mine. Now it's your turn."

"I think he's entitled to an explanation," said Sharon. "After all, he did save my life." Her puffy cheeks all but hid her dimples.

His eyes narrowed as he studied Sam's face. *Can we trust this guy? We don't know anything about him. Just how much should we share?*

He looked at Sharon again, and she nodded her head. "Go ahead, tell him everything. I think he's okay."

"Are you sure you want to hear this? It might take a while."

Sam nodded.

"Okay then, you may as well get comfortable."

He crossed his ankles, laced his fingers, and settled back in his chair. "I have nothing else to do this evening," he smiled. "I'm all ears."

Tylor dragged the guest's chair over from the second bed and sat next to him. "So, a few days ago, last Thursday, to be exact, I received a call from a friend of mine in South Dakota. Sharon was with him at the time..."

He outlined what he knew about Melvin Richard's disappearance and Sharon's quest to find him. She added details here and there to flesh out the story. And when he started talking about Melvin's job, Sam sat straight up.

"Hold on. Wait just a minute," he said. "Are you talking about NSR? North States Renewables?"

"Yes. Melvin worked for NSR. Do you know the company?"

"Hell, yes, I know the company. We've been buying cane billets from them for years; they're one of the reasons I'm out here. That, and of course, my girlfriend."

Sharon piped up, "Girlfriend? I'd like to hear about that. If you don't mind."

"Why not?" he said. "While we're swapping stories. It's a total and complete mess, and it would be nice to share it with someone."

Sam sat back in his chair and told them about the attack on the hybrid patch, the unknown body in the lab fire, Karen, and of course, her mother.

"So, you're in town to find the engraver and learn more about this Denver City Productions Company?"

"Right. And both of our stories seem to point to NSR and Billings. It's weird. But I think we might be able to help each other."

"Maybe so," said Tylor. "And I think there may be some connection with a project that I'm working on. If you have a little more time, I would like to tell you why I'm in town, apart from my meeting with Sharon, that is."

They looked at him expectantly.

"Well, in real life, I'm an engineering consultant, and one of my clients is located in Dusty Fork, Oklahoma.

"Dusty Fork?"

"Yeah, I know." He nodded. "But it's actually a real place." He continued, "Anyway, the company is Nelson Oil, and a couple of weeks ago, they called me for help."

"What happened?"

"Well, I was on my deck having my morning coffee when the phone rang. One of their tank farms was sabotaged, and they'd been up most of the night dealing with it."

He gave them a summary of the events that led to his review of the security footage and his visit with Mo that afternoon. When he was finished, Sharon said, "So, the security footage shows three guys at the terminal and a black SUV that might be from Montana?"

"Yes, and the guy who attacked you in the garage was a skinny black man, just like the one in the security footage, and he was driving a black SUV."

"That seems a bit thin. Don't you think? There are a lot of SUVs out there."

"I know," he said. "But you have to admit. It is one heck of a coincidence."

"Would you mind taking a look at the video footage? If it's the same guy, you might be able to confirm it."

"Sure, I'd be happy to," he said. "But in the morning, I'm headed over to Larimer Street to check out Denver City Productions... We could do it later in the afternoon, maybe."

"Would you mind if I took a look, too?" asked Sharon. "This is all very interesting."

"Not at all," he said. "And this time, I'd like to make sure you get there."

She tilted her head. "What do you mean?"

"Well, I think you should move into the Forsyth Grande for a few days; I'll get a room for you."

"No. Thank you, but no. I have a job to go to."

"I insist," he said. "That guy will probably try again, and I need to know you're safe. We'll call your office and explain the situation."

"I don't know. I don't see how I could possibly do that."

"I'll take you to your apartment to pick up a few things..."

She hesitated.

"Look, Sharon, if we are going to work together. I need to know you'll be all right. The hotel has great security, and there are surveillance cameras everywhere. I want to keep an eye on you."

"We're going to work together?" She managed a weak smile. "Okay, you convinced me."

"Great." He glanced at his watch. "You know what? It's getting late, and you need your rest."

Sam nodded. "Yeah, we should get out of here. We can continue this tomorrow."

He looked at Sharon. "Okay, I'll pick you up in the morning, and we'll drive out to your apartment. Then, in the afternoon, we'll meet with Sam and take a look at the video."

Chapter 28

Karen and Bud were in one of the environmental units checking on his latest oilcane hybrid. The temperature inside the unit was fifty degrees Fahrenheit, and the relative humidity was twenty percent.

"Look at that little bugger," he said. "It's growing like a weed."

"I see the pods," she said. "They are dozens of them, remarkable."

"I know. Right?" he said. "Exactly as advertised. They expand as they fill up. They should triple the terpenoid storage capacity."

"They look like leathery nodules. But they aren't very attractive."

The pods were the culmination of three years' work, and were indeed quite ugly. They resembled a tumor or an infestation on the plant's stem but were nothing of the sort. They were bioengineered storage chambers for farnesene accumulation.

"So, this hybrid will replace the one at the Owanka site?"

"On the next planting cycle," he said. "We'll start with a large test patch this year and then use the mature plants to produce the billets."

"But the hybrid in Owanka is already an oilcane."

"A modified version of the Broadview hybrid, actually. It's doing fine, but its oil storage is limited to cortical tissue. The pods will change that dramatically."

"Impressive."

"And the new facility won't even have a fermentation unit. No energy-intensive distillation."

"Fascinating. Dr. Nugent will be so pleased to see this."

"Dr. Nugent?"

"Yeah. I was talking with Jicard last week. He said he would set up a hands-on meeting for us."

"I don't think that's very likely," Bud said. "As far as I know, Dr. Nugent has never been here. At least, not in the past three years."

"Really? Jicard said he would arrange it the next time they talked."

"I'll believe that when I see it."

***

Later that morning…

"Here she comes," said Chip. "I could watch her all day."

"You *do* watch her all day," said Pedro. "You're hopeless."

Chip shrugged and kept his eyes on the monitor. "It looks like she's having lunch alone today… no wait, Dr. Jacobs is sitting down. I wonder what she sees in him? He's almost twice her age."

"It's not a romantic encounter," said Pedro. "They're probably discussing some boring research project or other."

"Did you know she runs on a different track every afternoon?" he said. "She uses our track on Wednesday and Saturday. Sometimes, I can see her from my apartment window."

"You need to get a different hobby, my friend. This is getting creepy."

He just kept watching.

***

"Hansen!" she said. "Over here! I'm so glad you could make it. How are things? I've been looking forward to talking with you."

"Oh, you know, in the Cave, every day's a holiday," he said. "But the food is outstanding." He scanned the room before he sat down.

"Yes, Maurice is a genius. But I meant with your research. You know, fuel additives, gelation compounds… It's all very exciting. I have so many questions… And I would love to chat a little about that door in the south wall of your chamber."

He straightened his back and placed both hands on the table. "Seriously, Dr. Wells," he said. "Duck confit grilled cheese? How does he come up with these recipes?"

"Okay, I get it. We'll talk about the food—my turkey-bacon club is delicious."

"I'm sorry," he said. "But I think we should stick to more mundane subjects… in public. Especially when it comes to the unfinished chamber." He dropped his head slightly and peered over the top of his glasses.

141

"What about it?"

"I've heard you've been asking around. People talk, you know."

"So, I am curious. What's wrong with that?"

"It's a very sensitive topic, and people could get hurt. It would be better if you'd just drop it, at least in public."

Not quite understanding, she said, "Okay,... I guess." She took a small bite of her club sandwich.

"It's important," he said. "I think you're the person I've been waiting for, and I know we could help each other. But we need to talk in private."

She was more than confused. "Okay, you have my attention. I don't know what you are talking about, but I'm game, I guess."

For the rest of their lunch, they chatted about the food, the ever-perfect temperatures, and some Cave gossip. When they were finished, he rose to shake her hand, and there was a small piece of paper in his palm.

"Thanks for sharing lunch with me, Dr. Wells. It was a true pleasure."

She smiled and nodded, "I enjoyed it too. I'll see you later."

She put her hand in her lab coat pocket and strolled back to her golf cart.

***

That evening, in her bedroom, she took the note from her pocket:

Things are getting very strange. Meet me in my room, #214, Thursday morning, at ten. But we need a pretense, so wear something suggestive.

She whispered to herself, "Suggestive?"

Chapter 29

Christi was sitting at their table in the coffee shop when BJ limped over.

"Hi Christi," he said. "How are things on this fine morning?"

He pulled out a chair and winced as he sat down.

"You look like you've been run over," she said. "What happened? I got you a chocolate croissant and a cup of dark roast."

"It's a long story," he said. "And thanks for ordering."

His face was bruised, and he had two black eyes—the left was swollen nearly shut. His lower lip was thick, and there was a scab in the corner of his mouth.

"Did Wagoner do that to you? She must be tougher than she looks." Her lips formed a thin smile.

"Ha, ha, very funny."

"I tried to call last night, but you didn't answer."

"I was in the emergency room, getting patched up. The doc says I have two cracked ribs."

"Ouch."

"Yeah, ouch." He winced as he reached for his coffee. "Son of a bitch!" he said. "That's hot."

Christi didn't react. "So, what happened? It looks like things didn't quite go to plan."

He took another sip and a bite of his croissant. "Everything was going fine," he said. "We were in the parking garage, having a nice chat—I had her full attention. And just as I was making my point, this big guy appeared from the shadows. I never saw him coming."

"Who was he?"

"I don't know. He sounded like he was from down south somewhere, Texas, maybe. He was a big bastard, he almost knocked me out with his first punch." He cradled his cheek in his right palm. "But if I ever see him again, the outcome will be different. You can count on that."

"I'm sure it will," she said. "Were you wearing a mask? Did he get a look at you?"

"A ski mask, actually. And no, he can't identify me. I'm not that stupid."

"Do you think he knew Wagoner?"

"No, it didn't seem so. I think he was just some do-gooder Samaritan asshole who happened to be in the wrong place at the wrong time."

"Well, we need to find out," she said. "This is one loose end that we can't just ignore."

BJ took another bite of his croissant while she went on.

"And what are we going to tell Jicard? He expects us to get the job done."

"What he doesn't know won't hurt us," said BJ. "He doesn't know about the parking garage. And I did manage to get several strong points across before the guy showed up."

"There is no way we can keep this from Jicard. If he finds out later, we're finished, literally."

"You worry too much, Christi. How is he going to find out?" He took another sip of coffee. It was a little cooler. "I think we should continue to follow her for a few days and see if she meets up with this guy," he continued. "If she does, then we'll take care of them both. And if she doesn't, then I'll have another talk with her, this time without interruption."

She shook her head slowly. "You're in no shape to take care of anyone—you can hardly stand up. No, we need to tell Jicard and recruit more help."

"Bullshit," he said. "I can take this guy out all by myself. I just need a couple of days to rest up. We don't need more help."

***

When she reached her hotel room, she was uneasy. *BJ is in over his head. He's delusional! If he meets that guy again, he'll blow the whole job. And he just might get himself killed in the process. No, I have to tell Jicard.*

She poured herself a glass of chardonnay and took a seat at her kitchen table. *I don't want to be too comfortable for this call, but a little wine won't hurt.* She took a sip.

Her watch read 11:05 a.m. *Okay, he should be back from his morning run by now.* She picked up her phone, found his number, and hit the 'Call' button, seconds later, he was on the line.

"Christi! It's nice to hear from you. What's up?"

"Morning, Jicard. I'm glad I caught you in—we need to talk. Do you have a minute?"

He was at his desk, reviewing some reports. "I always have time for you, Christi. What's up?" He leaned back and put his feet up.

"You know, we've been working on the Wagoner situation."

"Yes. I'm aware. How's it going?"

"Not so good, I'm afraid."

"Why is that? She should be easy."

"She should be, I agree. But BJ is losing perspective. I think he's in over his head."

"Really? Tell me more."

She took a deep breath. *Yes, I need to do this.* She took another sip of wine.

"Well," she said. "I went to meet with him on Sunday, as you suggested. And when I got there, he was already drunk. He looked terrible—he was loud and disgusting. He went on and on about you and that screw-up in Dusty Fork. I think that job with Junior and Tiny really shook his confidence."

"I see."

"He just wouldn't shut up about it. So, after a few minutes, I got up and left." She shifted her sitting position and drained the glass. "He texted me that night and suggested we meet on Monday morning, so we did. And by that time, he was back to normal. It was like Sunday never happened."

"Hmm. So, what did you come up with for Wagoner?"

"BJ watched her apartment and followed her for a couple of days to get her routine. And then last night, he cornered her in a parking garage."

"Okay," he said. "A parking garage is usually a good choice, not many people around."

"Well, not this time," she said. "As he tells it, they were in the middle of a serious heart-to-heart when they were rudely interrupted."

"'Interrupted'," said Jicard.

"That's his story," she said. "But if you ask me, He wasn't thinking straight. He's better than that."

"He always has been."

"Anyway, this guy came out of nowhere and changed the game. BJ took quite a beating before he could get away. He ended up in the emergency room."

"Is he okay?"

"He will be. But at the moment, he has two black eyes, a cut lip, and a two cracked ribs."

"It serves him right, the stupid son of a bitch. He let his guard down. So, what do you need from me?"

"I thought we could call in Junior or Tiny to give him a hand. Or, maybe you could have Forgue come out from Louisiana."

He thought for a moment. "No, I don't think so. Miss Wagoner is not worth the resources. She's a minor irritation at best. Besides, pretty soon, we'll need all hands on deck, including you and BJ."

She paused. "Kentala-Ridge?"

"That would be the one. The job in Dusty Fork proved the formula, so now it's only a matter of time."

"How much time, do you think?"

"I don't know yet, two or three weeks, maybe. It will take time to plan it."

"Okay, thanks. Just let me know when it gets close."

"Oh, I will," he said. "And as far as BJ is concerned, let him run with it for a while. If he's successful, then it's a good thing. And if he gets hurt again, well then, he gets hurt. Either way, he'll have a chance to redeem himself."

Chapter 30

"Pack enough clothes for a couple of weeks," said Tylor. "We don't know where we'll be going or how long we'll be there. And take a small bag for Melvin too—a pair of gloves, a shaving kit, and a winter hat, if possible."

"Why?"

"Well, we have no idea where he's been all this time. And when we find him, he'll appreciate a few personal items. I know I'm always glad to get home to my own stuff."

"Okay, sure. I think he has a small duffel in the bedroom closet—I'll toss in a few things."

"Excellent," he said.

***

They loaded everything in the trunk of Tylor's rental car and headed out. Seconds later, a black SUV stopped across the street. Tylor watched in his rearview mirror.

***

When they reached the hotel, they were greeted by a bellman pushing a brass luggage cart. He wore a crisp-blue uniform with a gold stripe down the pant leg and white gloves. "Good afternoon, folks," he said. "Welcome to the Forsyth-Grande. May I be of assistance?"

Tylor nodded and sat their bags on the cart. The bellman smiled, bowed slightly, and led them to the check-in desk.

"Good afternoon," said the desk clerk. "Two to check in?"

"Just one, actually," said Tylor. "I'm already registered."

"I see."

"Could we find Miss Wagoner a room on the eighth floor? Sharon Wagoner."

"Let me check," said the clerk as he scanned his computer screen. "Ah, yes. We seem to have two rooms available, 804 and 823. Does the lady have a preference?"

Sharon shrugged and looked at Tylor. He turned to the desk clerk. "823 would do nicely," he said.

"Fine, Room 823 it is," he said. "And how long will she be with us?"

"Two weeks. And please charge the room to my account. My name is Tylor York—I'm in 814."

"I would be happy to, sir," he said. "I have her in Room 823 for fourteen nights. Check-out will be on the eighteenth."

"Thank you."

"Excellent." The clerk handed a key card to Sharon. "Welcome to the Forsythe-Grande, Miss Wagoner. I hope you enjoy your stay." He gestured to the bellman. "Franklin will take your bags to the room."

"Thanks, but we were planning to have lunch first."

Tylor turned to the bellman, took out his wallet, and peeled off a few bills. "Take good care of the bags."

The bellman nodded, bowed again, and stuffed the cash in his pocket. "My pleasure, sir. They will be in the room waiting—I'll take them up right away."

As they walked toward elevator, Sharon said, "Two weeks?"

"I always say two weeks," he said. "If we need to leave early, we can. But sometimes, it's hard to get a room if you need to extend your stay."

"Oh, okay, I understand."

***

Up on the 'Patio', they enjoyed a leisurely lunch. Sharon was still feeling rough, so she opted for a bowl of clam chowder. Tylor enjoyed a fresh chopped salad with smoked salmon and a light apple cider vinaigrette. They talked for nearly two hours—mostly family stories and childhood experiences. And by the time they were finished, it was like they'd known each other for years.

"This has been a lovely lunch, Tylor. Thank you so much. Of course, I've heard about this place, but I've never been here—it's a little out of my price range."

"I love it," he said. "I always stay here when I'm in town." He opened his hand and turned it to the west. "The sunsets are spectacular."

"We're having dinner here tonight. Right?"

"Yes, with Sam. He said he would get here about five-thirty. So, we'll spend some time talking and looking at the security footage, and then we'll enjoy the sunset."

"I can't wait," she said. "This is so exciting."

***

Later in the afternoon, they were in the lounge when Sam showed up. He was right on time.

"Hey, Sam. We're over here," said Sharon, waving her hand. She was dressed in a smart-looking suit, pale green, with a pearl necklace. She was stunning, despite her bruises.

He moved toward their table. "Hello, Sharon. How are you feeling?"

"Still pretty sore, and the bruising is entering its purple phase," she said. She turned her head so he could see her face in profile. "It's quite lovely, I think—it coordinates nicely with my blue eyes. Am I right?"

"I'm speechless," he said. "And you're beautiful."

"Good answer." She smiled. "Can we order you a drink?"

"I think an ice-cold vodka tonic is in order," he said. "But I'm buying." He turned toward the bar and got the waitress' attention—she was at the table before he got situated.

"May I help you, sir?" She was smartly dressed in a close-fitting black uniform, tie, and pumps. The hemline of her skirt was about two inches higher than it had to be.

"Vodka tonic on the rocks for me (top shelf), make it a double, and another round of whatever they're drinking." He gave her his card. "And start a tab."

"Thank you, sir. The drinks will be right out."

He turned to Tylor and Sharon. "So, how did your day go? Mine went pretty well."

"We had a great day," said Sharon. "Tylor and I went to my apartment to pack a few bags, and he got me a room here in the hotel. Then we had lunch, and I spent the rest of the afternoon recuperating."

"Anything new with you, Tylor?"

"It was pretty much what she said, but I have one additional item to report."

"What's that?"

"When we were pulling away from her apartment to come downtown, I saw a black SUV in the rearview mirror."

"Really?"

"Yes. It stopped across the street from her apartment, and it had Montana plates."

"In front of my apartment! Why didn't you tell me?" Her eyes went wide, and she started to shake. "You should have told me! Oh my God, he's following me again. I know it!" She scanned the room, back and forth, as if he might pop out at any moment.

"It's okay, Sharon, it's okay. Calm down. He has no idea where you are." He turned in his seat. "He doesn't know my car, and we got away before he showed up. So, he can sit out there all night if he wants."

Sam reached over and touched her hand. She relaxed a bit.

"I'm sorry," she said. "Really, I am. It was just so awful. Just the thought of him sitting on top of me…"

"We understand," said Tylor. "But you're safe with us. We won't let anything happen to you."

"He's right," said Sam. "We won't let that scum bag anywhere near you."

She smiled thinly, and her breathing slowed. "Thank you both so much. I don't know how to thank you. I'll be all right, honest. It's just so fresh in my mind…"

She gulped down half of her wine and then paused to look at the glass. "And," she said. "I can see I'm going to need another one of these." She raised her hand to flag down the waitress.

Sam kept his left hand or hers and turned back to Tylor. "So, did you manage to get the plate number?"

"No, I couldn't. We were too far away at that point, but it was dark blue with white numbers and a white border. I thought about circling back, but I didn't want to risk it." He gestured toward Sharon.

Sam nodded.

"And what happened to you today? It went well. I believe you said."

"Yes, it did," he replied. "So, after breakfast this morning, I went to that address on Larimer Street—1531, Suite 2A. There was a door at the street level and a narrow stairway leading up to the second floor." He took a sip of his drink. "When I got to the office, it was locked, and there was no movement inside. I knocked on the door, but nobody answered."

"Really? That doesn't sound so good."

"It wasn't. But the door was glass, so I got a pretty good look inside. There was a reception desk with a small office in the back, but no people. In fact, I don't think anyone has been there in quite a while. Papers were strewn about, and everything was covered with dust. The place was deserted."

"Somehow, I'm not surprised."

"I think Denver City Productions is a sham."

"But if that's so, then who paid for the ring?" said Sharon. The waitress picked up her empty glass and replaced it with a fresh one.

"I can't be sure," he said. "But we may have a clue."

They were hanging on every word.

"Next door, in Suite 2B, there is a small investment firm. So, I stopped and talked with the receptionist for a while. Her name was Ms. Marla Tripsan—a lovely lady. Anyway, she's worked there for three years and told me the nobody ever visits. Apparently, the suite was leased about six months ago, and since then, the only person she has ever seen, and Tylor, you're going to love this one, was a skinny black man."

"No kidding."

"Her words, not mine, a skinny black man."

"This is so weird," said Sharon.

He took a sip of his vodka and tonic and continued, "So, let's take a look at that footage."

Tylor opened his laptop and moved to the other side of the table so they could all see the screen. He cued up the video from the main gate first.

"Ok," he said. "Here we go. This was recorded at three o'clock that morning."

As they watched, a black SUV suddenly appeared in the frame. Tylor paused the video. "There's the SUV. It's a little grainy, but if you look closely, you can count three men riding in the vehicle."

Sam leaned forward to take a better look.

"And you can see part of the license plate. It's dark blue with a white outline."

"But you can't tell who they are," said Sharon. "They're too far away."

"I know, but at least it's something," he said, "and it gets better." He cued up the pumphouse footage, fast-forwarded to 3:21 a.m., and pressed 'Play'. "Now, check this out…"

On the screen, they saw three men running across the driveway to huddle against the pumphouse wall. The skinny black guy was carrying a canister.

"There he is!" said Sam. "I can't see his face, but he certainly moves like the guy in the garage. He has the same build too."

"Okay, now we're getting somewhere," said Tylor. He stopped the playback at 3:23:43.4.

"I spotted this frame yesterday morning and sent a screenshot to Sheriff Mason. For about a half-second, the big guy looks straight at the camera."

"The video isn't all that great. Is it?" said Sharon. "I mean, the quality. It's not like in the movies."

"No, I guess it wouldn't win any awards in Hollywood. But keep watching."

He played the rest of the video, showing the big guy working on the lock, their entry to the pumphouse, and their hasty exit. And then, they watched it a couple more times.

"Well, I can't be one hundred percent sure," said Sam. "He never looked directly at the camera. But I think he was the guy in the garage."

"Good. I'll call Sheriff Mason in the morning and bring him up to speed. I'll ask him to contact the Denver Police and get them to check out Denver City Productions. Maybe he left some fingerprints."

"And what about Melvin? What do we do next?"

"Well, it all seems to be tied together, somehow. And part of the answer may be in Billings."

She said nothing.

"So, I think we should fly up there on Friday morning," he said. "We could stay a couple of days and nose around a bit. I would like to meet the people you interviewed. And I will also check the local newspaper to see if anything unusual happened the day Melvin disappeared."

She nodded. "That sounds good."

Chapter 31

The detective assigned to Molly's case was Quinton Reeves, an all-business sort-of-a guy with the Fort Collins Police Department. He was wearing a blue-stripe suit and wingtip shoes when he entered the examination room.

"Good morning, Parker, How are things going with our lady?"

"Hey, Quinton," he said. "You're in early this morning."

"I couldn't sleep. So, about five o'clock, I decided to stop trying."

Dr. Simon looked up from his work.

"I got here about six-thirty, and I've been working on Miss Greene's file ever since." He pulled a manila envelope from his briefcase and opened it on the table.

"Miss Greene?"

"Yeah," he said. "Her name is actually Molly Greene, with an extra 'e'—her fingerprints happened to be on file."

"She was in the system?"

"Well, sort of," he said." She didn't have a record, but she did have a license to sell real estate, so we had a bit of luck there."

He looked at the body and said, "I see. Well, hello, Miss Molly Greene. I'm very sorry that this happened to you. But we'll do everything we can to find the guy who did it." He turned back to the doctor. "So, what are we looking at?"

"Well, there was no smoke in her lungs, so she died before the fire ever reached her. The cause of death was blunt force trauma to her face, by something large and heavy, with a rounded surface."

"We believe the murder weapon was a compressed gas cylinder."

"That would be consistent," he said. "From the damage it caused, it's clear she was struck several times. But the first blow was the one that killed her. It drove several bone shards directly into her brain."

"So, the extra blows were meant to mask her identity."

"It seems likely," he said. "And from the condition of her hair and fingernails, I am pretty sure she had a makeover the day she died."

"A makeover?"

He shrugged, "It looks that way. But the rest of her body shows evidence of malnutrition and overall poor health. Take a look at this."

He pulled the sheet back, and they both stepped closer. "Her teeth are in horrible condition, and her skin is rough, especially her hands."

"I see that," said the detective. "Anything else?"

"Yes." He pointed to four nasty-looking scratches about an inch above her ankle. "See these? They're at least six months old, maybe more, and never healed properly. It's a fairly common occurrence among homeless people—I think she spent some time on the streets."

"I came to the same conclusion," he said. "According to the file, she grew up in Denver and had a seemingly normal life until about three years ago."

"What happened three years ago?"

"Her real estate agency went under, and she lost her job."

"I see."

"Shortly after that, she was evicted from her apartment and has been missing ever since."

"And now, she's lying on my table with a crushed face." He shook his head and looked at Molly. "Nobody deserves this, my dear, nobody. I am so sorry."

He turned toward the detective. "So, why do you think the coroner wrote it up as an accident? This was no accident, Quinton. This was clearly murder."

"I wonder the same thing," he said. "And we'll look into it." He stepped closer and studied her face. "He did a thorough job, that's for sure. Did you get anything from her stomach contents?"

"Yes," he answered. "She had barbecued pork, coleslaw, and a beer, about an hour before she died."

"Hmm, barbecue... okay, then. There are only a handful of barbecue places in town..." He turned to leave. "Thanks, Parker. I think I have enough to get started."

"We need to catch this animal, my friend," he said. "We really do. I'll let you know if I find anything else."

***

Later that day, Detective Reeves approached the Roberts Barbecue serving counter and showed his badge to the cashier. "Good afternoon, Miss. I would like to speak with the manager, please."

The cashier looked at the badge and said, "I think he's in the back. I'll get him." She stepped away from her computer monitor and went into the kitchen.

It was one o'clock in the afternoon, and the place was packed. Every table was occupied. It smelled of charred meat and hickory smoke.

A man came through the swinging saloon doors and stopped opposite the detective. "I'm Carl Roberts, the owner. How can I help you?"

Mr. Roberts was about five feet six inches tall and weighed at least two hundred pounds. He wore a plaid shirt with a bolo tie.

"Good afternoon, I am Detective Reeves with the Fort Collins Police, and I would like to ask you a few questions." He flashed his badge.

"Of course," said Mr. Roberts. "What's this about?"

He took a picture from his pocket and put it on the counter between them. "Have you ever seen this woman before?"

Mr. Roberts looked at the photograph for a while and then said, "Yes, I'm sure I have. She's one of our regulars, some kind of scientist, I think. Why? Is she in trouble?"

"We believe she may have had dinner here on the twenty-third. Do you remember seeing her that day? It was a Friday."

"You mean a week and a half ago?"

"Yes."

"A lot of people have dinner here, Detective, and Friday is one of our busiest days. I can't say for sure."

"Perhaps one of your servers might remember. Could I speak with them?"

"Let me check the schedule and see who was working that day." He tapped a few keys on the computer and pulled up a calendar. "Hmm, let's see… yes, here it is," he said. "March twenty-three. The server that day was Travis Coleman."

"Is he working today?"

"One moment." He turned and pushed open the swinging doors. "Travis? Travis Coleman. Come out front, please."

Fifteen seconds later, a young man appeared. "Yessir? Do you need something?" His eyes flicked back and forth between the detective and his boss.

"Relax, Travis, you're not in trouble," he said. "The detective, here, would like to ask you a few questions. That's all."

"Questions? Detective?" he said. "Have I done something wrong?"

"Good afternoon, Mr. Coleman. I am Detective Reeves. And no, you've done nothing wrong."

"Okay…"

"I just have a couple of questions."

"Okay…"

"Were you working here on Friday, the twenty-third?"

He paused, "Probably. I work most Fridays. Why?"

The detective pointed to the picture on the countertop. "Do you recognize this woman? And do you remember seeing her on that day?"

Travis glanced at the picture. "Sure, I know her. That's Karen Wells. She comes in a lot. She's a real looker. A biochemist, I think she said. We talk a little, sometimes."

The detective smiled. "That's great, Travis. Do you remember seeing her on the twenty-third? About a week and a half ago."

He paused and gazed at the ceiling for a minute. "Maybe… I think so. Yes. For sure, she was here. She had a bad cold that day."

"A cold?"

"Yeah. Her voice sounded real rough, gravelly-like, and she was coughing a lot. I tried to talk to her, but she didn't feel like it. She just sat in the back and waited while I got her order. I was a little worried."

"You like her, then."

"Oh, sure. She's very nice to me. We talk sometimes. She's a dream. She's not like anybody else."

"She is beautiful," said the detective. "Do you remember anything else about that day?"

"Yeah, I do. She came in really early."

"How do you mean?"

157

"Well, she usually comes in after work, you know, about seven or so. I kind of keep a lookout for her, you know. But that day, she was here about five-thirty. I asked her about it, and she said she left work early because she wasn't feeling well. You know, the cold and all."

Travis looked at Mr. Roberts and then back to the detective.

"Do you remember what time she left?"

"Not exactly, no. But she wasn't here very long. Maybe twenty minutes or so."

"Twenty minutes?"

"Yeah. I remember we weren't real busy yet. So, I was able to get her order out really quick."

"Okay, thanks… She was here early that day, about five-thirty, and left about twenty minutes later. And she had a bad cold. This is great stuff. Thank you, Travis."

He put his notebook in his pocket and stepped back from the counter. "Thank you both for your time. And especially you, Travis." He handed each of them a business card. "If you think of anything else, please let me know."

"Wait a minute, detective," said the owner. "Why are you asking these questions? Is she okay?"

"We don't know for sure," he said. "She went missing on the twenty-third, and we're trying to trace her movements."

"Missing? That's terrible."

"Yes, but we're working on it. I'll come back if I have more questions. And thank you again."

"Hold on, Detective. I think I may be able to help."

He paused. "How is that?"

"There should be a video from that day."

"You have security tape from two weeks ago?"

"We should have," he said. "Our system stores thirty days' worth on a rolling basis. It will only take a few minutes to check."

The three of them walked through the kitchen and crowded into his tiny office. There was a small desk cluttered with papers, a filing cabinet, and two shelves on the back wall. Framed pictures of his wife and son sat next to his computer.

He sat down, cued up the afternoon of March twenty-three, and fast-forwarded until the time stamp read 5:21 p.m.

Travis pointed at the screen, "There she is, just as I said."

The video showed Molly Greene, disguised as Karen Wells, entering the dining area. She took a table in the back of the room, and Travis waited on her. At 5:54 p.m. she finished and left.

But the more interesting video was from the parking lot camera. It showed a black man waiting in an SUV with blue and white Montana plates. The detective took some notes and recorded the plate number in his book.

"Could I have copies of these videos?" He reached into his pocket and retrieved an empty jump drive.

The owner took the drive and plugged it into his computer. "Of course," he said.

While it was copying, the detective turned to Travis and shook his hand. "Thank you so much. You have really made a difference."

A little embarrassed, he said, "You're very welcome, Detective. Gee, wait until I tell the guys."

The owner stood up and handed him the jump drive. "Here you go," he said. "I hope you find it helpful."

***

When the detective was back in his car, he thought about the Montana plates and decided to make a call. He opened the contact list on his cell phone, found the person he was looking for, and then touched the number. It rang only once.

"Federal Bureau of Investigation. How may I help you?"

"This is Detective Reeves with the Fort Collins Police Department. Is Special Agent Harris in the office today?"

Chapter 32

The next morning, Karen stood in front of her mirror to make sure everything was just so. She was excited about her meeting with Hansen.

She wore a black pencil skirt with a four-inch slit on her left thigh, a white button-down shirt, and black high heels. She put her hair up and selected a gold necklace with matching earrings.

"This should be suggestive enough," she said to herself. She undid the top three buttons of her blouse. "Yep. This outfit will do just fine."

***

Twenty minutes later, she walked into the lab. "Good morning, Bud. How are you this morning?"

"Wow, Karen. You look fantastic. Any special reason?"

"Not really," she said. "I just felt like dressing up a bit."

She was mesmerizing.

"Well, I'm glad you feel comfortable expressing yourself, but please don't make a habit of it."

"Why not, Bud?" she said with a smile. "Is something wrong?"

"There is nothing wrong," he said. "It's just very… distracting."

She sat down and crossed her legs. "Are you sure?"

Bud forced himself to look at his computer screen. "Yes, Karen. I'm quite sure."

She chuckled, "Oh, all right." She put her lab coat on. "Is this better?"

"A little," he said. "At least now I can get some work done."

***

The clock read 8:55 a.m. on Chip's monitor.

"Oh my God," he said. "Have you seen what she's wearing this morning?"

"No, I haven't," said Pedro. He leaned over to take a look. "Very nice."

"Show a little respect, man," said Chip. "She is the most stunningly beautiful woman I have ever seen."

"You're beyond help."

***

An hour later, Karen glanced at her monitor clock and said, "I have to go out for a while, Bud. I might be a couple of hours."

"No problem. I'll hold down the fort."

"Thanks."

She hung up her lab coat, walked outside, and climbed into her golf cart.

***

"Look, she's getting into her golf cart."

Pedro ignored him.

Chip was glued to his monitor as Karen drove from her office to the petroleum research chamber. He switched from camera to camera to keep her in view. When she reached the lab module, she left her cart and entered the elevator. He toggled a switch to bring up the apartment module cameras.

***

She stepped from the elevator, proceeded to Room 214, and knocked softly. Hansen opened the door immediately.

"So nice of you to come, Doctor Wells," he said. "Please come in."

She stepped past him and entered the apartment.

"Well, I see you took my note seriously."

"Thank you, Hansen." She did a spin so he could see the whole outfit. "Is this suggestive enough?"

He smiled and bowed slightly, "It's great to see you. Please come through."

She followed his gesture and entered the bedroom. He joined her and closed the door.

***

"They went into his bedroom!"

***

"This is very strange, Hansen," she said. "What's up?"

"I needed a ruse, and I figured a sexual liaison would be just the ticket."

She just looked at him. "Why do we need a ruse?"

"Because I wanted to talk with you out of earshot and away from the cameras. By the way, you do look fabulous."

She smiled. "Thanks, you're not bad yourself."

"You really think so?"

"Absolutely," she said with a grin. She buttoned her blouse, kicked off her shoes, and sat on a chair beside the bed. "So, what's going on?"

"Well, you haven't been here long enough to get fully indoctrinated, and you seem like a no-nonsense kind of a person."

"I'd like to think so."

"Good." He nodded. "I need to talk to someone."

She sat quietly.

"Can I trust you?" He peered over his glasses.

"Of course, Hansen. Of course, you can. What is it?"

He hesitated. "Can I get you something to drink? I think I have some coffee."

"Hansen." Her eyes narrowed.

"Oh, okay then." He opened the top drawer of his dresser, took out two small bottles, and held them out. "Take a look at these."

Cautiously, she leaned forward and accepted the bottles. The first, labeled #1, contained an orange spongy material that quivered like jelly when she shook it. The second held a dull-gray material, like oily sand. When she tilted the bottle, it slid back and forth like a wet clump.

"Fascinating," she said. "What am I looking at?"

"That's the thing. I'm not exactly sure," he said. "Those are supposed to be identical."

She looked at the bottles again. "Okay," she said slowly. "I'm going to need a little more."

***

"They've been in there over fifteen minutes. I'm starting to get worried. What could they possibly be doing?"

"Relax, man. The techs are always shacking up with each other. You know that."

"Yeah, but this is Dr. Wells," he said. "She would never…"

"Oh, grow up, man."

***

Hansen continued, "About a week ago, I was talking about the gelator with Stephen. He's one of my technicians."

She nodded.

"You know, when it's mixed with oil, it produces that orange sponge-like material." He pointed to bottle #1.

"Yeah. Go on."

"Well, he was excited because sales are going well, and Dr. Nugent contracted with a plant in Houston to make it in commercial quantities. They are calling it NuAge OilSorb."

"That's great news."

"Yes."

"But then, on Tuesday afternoon, we found something strange."

"This gray material?"

"Well, sort of, yes," he said. "We were running some tests on our lab batches, and we found a container that didn't have a label. We assumed it was just another batch of a gelator, so we tested it like the rest. But when we mixed with oil, it produced the stuff in bottle #2."

"Huh." She looked at the bottle again and held it up to the light.

"So, where did it come from? What is it? Is there an error in the formulation?"

163

"We don't think so," he said. "Stephan did a full workup, and it appears to have the same composition as our gelator, except for a few extra polymer chains and a trace amount of tellurium."

"Tellurium? How odd."

"Exactly," he said. "We don't use tellurium in anything."

"So why would anyone do this? What good is it?"

"It looks like sabotage. This stuff sinks like a rock. And if somebody used it on an oil spill, it would cause an ecological disaster."

"I see. The oil would sink to the bottom and make its recovery virtually impossible."

"Right," he said. "I don't know about you, but I've always been a company man. I believe in what we're doing, and if somebody is messing with our research, I need to know who's doing it. I want to tell Dr. Nugent about it, but first, I need to be sure."

She nodded. "But it can't be sabotage. Jicard would never allow it."

"Maybe. Maybe not. Who knows? I've never really trusted him."

"But if he's involved…"

"Then we need to be extra careful."

***

"It's been almost an hour, Pedro. I'm going to have them checked out." He reached for his phone.

"Cool your jets, Chip. You might catch them in the middle of something. It could be very embarrassing for Dr. Wells."

He considered that for a moment and then pulled his hand back. "Okay, I'll watch a little while longer."

***

Karen looked at Hansen. "Okay, you've piqued my interest," she said. "How can I help?"

"Well, the other day, I was jogging on the track, and I heard a noise from inside chamber nine."

"Really? What kind of noise?"

"It was a sharp, metal-clanging noise. Like something heavy falling on a concrete floor."

"But the chamber is empty—Jicard told me so."

"Yeah, that's what everyone believes. But there was no mistaking that noise. I heard what I heard."

"It's that door again. I've wondered about it since day one."

"I know. Bud told me."

"That rat. It's impossible to keep a secret in here."

He nodded. "I know. But we're going to keep this one."

She nodded. "Cross my heart."

"Okay. In addition to the noise I heard, there is something else."

"What?"

"Well, there's a door in our lab suite with a 'Security Personnel Only' sign that has never been used. At least, not since I've been here."

"And you think it leads to chamber nine?"

"I don't know. Probably not."

"Then, I don't understand."

He went on. "Last weekend, I was putting some samples away and happened to notice some footprints in front of the door. They weren't obvious, but I could see them where the ceiling lights reflected on the tiles."

"And you think they have something to do with this gray crystalline material."

"Who knows? But I've been thinking about checking it out."

"I want to go with you," she said quickly. "I'm in."

"I was hoping you would say that," he said. "But we need to consider the risk. You know how Jicard is about breaking the rules, especially security rules."

"Right, the cameras," she said. "They'll see us in a minute."

"Maybe not," he said. "There is only one camera near the doors, and Stephan thinks he can replace its feed with some prerecorded video."

"Really? Is he coming with us?" she said.

"No, he'll hang back and keep watch while we're inside."

"Okay, so, when do we do this?"

"Tonight, about eleven."

"I'll be there."

"We'll need a good reason to meet," he said.

"Let's see," she mused. "I haven't been sleeping well recently, and I am very interested in your research. So, you could invite me over to see one of your experiments."

"Okay, I like it. Consider yourself invited," he said. "Yes, that could work."

"Great. Then, I'll see you at eleven."

Chapter 33

After dinner, Karen returned to her apartment, rested for a while, and thought about the evening ahead. She was giddy with anticipation. *Maybe it's a hidden laboratory or a secret passage. Can Stephan really rig the camera? What if Jicard finds out?*

At ten-thirty, she got up, swept her hair back in a ponytail, and washed her face. She selected a pair of blue jeans, a black crew neck sweater, and a denim jacket.

"This should do nicely," she said as she glanced in the mirror. "Sort of a classy ninja look!"

She put on her running shoes, grabbed a flashlight, and tiptoed through the door. It swung closed with a click. Outside, the hallway was completely empty—the only sound was the gentle whoosh of air from the ventilation system.

Eerie.

Her hand quivered as she locked the door. She closed her eyes and stood motionless to calm her nerves.

As she approached her golf cart, a shuffling, scraping sound broke the silence. She turned with a start and almost dropped her flashlight.

"Good evening, Dr. Wells." It was Maurice. "Going for an evening drive?"

"Oh, a... hi, Maurice, something like that." She stepped in and sat down. "Were you coming to see me? Do you need something?"

"No, nothing. I'm fine," he said. "We just finished up in the kitchen, and I thought a stroll might help me unwind."

"Oh, okay then." She smiled. "Enjoy your walk." She took a deep breath and headed out. It was after ten o'clock, so the temperature in the Cave was dropping. The air felt cool on her neck.

Why was he in my hallway? What in the hell was he doing there? Does he know? How could he possibly know? Maybe he always walks in the evening... Get a grip, Karen! He was just taking a walk, for God's sake!

***

Hansen was waiting at the side door when she pulled up. "Hi Karen," he whispered. "Are you all set?"

"Yep," she answered. "I have my flashlight, my jacket, and my running shoes. This is so exciting."

"Okay, then, follow me." Twenty seconds later, they were through the door. He closed it behind them.

It was as black as coal. She swept her head from side to side—there was no light at all.

"Wow," she whispered. "I've never experienced such darkness."

Hansen switched on his flashlight. "Let's get going."

They moved single file along a narrow concrete path, barely wide enough for his shoulders. The walls and ceiling were carved granite, cold and damp to the touch. The air was still and humid. And they heard no sound, nothing, save a steady drip, drip, drip from somewhere in the darkness.

"What is that smell?" she whispered.

"I don't know," he said. "But it's rank. It smells like something died... Let's keep moving."

A few more yards put them at the top of a steep concrete stairway. It was wet and slippery with a thin coat of mud.

"Are we going down?" she asked. "Maybe we should go back."

"We're just getting started, Karen. A little backbone, please."

She stood motionless.

"You wanted to come along," he said. "So, let's explore." He led the way down, and she followed.

Soon, the path joined a larger tunnel. It was wide enough for two golf carts and extended in both directions, well beyond the reach of their flashlights.

"Which way?"

"The dripping sound is from the right, so let's go that way."

The smooth concrete was covered with a thin layer of dirt, and each footfall returned a gritty, scraping sound, like sand on a polished marble floor. It was impossible to walk without making noise.

"Look at the floor," as he swept his flashlight from side to side. "There are very few footprints and no cart tracks at all. Maybe we went the wrong way."

As they moved slowly down the tunnel, moisture on the walls glistened, and the sound of dripping water grew louder. Countless tiny insects scurried to avoid their lights.

"Talk to me. I'm a little nervous."

"Okay, so, Karen, I understand you're from Ohio."

"Yes. Sandusky, a couple of miles from Lake Erie."

"Really? How did you end up way out here?"

The ceiling sloped lower. He could almost touch it with his hand. They continued down the tunnel.

"Oh, school mostly. I did graduate school at Colorado State. And I liked the area, so I decided to stay."

"So, you were all alone in Colorado when your family was in Ohio? That's brave."

"Well, I wasn't all alone, not for long anyway. My mom came out to be with me. She got a job at Loveland High School."

"And now that you're here in the Cave, what is she doing?"

"Well, actually, I was worried about that. But Jicard is taking care of her financially, and Christi visits a couple of times a week."

"Christi?"

"Christi Snow. She was my lab assistant before Jicard drafted me. She'll be the acting director until I get back."

The dripping water was slightly louder. "It seems like we're getting closer," Hansen said. They took a few more steps, and then he continued, "Huh, Christi Snow, you say. I'm not sure I would trust her. I've heard rumors."

"I'm not worried. We worked together every day for over five years. She and mom are great friends, and I'd trust her with my life."

His light obscured his face. "I hope you're right."

"Why, what have you heard?"

They stopped and listened. Karen directed her beam to the right. A narrow rivulet of water was flowing along the wall. Soon, the dripping sound was joined by a chorus of slithering and clicking sounds.

"Oh my God, Hansen," she said. "Look at that!"

He swept his beam to join hers.

"What is it?"

"A furry rodent of some kind. A rat, I guess."

The carcass was covered with hundreds of tiny scavengers, millipedes, beetles, and other troglobites—some nearly transparent.

"Eww…"

"Look, I don't see anything of interest down here, and it's been nearly thirty minutes. I think we should be getting back."

"I agree," said Karen. "This is too creepy."

"Wait a minute! Stop!" He gripped her forearm.

"What?"

"Shush… I thought I heard something," he whispered. "Turn off your light and listen." Again, total darkness.

For several moments, there was only dripping water and insects. And then… a soft *crunch*.

"There! Did you hear that?"

"Yeah," she whispered. "Someone's coming. Shit. Let's get out of here!"

"I agree. It's definitely time to leave."

They hurried back toward the passageway—the footsteps drew closer.

"There are more now, and they're coming faster."

"Yes," he said. "And look ahead. Do you see that?"

"It's a flashlight! Oh, God!"

"We're here!" he said. "You go up first."

Karen dashed into the narrow passageway and nearly fell on the steps.

"Are you okay?"

"Yeah. I just slipped, that's all. Keep moving."

They made their way back to the door and stepped into the laboratory hallway.

"Where have you guys been?" said Stephan. "I'm almost out of the video."

"Sorry, we got held up a bit. But everything's fine now." He pointed to the floor. "Give it a quick polish and then shut everything down. I'll tell you about it later."

***

A text message appeared on Jicard's phone:

We had two visitors in tunnel N-7 this evening, infrared sensors. They used N-7B.

He responded:

Did they see anything?

Response:

Nothing. They went north in the tunnel. Should we track them down?

Jicard replied:

No. I'll handle it.

He picked up his phone and called the control room—the supervisor answered.

"Yes, Mr. Jicard. What can I do for you this evening?"

"I need copies of all videos from the petroleum chamber for the last four hours. Save them to my folder."

Chapter 34

Late Friday afternoon, Tylor, Sharon, and Sam met in the Riverview Skyline Lounge in Billings. Sharon was exhausted, and Sam was checking his email.

"It's been a busy day," said Tylor, and one thing is crystal clear—Robin really likes Melvin. She couldn't stop talking about him."

Sharon nodded. "Yes, we had a lovely chat last week, and I like her a lot. She'll do anything she can to help us."

"And Tony was nice enough, I guess. But he didn't tell us much. He got very nervous when we asked about the Malibu."

"I noticed that too—he kept checking his text messages." She looked at Sam. "Maybe Meagan will have more for us in the morning. I'd like to know what she thinks about Paul's idea."

Tylor perked up. "And Sam," he said. "Any news from Mowata?"

"A bit," he answered. "The field is a total loss, and the sheriff's lab is checking into the cause. But they are pretty sure it was herbicide."

"The same one they used on the hybrid?"

"That's the assumption. They're checking into it." He stared out the window and was silent for several moments.

Sharon and Tylor exchanged glances but said nothing.

"Sorry. I was thinking about Karen. I'm so worried. I should be back in Fort Collins searching for her."

"We understand, Sam. We're worried about her too. But the police are on it. And if there's a connection to NSR, this might be the place to find it. That's one of the reasons we're up here."

"I know, I know." He fell silent again.

"Did James have anything more?"

"Uh, yes, as a matter of fact. The sheriff had his team search the field."

Sharron perked up. "Did they find anything?"

"They did," he said. "In the southwest corner of the field, they found a damaged drone. It must have crashed during the attack."

"Wow. No kidding?"

"No kidding. It's in pretty bad shape, but it has an onboard tank, and it's empty."

"For the herbicide, I suppose."

"Probably. In any case, the forensic unit hauled it back to their garage. They'll sample the residue in the tank and try to figure out where it came from."

***

The following day, they went to The Happy Omelet for breakfast. Tylor had a western, Sam had cheese and onion, and Sharon had her favorite, mushroom and cheddar. When they were finished, Tylor talked with the manager, and he agreed to let Meagan visit for a while.

"Hi Sharon," she said. "It is nice to see you again. Do you have any news?" She joined them in the booth.

"Hi Meagan, thanks for meeting with us."

"My pleasure."

"Please, allow me to introduce my friends, Tylor York and Sam Wilson. They're here to help me find Melvin."

"It's lovely to meet you, both." She reached over and shook their hands. "I've been thinking about him ever since Sharon and I talked. But I don't know what more I can say. I already told her everything I know."

"We understand," said Tylor. "But if it's okay with you, we would like to hear the story one more time. We have a couple of ideas that we would like to share."

"Sure," she said. "I'd be happy to. Where should I begin?"

"Why don't you start with how you know Melvin and then end with that funny business about the Malibu?" suggested Sharon.

"Okay, but it might take a while. So, let's get a little more coffee first." They nodded in agreement.

For the next half hour, she talked about Melvin's many trips to Billings and how she always looked forward to seeing him. Tylor and Sam asked questions along the way, and she was happy to clarify. Finally, she came to his January 15 visit and his disappointment with the Malibu that day.

"You know, it still seems strange that there were no SUVs available. We always had two or three on the lot. They were very popular."

"Maybe there *were* some, but they just didn't show up on the computer," said Sharon.

"I'm not sure I know what you mean."

"Well," she looked at Sam and Tylor. "We think someone may have faked the computer entry that day." Then she shared what Paul had suggested.

"Of course! That would explain it. And it also explains why the car disappeared the following day," she said. "Sure, if someone really wanted to, they could easily hide the SUVs in the inventory and substitute a Malibu. But I can't see why anyone would do that. The company makes more money from SUVs."

"But you do think it's possible, then."

"Absolutely! Yes, it is definitely possible."

Tylor looked at Sam and Sharon and then back to Meagan. "Well then, I guess that's all we have for today," he said. He took both of her hands in his. "We are genuinely grateful for your help, and thank you for talking with us."

"It was my pleasure," she said. "So, where do you go from here?"

Tylor responded, "Our next stop is the County Library to check out some newspapers from that week. It's a long shot, but he may have been in an accident. And if he was, there might be some mention of it."

"I see," she said. "Well, I wish you luck. And when you find him, Sharon, please let me know".

"I promise."

***

That afternoon, they visited the Yellowstone County Public Library and asked the attendant for back issues of 'The Billings Recorder'. The week in question had already been microfilmed, so they each chose a separate viewer and sat down to browse. Sam found it first.

"Here's it is… Oh, it's terrible," he said. He looked up and turned to Sharon. "I'm sorry, Sharon, I am so sorry. It's in the January seventeen issue, page eight, upper left corner." They scrolled to find the article.

Driver Dies in Fiery Crash

According to the Billings Police Department, at approximately 5:30 p.m. on January 15, a red Chevrolet Malibu was traveling eastbound on Route 3. About one mile east of Zimmerman Trail, it left the pavement and crashed at the base of The Rims. The driver was pronounced dead at the scene, and no other vehicles were involved. The reporting officer suggested excessive speed and icy road conditions as probable factors. The driver remains unidentified, and the accident is under investigation.

"Oh my God, noooo," said Sharon. "This can't be true… What am I going to do? What about our plans?" She stared at the screen for several moments… "Tylor! Sam! This can't be my Melvin. It just can't." She rested her forehead on her hands and sobbed uncontrollably. "It can't be him…"

Tylor and Sam looked at her, speechless, uncertain how to help.

Then she turned to Tylor, her eyes red and full of tears. "It has to be wrong, Tylor. He is an excellent driver. There is no way he would have been speeding. And he grew up in Colorado, for goodness' sake, a little ice on the road would be no big deal. There must be some other explanation."

He stepped to her cubical and put his arm around her shoulders. "This is a terrible shock, and I can't begin to know what you're feeling."

"It's wrong, Tylor. The article is wrong! Melvin is an excellent driver." She looked him straight in the eye. "You'll check into this for me. Won't You?"

Tylor nodded. "Yes, I'll make some calls."

"Promise me!"

He looked at Sam and then back to her. "Yes, I promise."

She nodded. "It must have been some other Malibu! It must have been!"

He leaned over and spoke softly, "I think we should go back to the hotel and rest awhile."

He looked at Sam. "Would you shut down the viewers? I'll walk her out."

He nodded, "Sure thing."

"Let's go, Sharon." He reached for her forearm.

"No! No! Not yet." She pulled her arm away. "I need a printout of the article."

"Don't worry about that. I'll take care of it. You go with Tylor… I'll be out in a few minutes."

"Well, okay, then. Thanks, Sam."

She rose slowly from her chair, and Tylor held her arm for support. "Let's go," she whispered. "Let's go."

***

"I just got a text from Tony. Apparently, Sharon Wagoner is back in town, and this time she has company."

"How? What company? Who's with her?"

"Those are excellent questions," Jicard said. "It seems that BJ screwed up again. He was supposed to have a serious talk with her."

"I know that he and Christi were working on it," said Dan. "I'll find out and get back to you. But who is she with?"

"Sam Wilson and some guy named Tylor York. How in the hell did she meet Sam Wilson?"

"I don't know."

"Well, you damn well better find out, and you had better do something about it. Miss Wagoner is becoming a nuisance, and Kentala-Ridge is only one week away. We can't have her nosing around." He paused. "They're staying at the Riverview in Billings. Get rid of them."

"Yes, sir!"

"Good. Call me when it's done!"

***

Jicard was pacing his office to cool down. *Those idiots. Do I have to do everything myself?*

He was about to sit down again when his phone rang—the caller ID read, 'Private Number'. He eased into his chair and picked up the handset.

"Jicard here."

"Ah yes, Mr. Jicard," said the voice. "We are pleased that you are in your office. We decide to purchase one thousand kilograms of Gelator-T. You ship to our warehouse in Munich."

"Good afternoon, Fazal," he said. "And yes, we can do that."

"We pay only agreed price, one thousand two hundred American, no more."

"That is correct. The price is twelve hundred dollars per kilo, one point two million total. Send fifty percent now and fifty percent upon shipment. We can have it ready in two weeks."

"First, we want proof. We send money when we have proof."

"Fine," he said. "Watch the news for the Kentala-Ridge pipeline on Sunday morning, the 15th. You will have your proof."

"We watch."

Chapter 35

Tylor and Sam met in the Skyline Lounge for the hotel's 'Weekend Breakfast Buffet'. Sharon opted to stay in her room.

"This is really hard for Sharon," said Sam. "She obviously loved him very much... it's dreadful."

"I know. She spent all that time searching, only to find..." He shook his head. "I wish there were something more we could do."

Sam nodded. "Me too."

"Do you think she'll want to go with me this afternoon?"

"It's hard to say. She might."

Just then, Sam's phone started to vibrate. The caller ID read, 'Susan Wells'. He pressed the "Answer' button.

***

"Hi, Susan. Is everything all right?"

"Well, okay, I guess," she said. "The FBI was here."

"The FBI? When? This morning?"

"Yes, this morning. There were two of them."

"Really? Are you okay?"

"I'm fine," she said. "I can tell you. I was a little scared when they knocked on the door. But after we started talking, they turned out to be very nice. I actually feel a little better now."

"You said there were two of them?"

"That's right, they gave me their cards." She picked them up from the coffee table. "Special Agents Evelyn Harris and Sydney Baker. I didn't know they had female agents.

Anyway, they wanted to talk about Karen and the fire at the lab. And they told me the body in the morgue has been identified."

"Really? Who was it?"

"Her name was Molly Greene, the poor girl. They say she was a homeless person in Denver."

"But she looked so much like Karen… Apparently, there was already a strong resemblance, and all they needed was a makeover, some hair color, and a lab coat to complete the illusion."

"It was so convincing, right down to the fake ring," he said.

"Right," she said. "I also told them about the ring and Denver City Productions, and they would like to talk with you about it. Could you come back to Fort Collins for a couple of days? Maybe we could talk with them together."

"Of course, I can," he said. "I'll book a flight this afternoon."

"Good. I'd feel better if you were here."

"Did they have any new information about Karen?"

"Not much. They searched her apartment but found nothing. We still don't know what happened to her."

"I was hoping," he said.

"Me too. But they said it's still early. Today, they're talking with people in her neighborhood."

"Maybe they'll turn up something."

"Let's hope so," she said. "What time tomorrow should I expect you?"

"About eleven, I think. I'll take you to lunch."

"It's a date."

***

He ended the call and turned to Tylor. "Would you mind doing this on your own for a couple of days? I need to get back to Fort Collins."

"Has something happened?"

"Not much," he said. "But the FBI has picked up the case, and they would like to interview me. I think I'll catch a flight this afternoon."

"What about our trip to the accident site?"

"It looks like you'll have to do it by yourself." He gave him the highlights of his conversation with Susan. "So," he said. "I need to go as soon as possible."

"I agree. You need to do what's necessary."

"Maybe Sharon *would* like to go with you."

"Maybe," he said. "If she feels up to it."

"Okay, then. I'm going to call the airline and then check out. I'll catch up with you sometime tomorrow." He headed for the elevator.

***

Tylor took a sip of coffee and composed a short text message:

Hi Mo,

Anything new on the gelator problem?

Please let me know.

Tylor

As he pressed the send button, and moments later, Sharon appeared. She wore a sweatshirt, blue jeans, and sneakers, and her hair was pulled back in a ponytail.

"Good morning, Tylor," she said. "Anything good on the buffet?" She smiled weakly.

"Hi, there! It's good to see you up and around. And ah, yes, the buffet is very nice. I could definitely recommend the cinnamon rolls and the quiche Lorraine, and if you want an omelet, they'll make one while you watch."

"Okay, I'll check it out. Please wait for me. I need to talk."

He said, "I'd be happy to."

As she moved toward the buffet, his phone vibrated. It was Mo:

Things are going well. The polymer breaks down pretty fast under ultraviolet light (302-310 nm). I think we'll have a workable solution in another day or two.

Tylor responded.

Excellent news, Mo. You're the best; please keep me posted. If you can't reach me, leave a message at the Riverview in Billings. I will be here for the next week or so.

He then sent a text to Jack Nelson:

Sorry for the extended silence. We've been a little busy. But we have excellent news, Mo is getting close. He thinks he'll have something for us in the next few days.

How are things in Dusty Fork?

Jack responded almost immediately.

I am glad to hear that Mo is making progress. Please ask him to hurry. With the pipeline out of service, we are using trucks to haul the crude. It is very slow. We are loading around the clock, but we can only manage about ten percent of our normal volume.

Our credit line at the bank is near the breaking point; we have barely enough for one more payroll. After that, we will start laying off people. Remember, we have sixty families to support. We're desperate.

Tylor sent another text to Mo.

Hi, again Mo.

I just heard from Jack, the situation in Dusty Fork is near critical. We need the solution as soon as possible.

Sharon returned with a cheddar and mushroom omelet, a side of potatoes, and a glass of orange juice. She settled in across from Tylor.

"So, where's Sam?" she said as she sat down. "I thought he was having breakfast with you."

"He did, but he left for Fort Collins a few minutes ago."

"Fort Collins? Why?"

"The FBI has picked up the case, and they want to talk with him. They interviewed Karen's mom this morning."

"Wow," she said. "Really? Did they go to her house? Is she okay? If the FBI came to my door, I'd probably freak out."

"She's fine. She said they were very friendly, and she felt better after they left."

"So, what's next for us? I think I would like to see where the accident happened."

"Are you sure?"

"Yes. I am sure. I need to see it."

"It might not be the greatest of ideas, Sharon. There is no telling what we may find."

"I need to see it," she said. "When were you planning to go?"

"Pretty soon, I guess. I was going to drive out after breakfast."

"That's good for me. I will need a few minutes to get ready. How about eleven-thirty?"

"Eleven thirty will be fine," he said. "I'll wait for you at the garage entrance."

"Thank you," she said. "I need to see it—I think it'll help me process this whole ugly nightmare."

***

When Sharon opened the door to her room, she found an envelope lying on the floor. It read:

Miss Wagoner,

You are in danger! They know you are in town, and they are watching. Save yourself and your friends; Leave Billings now. Forget about Melvin's 'accident'. I won't be able to warn you again.

Chapter 36

Sheriff Pierre LeBlanc was standing in the forensics garage when James pulled up in his pickup truck. Behind him was a large workbench covered end-to-end with pieces of the recovered drone.

"Good afternoon, Sheriff," he said. "Do you always work on Saturday?"

"Hi, James. Thanks for driving down. And yes, I do. My kids don't even recognize me any more."

"I doubt that," said James, with a smile. "So, my friend, what have you found?"

"Step inside and take a look."

James walked into the garage and approached the workbench. The team had taken the drone apart and arranged its parts neatly for inspection. On the left end were six rotor arms; two were bent nearly in half, and one was missing its blade.

He looked at the sheriff and said, "I guess I didn't expect so many pieces."

The sheriff nodded. "Me neither," he said. "Go ahead and check them out."

Next were twelve spray heads and associated plastic tubing. Several still had liquid inside.

The third group of components included the battery case and battery and a large plastic tank with lines inked up its side. The line at the top read: '3 Gallons'. It was empty, except for an oily film smeared around the fill port.

The last group included the aluminum frame with the drive motor, electric pump, and control package.

"So, it looks like it was designed for the task," said James. "Did you find any fingerprints?"

"Quite a few, actually. They were all over the frame and rotor arms, and there were several different sets on the tank and battery pack."

James tried to picture the operator refilling the tank and replacing the battery. "Yes, there would be," he said. "I wonder how many acres they could cover with three gallons of herbicide. How long would the battery last?"

The sheriff walked down the end of the bench and pointed at the frame. "The model and serial numbers are stamped here, next to the motor mount, and we looked it up on the internet."

"I see."

"It was built by TruPath Flyers in Houston," he began. "According to their website, this model can carry twenty-five pounds of chemicals and spray about thirty acres per hour. The battery appears to be the weak link. It only lasts about fifteen minutes when the tank is full."

"So, they would have to stop quite often to fill the tank and replace the battery."

"I guess so."

"That explains all the prints on the tank and the battery case."

"And," he said. "Their multi-unit controller can handle up to forty drones at once. GPS navigation is standard."

"Wow," said James. "So, they could have dozens of these in the air at the same time."

"It seems so."

"And as long as they have enough charged batteries, a small group of people could cover an eighty-acre field in no time." He stood back and scanned the bench. "Where did this particular unit come from?"

"The team is working on that," said the sheriff. "They will contact the company on Monday and find out who bought it. I'm guessing it was a large order."

***

Dr. Nugent's phone vibrated; it was a message from Fu Tong.

The Governor, the Mayor, and I are meeting at my home tomorrow afternoon. We will be discussing the upcoming expansion in Stillwater County. Plan for an overnight stay. The meeting will begin at 2:00 p.m.

He responded:

It is on my calendar, and the pilot has been alerted. I'll see you then.

Chapter 37

Tylor turned into the neighborhood and stopped his car along the curb. Across the street was a sprawling ranch house with a long curved driveway, and towering pine trees on both sides. A granite sculpture stood guard at the entrance.

"Are you sure this is the right place?"

"I think so," said Tylor. "According to the satellite map, this should be it." He turned off the engine. "Besides, what's the worst that can happen?" He reached for the door handle, and Sharon stopped him.

"Wait a minute. Before we go in, I need to show you something."

He settled back in his seat. "What?"

She opened her purse and extracted a folded piece of paper. "Here, read this. I found it in my room this morning. Someone slipped it under my door while we were at breakfast."

He took the note and opened it. "Just this morning?"

"Yes," she said. "I'm frightened, Tylor. Maybe we should just go home."

After scanning the note, he looked into her eyes. "Sharon, if you want to stop, we will. I know this is difficult for you."

Tears welled up. "It's not that I want to stop, but maybe we should. I don't think these people are kidding."

"I understand how you feel," he said. "But this whole thing smells like rotten fish, and I never thought Melvin's death was an accident." He held up the note. "And this proves it!" He glanced at the house. "I intend to press on."

She sat silently for a moment.

He turned in his seat and put his right hand on her shoulder. "But if you want to return to the hotel, we can leave right now."

She looked at him, then the note, and then past him toward the house. "No. If you're that sure, then I'm with you. Let's go in. But promise me you'll be careful."

***

Harry and Mavis Walton were tidying up in the kitchen when the doorbell rang.

"Honey, could you get that?" she said. "I'll finish up in here."

"Sure," he said. He tossed his dishtowel on the counter, walked to the front door, and opened it a crack. "Yes? Can I help you?"

"Good afternoon, sir, my name is Tylor York, and this is Sharon Wagoner. Would you mind if we asked you a couple of questions?"

"I'm sorry, whatever it is you're selling, we are not interested." He started to close the door.

"Please, sir, please wait!" said Sharon. "We're not trying to sell anything, I promise. We just want to ask about the car crash. The driver was my fiancé."

He paused. "Do you mean the one in January?" He opened the door a little more to get a better look at Sharon.

Mavis joined him. "Who are these people, Hon? We don't need any more magazines. Tell them to go away."

"No, Mave, they want to ask about the accident."

"No kidding. Who are they? Reporters or something?"

He raised his eyebrows and looked at them.

"No, we are not reporters," said Sharon. "Ah, the man who died in the crash was my fiancé." Her eyes began to water. "I just need some information."

"Are you serious? He was your fiancé?" she said. "Oh, my dear, dear girl, please come in." She pushed the door open and gestured toward the living room. "Please, come in and have a seat. I'll get some coffee."

"Harry," she said. "Make them comfortable. I'll be right back."

The living room was bigger than most, with a high cathedral ceiling. The walls were a warm beige, and the carpeting was off-white. There was a long leather sofa facing the fireplace and an overstuffed chair on each end.

"Please make yourself comfortable," said Harry. He directed them to the sofa.

"Thank you," said Tylor.

"You have a beautiful home, sir. This is very good of you."

"Please, my name is Harry, Harry Walton, and my wife's name is Mavis. "I'm sorry about the thing at the door. We get so many salesmen in this neighborhood..."

"Don't give it a thought, Harry," said Tylor. "We completely understand."

He looked a Sharon. "I'm glad you like it."

"Sir?"

"The house," he said. He swept his arm around the room. "We love it too. We've been here for eight years now."

"It's charming."

"Did you say your name was Sharon?"

"Yes, Sharon Wagoner. And this is my friend, Tylor York."

"Nice to meet you," he said.

Sharon looked toward the back of the room, "The windows are magnificent..."

At that moment, Mavis returned from the kitchen with a serving tray and four steaming cups. She placed it gently on the coffee table and said, "Cream or sugar?"

"A little sugar, please. And thank you, Mrs. Walton."

"Oh, please, dear, call me Mavis." She handed a cup to Sharon.

"Okay, thank you, Mavis. It smells delightful."

Mavis handed cups to Tylor and Harry, took one for herself, and then eased into her favorite chair. "Now, how can we help you?"

"Well, we are trying to find out exactly what happened, and we thought you might remember something," said Tylor. "Were you at home that day?"

"Were we home? You're kidding, right?" he said. "Of course, we were home. It crashed in our back yard," He pointed at the windows Sharon had been admiring. "It crashed right there. We saw everything, it was horrible. The fire was so hot. It damaged our pine trees. We don't know if they're going to make it."

"Harry! Stop talking!"

Sharon's face had gone pale, and she was visibly shaking.

"Take it easy, Hon!"

Harry realized what he'd said and dropped his eyes. "My big mouth! I am so sorry, my dear. I didn't mean to…"

Sharon sat up straight and looked at him. "It's all right. Really, it is." She shook her head back and forth and grasped Tylor's hand. "It's a lot to take in, that's all. Please, tell us more."

"This is obviously very difficult for you," he said. "Maybe if we knew a little more of your story?"

Sharon said, "Oh, I don't think I should."

"Please, we want you to feel comfortable," said Mavis.

"But you don't even know me."

"Please, trust us. We have a reason, I promise."

"Well, okay, if you're sure, we don't want to take up your whole afternoon."

Mavis said, "Don't worry about that, dear. We would like to help."

Harry nodded.

"Well, okay then. Melvin, my fiancé, flew up for a business meeting on the fifteenth of January. We live in Denver. That is, we did live in Denver…" She shook her head. "No, I can't do this."

"Please, go ahead," said Harry softly. "Take your time."

Sharon nodded and continued, "Well, he, Melvin, arrived about three o'clock in the afternoon, and he sent me a text message. And that was the last I heard from him. It was supposed to be a one-night trip."

She continued with the story's highlights but left out some key details, like the garage attack, Karen's disappearance, their suspicions about the accident's cause, and the note she received that morning.

"Oh, my dear child," said Mavis. "Now I understand why you're here. You are trying to understand how this could have happened. You need some closure."

"I guess so."

"Well, first, I'd like to apologize for what Harry said earlier," she said. "He's really not that kind of a person."

Sharon nodded. "He couldn't have known."

"Nevertheless, he should have been more considerate."

"She's right," said Harry. "I should have. I'm sorry."

"Anyway," continued Mavis. "Harry and I have thought a lot about that day, and we're pretty sure it was no accident."

"Really? Why would you say that?" said Tylor.

"It was that pop at the end. It just wasn't right."

"What pop? What are you talking about?"

"We tried to tell the police that day, but they didn't seem to be interested. And the coroner, well, he always had better things to do."

"What are you talking about?" repeated Tylor.

"The pop!"

"What pop?"

"On the recording. We've watched it dozens of times. It just wasn't right."

"You have it on video?" Tylor was dumbfounded. "How is that possible?"

"It's on Harry's computer, come, we'll show you."

Harry led them to his den and turned on his computer.

"We have surveillance cameras all around the house," he said. "And the one that covers the backyard recorded the whole thing. I saved it to my hard drive in case the police wanted to look at it. But they never did."

"Could we see it?"

"Of course," he said. "But I must warn you, it's pretty graphic." He turned to Sharon. "You might not want to see it."

"No. I *do* want to see it. Please."

"Okay, but if it's too much, just let me know."

Harry turned back to the monitor, opened a video file named 'Accident-Jan-15', and then pressed play.

Instantly, the screen was filled with a view of their backyard. Everything was covered with a thick blanket of snow, and pine tree branches swayed back and forth. The dark green of the trees stood in stark contrast to the brilliant white landscape.

"Here it comes," he said. "Watch the upper left corner of the screen." He paused the playback. "Sharon, my dear, you might want to look away."

"Please continue," she replied. He clicked 'Resume'.

In a fraction of a second, the car was in the frame, unbelievably fast. It was upside down when it hit the ground. The body flattened on impact. It bounced a couple of times and then came to a stop. Then, there was no movement. A plume of steam rose from the engine compartment, but otherwise, there was nothing, no fire, no smoke, nothing.

Harry paused the playback.

"That was horrible," said Sharon. "My dear sweet Melvin. There is no way he survived that." Tears ran down her face. "But what about the pop? You said there was pop."

"I truly don't want you to see the rest," he said.

"Harry, we've come this far," she said. "Please. I need to know everything."

"Okay, then. But Tylor, you stay close to her." He shook his head slowly and continued, "Now watch the timestamp in the corner of the monitor. It will happen in about nine seconds."

The timestamp ticked on, and then they saw it—a flash of light at the rear end of the car. It was small, no larger than a firecracker. And then the fuel ignited.

Sharon's chest felt tight, her knees gave out, and she sank to the floor. "Oh, dear God!"

***

Ten minutes later, she woke up in the living room. "Where am I?" she said. "Where's Tylor? Did I faint?"

"I'm right here," he said. "You had us worried for a few minutes."

"I am so embarrassed."

"Don't you worry about it," said Mavis. "You've had a terrible shock. I almost fainted the first time I saw it."

"I have never seen anything so terrible in my whole life," said Sharon. "I don't think I will ever forget it."

"None of us will."

She looked at her watch. "Oh, look how late it's getting. We have to go."

"Give yourself a couple more minutes," said Harry. "We're worried about you."

She sat up on the sofa. "No, we have to get going. You have been so generous with your time. But we never meant to stay this long."

She stood up and moved toward Tylor. "Come, let's go. There is still one more thing we need to do." She tugged on his arm.

"Relax a little, Sharon. Calm down." Tylor stood up and turned to the Waltons. "Thank you so much for your time. We are grateful. And we're sorry we were so much trouble."

"It was nothing," said Harry. "We're happy to have helped." He handed a thumb drive to Tylor. "This is a copy of the video. Please make good use of it. Someone planted that explosive device. It was no accident."

"I agree, Harry, and we will find the person who did it."

***

Back in the car, Sharon was anxious. "I want to go up on the ridge and see it from above. I need to have the whole picture in my mind."

"Whatever you say."

Tylor started the car and left the neighborhood. They drove west on Rimrock Road, wound up Zimmerman Trail, and then turned east on Route 3. One point seven miles later, they pulled into the overlook. A section of the guardrail was still missing.

"This must be the place."

"Okay," said Sharon. "Turn off the car, and let's take a look." She opened her door and stepped out. A gust of wind caught the door, but she grabbed it and pushed it closed.

"Don't get too close," he said. "Be careful!"

"I'll be fine." She walked through the opening and peered down. Tylor joined her.

It was easy to see where the Malibu had crashed. The vegetation was all gone—incinerated. Charred stumps and naked tree trunks rimmed the burnt-out circle.

"My God, Tylor, who would do this? What possible reason could they have?"

"I don't know yet, but we are going to find out. I promise you."

They lingered for a few moments in the chilly breeze and then returned to the car. Sharon was still crying. "Thank you for doing this, Tylor. I truly appreciate everything you've done. I needed to know what happened, and you helped me find out. I couldn't have done it without you." She turned to face forward. "But I think I've seen enough. So, if it's okay, I would like to go back to the hotel."

"Absolutely. I think we've had enough for one day."

But before he could start the engine, a man appeared outside his window. He made a cranking motion with his hand.

"Please, sir, roll down your window," the man said.

Tylor obliged and said, "Can I help you? Do you need something?"

The man answered, "I certainly do, Mr. York." He raised his left hand and shot two taser blots into his chest.

Tylor's body convulsed uncontrollably for several seconds. Every muscle in his body cramped at the same time. Finally, the pulses stopped, and the man pulled out the probes. He then grabbed his neck and used a syringe to inject a strong sedative. Tylor slumped in his seat and passed out in seconds.

Watching from the passenger seat, Sharon was catatonic. She tried to scream, but nothing came out.

"You're next, Miss Wagoner. You should have left all this alone." He loaded a new cartridge in the taser and fired again. Seconds later, when she stopped convulsing, he walked around the car and dragged her to the pavement. He held her head in the crook of his left arm, pushed a syringe into her neck, and then placed her limp body in the rear of his SUV.

To finish the job, he started his engine and pushed Tylor's car off the cliff. His text message read:

TY complete.

Chapter 38

It was half-past two on Sunday morning when Paul Betson's phone began to vibrate. *What the hell! Who could be texting me at this time of the night?* He rolled over and touched his phone. "Tylor!" he said aloud. "Couldn't you wait until morning? What could possibly be this important?"

He opened the message. It looked like gibberish:

ss t oomp eer.

"Stomper!" he said aloud. In less than five minutes, he was out of bed, dressed, and in his car. He checked the GPS location of Tylor's phone and then headed west. *Five and a half hours... I should be there a little after eight.*

***

At seven-thirty, Sharon awoke in darkness. The air was chilly and smelled damp. "Where am I?" she said quietly. There was no response. "Hello! Is anybody there?" Her head felt like it was in a vice. "Hello?" There was no sound.

She stood up and shuffled slowly forward, sweeping her outstretched hand back and forth. Eventually, she touched something. Using both hands, she carefully examined the object. It was a lamp on a small table. She felt around until she found a switch and turned it on.

Light flooded the room, and her head exploded with shooting pain. Needles pricked the back of her eyeballs, so she closed them immediately. Moments later, she opened them slowly and used her hand to block the light. She quickly scanned the room.

It was tiny, like an examination room. There was a chair, a table, and a small bed. The stone walls were dripping with moisture, and the blanket on the bed was old and thread-worn. *What is this place, some kind of jail cell?*

Where in the hell am I? That man! He shot me with a Taser. He drugged me! And Tylor too! Oh, my God! Tylor, where are you?

Suddenly she felt ill. She fell back on the bed, covered herself with the blanket, and passed out.

***

At eight-fifteen, Paul arrived at the overlook, but Tylor was nowhere to be seen. He stepped out and called his name—nothing. He rechecked the GPS location. *This is the right spot. Come on, Tylor, where are you?* He noticed a gap in the guard rail and walked over to take a look. *Oh my God! How in the hell did you get down there?*

About forty feet below his feet, stuck on an outcrop, was a blue sedan. It appeared to be undamaged, but there was no movement inside. "Tylor! Are you in there? Hang on. I'm coming down."

He dropped to his stomach, extended his legs, and eased himself over the edge. Countless roots and small rocks protruded from the cliff-face, so finding handholds was easy. He reached the car in about twenty minutes. Tylor was just waking up. "Hey, buddy. How did you end up down here?"

He looked past the hood of the car and saw nothing by open space. Another six feet and things would have been much different.

Tylor turned his face toward the window and forced a tight grin. "Hey, man, nice of you to stop by. What took you so long?" He slumped forward against the airbag. "My neck hurts like hell, and I think there's a railroad spike in my left temple." He rubbed it gently.

Paul pulled the door open to help him out.

"Wait a minute," he said. "Help Sharon first. I'll be okay for a few minutes."

"You're alone, Tylor. There is no one else in the car."

"She has to be here." He twisted around to look at the passenger seat. "Where is she?" He turned back. "He took her, Paul! That bastard kidnapped Sharon!"

"Calm down a little. We'll find her." He helped him from the car. "But we need to find a hospital first."

Chapter 39

Fu Tong's estate was on twenty-thousand acres of mountainous terrain by Holter Lake, thirty miles north of Helena. There was a private airstrip for corporate jets and two helipads, one at the airstrip and one a mile to the east near the mansion. The rest of the property was undeveloped wilderness extending along the north shore.

The mansion was built on a plateau, eleven hundred feet above the lake. There were three ways up; a paved driveway from Beartooth Road, a maintenance access road across the top of the dam, and a cable lift gondola from the airstrip. Most visitors used the gondola.

The architect's design included two and a half levels, with more than twenty-two thousand square feet of living space. There were nine bedrooms, twelve baths, an indoor swimming pool, two gourmet kitchens, offices, meeting rooms, a library, a billiard room, a gallery for small groups, and a grand ballroom for entertaining. The west side of the house was graced by a sweeping veranda that afforded breathtaking views of the Rocky Mountains and the lake, below.

Fu Tong was watching from his office when the plane touched down. With him were Mayor Dellinger and Governor Olsen.

He pointed toward the airstrip, "That's Nugent's plane now—he'll be up in a few minutes. Refills anyone?"

The governor said, "Sure, another scotch, for me."

"And I'll have a gin and tonic, please" said the mayor.

Mr. Fu nodded to the server, "Drysdale…" Almost unnoticed, their glasses were collected and replaced with fresh drinks.

The governor took a sip and turned to Mr. Fu. "So, is he on board? I met him at the ribbon-cutting last fall, but we never had a chance to talk."

"Absolutely, he is very excited about the expansion."

"And so are we," said the mayor. "I've been in discussions with the Stillwater planning board, and between our two counties, we can commit nearly one hundred thousand acres to the project."

"Fabulous," said Mr. Fu. "That's more than we anticipated."

***

Dr. Nugent shivered as he stepped from the plane—it was much cooler than he'd expected. He walked quickly to a waiting a golf cart shuttle, and minutes later he arrived at the gondola lift.

"Make yourself comfortable," said the attendant. "You'll be there in four minutes." He closed the door and pressed a button to engage the drive motor.

The aerial ride was smooth and nearly silent. *This so much better than those sky lifts at the amusement park. And what a view!* To the south he could Holter Dam and the lake beyond, and beneath him, the Missouri River.

When he reached the top, a second shuttle was waiting. "Is this your first visit?" said the driver.

He nodded. "Yes, and it's all very impressive."

"Did you know it's over twenty thousand acres? There are actual mountains on this property. "He pointed to the east. I've been here almost two years and I still can't believe it."

"It is amazing," agreed Dr. Nugent.

"Well, anyway," he said. "Welcome to the Fu Tong Estate."

"Thank you."

They arrived in less than a minute, and the driver escorted him to the front door.

"Here is your briefcase Dr. Nugent. Your bag will be in your room."

A young man wearing a black suit escorted him to Fu Tong's office. When he reached the door, Drysdale rang a small bell.

"Excuse me, gentlemen, Dr. Nugent has arrived."

***

Mr. Fu stepped forward, "Welcome, Amil. It's nice to see you again. What do you think of the place so far?"

He nodded. "It's great to be here. Thanks for inviting me. And to be honest, it's a little intimidating."

He smiled. "You already know Governor Olsen and Mayor Dellinger…"

He turned to them and nodded. "Gentlemen. Good afternoon."

"I'm afraid we got started without you, my friend. What would you like?"

He rubbed his arm briskly. "It's a bit chilly, so maybe some cognac if you have it."

"I have nice Hennessy Paradis. I think you'll enjoy it."

He grinned. "I'm sure I will. Thank you."

Mr. Fu glanced at Drysdale.

"Immediately, sir."

Mr. Fu moved toward the conference table. "Now, gentlemen," he said. "Please find a seat. We have things to discuss."

***

Christi Snow was in her apartment reviewing plans for Kentala-Ridge when her phone rang. It was Jicard.

"Good afternoon."

"Hi Christi, how's it going?"

"I was just reviewing the plan for next weekend. It looks pretty good."

"That's fine, but I have something else I need you to do first."

"What's that?"

"There is a lab in Denver working with Nelson Oil. They are close to a countermeasure for our Gelator-T…"

***

"Dr. Nugent," said the governor. "Thank you for coming. I'm anxious to learn more about the hybrid."

"It's a pleasure," he said. "I'm pleased to be here."

"Mayor Dellinger, I understand you've been talking with the planning board in Stillwater. What do they think?"

"They're definitely on board. Their acreage is mostly under-utilized grassland. So this project will be a big shot in the arm for the farmers."

"Terrific. That's good to hear."

"So," said the governor. "Tell us about the new hybrid. Is it similar to the sugarcane in Broadview?"

"It's actually quite different," he said. "The Broadview hybrid is cold-tolerant sugarcane. This expansion will feature an oilcane—we plan to produce farnesene."

"I never heard of it, said the governor. "What's far-neh-seen?"

The mayor piped up, "It's a renewable fuel, like diesel. Right?" He looked at Dr. Nugent.

"Right, Mayor," he said. "Well, almost."

He opened his laptop. "I have a presentation with me that I used at a conference last month. I think it may be helpful."

"Mr. Fu, can we plug this into a monitor?"

He pressed a button, and a sixty-inch flat screen descended from the ceiling. Drysdale provided a power adapter and a cable, and within minutes, the laptop was up and running. The NSR logo was rotating slowly on the screen.

"Thank you," said Dr. Nugent. He placed his hand on the laptop and pressed 'Play'. The mayor and governor turned their attention to the screen.

The first few slides addressed the current demand for gasoline and diesel fuel in the United States and the existing capacity to produce renewable alternatives, specifically ethanol and biodiesel, and more recently, farnesene. The fourth slide outlined NSR's cold-tolerant sugarcane hybrid in Broadview and its newest oilcane hybrids.

"You are familiar with the sugarcane hybrid," said Dr. Nugent. "We have over a million acres in Montana, North Dakota, and South Dakota. And now we have two oilcane hybrids specifically engineered to produce farnesene in addition to sugar. The first field trial was planted in Owanka, about fifty thousand acres so far, and the newest will be used in the Stillwater-Yellowstone expansion."

"Tell us about this farnesene," said the governor. "What it is exactly."

"Well, technically, it is a sesquiterpene that is produced naturally in most plant cells. We modified our oilcane hybrid to produce it in high concentration. All we have to do is squeeze it out."

"Should I know what a sesquiterpene is?"

"I wouldn't think so, Governor. Most people don't," he said. "A sesquiterpene is a class of terpenes made up of isoprene units. But the most important thing is its chemical formula, $C_{15}H_{24}$, the same as a typical molecule of diesel fuel."

"So we can use farnesene to replace diesel fuel, and all we have to do is squeeze it out of the oilcane plant."

"Almost," said Dr. Nugent. "Farnesene oxidizes too easily to be used directly. So, we hydrotreat it first to remove its double bonds. The end product is called *farnesane*—without the double bonds."

The following slide had structural diagrams for farnesene and farnesane to illustrate the hydrotreating step.

"The refinery in Billings will do the conversion for us. At least until we build our own unit."

The mayor smiled. "So, we squeeze the farnesene out of the oil cane, extract it from the sugar syrup and then hydrotreat it to make farnesane. What happens to the syrup?"

"We will send it to Broadview for ethanol production."

Mr. Fu had been listening quietly. "Gentlemen," he said. "If you don't mind, I think it's time for a short break."

He nodded to Drysdale, and a serving tray appeared on the conference table.

"Excuse me, gentlemen," said Drysdale. "This afternoon, we have an assortment of pastries, small sandwiches, and fruit. Please help yourselves." He handed out plates and napkins. "We also have coffee and tea, or I could freshen your drinks if you prefer."

Dr. Nugent grabbed a ham and cheese finger sandwich and walked to the French doors. A light snow was falling on the veranda, but the lake and airstrip were still visible. The view was incredible. *It is so peaceful here! What a lifestyle he has.* The wind gusted a bit, and a few flakes swirled near the window. He lingered for a few more moments and then strolled back to the conference table.

"I think I would like a refill," he said. "Would you mind?"

Drysdale had anticipated the request and replaced his cognac without comment.

"Thank you, Drysdale."

He nodded. "My pleasure, sir."

"Okay, gentlemen. If we're all ready, let's get back to it. Dr. Nugent, if you please…"

"Thank you, sir."

"So, what does this latest hybrid look like?" said Mr. Fu.

Dr. Nugent put up a slide showing two photos: the Owanka hybrid and the upgraded version with the accumulation pods.

"That is one ugly-looking plant," said the mayor. "It looks like it has a disease."

"I agree, it's not very pretty. But the little pods on the stem more than triple the plant's storage capacity. They balloon out as they fill with farnesene."

"And this is real?"

"Yes. The Owanka hybrid, on the left, looks like a normal sugarcane plant, but product storage is limited to its stem tissue. The latest hybrid, the one on the right, was engineered to grow those special storage pods. They work beautifully."

"So, how much farnesene can we expect to produce?"

"That's an excellent question," he said. "Let's take a look at the last slide in the deck."

Mr. Fu was particularly interested in this slide. It even caught Drysdale's attention, who had been watching from the back of the room.

"You remember the first slide? It listed a daily demand in this county for one hundred thirty million gallons of diesel fuel. Well, we expect to take a bite out of that."

He moved the cursor to the first bullet point.

We expect to produce over seven hundred million gallons of farnesene per year on your acreage. That would be about one and a half percent of total US demand."

"That much," said the mayor.

Dr. Nugent continued, "And from the same plants, we expect to produce about five hundred million gallons of ethanol. About half of that will be from the sugar syrup via conventional fermentation, and the rest will be from the bagasse via cellulosic fermentation."

"Incredible," said the mayor.

Mr. Fu piped up, "Thank you, Dr. Nugent. Thank you very much. We are all very excited about the expansion."

He stood to address the table.

"You and your team have accomplished something truly remarkable. And it's going to make a real difference, not only for this country but for the entire world."

The mayor and the governor nodded in agreement.

"We want you to know that it's appreciated, and we intend to do everything possible to make it happen."

"Thank you, Tong."

"The governor and the mayor are working on tax incentives for the processing plants. And we are talking with North Dakota and South Dakota about future opportunities."

"That's right," said the governor. "And the best part about this whole project is its low cost. It will be the first renewable fuel to compete directly with petroleum diesel without federal subsidies. The public will lap it up."

***

Later that evening, Mr. Fu and Dr. Nugent were alone in the gallery.

"So, Amil, how are things going at the Cave?"

"Fairly well, I would say. Billet deliveries are up, and they seem to be back on track with the farnesene hybrid."

"What about the oil spill product, the OilSorb?"

"Yes, NuAge OilSorb. We're expecting great things from that product. Demand is going through the roof. The plant in Houston will make its first batch next week."

"It sounds like things are well in hand."

"Pretty much, I guess. The only thing that seems a little off is the management."

"You mean Jicard?"

"Yes, Jicard. He's been very flippant of late, stubborn, and difficult to read. It seems like he's doing a decent job on the surface, but he's spending far more money than we ever anticipated. I may have to pay him a visit and check things out myself."

"Don't worry about the cost, my friend. As long as he's meeting our objectives, it's okay with me. Just let him run with it."

"But Tong, we are talking about millions of dollars here. I know it's your money, but he is out of control."

"Amil, trust me. I know the Cave is an expensive place to operate. But from where I stand, it's well worth it."

Chapter 40

The fire started in the solvent storage room and spread quickly to engulf the whole building. At five-thirty, Mo's telephone started ringing.

"Hello?"

"Is this Mr. Finkelman?"

"Yes. Who is this?"

"I am calling from the Denver Police Department. Do you own a building located at five twenty-five thirty-eighth avenue?"

"Yes, that's my laboratory. Is there some kind of problem?"

"Yes, sir. I am sorry to say. There is a structure fire in progress at that address. Station number seven has responded and is on site as we speak."

"No, that can't be. You must be mistaken. My building is called avenue thirty-eight labs. You have the wrong address."

"There is no mistake, sir, and it looks bad. You might want to drive over and see for yourself."

"A fire! Oh my God. Okay. Ah, thanks for calling. I'll be there in fifteen minutes."

***

"Trupath Flyers. How can I help you?"

"Good morning. I am Deputy Sheriff Alice Montgomery calling for the sheriff's office in Crowley, Louisiana. May I speak with your manager?"

"Deputy sheriff, you say?"

"That's right. I would like to speak with your manager, please."

"Okay, ma'am, just a minute. Please hold on."

The receptionist buzzed the owner, Charles Ebert. "Sir, there is a deputy sheriff on line one. Do you have a minute to talk?"

"Certainly, patch him through."

"She's a woman, sir."

"Oh. Thanks for letting me know."

"Ma'am? Thanks for waiting. I will transfer you to Mr. Ebert."

"This is Charles Ebert speaking. How may I help you?"

"Sir, this is Deputy Sheriff Alice Montgomery calling for the sheriff's office in Crowley, Louisiana."

"Yes, ma'am. Are we in some kind of trouble?"

"Oh, no, sir. Don't be alarmed. I just need some information, that's all."

"Fine. I am always happy to assist law enforcement. Please, ask away."

"Great. Well, I am calling in reference to an ongoing investigation concerning one of your drones. It was recently used in the execution of a crime, and we would like to know who purchased it from you. It was a model XT-955. I have the serial number when you're ready."

"What kind of crime?"

"I am not at liberty to say, Mr. Ebert. Are you ready for the serial number?"

"Oh... sure. Go ahead. I'm ready."

She read out the serial number, and he entered it into his computer.

"Yes, here it is," he said. "We sold that unit to Denver City Productions, 1531 Larimer Street, Denver, Colorado. There were fourteen drones in the order."

"Thank you, sir. You've been very helpful."

"Wait a minute, Deputy. I have a little more."

"And what would that be, sir?"

"I should mention that they are one of our best customers. They have done a lot of business with us since that order."

"Really. How so?"

"The unit that you mentioned was shipped last year, but they gave us a much larger order in January."

"Really? Can you elaborate?"

"Certainly," he replied. "It was the largest single order we've ever had, almost six million dollars. We shipped seven hundred drones, ninety-eight controllers, and fourteen hundred battery packs. The last truckload went out a couple of weeks ago."

"That was a very nice order indeed. Do you have the shipping address?"

"Of course," he said. "The entire order was shipped to an address in Billings, Montana; Snowpack Warehousing, Sixty-two fifty Titan Avenue."

"Thank you, sir. You've been very helpful. I may call again if we have more questions."

"Feel free," he said. "I am happy to help."

***

Dr. Nugent was sitting in his office when his phone buzzed. It was the receptionist.

"Good morning, Millie," he said. "I'm sorry I didn't stop by this morning, but I had some urgent emails to deal with."

"It's fine, don't give it another thought."

"Okay. So, what's up?"

"Oh, there are a couple of men here from the FBI. Do you have time to talk with them?"

He hesitated for a moment. *The FBI? I wonder what they want. Should I tell them to make an appointment? No, I guess I should give them a few minutes.*

"Sure thing, Millie. I think I can spare a few minutes. Send them up."

"Thank you, Dr. Nugent." She hung up the phone and turned the agents. "He can give you about twenty minutes if you care to go up." She pointed at the door in the back of the reception area. "Take the elevator to the second floor and then turn to the right. His office is at the end of the hall. I'll buzz you through."

Dr. Nugent was standing outside his office when the agents approached. "Good morning, gentlemen. My name is Dr. Amil Nugent. Please come in." He stepped back and held the door.

The agents made their way to the conference table. Dr. Nugent walked to his credenza, grabbed a carafe of coffee, and then joined them. "Can I offer you a cup? It was brewed fresh this morning."

The older or the two agents spoke first. "Please."

He handed out mugs with the NSR logo, filled them to the top, and sat across the table. "So, gentlemen. How can I help you?"

Again the older agent spoke first, "I am Special Agent Dave Lyons with the FBI, and this is Special Agent Peter Stanton." They showed him their credentials. "Thank you for giving us a few moments this morning."

"I am happy to do it," he said. "But it's not every day that I have two FBI agents in my office. Can you tell me what this is about?"

"Of course, sir," said Agent Lyons. He retrieved a notepad from the inside pocket of his suit jacket and sat forward in his chair. "We have a few questions concerning our ongoing investigations. Special Agent Stanton will lead off."

Dr. Nugent sat quietly and sipped his coffee. Agent Stanton took out a notepad and found the first item on his list. "Dr. Nugent, on the twenty-third of March this year, there was a fire at your laboratory in Fort Collins. The building was destroyed, and a woman died. What can you tell us about that incident?"

"Oh," he said. "The Fort Collins fire." He sat forward in his chair and put his mug to the side. "It was a terrible accident, just terrible. I still can't believe it happened. We lost one of our best people that night, Dr. Karen Wells. It was a tragedy."

"Did you know Dr. Wells?"

"Only by reputation, we never actually met. But she was one of our best."

"Why do you say that?"

"She developed our cold-tolerant sugarcane hybrid." He waved his arm toward the window. "You may have noticed that ocean of green out there. That's her legacy."

"Do you mean that she...?"

"Yes. Her research made all of this possible, the sugarcane, this plant, even this office. She is greatly missed."

"I see," said Agent Stanton. "What can you tell me about her?"

"Not much, I'm afraid. I think she grew up somewhere in the Midwest—Ohio, maybe. We hired her straight out of CSU. That's where she got her Ph.D. She was a brilliant scientist, such a waste."

"Who did she report to?"

"She was independent, mostly, she didn't really need supervision. But on paper, she reported to our Broadview Plant Manager, Dan Turner."

"Does he work in this building?"

"Yes, normally. But he's out today. You can make an appointment with the receptionist."

"Thanks. We'll do that." He paused for a moment. "Special Agent Lyons has the next question."

Dr. Nugent took another sip from his mug.

"Sir, this question concerns one of your former employees, a Mr. Melvin Richards," he began. "We understand he was one of your engineers. What can you tell us about him?"

"Melvin Richards! That son of a bitch! How do you know about him? Have you been talking to Sharon Waggoner? So, she brought her sorry, poor-little-me story to the FBI. Well, I should have guessed. You *have* been talking to her. Haven't you?"

Agent Lyons just looked at him. And repeated the question, "What can you tell us about Melvin Richards?"

"He's a son of a bitch. That's what he is. He quit his job without warning and left us in the lurch. He cost us more than two million dollars."

"What do you mean, he quit?"

"I mean, he quit! And I told that little bitch, Miss Waggoner, the same thing. He was supposed to show up in Rapid City on January sixteen and never did. It cost us weeks of delay in project costs. We even sent the company jet to pick him up."

"When did you send the jet?"

"On January fifteen. He was supposed to meet the plane at general aviation in Billings, but he never showed up."

"So, you talked with him on the fifteenth?"

"No. I didn't talk with him. Dan Turner did."

"Dan met with him in Broadview, gave him the good news about Rapid City, and then sent him on his way."

"But he never made it to Billings?"

"Right, I already told you that." Dr. Nugent glanced at his watch. "Do you have any more questions? If not, I need to get back to work."

"Just a couple more. They are short, I promise."

"Okay, then. But let's move on."

Agent Stanton continued, "What do you know about a company called Denver City Productions?"

"Nothing. I've never heard of it."

"Do you know a person by the name of Molly Greene?"

"No."

"How about Linda Johnson or Byron Jameson? He is also known as BJ."

"No, and No. I don't know any of these people. What is going on here?"

"We are sorry, sir. We are only doing our jobs."

"That's okay, and I'm sorry for the outburst. But if we're finished, I need to get back to work."

"I think we have enough, for now," said Agent Lyons. "We appreciate your time." They rose from their chairs and turned toward the door. "We'll see ourselves out."

At the receptionist's desk, they made an appointment to meet with Dan Turner the following day. Then, they left.

Millie told Dr. Nugent about the appointment, and he called Dan.

"Hello, Dr. Nugent. Good morning."

"Yes, good morning, Dan. Guess who just left my office."

"I have no idea. Who?"

"The FBI, that's who."

"What did they want?"

"They had some questions about Melvin Richards."

"Wow! That will just not go away. Will it?"

"No. It appears not."

"It still puzzles me why he just disappeared like that."

"And they also wanted to know about Dr. Wells' death. I told them what a loss it was and how much we miss her."

"It was a tragedy, that's for sure. Was there anything else?"

"Not really. I just wanted to give you a heads-up. They talked with Millie on the way out and made an appointment to see you tomorrow morning. Be careful what you tell them."

"You can be sure of that."

***

Special Agents Lyons and Stanton were in their car, headed back to Billings.

"Well, Peter, what do you think about Dr. Nugent?"

"He sounded sincere to me. If he's lying, he is awfully good at it."

"I agree," said Dave.

"And he certainly didn't like Mr. Richards."

"You're right. There was no love loss there," he said. "But on the other hand, if what he said about him is true, then his feelings may be justified."

"Perhaps, but my gut tells me there is more to the story."

"Yes. It will be interesting to see what Mr. Turner has to say in the morning. Maybe he'll fill in some of the blanks."

Chapter 41

"Good morning," said Paul. "You were out for quite a while."

"Was I? What time is it? I feel like shit. What did that asshole shoot into me."

"It's almost noon on Monday, and the doctors aren't sure. They think it was just a strong sedative. Apparently, you were never in any real danger, except for when you drove your car off the cliff."

"Yeah, except for that. Monday noon? Wow, we lost a whole day. We need to get out of here and find Sharon. Hand me my clothes."

Paul opened the wardrobe and obliged.

"Tell me what happened. What do you remember?"

"Well, you know we were planning to check out the accident site."

"Yeah. That was in your last text."

"Well, we did. Sharon and I had a nice visit with the Waltons on Saturday afternoon."

"The Waltons?"

"Yes, the Waltons. Their house is below the Rims. Melvin's car crashed in their back yard."

"No kidding! That's something they'll never forget."

"For sure. But it gets better—they caught it on video."

"What? The crash? How is that possible?"

He glanced out the window while he buttoned his shirt. "They have surveillance cameras around their house, and the one that covers their back yard recorded the crash."

"Wow. It must have been horrible to watch."

"It was," he said. "Of course, Harry and Mavis, the Waltons, had watched it many times, and they found something... unexpected."

"What was that?"

"When the car crashed, it was upside down and crushed, but there was no fire. It was just lying there with steam coming from the radiator. But after a few seconds, a tiny explosive device detonated, and the fuel ignited. We saw it in the video. It was unmistakable. Harry gave me a copy on a thumb drive.

"So, you were right—it was not an accident."

"No, it wasn't. Somebody rigged the car and caused it to crash—it was murder. It was horrible to watch—Sharon actually fainted."

"She fainted? Is she all right?"

"Yeah, she passed out when she saw the fire erupt. Harry helped me carry her to the couch."

"How long was she out?"

"About ten minutes, I guess. It was quite a shock."

"How did the Waltons take it?"

"They were concerned, of course. But they were very nice about it. When she woke up, she was disoriented and a little embarrassed. It took her a few minutes to gather her wits. They asked her to stay for a while and rest up, but she would have none of it."

"And that's when you went up to the cliff."

"Right, she said she wanted to see it from above."

"But how did you end up driving off?"

"That part is a mystery. I'm not sure, exactly."

Paul said nothing.

"We were at the edge, looking down at the crash site. It was difficult for Sharon, but she stood there and took it in. After a few minutes, she had seen enough, and we walked back to the car. That's when it happened."

Paul was hanging on to every word.

"I was getting ready to start the engine when a man walked up and asked me to roll down the window. He seemed innocent enough, so I did. I remember him saying my name, and then he shot me with a taser and kidnapped Sharon. After that, things got fuzzy. He must have pushed the car over the edge before he left."

"You're lucky that outcrop was there."

"Indeed."

"He actually said your name?"

"He did. I asked if he needed something, and then he said, 'Yes, I certainly do, Mr. York'. Somehow, he knew we were going to be there. He must have bugged the car."

"Do you remember what he looked like?"

"No, I didn't see his face. It all happened too quickly…"

"But you do remember him taking Sharon."

"No, I don't, not really. I guess I was already unconscious. But he must have. It is the only thing that makes any sense."

"Do you think he was the same guy that caused Melvin's accident?"

"Maybe… I don't know. I need to tell Sam about this right now."

"Fine. But then we need to call the police. These guys are not fooling around, Tylor."

"I agree." He pointed to the stand next to his bed. "Hand me my phone, and let's get out of here."

***

The parking lot was a short walk from the hospital door, and Paul's car was in the second row. "It's over there," he said. "The red one, the last spot in the row."

"The Charger? I thought you drove a company pickup truck."

"I do. But that's for work. This is my personal car. Besides, who wants to drive a pickup truck three hundred and fifty miles in the middle of the night?"

"Yeah, I'm sorry about that. Did you bring me to the hospital in this?"

"I did, but you were pretty out of it. I doubt if you remember."

"I am sorry to say. I don't. But now that I'm awake, you should know that I totally approve. This is one sweet ride, my friend."

"Thanks. I've only had it a month, or so. It still has that new-car smell."

"And I am sorry about the Stomper call. But I am glad you showed up and saved my ass."

"Don't mention it. Next time, it's your turn."

"Count on it."

"So, where do you want to go first?"

"Let's head for the airport," he said. "I need to replace the rental car— I am sure there will be some paperwork. And on the way, I'll make a couple of calls."

"Your wish is my command, sir." He started the car and backed out of the parking space. The big V8 engine rumbled with power.

They left the parking lot and drove east on 12th Street.

Tylor opened his phone and found two missed calls. The first was from Mo, and the second was from Sam. Mo answered on the first ring.

***

"Tylor! Where have you been? I've been trying to reach you."

"Sorry, I've been a little occupied," he said. "Has something happened?"

"They set us on fire! The lab is gone."

"What are you talking about?"

"I got a call from the police at five-thirty this morning and then rushed right over there," he said. "The fire department did what they could, but it's a total loss. Everything is gone, my equipment, all of my samples, the computer system… everything. Fortunately, no one was in the building at the time."

"Mo, I am so sorry. What can I do to help?"

"There isn't much that anyone can do at the moment, I'm afraid. But I do have a plan."

"What sort of plan?"

"Well, nobody got hurt, and the building is insured. So eventually, everything will get rebuilt. And in the meantime, I'll move back to the garage."

"The garage?"

"I call it a garage, but it's really a large shed on the back edge of my property. It used to be my laboratory before I moved to the new building. The computers will have to be updated, and I'll need some new furniture, but the old equipment is still there. I should be up and running in no time."

"Is Pat okay?"

"She's a little shaken, but she'll be fine. She had a few tchotchkes on her desk, but nothing that can't be replaced. She'll be my assistant again— she's already on the phone ordering supplies."

"Good. I'm glad she's okay. Let me know if I can help."

"Thanks. I'll call you in a few days."

***

Paul stopped at a traffic light and turned to Tylor. "Did I hear right? They torched Mo's lab?"

"It appears that way. The fire department suspects arson."

"These people are seriously evil. What's he going to do?"

"I'll tell you later. First, I need to call Sam."

He picked up his phone, located the missed call, and touched the 'Call' button. Within seconds, he was on the line.

***

"Hey, Sam. How are things going?"

"Oh, not too bad. I'm visiting with Karen's mom this afternoon."

"Is she okay?"

"She's fine—a little anxious, I guess. But then, aren't we all? And what about you? I called yesterday, but you didn't answer. I have some news."

"I am sorry for not calling back. I was, ah, indisposed, you might say. Anyway, what's up? How was your interview with the FBI?"

"I'll start with Mowata," he said. "I had a chat with my brother yesterday. He's been working with the sheriff in Crowley."

"What did he say?"

"It turns out the drone they found in our field was purchased by a company we're familiar with, Denver City Productions."

"No."

"Yes, and total of fourteen drones were purchased at the same time."

"Fourteen drones could do a lot of damage."

"There's more," he said. "In January, they ordered seven hundred."

"My God! They could wipe out a whole county with that many."

"At least," said Sam. "And guess where they were shipped?"

"Denver?"

"No, Billings. Some warehouse on the east side of town. I think NSR is in this up to their eyeballs."

"Wow. And what about your talk with the FBI? How did that go?"

Paul stopped in the airport parking lot and turned off the engine.

Sam continued, "Detective Reeves has been working with the Denver Police to find out about Molly and her friend Linda Johnson. It turns out they were both killed on the same day. Linda died in Denver. Somebody drugged her and then left her outside in the weather—she froze to death."

"How horrible."

"They have a description from some of the homeless people, but little more. They're searching for a motive. These ladies were living together on the street, in a packing crate, for God's sake."

"There must be a connection."

"They assume so," he said. "It seems that Denver City Productions has no employees but still manages to do over ten million dollars per year in sales."

"A clever business plan."

"And they found fingerprints in the office on Larimer Street, those of a Mr. Byron Jameson. According to their files, he's an Afro-American, six feet tall, thirty-two years old, and about one hundred thirty pounds. He is also known as BJ."

"So, a skinny black man!"

"Right. He's been in trouble with the police since he was a teenager."

"So, what have they learned about Karen?"

"I am afraid the news on Karen is not as good," he said. "Her disappearance is still a mystery."

***

Paul shifted in his seat and pointed at his watch. Tylor held his index finger in the air.

"Be patient," he said. "We have a lot to catch up on."

***

Sam continued, "But the FBI believes Christi was directly involved, and they suspect NSR is behind it somehow. A couple of their agents are in Broadview this morning, talking with Dr. Nugent."

"From the Billings office?"

"I suppose so."

"I was planning to call the Police myself, but now I think I'll visit the FBI instead."

"Why do you need to call the police?"

Tylor told Sam about his visit with the Waltons, the crash video, and the incident at the overlook. Then he updated him on the situation in Dusty Fork and the fire at Mo's lab."

"Wow, these guys have been busy."

"They certainly have," he said. "It seems they don't like us very much. And the whole thing with Mo's lab is highly suspicious."

"But you're okay. I mean from the attack."

"Yes, I'm fine. I have a little headache, but Sharon has been kidnapped!" he said. "Paul and I are going to start searching, but we'll need some help. So, I am going to talk with the FBI this afternoon— I want to give them Melvin's duffel bag, and I also want to tell them about the gelator. It looks like NSR is involved in that as well."

"Well, you can count me in. I'll be back this evening."

Chapter 42

Maurice had outdone himself again. Lunch featured a light spinach pasta salad with crispy mushrooms, chunks of butternut squash, and a lovely pumpkin seed pesto. Karen was delightfully sated when she pulled up to the lab.

"Mondays are the best," she muttered to herself. "And Maurice is amazing." She strolled into her office.

"Good afternoon, Bud," she said. "Did anything interesting happen while I was out?"

"Yeah, a little bit. We received a cavecast from Jicard. Apparently, Dr. Jacobs was promoted this morning and has been reassigned to Haynes. He is gone."

"Hansen is gone? No. That can't be true. He would have said something."

"This sort of thing tends to happen quickly around here—I doubt they gave him much warning. It's like that chemist who disappeared last summer—Dr. Gilford."

She stopped smiling.

"He left suddenly, as well. One day he was here, and the next day, he wasn't. Anyway, Hansen is gone, and he's probably better off being away from this place." He turned his attention back to his computer monitor. "And oh yeah, somebody left an envelope on your desk."

She opened it, and found note inside.

Destroy this after you read it. Dr. Wells, you are in danger. Jicard knows about your walk in the lower tunnel, and he is watching you.

When you get back to your room, charge your cell phone and send a text message to someone for help. Hide it behind the drainpipe, seventeen feet east of your apartment door. It's a dead spot in the camera coverage. I will pick it up later tonight and send it out on the next truck of billets. When it finds a cell tower, it will transmit automatically. Please be careful.

She read the note a second time, folded it in half, and placed it in her pants pocket.

"Anything important?" he said.

"Not really. No, it's nothing. Let's get back to work."

***

At two o'clock, she feigned a headache and returned to her apartment. She entered her bedroom, closed the door, and scanned the note again. *Who sent this? Should I trust it? It may be a trap. No, things don't feel right. I think it's real.*

Her cell phone charger had been plugged in since the day she arrived. She used it every night to look at old photos and re-read old messages, especially those from Sam. So, it was to him that she wrote the text.

My darling Sam,

I do not know where I am. When I arrived, the plane landed in Billings, and I believe I'm some distance south of there. I am with a group of scientists in a secret NSR research facility called the Cave.

The man who runs the place is Louis Jicard. He's a psychopath. When I arrived, he said we were under a mountain at the east edge of the Bear Tooth Plateau, close to the Wyoming border. We have no way to contact the outside world.

This place is built like NORAD—it is a fortress. They are armed, and they have cameras everywhere, inside and out.

But occasionally, we ship out truckloads of sugarcane billets, and I am sending my phone out on the next one. I pray that you receive this message.

Sam, I believe I am in grave danger, and I need your help. Please find me.

All my love,
Karen

She unplugged the phone, carried it into the hall, and placed it behind the drainpipe. She then walked back to her apartment door, stepped into her golf cart, and returned to her office.

When she arrived, Bud looked up and smiled. "I am glad to see you back. Are you feeling better?"

"Yes, much better, thank you. I just needed to lie down for a while." She walked to her desk and eased into her chair. "I'm going to miss Hansen a lot. We were just getting to know each other. I hope he enjoys the new job."

As she leaned forward to switch on her monitor, Max walked in. "Hi, Max. What can I do for you this afternoon?"

He stood next to her desk in his monolithic way and said, "Please come with me, Dr. Wells. Mr. Jicard would like to speak with you."

She swallowed hard and said, "What about?"

"He did not say, ma'am. He just wants to talk with you."

"Oh. Okay, I guess." She stood up and looked at Bud. "Apparently, I have been summoned. Hold down the fort until I get back. Tomorrow morning, I would guess."

"Aye, aye, commander, I'll take care of everything."

***

Eight minutes later, Max knocked on Jicard's door.

"Come," was the reply.

Max opened the door and ushered her inside.

"Thanks for coming." He gestured toward a chair at the end of his desk. "Please, have a seat."

Karen moved to the chair and sat down.

"Good afternoon, Dr. Wells. Are you comfortable?"

"I guess so," she answered. "What would you like to talk about?"

"You know, Dr. Wells, it has been eighteen days since you joined us. What do you think of that?"

"Really, that many? I haven't been keeping track."

"Well, I have. And I must say you've made a real difference here. You are very popular with your staff, and you seem to be making friends everywhere. Morale is up, production is up, and your work is exemplary."

"Thank you, sir."

"Oh, there is no need to thank me. I am merely stating the facts. But there is one area where you have not excelled."

"Sir? Have I done something wrong?"

"I am talking about respect, Dr. Wells."

"Sir? I am not sure what you mean."

"I don't think you appreciate what it takes to run this facility. We have two hundred researchers here, intelligent, independent, very talented people."

"I'm aware of that. I feel privileged to be among them."

"You should—getting them here was no small feat."

She nodded in agreement. "I can believe that."

"And I think you would agree that we do a lot to keep them happy—a pleasant working environment, good pay, good food, medical benefits, exercise facilities, and the like."

"I do."

"And the only thing we ask in return, Dr. Wells, is that they obey our rules—a reasonable request, we think. Are you with me so far?"

"I think so. But I am not sure where you're going, Mr. Jicard."

"Oh, I am certain you know 'where I'm going', as you put it, but I will make it perfectly clear."

She shifted in her seat.

"Dr. Wells, I know that you and Dr. Jacobs intentionally ignored a security-personnel-only sign and entered the tunnel system beneath his lab. Your presence was detected with infrared sensors. Do you deny that?"

Karen straightened her back and swept a long hair from her right cheek. "No, sir, I do not deny that. Hansen and I were down there for about twenty minutes. And I must say, there was nothing to see. It had not been used in years, maybe decades."

"Hansen? I think you mean Dr. Jacobs."

"No. I mean Hansen. He and I have become friends. By the way, was he really promoted? Where is he exactly?"

Jicard smiled and raised his index finger in the air. "You see, this is precisely what I mean. You are a dangerous combination, Dr. Wells. You are physically attractive, personable, and extremely intelligent. People are naturally drawn to you, and I imagine you almost always get what you want. Well, I am sorry to disappoint, but it is not going to happen this time."

"I resent that!"

"I don't care what you resent," he said. "In this facility, I have the final word. And there is a zero-tolerance policy for breaking security rules. This fact was made clear the day you arrived. People are not allowed to enter restricted areas without permission, period."

"What are you saying?"

"I am saying I can no longer allow you to foment disobedience in this facility, and you have left me with no alternative. Effective immediately, I am terminating your employment."

He looked toward Max and nodded. "Take her to chamber ten."

"Yes, sir."

She held out her right hand to keep Max away. "Mr. Jicard. What are you planning to do?"

"I may not see you again, Dr. Wells. Goodbye."

Max stepped behind her chair, grasped her upper arms, and lifted. She winced—his grip was like steel. Together, they walked to the rear of Jicard's office and stepped through a side door—it was a private elevator.

Chapter 43

Paul and Tylor were lounge when Sam arrived. "Good morning, gentlemen." He took a chair across from Tylor. "How do we proceed?"

"We're glad you could make it, Sam. Paul and I were just getting started." He pulled out his cell phone and opened his map program. "Today, we want to go to the airport and talk to that rental agent again, Tony. He's the one who sent the text to Sharon. I'm sure he knows more about the Malibu.

And second, we think we should visit that warehouse and see if we can learn anything about the drone shipments. Maybe they are still in the warehouse. But if they aren't, then we need to find out who picked them up."

"Okay. Just tell me what you want me to do. I am all in," he said. "I thought a lot about it on the way up last night, and I'm convinced that they have Karen as well."

"We are too."

***

That same morning, in Broadview, Special Agents Lyons and Stanton arrived at the North States Renewables facility. They parked their car in the visitors' section and walked into the reception room. Millie was behind the desk and smiled as they approached.

"Good morning, gentlemen. You are right on time."

"Good morning, Ms. Carson," said Agent Lyons. "It is nice to see you again. Is Mr. Turner available?"

"He is," she said. "I'll let him know you're here." She punched in his extension.

"They are here, Dan. Should I send them up?" There was a short pause, and then she hung up the phone. "He'll see you now. His office is the second door on the right, just past the elevator."

The agents started for the door, and Millie buzzed them through. Dan was waiting for them.

"Good morning," he said. "I am sorry you had to make a second trip."

"It's not a problem, sir," said Agent Lyons. "May we come in? We have a few questions."

"Actually, my office is a little small for the three of us," he said. "Let's use the conference room instead."

They followed him to the conference room and took seats at one end of the table.

Agent Lyons made the introductions. "I am Special Agent Dave Lyons with the FBI, and this is Special Agent Peter Stanton." They showed him their credentials. "Thank you for giving us a few moments this morning."

Dan nodded. "It's okay," he said. "What sort of questions would you like to ask?"

Special Agent Stanton began. "The first couple of questions are about the fire at your laboratory in Fort Collins."

"Oh, the fire. Okay, go ahead."

"The fire occurred on the twenty-third of March, the building was destroyed, and women died. What can you tell us about it?"

"Well," he said. "It was terrible. The woman who died was Dr. Karen Wells, a brilliant biochemist. She is the one who developed our cold-tolerant hybrid." He pointed at lush green fields outside the window. "We owe everything to her."

"What would you say if we told you that the person who died in the fire was a lady named Molly Greene and not Karen Wells?"

"That's impossible," he said quickly. "I attended her funeral." He sat back in his chair. "What are you saying?"

"We are saying that Dr. Karen Wells did not die in that fire. We believe she was kidnapped."

"Karen is alive?" he said. "Give me a second to think about that."

"Do you know the name, Molly Greene?"

"What?" he said. "Molly Greene? Ah, no, I'm sorry. I don't know that name. Who is she?"

"Does the name Linda Johnson mean anything to you?"

"No."

"How about a man named Bryon Jameson? He is also known as BJ."

Dan hesitated for a second and then said, "Jameson? No, I don't know that name either."

"Perhaps you know him as BJ?"

"No, I'm sorry. I've never heard of him."

"Do you know a woman named Christi Snow?"

"Of course," he said. Christi was Dr. Wells' assistant in Fort Collins. She disappeared after the fire, and we haven't heard from her since. Do you think she kidnapped Karen, ah, Dr. Wells?"

"How well did you know Miss Snow?

"Not very well," he said. "She worked for Dr. Wells, so I met her a few times. You know, at the lab."

"I see," said Agent Stanton. He jotted down a few notes. "So, you have no idea what happened to her?"

"No. I wish I did."

"Thank you, sir. Now, Special Agent Lyons has a few questions."

"Mr. Turner. What can you tell me about a company called Denver City Productions?" He watched his face closely for a reaction.

Dan showed none. "I don't know that company. Should I?"

"Not necessarily," said the agent. "It pertains to another line of inquiry we've been following." He made a note in his book and then went to the next question.

"Do you know a man named Melvin Richards? We believe he used to work for you."

"Yes, I know Melvin Richards. He is an exceptional engineer." He spread his arms wide. "He designed this processing plant, the whole thing, from the ground up. He was supposed to do our next plant in Rapid City. But he up and quit on us. It was quite a blow to the project."

"How so?"

"It cost us millions. And to make matters worse, I kind of liked the guy. So, I have a lot of mixed feelings about it."

"He quit?"

"Yes, and it was very strange."

"Strange?"

"Well, I met him at Lucky's that day and told him about his promotion—that's in Broadview. After that, we said goodbye, and I sent him on his way. He was supposed to meet the company jet in Billings, but he never showed up. That was on January fifteen."

"You remember the date exactly?"

"Yes, I certainly do. His fiancée, Sharon Wagoner, keeps reminding me. She has called at least a hundred times. I had to set a filter on my computer to block her emails—she's a royal pain in the ass. She thinks we know where he is, and should drop everything to help her find him. But we don't know where he is. We only know he left us in the lurch."

"I see," said Agent Lyons. "Thank you, Mr. Turner." He made some more notes in his book. "I have one more question."

"Okay, shoot."

"What would you say if I told you that Melvin Richards died in a car crash?" Again he watched Dan's face for a reaction.

"What? Melvin's dead? How, when?"

"He died on the way to the airport that day. Apparently, he lost control of his car and drove off The Rims, a couple of miles past Zimmerman Park."

"No, that can't be true." He paused for a moment. "Melvin Richards is dead?"

"We believe so."

"Then, that's why he never showed up at the plane. He died in a car crash." He paused. "Oh, I feel terrible. We've had nothing but bad thoughts about him. I cursed his very existence. And all this time, he's been dead…" He paused again. "Thank you for telling me. I'll share this with Dr. Nugent as soon as we are finished. He'll be crushed."

"I am sorry to be the one to tell you, truly." He looked at Agent Stanton and then back to Dan. "You know what? I think we have all we need for today. We'll let you get back to it."

They rose from their chairs and walked toward the door. Agent Lyons turned. "We'll be in touch, and thank you for your time."

***

A few minutes later, they were back in the car headed south on Route 3. Halfway through Broadview, Agent Stanton glanced to the left. "That's the restaurant Mr. Turner talked about, Lucky's Bar and Grill. Do you think we should stop?"

"Not today," said Agent Lyons. "We need to get back to Billings."

"It would only take a few minutes."

"No. We need to drop off those DNA samples and then get back to the office. Fort Collins is waiting for our report."

"Okay," he said. "But I think we should definitely come back and interview the owner. She may have overheard their conversation."

"We will if we have to," he said. "But in the meantime, let's talk about Turner. What was your impression?"

"I think he's lying. He had answers for every question, perfect, well-rehearsed answers. He never batted an eye."

"I agree. He is definitely hiding something."

"And he didn't seem surprised when we told him Richards might be dead."

"Yeah. I am pretty sure he knew about Richards. In fact, I'd bet he was in on it from the beginning."

***

Tylor went to the airport alone, while Sam and Paul went to the warehouse. Tony Waterson was at the rental desk when he arrived.

"Tony? Good morning."

"You again? I have already told you everything I know. Please go away." He looked nervously around the room.

"I am sorry to keep bugging you, but we need your help. Susan has been kidnapped."

"Kidnapped! I was afraid that might happen. Why didn't she just leave town."

"What do you know about it? Would you please tell me? She needs your help."

"I was worried about this from the first moment I saw her. She such a slip of a thing."

"Please, Tony. Please talk to me."

Tony looked down and was silent for several seconds, then he looked directly at Tylor.

"I can't stand by and let it happen again." He had a determined look on his face. "But we can't talk here," he whispered. "It's too dangerous."

"What? Why not?"

"I can't say." He thought for a moment and then whispered, "Meet me tomorrow afternoon at the coffee shop at twenty-seventh and twelfth, at two." We can talk then.

"Tomorrow?"

"Yes, tomorrow." His hands were shaking.

Tylor searched Tony's face and decided to trust him. "Okay. Two p.m. tomorrow. I'll be there."

"Seriously, we can't talk here." His voice was barely audible.

"Okay, then, thank you," said Tylor. "Do you have an extra map?"

Tony exhaled. "Lewis and Clark Caverns, you say? Of course, sir." He reached over and pulled out a Billings area street map. "Here you go, sir. You go through town and then take I-90 west for about two and a half hours to Route 287. Just follow the signs—you can't miss it." He circled the location of the coffee shop.

"Thanks so much. I'll see you tomorrow afternoon..." Tylor folded the map in half and walked out of the airport.

***

Sam and Paul stopped in the visitors' parking area next to the 'Snowpeak Warehousing' sign—the loading area was packed. At least twenty semi-trailers were parked against the building's north wall. They exited their car and walked into the reception area—a handsome middle-aged lady was behind the desk.

"Good morning gentlemen, can I help you?"

"I hope so," said Sam. "We need little information on an order we placed in January."

"And what company are you with?"

"North States Renewables," said Paul.

"Oh, NSR, I see," she said.

"And what order are we talking about?"

"It was placed with Trupath Flyers in Houston. The last partial shipment arrived about two weeks ago. I have the order number if you need it."

"That won't be necessary. What do you want to know about it?"

"Is it still here in the warehouse, or was it picked up already?"

She glanced at her computer screen. "Oh, it went out the same day, Friday, the thirtieth. Your company is always prompt."

"Can you confirm the name of the freight company? We want to make sure they get paid on time."

"Of course," she said. "The shipment was picked up by Triple-B, ah, Bison-Black Bear Express."

"Great," he said. "That agrees with our records. Thank you very much for your help."

"Don't mention it."

Sam and Paul walked back to the car and headed for the hotel.

Chapter 44

When Karen woke up, she was starving. Her left arm ached, and her knees were jammed up against her chest. "Where am I?" she muttered.

She was in a steel-framed box covered with rusty chicken wire. Above her head, a single light bulb hung on a long, twisted cable, and dripping water echoed in the darkness. She tried to straighten her legs but could not.

"Hello!" she cried. "Is anybody there?"

There was no reply.

"That's water dripping," she said quietly. "I must be in the tunnel again. How did I get here? Nothing looks familiar." *I was meeting with Jicard in his office. He actually fired me! The asshole. Then Max brought me down in the elevator. Why does Jicard have a private elevator? Why did Max shove me against the wall like that? He nearly broke my arm. What is going on?*

Suddenly she heard a woman's voice. It was faint. "Hello? Who are you? Can you help me?" It seemed a long way off. She cupped her ears to concentrate. But before she could answer, Max appeared.

"I see you're awake, Dr. Wells. That's great." He reached down and opened the door. "Please, let's get you out of that nasty, dirty place. We have things to talk about."

He grabbed her left arm and pulled hard. On the way out, the frayed chicken wire scratched her leg. "Good morning, Dr. Wells. I am here to make you a proposition."

"Why did you put me in there? You can't treat me like this!"

"Oh, Dr. Wells, I can treat you any way I please. But I would prefer that you accept our proposition."

"What are you talking about?"

"Our proposition is this. You will assist Dr. Gilford in his work, and in exchange, we will let you live."

"Now you are threatening me? Who's Dr. Gilford? *Is that the chemist Bud was talking about?* "Go to hell, Max."

He picked her up with one hand and threw her against the wall like a rag doll. Her face scraped on the carved stone as she slumped to the floor. "You will accept our proposition sooner or later, Dr. Wells. And I suggest you do so now—it will hurt less that way."

"I do not respond to threats or force," she replied. "And as I said before, you can go to hell, Max!"

He lifted her from the floor, held her in mid-air with his right hand, and struck the left side of her face. Her head snapped to the right, and her mouth filled with blood. He then delivered a massive blow to her stomach. She gasped for air and slumped back on the floor.

"I can do this all day," he said. "You will agree to our proposition, and it would be easier if you did so now."

"Over my dead body. She spat out the blood and watched it mix with the dirt on the floor."

"Well, maybe not dead, but certainly bruised." He picked her up again and held her off the floor. She could hardly breathe. He then struck her from the opposite side, and her head snapped to the left. Blood sprayed from her mouth and streamed down her chin. "You will agree," he repeated.

"Let go of me, you asshole. Put me down!"

He then stuffed her back in the cage, locked the door, and walked away. "Give it some thought, Dr. Wells. I will be back."

She could manage only short breaths. *Like hell, I will! Dr. Gilford? Has he been down here all this time? I guess he wasn't transferred after all. He must be working with Jicard. And he's probably the one who's been messing with Hansen's research. Like hell, I'll help him. There is no way!*

Again, she heard the woman's voice, far away, very faint. "Who's out there? Please help me."

Her face was burning. She passed out.

***

Twenty minutes later, Max returned, dragging a body behind him. He rapped on the cage with his fist. "Wake up, Dr. Wells. It is time for our second chat." He tossed the limp body against the wall and dragged Karen from the cage. Her face was bruised, her lip was bleeding, and a long scab was forming on her left leg.

"Stand up. I have someone with me."

Karen staggered to her feet and opened a swollen left eye. "Hansen! What has he done to you?" She stepped toward him, but Max pulled her back.

"Not so fast, Dr. Wells," he said. "You are not going anywhere."

"Let me help him!"

"I am afraid not. You see, Dr. Jacobs, here, has refused our proposition, 'categorically', to use his words."

His right arm twitched slightly, and he managed a low groaning sound.

"Hansen! You're awake! Hansen!"

"Forget it, Doc. He is beyond help."

"What are you talking about? He's hurt!"

Max handcuffed Hansen to the cage and then dragged Karen down the tunnel. "You need to see something."

Hansen stirred and jerked at his handcuffs. Weakly, he cried out, "Karen…"

Max pulled and dragged her along until they came to a solid steel pole embedded in the rock floor. He stood her against it and secured her with a second pair of cuffs. The steel was cold and wet against her back.

"What in the hell are you doing, Max? Let me go at once. And what is that smell?"

"Shut up, Dr. Wells, and pay attention. I am about to give you a valuable lesson in persuasion."

Max walked back to the cage and returned with Hansen. He was conscious but too weak to resist.

"Release him, Max. Can't you see he's hurt?"

"I told you to shut up, Dr. Wells." He flipped a switch on the wall, and suddenly the tunnel was flooded with light. Ten feet from the steel pole, directly in front of Karen's feet, a large pit loomed from the darkness.

"What are you doing, Max?"

"I thought I told you, Dr. Wells. This is a lesson in persuasion," he said. "You see, a cave can be a very dangerous place. Over millions of years, dripping water can accomplish remarkable things. It can turn the tiniest crack into a gaping trench or a shallow hole into a deep dark cavern, like this one." He picked up a rock and tossed it toward the center. "If you listen quietly, you will hear it hit the bottom."

Moments passed, four, maybe five seconds before they heard a distance thunk, the sound echoed in the cave. "There, did you hear it?"

"Max! You're crazy. Please stop this at once and let us go."

"Crazy, you say. No, ma'am, I am not crazy. I am simply doing my job. Mr. Jicard needs to ramp up production, and Dr. Gilford will need some help. You, Dr. Wells, will be that help. "

She said nothing.

"You will agree to our proposition and pledge to help Dr. Gilford, willingly, without resistance, until the project is finished. You must agree right now." He paused for a few seconds.

"What project and what will happen to me when it's finished?"

"Wrong answer, Dr. Wells." He picked up Dr. Jacobs and held him above his head.

Hansen flailed his arms, but it was no use. The grip was unyielding, and his strength was gone. He looked at Karen with wide soulful eyes and mouthed her name.

"Okay, okay," she cried. "I agree!"

"Too late, Dr. Wells. You had your chance." He angled toward the edge and launched Dr. Jacobs toward the left side of the hole. His scream was pitiful.

The walls of the chasm were festooned with hundreds of rocky outcrops and small ledges. So as Dr. Jacobs fell, he bounced back and forth across the void. He shrieked like a wounded animal as long bones snapped, and strips of flesh were torn from his body. But after the third bounce, he stopped screaming—nothing more was heard until he hit the bottom. The last sound was a wet crunch, like a watermelon hitting a concrete floor.

"Oh my God, you murdered him! Max! What is wrong with you?"

"He was a stupid man. He could have accepted our proposition, but he refused. He died for his principles. He was a foolish, stupid man."

Karen stared in utter disbelief.

"And now, it's your turn, Dr. Wells. Are you a stupid woman, or will you agree to help Dr. Gilford?"

"You would do that to me?"

"Without hesitation," he replied. "But I am pretty sure you'll agree. Because in your case, I have more cards to play."

"And what cards would those be? You have no leverage over me, and my principles are just as important as Hansen's were. You can go to hell."

"Oh, I may well end up there, but not for some time, I think. And in the meantime, I do have cards to play."

"What cards?"

"Well," he said. "The first card would be your colleagues upstairs. If you refuse to cooperate, you will die, and then we will have to recruit someone else. Our first choice would be Dr. Jacobs' assistant, Stephan. He is quite knowledgeable in the field and would be an excellent choice. In fact, he would be here right now if you hadn't decided to take that walk with Dr. Jacobs."

"Stephan."

"And if he refuses, then we will draft Bud, ah, Dr. Xavier, and so on. Eventually, we will find someone who wants to live."

"And your other card?"

"Cards, Dr. Wells. Cards... ss," he replied. "My next cards will be the people you love, like Sam Wilson, for example, and your dear sweet mother. She lives in Fort Collins, I believe."

"You leave them alone! You wouldn't hurt my mother!"

"Oh, I would. Without hesitation," he said matter-of-factly. "If you refuse our proposition, then next week, Mr. Wilson will die in a car crash. And as for your mother, I haven't yet decided. But she will most certainly die. There might be a gas explosion in her basement, or perhaps a poisonous snake will find its way into her bed. There are so many possibilities..."

***

When Karen woke up the following morning, she thought she was going blind. She could see only a faint glow of light in the room. *This isn't my room. What is that smell? My lungs feel heavy.* She put her right hand on her chest. A little pressure helped a bit. She then touched her left cheek. *Ouch! What the hell?* Then she remembered. *Max killed Hansen. That unbelievable bastard!* "Hansen!" she screamed.

"Oh, good, you're awake, thank God." Again, it was a woman's voice, but closer this time. "Who are you? Can you help me?" It was the same voice she heard when she was in the cage. "Who is Hansen?"

"My name is Karen," she said. "Who are you? What is this place?" She tried to sit up, but her body screamed in protest. Finally, exhausted, she eased back on the bed. "I'm Karen Wells."

"My name is Sharon, Sharon Wagoner. I am so glad you woke up. You have no idea," she said. "Do you know what day it is?"

Chapter 45

Tylor was in a booth toward the rear of the coffee shop when Tony arrived. He stepped through the door and quickly scanned the room. When he spotted Tylor, he shuffled to the booth and sat down.

"Were you followed?" he whispered.

"I don't think so."

"Did you check your car for bugs or a tracking device?" Tony hunched down and peered out the window. "We have to be very careful. If they catch us together, they will kill us."

"I believe we're safe," he said. "Who are *they*?"

"I am not sure. But they don't want me to talk with anyone, especially you," he said.

"I can see that you're worried," said Tylor. "But I can assure you that nobody followed me."

"Well, okay then. But we need to be careful."

"Tony. What can you tell me?"

"I don't know anything about any kidnapping," he said. "Oh, God. They are going to kill her. I've been scared to death ever since that Malibu thing. I can't sleep. I can't eat... I have nightmares, Mr. York!"

Tylor made a patting motion with his hands. "Calm down, and talk to me..."

He bowed his head close to the table and spoke in a low voice. "The Malibu was rigged with remote-controlled explosives. And when it didn't come back the next day, I knew it was bad. They killed him, Mr. York."

But Meagan says it *did* come back. It was listed as 'Returned' on the computer.

"No, it didn't. They faked the entry. It never came back. And when I heard about the crash on route 3, I knew what happened."

"Was Meagan involved?

"Dear sweet Meagan? No. No way. I am sure she wasn't."

"Why didn't you call the police?"

"I wanted to, so much. I picked up the phone a hundred times. But I knew they'd kill me if I did. And then she showed up and started asking questions. I knew they'd kill her too. She is so sweet and innocent. I just couldn't let that happen, so I tried to help—and now they have her. Oh my God. Why didn't I do more?"

"You are the one that sent the anonymous note. Aren't you?"

"Yes, it was me. I sent the note. I hoped she'd leave town. I should have done more."

"Who are they?"

"I honestly don't know. I get text messages with instructions, and then I text back to the same number. I never know who is on the other end." He opened his cell phone and pointed to the messages. Tylor wrote down the number.

"So, where do you think they took her?"

"You like her. Don't you? I can hear it in your voice."

"Yes. Quite a bit, actually."

"Well, she seems like a keeper, that's for sure. You be sure to take good care of her."

"I want to," he said. "But I need to find her first." He looked at him expectantly.

"I don't know exactly where they took her. But I get the sense that it's somewhere south of here. Out toward Red Lodge, I would guess…"

"Out toward Red Lodge. Okay, we'll check it out." He made a couple of notes.

"Look, Mr. York, I think we need to wrap this up now."

"I understand, Tony. And thank you so much for meeting with me. You've helped us more than you know."

"I needed to do it. I couldn't stand it any more. I only hope it was worth the risk." He looked straight into Tylor's eyes. "You catch these people, Mr. York, and make them pay. They are bad people."

"We will. And I promise to call you when it's over."

"Thanks. Now, you must leave first. I will order a cup of coffee and hang out for a while. We can't be seen together."

***

"Where is she? I have checked her room, her office, the cafeteria— everywhere."

"She's gone, Chip. Didn't you see the cavecast? She's been promoted and reassigned to Roscoe. She is going to be their new plant manager."

"Dr. Wells and Dr. Jacobs, both? I don't think so."

"What do you know?"

"I pay attention to what goes on around here, and this is very strange."

"You're infatuated with the woman, Chip. You have been since the first time you saw her."

"Okay, Yes. You're right. But it still seems strange that two top-rung docs would leave at the same time. And," he said, "how did they manage to get out of here? We have cameras everywhere, and there is no video of them leaving."

"Forget it, Chip. Just, forget it."

"No, I won't forget it," he said. "The last video we have, shows Max escorting Dr. Wells into Jicard's office, and she never came out. And the night before that, the same thing happened with Dr. Jacobs. That is strange, Pedro. That is very strange, indeed."

***

He knocked three times on Karen's cell door, "Dr. Wells?" he said. "Good afternoon. May I speak with you? I am Dr. Arthur Gilford."

She used the peak-hole to check him out. *He doesn't look like a monster.* He was wearing a white lab jacket and silver-framed glasses. He was about fifty years old, with dark skin and short curly hair. His smile was enchanting.

"Good afternoon, Dr. Wells," he said. "I am sorry we had to meet under these circumstances. May I come in?"

"What makes you think I won't just run away when you open the door?"

"You are too intelligent for that. And even if you did, you wouldn't get far. Our guard would see to that."

Karen considered her options and realized she had none. "Please, come in," she said. "I have been looking forward to meeting you."

Dr. Gilford unlocked the door and walked inside. His smile vanished immediately. "My dear girl," he said. "I see you've had a session with Max. I am so sorry."

"Is this how you recruit assistants? He almost killed me. He *did* kill Dr. Jacobs."

"Yes, I was afraid it would come to that. Dr. Jacobs was unrealistic."

"Unrealistic? And that's reason to kill a man?"

"Under normal circumstances, of course not," he whispered. "But circumstances down here are anything but normal. If we disobey, they will kill us, period. So, calm down a little and trust me. I mean you no harm." He placed his hand lightly on her shoulder.

She studied the man and decided he was telling the truth. "All right, Dr. Gilford, what do I need to do?"

"That's better," he said. "First, we need to get you cleaned up a little, and it looks like your leg could stand some attention. Come with me."

He turned to leave, and Karen said, "What about Sharon?"

"You mean Miss Wagoner? Oh, I can't help her." He tilted his head toward the guard. "She is here for a different reason. I am not authorized."

"But she's starving. She hasn't eaten in days."

"I am sorry," he said. "We must go now. You can bring something to her later." He placed his hand on the small of her back. "Let's go."

Karen looked to the right when they left her cell. At least a dozen more were carved into the tunnel wall, but only the first two were occupied. As they passed Sharon's, her face was in the peep hole. "I'll be back," she said.

Soon they came to a sealed door. Dr. Gilford opened it, and they stepped through. The guard followed and closed it behind them.

"Welcome to chamber nine," said Dr. Gilford. "Your new home away from home."

Her mouth dropped in awe. *Another lie!* It was almost as large as the main chamber upstairs. The floor was a mixture of polished white tile and concrete, and the lighting was brilliant. There was a truck loading area on one side, stainless steel equipment in the center, and several hundred drones lined up against the other wall. Next to the drones was a huge pile of shipping crates.

"Jicard said this chamber was unfinished. He told me it was unsafe, security personnel only."

"Yes. That is their standard verse. They are doing things down here that they don't want anyone else to know about."

"What sort of things? What are those drones for?"

"All in good time, my dear." He raised his hand to point the way. "Let's get you to the shower, and then we'll work on your injuries."

While his hand was in the air, she noticed that three of his fingers were severely disfigured. "What happened to your hand?" she said.

"Oh, that." He held it so she could get a better look. "Pliers at dawn can be an effective form of persuasion."

"Oh, my God. That's horrible." She looked at her own hand and wiggled her fingers.

"It was," he continued. "When I first arrived, they put me in the cells, too. And for the first couple of weeks, they tried to convert me with daily beatings. But when that didn't seem to work, they got more creative and came up with the pliers-idea. They strapped my arm to a table and went to work on my fingers, one at a time. When they started on the fourth, I acquiesced. It took over three months for them to heal."

"I am so sorry, Dr. Gilford. I thought you were working for Jicard."

"Water under the bridge, my dear," he said. "But would you mind calling me Gil? My friends call me Gil."

"Of course. I would be honored," she said. "And please call me Karen."

Chapter 46

"You look like hell, Forgue, and that is one nasty-looking ponytail. Don't you ever wash your hair?"

"Screw you, Jicard."

Christi and BJ joined the call.

"Good morning, Jicard," she said. "Is this about the pipeline job?"

"Hang on for a couple of minutes, Christi."

Dan Joined.

"Good morning, Dan," he said. "Great. So, we're all here."

They all nodded.

"Listen up, people," Jicard said. "The time has come to tackle the big one, the Kentala-Ridge Pipeline."

No one said a word—they just stared at their screens.

"We proved the formula with the Dusty Fork project, so we know it works. Since then, we've been preparing for Kentala-Ridge. Canisters have been shipped to each of you, and now we need to make sure that everyone is on the same page." Jicard studied their faces. "Dan, let's review the assignments."

"Check," he said. He picked up a sheet of paper and held it between him and the computer monitor. "Of course, we have all talked about this before, but just to confirm, I'll read through the list." He sat back in his chair.

"Christi, you and Tiny have the alliance terminal. Pick him up in Denver and drive out there Saturday. Get a room and rest up."

"Got it."

"BJ, you and Junior will hit McCook."

"We are ready," he said. "Junior will be at my apartment first thing Saturday morning, and we have rooms booked at a motel on the south side."

"And Forgue," he said. "You will fly up to Wichita Friday, ah that's tomorrow, and rent a car. Get a room in Wichita for the night, then drive to the terminal Saturday afternoon. Jetmore is about three hours away."

"I already made the reservations, and I'm bringing one man with me."

"Excellent. Okay, that's the list," said Dan. "Jicard?"

"Thanks, Dan. Are there any questions?"

Nobody said a word.

"Good." Dan continued, "They have no idea we're coming, so we shouldn't have any problems. But be careful anyway. I already sent photos and video files to each of you. Study them carefully and plan your attacks well. Call me if you have questions."

"So," said Forgue. "It seems to me that timing will be the key issue."

"That's right," he said. "To get the maximum effect, we need to inject simultaneously while the oil is flowing. If we can hit all three terminals at precisely the same time, we will shut down more than one hundred and fifty miles of pipeline."

"So, each injection will clog up fifty miles of pipe?" said BJ.

"Correct," said Dan. "Fifty miles, more or less. It depends on the flow rate and the temperature of the oil in the pipe."

"Wow, fifty miles!" BJ turned his eyes upward and stared at the ceiling. "Incredible! That's like from here to Greeley!"

"Right… So then, to wrap things up," he continued, "make sure you're in position no later than two-forty-five. When you're ready, send me a text to confirm, and then standby. I will transmit the go-message at three."

Everyone remained quiet.

Jicard closed the meeting. "Okay then. Thank you, all, for your attention. Stay focused and don't make mistakes. Dan will be available by cell phone if there are problems." He paused. "And one more thing, no rough stuff. We want a clean in-and-out operation, no casualties."

Chapter 47

Sam, Paul, and Tylor were in a minivan headed south on Route 212. The road sign read, 'Red Lodge 44 Miles'. Paul said, "Tell me again. Why are we going to Red Lodge?"

"Because," said Tylor. "Tony thinks she's out there. And if NSR is involved, then Karen may be there as well."

"But we don't know that."

"True. But at the moment, it's the best lead we have."

They reached the hotel at six-thirty and checked in. An hour later, they met in the lobby.

"Let's find a bar and get to know the locals," said Tylor. "We need to know if anyone knows Dan Turner, Dr. Nugent, or someone named BJ."

They started for the door. "And make sure to ask about Triple-B Express," said Sam. "You never know. Maybe one of their drivers lives here."

"Now who's dreaming?" said Paul.

***

Karen stepped out of the shower, toweled off, and checked out the damage in the mirror. *You would never win Miss Sandusky South today. That's for sure. Where is that beaming smile?* She tried, but it hurt too much.

The scratch on her leg was a nasty rust color, there was a massive bruise on her chest, and both sides of her face were red and puffy. She had two black eyes, the inside of her left cheek was cut, and her lip was bruised and swollen. *It looks perfectly awful, but no permanent damage, I think. Everything should heal up, eventually.*

Dr. Gilford had laid out a jumpsuit and a pair of canvas shoes, so she stepped over and slipped them on, the fit was adequate, and it felt good to be clean again. He knocked on the door.

"Are you about done in there? I have some food for you."

"I'll be out in a minute."

The lunchroom was equipped with the barest of necessities; a small refrigerator, a sink, a microwave, and a storage cabinet. A round table with four plastic chairs sat in the middle of the room. He was standing near the table when she entered.

"I gather Maurice doesn't cater down here."

"You gather correctly," he said. He pulled out a chair so she could sit and then took one across from her.

"I have to say. This is a real treat—I haven't had anyone to talk with in a very long time."

"I don't know how to respond to that," she said.

"It was pretty difficult at first, especially while my hand was still mending. But the work saved me. As long as I stayed engaged, it was tolerable."

"I get that," she said. "There have been times when I've worked alone on a project for weeks."

"Exactly," he said. "But it is much better to have another person handy, you know, just in case you get lonely or something."

She grinned. "Ouch, that hurts," she said. "Don't make me smile."

"My apologies. And I am very sorry about Max and the way he recruited you. But a selfish part of me is glad you're here."

"Well, no part of me is glad I'm here," she said. "And I intend to get out as soon as possible."

He said nothing.

"But first things first... I am famished. What culinary treat have you prepared for us?"

Dr. Gilford replied, "I wouldn't call it a treat, exactly, but its edible—for the larder, you see, is rather limited." He stepped to the storage cabinet. "Nutritional delicacies include rice, beans, canned vegetables, and once in a while, a little tuna. And for beverages, we have water or coffee. Today's selection is beans and rice with coffee."

"So, no chateaubriand or shrimp with lobster sauce?"

He smiled. "I am afraid not."

"Well then," she said. "Please pass the beans. I'm starving."

They sat together and talked for another hour. Dr. Gilford brought her up to speed on Gelator-T and the drones, and she told him about her work upstairs. When the subject of Sharon came up, she told him everything they'd shared the night before.

"So that's what they're doing," he said. "I suspected as much." He took a sip of coffee. "They're using the gelator to shut down pipelines and drive up the cost of oil. And the drones are being used to wipe out the competition."

He sat back and looked out the window.

"I'd say it was a clever plan if it wasn't so horrific."

She listened intently.

"For better or for worse, the world's economy runs on oil. Any significant interruption will be devastating. Millions of people work in the petroleum industry, and oil is used for virtually everything, from transportation and chemicals to food preparation and bug spray."

He sat forward in his chair. "And shutting down the oil industry will not reverse global warming. Nothing will do that. Since its creation, the earth has cycled through numerous ice ages and warm periods, and we are little more than spectators. It is currently entering a warming period, and there is nothing we can do to prevent it. We may have helped it along a bit, but it's going to happen, regardless."

"You believe that?"

"Absolutely," he said. "We could stop all industry and eliminate man from the face of the earth, and it would still happen. Don't get me wrong. I have no problem with our efforts to clean up the air and make our existence on the planet a little more pleasant. But trying to prevent the inevitable is a waste of time. Instead, we should be working on ways to adapt."

"I see…"

"Oh, I am sorry," he said. "I didn't mean to pontificate. I've been trapped down here for so long. I guess I got carried away."

"No worries."

"But back to the present concern, I suspect that Jicard is up to no good. We sent out six more canisters last week, so he must be planning something big. Maybe a major pipeline."

"But there are thousands of miles of pipeline in this country. He can't possibly hit them all."

"He doesn't have to," he said. "I think he is looking for a psychological effect. If people hear about a major attack, they will panic and start hoarding."

"And that would cause chaos and drive up prices."

"It would, but there seems to be even more afoot," he said. "Last week, he told me to ramp up production. Instead of twelve liters at a time, he wants one-thousand-liter batches." He sat back on his chair and looked at the ceiling. "I think he is planning to sell the stuff."

"But who would buy it?"

"Anyone who wants to damage the oil industry—terrorists would be my guess. Imagine the havoc they could cause in the middle east."

"Oh, my God."

"Yes. And suddenly, this little problem of ours would become a global disaster. Nations would go to war, and millions of people would die."

"We have to stop him," she said. "What can we do?"

"Well, I've been working on a plan for a couple of weeks now. Tell me what you think…"

***

Sam parked the minivan at a small restaurant halfway through town, the 'Red Lodge Canteen and Grill'. "This looks like a possibility," he said. "Let's check it out."

The crowd inside was thin. There were three men at the bar—all wearing cowboy boots, a middle-aged couple sitting at a table, and two ladies standing near the slot machines. Tylor and Sam took stools at the bar, and Paul made a beeline for the slots.

"Good evening, ladies," said Paul as he approached. "Which is the luckiest?"

"That all depends, stranger. Do you want to lose a lot in a hurry, or do you want to play for a while?"

"I guess I want to play for a while."

One of the ladies had dark hair and wore a denim jacket. The other was a blonde with blue eyes. The denim jacket said, "In that case, I would recommend the second one. It's a nickel machine. It pays out pretty regular, but not very much at a time".

Paul dropped a nickel in the slot and pulled the handle. "Are you girls from around here?"

"I grew up in Billings and moved out here last year. Why do you ask?" said the blonde.

"Oh, no reason. Just making conversation."

"So, where are you from? You sound like you're from the Midwest—Michigan, or maybe Wisconsin."

"You're not too far off," he said. "I grew up in Illinois—Peoria, Illinois." He dropped another nickel and pulled the handle again.

"What are you doing way out here?"

"I am looking for a friend, but I'm not having much luck. So, I stopped in for a drink and maybe some dinner."

"What's your friend's name?"

"Her name is Sharon." He showed them a picture on his cell phone.

"Pretty," said the denim jacket.

"Have you seen her?" he asked. "She was traveling with some men. Dan Turner, a guy, called BJ, and a professor type named Dr. Nugent."

"Sorry. We haven't seen your girlfriend, and none of those names seem familiar." She glanced at her friend and said. "And I am afraid we have to be on our way now. Good luck with your search."

They dropped a twenty on their high top and made their way out. Paul lost a couple more nickels in the machine and then joined Sam and Tylor.

"Any luck?" asked Tylor.

"No, I'm afraid not, and I lost about forty-five cents. But the girls were nice."

"Sam's buying. Do you want a beer?"

"Sure thing," said Paul. "Do they serve dinner?"

The bartender overheard the question and handed them menus. "The steaks are good," he said. "And the huckleberry pie is topnotch. My wife baked it."

All three nodded their heads, and he jotted down the order. "It'll be about twenty minutes or so," he said. "In the meantime, I'll refill your beers."

***

While the bartender's wife was working on their dinner, Paul fed him the same story he used on the girls.

"Sorry, my friend. But I've never heard of them."

Then Sam piped up. "The guy, named BJ, used to work for a local trucking company, I think he called it Triple-P, or something like that. Have you ever heard of it?"

The bartender's eyes lit up. "Sure thing. But it's called the Triple-B. They're pretty big around here. My brother-in-law works for them."

"Really? Does he live in town?"

"No. He's over in Belfry. That's about fourteen miles east of here."

"Belfry?" said Paul. "Do we need to worry about bats?"

"Only if you go near the school. It's their mascot."

"No kidding," he said. "I love it, The Belfry Bats. That's great."

"Anyway," said Tylor smiling at the image in his head. "We sure would like to talk with him. Do you think he'd be home tomorrow?"

"He would. But he works the night shift, so he sleeps during the day. The best time to catch him would be about seven in the evening." He jotted down his address. "His name is Horace, Horace Gracely."

"Thank you so much," said Paul. "We'll drive over there tomorrow."

"Don't mention it. I hope he can help you."

When dinner finally arrived, and it was worth the wait. The steaks were grilled to perfection, and the huckleberry pie was extraordinary.

Chapter 48

Forgue and Wolf arrived at a small airfield about twenty miles southwest of Baton Rouge on Friday afternoon—the NSR jet was waiting in the hanger. They drove in, transferred their gear to the aft luggage compartment, and climbed aboard. Five minutes later, they were airborne.

Cyrus Wolf had been Forgue's right-hand man for the past five years. He had an athletic build; one-hundred-eighty pounds, six feet tall, with blond hair, and blue eyes. He had never been to Kansas.

"Wow, a Lear. I have never been in one—it's fabulous. So, how long will it take to get there? What's Kansas like?"

Forgue replied, "We'll only be there a couple of days. Just concentrate on the job."

"Wichita has a great aviation museum," he said. "I looked it up online. They have a couple of big bombers—a B-47 and a B-52D! I think I'll check them out first!"

"We will not have time for site-seeing."

"You know, I also read that Wichita has over one thousand restaurants. We should be able to find a great steak dinner."

"Cyrus. Shut the hell up. We are going to Kansas to do a job, that's all. We are not tourists, so please focus. We'll be there in a couple of hours."

***

On Saturday morning, Christi and Tony left Denver on schedule. The route took them north for about two hours on I-25 and then northeast across country for another hour and a half. *Four hours in the car with Tiny! What in the hell will we talk about?*

***

Junior was late. He didn't get to BJ's apartment until almost dinner time.

"Where have you been? We should have been on the road hours ago."

"I'm sorry, man. I got held up."

"McCook is four and half hours away, and it's in a different time zone. It will be after eleven by the time we get there."

"Well then, I suggest we stop talking and get started." He dropped his bag in the rear of the SUV, closed the hatch, and climbed into the passenger seat. "Where do you want to stop for dinner? I'll look it up on my phone."

***

Saturday afternoon Forgue and Wolf checked out of their motel and headed for Jetmore.

"Boy, that Learjet was sweet. That's the first time I was ever in a private plane. I think I'll get one when I get rich."

"You do that," said Forgue. "Maybe you should get two."

The drive took over three hours, northwest on Route 96 to Nickerson and then, straight west to Jetmore. They passed at least ten small towns along the way, and Cyrus looked up every one of them.

"Did you know that Yaggy, Nebraska had a post office in 1901? It was open for about three months, and then it closed on the thirteenth of May. Isn't that interesting?"

"I didn't know that," said Forgue.

By the time they reached Jetmore, he was thinking about homicide.

Chapter 49

Declan Kentala lived with his wife, Angela, on a sprawling two-hundred-acre ranch eight miles south of Boseman. It had commanding views of the city to the north and Mount Ellis to the east. His father, Kenneth Kentala, acquired the property in the early fifties and left it to Declan when he passed.

Kentala Petroleum was a family-owned multinational corporation. It's assets included oil wells and terminals in southeast Asia, crude oil processing plants, and several pipeline transportation companies. It was a dominant force in the industry.

It began with his grandfather, Joseph Kentala, a wildcatter, working in the waters off southeast Asia. For him, it was a cut-throat, dog-eat-dog existence. He focused on high-risk drilling ventures, which often failed. But he never gave up, and eventually, a few paid off. When he died, his son inherited a going business with a solid foothold in the industry.

Kenneth Kentala concentrated on terminal and transportation ventures with reliable cash flows and solid profit margins. Under his guidance, the business expanded substantially to establish operations in eight countries.

When Declan took the reins in his late twenties, he continued to grow the company, especially in the United States. He worked steadily to expand exploration in the Bakken Formation spanning Montana and North Dakota and later built a pipeline to transport the oil to Ponca City.

During the same period, demand for alternate fuels rose significantly, so he purchased large tracts of land in Kansas and built a corn-to-ethanol production facility. Over two hundred people were employed at the Quinter plant.

By any measure, he was a successful businessman. He was honest, possessed a strong work ethic, and truly cared about the people who worked for him. He put in long hours during the week and used Saturday mornings for emails and correspondence. It was on one of those mornings that the message arrived. He was finishing his last email for the day when his wife came strolling in.

"Angela, my dear. You are looking particularly lovely this morning. What have you been up to?"

"I was getting ready to fix some lunch when I heard a noise out front. I found this on the porch—it looks important." She handed him a white envelope with 'Kentala: Open Immediately' typed on the front."

"Hmm," he said. "I wonder what it could be." He took the envelope and slit one end with a letter opener. Inside, he found a single sheet of paper with a message typed in bold print. He scanned it once and then took a minute to re-read it.

Mr. Kentala:

I am writing this, so you will understand what is about to happen. It will hurt you financially, that is certain. But I hope you find it spiritually distressing, as well.

Consider it retribution, in small measure, for the incalculable harm your family has done to mine and the world in general. In short, this is personal. It is not business.

So, when you wake up tomorrow and find your world in ruins, you should think of your late father. For it was he who wronged my family. And it is for his actions that you will pay the price.

"Did you see who left this?"

"No, it was just lying on the porch. Why? What does it say?"

"I am not sure, exactly. Something about dad, I guess. And some kind of retribution? It says I will pay the price."

She took the note and read it herself. "What does it mean? What did your dad do?"

"He did a lot of things during his lifetime, and he made a lot of enemies. It could be anyone."

"Well, it isn't signed, and it doesn't mention anything specific. So, I don't see that we can do very much."

"I don't know," he said. "But it feels ominous. Maybe I should call Floyd. I should send him a copy, at least."

"And tell him what? We don't even know what it means."

"Well, I am going to send it anyway. He can tell his people to be extra cautious for the next few days."

He scanned the message and attached it to a brief email. "I guess that's all I can do for now. At least he'll know about it." He rose from behind his desk and put his arm around Angela's waist. "Now, did you say something about lunch?"

Chapter 50

Saturday evening, Sam and Tylor drove to Belfry. It was a quiet community, with a handful of businesses and about a dozen streets, in total. It didn't take long to find the address.

It was a large mobile home surrounded by towering pine trees, and the gravel driveway in front was fully occupied by a bright red Peterbilt 357 tractor. Tylor parked along the street.

"That is one good-looking truck. This is might be the place," said Tylor.

"It seems likely."

As they approached the front porch, Sam smiled. There was a 'Go Bats' banner hanging in the window. Horace was waiting for them.

"I heard ya pull up. You must be the men from Red Lodge," he said. "But Orville told me there'd be three of ya."

"Good evening, sir. My name is Tylor York, and this is Sam Wilson. The third member of our group is Paul Betson. He stayed behind in Red Lodge."

"Well, I'm Horace Gracely, and it's mighty nice to meet ya. I don't get a lot of company out here." He swung the door open and stepped aside. "Please come in and have a seat. It's not very fancy, but I have lots of cold beer."

They took seats at the kitchen table, and Horace grabbed three beers from the refrigerator.

"So," he said. "Orville told me you had some questions about Triple-B?"

"We'll sort of," said Sam. "We are looking for a guy who used to work for them. Have you ever heard of a man called BJ? We understand he used to be a driver."

"BJ, huh? No. I'm sorry. I've been with the company for about ten years now, and I've never heard that name. Are ya sure it was Triple-B?"

"Yes, we're sure."

"Well, then. I'm sorry, but I've never heard of him."

"How about his friends?" said Tylor. "He was traveling with a man named Dan Turner and professor type, a Dr. Nugent. Have you heard of them?"

Horace concentrated for a moment and took a swig of beer. "Nope, I don't know them either. Why are ya looking for these fellas? Do they owe ya money?"

"No," said Tylor. "A couple of our friends went missing, and we think they know where they are." He placed pictures of Karen and Sharon on the table.

"Wow, pretty!" he said. "If I had lady friends who looked like that, I'd be searching too."

"Yeah, Karen disappeared in March, and Sharon was taken a few days ago."

"What do ya mean, 'taken'?"

"We think they were kidnapped."

"No kidding. Kidnapped? Now, I definitely want to help. But why Triple-B?"

"Karen, the one who disappeared in March, worked for a company called North States Renewables, and so do the men we're looking for. We think they're involved. And a couple of days ago, Sam and Paul saw a Triple-B truck at one of their warehouses. So, we thought there might be a connection."

"North States Renewables, ah…" he mused. "You mean NSR. Right?"

"Yes, NSR."

"Sure, I know that company. They're one of our biggest customers. I don't drive for 'em, but we have a whole fleet of trucks dedicated to NSR."

"Do you know any of their drivers?"

"No. Sorry. That's a big secret inside the company. Nobody talks about it," he said. "But if I do hear anything, I'll let ya know." He held up his empty beer bottle. "I'm going for a refill. Do ya want another?"

"No," said Tylor, "Thanks, but we have to be on our way." They rose from their chairs.

"Well, okay then," said Horace. "I am sorry I couldn't be more help."

"Oh, you've helped a lot, and we appreciate your time."

"Don't mention it." He stepped out on the porch and held the door. "I hope ya find your friends. And if I can be of more help, just let me know. If I'm not home, Orville will know where I am."

Back in Red Lodge, Paul was walking back to the motel when he saw two Triple-B trucks drive by. He took out a pad and wrote down their trailer numbers.

***

Sam and Tylor were back at the hotel by eight-thirty. Paul was sitting in the lounge sipping a beer when they walked in. "Welcome back," he said. "Was Horace any help?"

"A little, we think." They found a couple of overstuffed chairs and eased in.

Tylor continued, "He's been working for Triple-B for about ten years, and he confirmed that NSR is one of their biggest customers."

Sam added. "And he told us they have a fleet of trucks dedicated to NSR."

"Interesting," said Paul. "On my way back tonight, I saw two Triple-B trucks headed south. If we see any more, maybe we should follow them."

Chapter 51

It was two o'clock in the morning when Christi and Tiny arrived at the Alliance terminal—they parked along the road, collected their gear, and walked toward the entrance. Moonlight was practically nonexistent—only a thin crescent was visible. They broke out their flashlights and found the front gate.

It was deserted. There were no cameras, and no people. The gate was a length of chain stretched across the driveway, so they stepped over it and walked in.

"Where is everybody?" said Tiny. "Dan's video showed a guard at the gate and at least two operators."

"Maybe we got lucky. Let's find the pump house."

When they reached the building, the door had only a cheap padlock—Tiny made short work of it. He pulled out his large bolt cutters and removed it with one snip. "No sweat he said. This is going to be a piece of cake."

"Don't get too comfortable," she said. "We have forty-five minutes to wait, and we're fully exposed."

He stepped outside and scanned the terminal. "There is nobody out here."

"Okay, then let's get hooked up, so we're ready when three o'clock gets here." She sent a text message to Dan:

C and T in position.

For BJ, things were a bit different. As usual, Junior was late, and it was past two-thirty before they arrived at the terminal.

McCook was much larger than Alliance and was lit up like a Christmas tree. There was a barbed-wire security fence surrounding the facility, a guard at the gate, and cameras were all over the place. His plan was to take out the guard first and then take care of the camera system. After that, the pumphouse would be easy.

Junior stayed in the SUV while BJ approached the guardhouse. He reasoned that his dark skin and oversized hoodie would make it difficult for them to see his face, and he was right. When he reached the guest window, he knocked on the glass and motioned for the guard to come outside.

"Who are you, and what are you doing out here in the middle of the night?" asked the guard. His hand was poised over the 'Emergency' button.

BJ reached for the glass and then collapsed out of sight. "I need your help. Please help me."

He pushed the button and then stepped outside. Two things happened immediately—the security system saved the last ten minutes of video to its backup drive, and then emailed the file to his supervisor.

"Can I help you?"

BJ reached up, pushed a syringe into the guard's neck, and then rolled away. The guard slumped to the ground, and BJ stepped inside. The first thing he noticed was a blinking red light.

"Shit," he said. "You son of a bitch." He kicked the guard in the ribs. "You just had to do that, didn't you!"

He found the camera system, turned it off, and motioned for Junior to come running. It was two-forty-five when they reached the pumphouse. "Hurry up," he said.

Junior had a sledgehammer with him. He hit the padlock once, and it disintegrated.

"Okay. Get set up, and I'll message Dan."

It was two-fifty-five when he sent the text:

B and J ready.

Like Alliance, Jetmore, too, was a small terminal. Forgue had no trouble getting to the pumphouse in time. Wolf connected the canister, and Forgue sent the message:

F and W in place. We are ready when you are.

At three o'clock, Dan Tuner sent a one-word text message to all three teams, 'Go', and ninety seconds later, it was done. The injections were nearly simultaneous.

***

On their way out, Christi and Tiny got an unexpected surprise. A hidden motion detector had tripped when they first opened the pumphouse door, and a roaming guard was alerted. So, when they were ready to leave, he was waiting outside.

"Good evening, folks," he said. "What do you think you're doing in there?"

"Actually, we were just getting ready to leave," said Tiny. "If it's okay with you."

"No. It's not okay. I'd like you to stay right here until the sheriff arrives." He stepped back and put his hands on his hips.

"I'm sorry, but we will not be able to do that." Tiny picked up his bolt cutters and swung them hard against the guard's left temple. He dropped like a sack of potatoes.

"You idiot!" said Christi from inside the pumphouse. "What have you done?" She knelt down to check the guard's pulse. "He's dead!"

"I meant to knock him out, that's all. He can't be dead."

"He is dead, Tiny. And you are an idiot! Don't you remember what Jicard said? No casualties!"

"I remember. But I didn't mean to do it. It was an accident."

"Somehow, I don't think the sheriff will buy that explanation." She stood up and started for the car. "We have to get out of here. Now!"

***

In McCook, BJ and Junior had a squad to deal with…

The guard's supervisor dispatched a security detail in response to the emergency message. Six men arrived at the guardhouse just as they were getting ready to leave.

"We'll never get past them," said Junior.

"You're right. We need a diversion."

BJ stepped behind the pumphouse, planted a small explosive device, and set the timer for thirty seconds.

"Hurry, come with me."

They ran to the nearest storage tank and circled around to the opposite side. Ten seconds later, the bomb detonated.

The men at the guardhouse heard the explosion and saw flames rising from behind the pumphouse. They ran to investigate.

BJ and Junior dashed from their hiding place, ran past the guardhouse, jumped into their SUV, and took off like a shot. They were a half-mile away by the time the security team figured it out.

***

Forgue and Wolf had no problems. When they were finished with the injection, they stowed their gear in the rental car's trunk and left.

"So, are we going straight back to Wichita now?" asked Cyrus.

"No, we are headed north to Quinter."

"What's in Quinter?"

"Our next assignment," he said. "We will be setting up for another drone attack."

"Just the two of us?"

"For now," he said. "We are going to rent some space and scope out the area. The rest of the team will arrive next week."

Chapter 52

Declan Kentala's phone rang at three-thirty. Angela punched his shoulder to wake him up. "Declan. The phone is ringing," she said. "Wake up and answer it."

The caller ID read, 'Ridge Security'. He picked it up. "This can't be good," he said. "Hello, this is Declan Kentala. What has happened?"

The security manager gave him a summary of the incident, and Declan listened.

"So you're telling me that Norris Hankin was killed. Oh my God! Have you called his family? His wife's name is Terra, I think. I'll be there as soon as I can."

Declan got out of bed and put his slippers on.

"And make sure that the authorities get everything they want," he said. "I want full cooperation, no exceptions. We need to find out what happened as soon as possible."

"What is it?" said Angela.

"I guess that note we got yesterday was real after all—the pipeline was hit this morning. They killed Norris Hankin in Alliance, and they drugged Homer Townsend at McCook."

"Did they blow it up?"

"No, that's the strange part. The pipeline wasn't damaged at all. But the pumps are locked up, and flow has stopped entirely. I need to get there and see it for myself.

"Okay," she said. "You grab a quick shower, and I'll pack you an overnight bag." She rolled out of bed and put on a robe. "And after that, I'll call the field and have them send the helicopter."

"Thanks," he said. "I wonder who sent that message."

***

Three and half hours later, he arrived at the Alliance terminal. The sheriff's van blocked the main entrance, so he parked along the road and walked in. Floyd was there from Ridge, and two maintenance men were working in the pumphouse.

"Mr. Declan," he said. "Thanks for coming so quickly." His coveralls were covered with oil and mud, and his shirt was soaked through with perspiration. He reached for a handshake but then thought better of it.

"What's going on here?"

"We got a motion detection alert in the pumphouse about two-forty-five, and Norris drove over to check it out. He sent a text message to let me know. After that, there was nothing."

He started for the pumphouse and motioned for Declan to follow. "When the motion detector stopped sending, we knew there was a problem, so we called the sheriff. He found Norris lying next to the pumphouse. They must have clocked him when they came out."

He stopped and pointed where the body had been.

"Norris was a good friend, Mr. Declan. I can't believe he's gone. And I'm worried about Terra and the kids—they'll be devastated."

"I am going to see her in a few minutes. But before I go, tell me. What did they do to the pipeline?"

"We don't know yet. There aren't any leaks, and we didn't see any actual damage. The sheriff's forensic team was in there for a while, looking for fingerprints and taking photos. And as soon as they were finished, we started checking."

"There was no damage? Then why did the pump lock up?"

"We couldn't figure it out either, so we decided to take it apart. That's when we found this…"

He reached for a sample container and held it so Declan could see inside.

"It was packed full of this gray sandy stuff."

"What is it?"

"Search me," he said. "I've never seen anything like it."

"What does the sheriff plan to do?"

"He said he was going to contact the FBI, especially since they also hit Jetmore. He thinks it might be terrorism."

"I guess it could be… Is that gray stuff inside the pipeline too?"

"We think so, but it will take a while to confirm."

"Well, do the best you can," he said. "And thanks for rushing down here this morning."

"Anything for Norris."

"Also, you better contact the production supervisor in Sidney and the refinery. Tell them we'll be out of service for a while."

***

Terra answered through the door when he knocked. She was alone in the house, and her voice quivered as she spoke. "Who's there?"

"It's Declan Kentala. May I come in?"

She opened the door slowly, peered out, and then stepped aside so he could enter. "Oh, Mr. Kentala, thank you for coming. I'm so worried. I don't know what I'm going to do."

"I came straight from the terminal," he said. "We're worried about you." He moved toward the living room.

"Oh, please, have a seat. Can I get you some coffee? Please excuse the mess. I haven't had a chance to tidy up this morning."

"Please relax, Mrs. Hankin," he said. "I don't need anything. Come, sit with me for a few minutes." He motioned toward an overstuffed chair.

She stepped to the chair and sat on the edge of the cushion. "I can't believe he's gone. We were married for thirty years. I don't know what to do."

"Have you talked with your kids yet?"

"They called about an hour ago. It's already on the news." She stared at him with watery eyes. "Soon, everyone in the country will know."

"It can't be on the news. I haven't released his name."

"Oh, they didn't say his name, just a security guard at the Alliance terminal. The kids connected the dots and thought it might be their dad."

"I am so sorry, my dear. So sorry."

"Who would do this? Norris wasn't a threat. He didn't even carry a gun. There was no reason to kill him."

"I know," he said. "I don't understand it either."

"I am so worried," she said. "How will I be able to keep the kids in college? We were barely able to afford it on Norris' salary, and now that will be gone."

"No, it won't," he said. "That is one thing you won't have to worry about."

"How do you mean?"

"Well, it's one of the reasons I wanted to come over this morning," he said. "I know nothing can bring Norris back, but I would like to help out if you'll let me, financially, that is."

She said nothing.

"He had some life insurance through the company, but that won't be enough to cover your kids' tuition. So, I would like to take care of that, personally, if you'll let me. You have two kids in school, is that right?"

"Yes, Martin and Charise"

"Please, tell me about them."

Terra Hankin spent the next twenty minutes talking about her children. Declan watched as the tension left her body and her eyes brightened. She told him how they grew up, their interests, and what they planned to do after college. "Martin loves animals and wants to be a veterinarian," she said. "And Charise is in the engineering program. I am so proud of them."

"And you should be," he said. "They sound like strong, intelligent kids with solid futures. Please let me help."

"Oh, Mr. Kentala, thank you, but I couldn't let you do that."

"You can, and you will. I want to do this for you, for Norris, and for Martin and Charise. He was a good man and an excellent employee."

She was dumbstruck. "But why? It isn't your fault that he was killed. You didn't even know him that well."

"It's true. I didn't know him—we only met a few times. But he died when he was working for me, and he shouldn't have. Please let me do this."

She took a deep breath and settled into the chair a little. "Well, I guess I'd be a fool to say no. He always said you were a decent man."

"Great. I will get in touch with you in a couple of weeks to iron out the details. But right now, I need to find out what happened to the pipeline and do everything I can to get things moving again."

"Thank you again for coming, Mr. Kentala. You've been a godsend." She took a deep breath, straightened her back, and held out her hand.

He took it in both of his and smiled warmly. "It was my absolute pleasure. But now I do have to go. You take care of yourself."

"I understand," she said. "If there is anything I can do, please let me know." She followed him to the door and watched as he walked toward his car.

***

Before starting the engine, he pulled out his cell phone to check the news. He was amazed at what he found:

At approximately 3:00 a.m. this morning, the Kentala-Ridge Pipeline was attacked without warning. No leaks have occurred, but all flow in the line has stopped. The coordinated attack hit pumping stations at Alliance, Nebraska, McCook, Nebraska, and Jetmore, Kansas. A security guard at alliance was killed, and a second at McCook was drugged and assaulted. The guards' names have not been released, and no other injuries have been reported.

The crude oil pipeline has a capacity of 200,000 barrels per day. It spans six states, from Montana to Oklahoma, and is 768 miles long. It was completed seven years ago for a little over $2 billion dollars and has operated without incident. It is a primary source of crude oil for the Kentala Refinery in Ponca City.

Company officials have refused to comment except to say the incident is under investigation.

He punched in a number and waited. Floyd Garrison answered on the third ring. "Mr. Declan. Did you talk with Terra? How's she doing?"

"She's having a rough time, Floyd. But I think she'll be okay. I want you to check in with her from time to time and make sure she has everything she needs."

"I will."

"We also need to find out about Homer Townsend. Have you made contact?"

"I called him this morning. He's doing okay. He has a couple of bruised ribs, but the doctor said he can go home this afternoon."

"That's good news," said Declan. "But I want to make sure that everything is covered, doctor bills, hospital, everything. And when he comes back to work, I want to give him a decent raise, or maybe a promotion if he's eligible."

"I'll take care of it."

"Have you seen the news? How did that happen so fast?"

"Things move quickly these days, sir. There is not much we can do about it."

"I guess," he said. "But I don't want any names released just yet."

"You can count on me, sir."

"Good," he said. "Now, let's get busy finding out what happened, who did it, and what we can do about it. Give me the sheriff's phone number."

Chapter 53

Dr. Gilford and Karen were working on the drone configurations. They finished number twenty-three and took a break.

They sat on an empty crate and leaned against the stack. "What are you going to do with all these crates?"

"I don't know," he said. "They're everywhere. Jicard told me to take them apart, but it's going to take a while." He pointed to a small pile of boards lying next to the wall. "And when I finish with these, there are more at the end of the truck tunnel."

"I don't know how he expects you to do that in addition to the drones," she said. "It will take forever."

He frowned. "It's not like I have many choices in the matter."

"Say, Gil. Do you think Jicard would let us recruit Sharon? She is very smart, and I'm sure she could help with the drones. Besides, if she were in here with us, we could make sure she gets something to eat."

"That's a good idea. He is pushing to get them out, so I don't see any harm in asking."

***

After a quick phone call with Jicard, Dr. Gilford retrieved Sharon from the cells. She was in pretty poor shape, so he took her to the showers to get cleaned up.

"Thanks for getting me out," she said. "Your Mr. Jicard is one disturbed man."

"First of all, you are hardly out—this is only a slightly better prison. And we are on very thin ice here, so keep your opinions to yourself. And finally, he is certainly *not my* Jicard."

"Oh, sorry. I didn't mean to offend," she said. "Nevertheless, I am sincerely grateful."

"And you are welcome," he said. "Now, grab a shower, put on a jumpsuit, and then go into the lunchroom. I will leave something on the table for you."

"Okay, thanks."

"And when you're ready, come join us— we'll be working on the drones. But don't take too long."

***

Karen was working on number twenty-four when he walked up. "Is she okay?"

"She needs a little food, but otherwise, I think she'll be all right. She'll be out soon."

"Good... I wish Hansen were here with us. He would know what to do. I keep thinking about his body just lying there in the pit."

"I shouldn't worry. I doubt if there's much of it left by now."

"Why is that?"

"Scutigera Gigante."

"What?"

"Scutigera—giant carnivorous centipedes—nasty little bastards. They live in the lowest parts of the cave, and eat virtually everything. I am sure his bones have been picked clean by now."

She shivered. "Oh, that's horrible. What a horrible thought."

"They are at the top of the food chain down here—very efficient hunters. They grow as long as your forearm, and there are thousands of them."

She glanced quickly around the room. "Do we need to worry?"

"No. I have never seen one in the chamber. They like dark, wet places. They hate bright lights."

"Thank goodness for that."

By the time they finished with number twenty-five, Sharon joined them. "Thanks again for getting me out of there," she said. "How can I help?"

Dr. Gilford explained what they had to do, and she dove right in. Her small hands could reach further into the electronics enclosures, which made the work go faster.

"Okay. You are catching on nicely." He reached into his pocket. "When you get to number thirty-three, stick this to the back of the circuit board." He handed her a small electronic device.

She looked at him.

"It's a cellular transmitter," he whispered. "And hopefully, our ticket out of here." He knelt between the girls and gave four to each. "I got the idea a couple of months ago when the drones started to arrive. I built twelve of them from the spare parts kit."

"How do they work?"

"I configured them to turn on when the navigation units power up. Then, when they find a cell tower, they will automatically call the police and send a series of preprogrammed messages."

"What if they don't launch the ones with the transmitters?"

"That's a chance we will have to take, I guess. But we can improve the odds by spacing them out across all seven hundred drones. That way, at least a few should be activated, no matter how many are launched."

Karen looked at him admiringly. "Brilliant idea."

"Thanks. But it won't work if we don't get them installed, so let's get a move on. Jicard plans to ship them out on Tuesday."

Chapter 54

Jicard was reading his newsfeed when the call came in. He put his glass of Macallan on the credenza and picked up the handset. It was eleven p.m. in Baghdad.

"Jicard here. Good evening, Fazal. How are things in Iraq?"

"We have seen the news. Congratulations."

"Thank you."

"We want the Gelator-T, but we want three thousand kilograms. Will the price be the same?"

"Yes. Twelve hundred dollars per kilogram."

"We will transfer first half of money now, and balance on delivery to Munich warehouse."

"No. The balance must be paid before shipment."

The line went silent for a few moments, and Jicard thought they had lost the connection. But thirty seconds later, Fazal was back.

"It will be as you wish. The balance will be paid before shipment."

"We expect it to be ready in two weeks."

"It will be ready."

"We will transmit funds immediately. Please, you verify receipt."

Jicard opened his bank account and watched the activity screen. Within a minute, a wire transfer arrived for one point eight million dollars.

"Fazal. The funds have arrived. It is nice doing business with you."

"Okay, Jicard. Two weeks from today, you ship, or we will find you."

"Don't make me laugh, Mr. Fazal al-Latif." Jicard chuckled. "You have a pleasant evening, now. We will be in touch."

He picked up the phone and rang Dr. Gilford.

"Yes? Mr. Jicard?"

"Dr. Gilford. We need to ship three thousand kilograms of Gelator-T two weeks from today. Put it in fifty-five-gallon drums labeled vegetable oil."

"But Sir, that is a lot to make in two weeks. You said it would be one thousand kilograms. You are talking about seventeen drums of material."

"Things change. You should know that."

"I'm not sure we can do it, Jicard. We might be able to make two thousand by then…"

"You will prepare three thousand kilograms in two weeks. I have confidence in you. I will even allow you to use Miss Wagoner. With her help and Dr. Wells, you should have no problem. And maybe Maurice will send down some decent food."

"What about the drones?"

"Nothing has changed with the drones. They must go out Tuesday evening. The truck will arrive at nine p.m."

"But Sir?"

"No buts, Dr. Gilford. You have your orders, and I expect you to carry them out. If you fail, then you and your helpers will be joining Dr. Jacobs."

"I understand."

Chapter 55

"Yes, Mr. Kentala, Mordechai Finkelman in Denver—we call him Mo," he said. "We have been working on a solution for several weeks now, and we are very close."

"I have known Jack Nelson for a long time, and he speaks very highly of you."

"He was one of my first clients. We've been working together on projects for years."

"Well, if he trusts you, then that is good enough for me."

"Thank you, sir."

"You are going to need some capital to build the delivery systems. How much do you need? I will send the funds today."

"Fifty thousand should make a good start, I think."

"Fine. But I will send one hundred thousand. Honest people always ask for less than they need. Send me your bank info."

***

Paul was filling the minivan when two Triple-B trucks rolled by. *They're headed south, but there's nothing but mountains out there... I've gotta know.* He swiped his credit card to pay for the fuel and jumped into the van.

When he pulled into traffic, the trucks were two blocks ahead, but he caught up at the next light. When it turned green, he stayed close and followed them out of town. They continued south on Route 212. *Where are they going? There is nothing out there. I checked the maps.*

It was a two-lane road with very little traffic, so he stayed well back. At one point, a blue pickup truck appeared behind him, and he let it pass. Then about ten miles out of town, he rounded a curve, and the trucks disappeared. The road ahead was empty, and they were gone. The blue pickup was also out of sight. *They couldn't have sped up that much. Where did they go?* He increased his speed for a mile or two and eventually caught up with the pickup, but the semis were nowhere to be found.

"What the hell?" he said aloud. "How can two semi-trucks just disappear?" He drove back to the hotel.

***

"We are wasting our time out here, Tylor. We have no evidence that Karen or Sharon are anywhere near Red Lodge."

"But Tony thinks they are, and we've learned a lot more about Triple-B since we got here. We might be very close."

"Maybe," he said. "But I'm sorry. I just don't see it."

"Give it a couple more days. We're on the right track. I'm sure of it."

Tylor heard a noise and looked up—it was Paul. He walked into the lounge and took a chair next to the fireplace. He looked dazed.

"Hey guys," he said. "You'll never guess what just happened."

***

"Where have you been, Chip? You were off camera for almost twelve minutes."

"I had some personal business to take care of."

"In the main chamber? What kind of personal business?"

"I can't tell you, Pedro. It's a secret."

"You're keeping a secret from me? I'm your best friend."

"I did a favor for someone. That's all. So, can we please drop it?" He sat down and resumed his surveillance duties.

"Sure. I guess so. Jeez!"

Chapter 56

It was three and a half hours from Billings to Ridge, so Agents Dave Lyons and Peter Stanton started early. The best route took them down I-90 for about an hour and then across country on Route 212. Along the way, they passed through several small towns and encountered a fair amount of truck traffic. By the time they got to Broadus, Dave needed a break.

"That looks like a decent cafe. Let's stop for coffee."

"Sounds good to me," said Peter. "I thought we would never get around that truck. How much farther?"

"About an hour."

In the parking lot were six Kentala Petroleum tanker trucks. They were beautiful. They were bright blue with white details—the paint was clean and waxed. Bumpers and wheels were polished chrome, and the stainless steel tanks were brilliant in the sunshine.

"Wow, good-looking trucks," said Peter. "They look brand new." He and Dave walked into the cafe and found a booth near the windows. The place was packed.

The waitress appeared in seconds. "How can I help you, gentlemen?" she said. "We don't get many suits in here. Perhaps a nice slice of huckleberry pie?"

Dave said, "Two coffees, please, and yes, the pie sounds good—one for each of us." He motioned toward Peter.

Peter nodded, "Pie sounds great. Maybe with a little whipped cream?"

"No problem," she smiled. "I'll be right back."

The tone in the dining room was subdued. The drivers were all talking about the pipeline and grousing about driving all the way to Billings to unload. They were angry, but not at Kentala.

"It feels like a powder keg about to explode," said Peter.

"I agree," said Dave. "It's lucky the people responsible aren't here. They'd be skinned alive."

The waitress returned with their pie and coffee. "I hope you enjoy it," she said. "It's still warm from the oven. I baked it this morning." She placed a small caddy with sugar, sweeteners, and non-dairy creamer on the table and returned to the kitchen.

"It looks delicious," said Peter as he took his first bite. "Too bad it's so far from Billings."

Dave sampled it as well. "I agree. That is one good piece of pie," he said. "Some of the best I've had."

**

An hour and a half later, they arrived at the Kentala Ridge terminal. The security guard directed them to the operations building, and Floyd Garrison was waiting—he'd flown back from Alliance the night before.

"Good morning, gentlemen. I am Floyd Garrison, Manager of Security. Welcome to the Ridge terminal. The agents introduced themselves and showed him their credentials. "Please," he said. "Come in and have a seat." He pulled out a chair and paused. "Would you like some coffee? I could make a pot."

Agent Lyons looked at Agent Stanton and said, "Not right now. I think we're good."

"Fine," said Floyd. "Then, let's get started."

They spent a half hour reviewing what Floyd had learned about the attacks at the three terminals and the fingerprints and photos collected by the sheriff. They also discussed the attacks against Nelson Oil.

"Can you think of any reason why someone would target Kentala? Maybe a disgruntled employee or an ex-business partner?" asked Agent Lyons.

"No. It certainly wasn't a disgruntled employee," he said. "At Kentala, there is no such animal. I have been here more than fifteen years, and I have never heard a single person complain about the company."

"That's hard to believe," said Agent Lyons.

"I would agree if were any other company. But everyone loves working for Declan Kentala. He is always looking for ways to help his employees."

"Really? How is that?" said Agent Stanton.

"Well, how much time do you have? He pays more than the industry standard, and benefits are covered one hundred percent. Everyone is eligible for advanced training classes, and he goes the extra mile to ensure safe working conditions. There are employee picnics, softball leagues, and a college scholarship program. The list goes on—there is nothing for people to complain about. Last year he even attended my nephew's graduation."

"It sounds too good to be true."

"Maybe it does," he said. "But you can ask anyone. Nobody ever leaves this company unless they retire. And when new jobs open up, we get a thousand applications the very next day."

Chapter 57

"Are you sure we need all of this stuff?" said Sam. "It's not like it's below zero out there."

"I'm sure," said Tylor. "I grew up in Minnesota, and we camped out a lot. Believe me, twenty degrees at night can be very uncomfortable if you are not prepared for it. Especially if it's windy."

"But wool socks? I always wear cotton."

"We need a fabric that will wick away moisture. If you can't wear wool, then we'll get polyester. Cotton will soak up perspiration, and your feet will get cold. I've been there—trust me. And remember, we'll be out there all night with no fire. So, we must conserve body heat."

***

A couple of hours later, they arrived at the spot where the trucks disappeared. Paul found an open path between the trees and pulled off the highway—he drove in about fifty yards before he stopped. They'd rented a minivan for the night.

"This is where I lost them," he said. "And I want to make sure we're out of sight." They got out and walked back to the road. The woods were dense and chilly, but the trees sheltered them from the wind. They also blocked most of the afternoon sun. Precious little made its way through.

"That spot has possibilities," said Tylor. "Let's set up over there." He led them to a flat-top rocky outcrop that overlooked the highway. It was screened on both sides by short pine trees, and there was a lot of leafy undergrowth in front. "I'll take the first watch. You two go back to the van and stay warm." He put a stadium pad next to a tree and settled in.

"I'll relieve you in about two hours," said Sam.

"Fine," he said. "Two hours."

There was virtually no traffic on the highway. Tylor saw eight cars, a tourist bus, and two recreation vehicles in the first hour but no semi-trucks. After that, there was nothing. He was glad when Sam showed up.

"I'll take it for a while," he said. "Have you seen anything?"

"Not really," he said. "It's been pretty boring. Less than a dozen vehicles have gone by—mostly cars." He gave him the notebook, a pen, and his binoculars. "Here you go. It will be dark in about an hour, so stay sharp." As he turned to leave, Sam stopped him.

"Tylor! Wait. Take a look at this." He put the binoculars to his face, and Tylor peered over his shoulders.

Across the road, about one hundred and fifty yards away, a truck was entering the highway—it drove out of the woods and turned north. A minute later, it passed their position and proceeded toward Red Lodge. It was a Triple-B truck.

"My God. Did you see that? Where did it come from?"

"I couldn't tell—it was too far away. But I vote we walk up there and check it out."

"I agree," he said. "I'll get Paul."

Twenty minutes later, they stood where the truck had come out of the wood, but there was no road or driveway. The sun was dropping quickly behind the mountains.

"I am sure this is the right place," said Sam. "But I don't see anything."

"Let's take a closer look," said Tylor. "It will be dark soon."

They walked across and entered the woods—Tylor led the way. "Check this out, guys," he said. "It's a camouflaged panel—it matches the undergrowth perfectly. And look, it runs on a track of some sort." They huddled together to inspect the panel.

Paul turned on his flashlight. "You're right," he said. "The track extends well into the underbrush, and look behind it—a driveway. That's where the truck came from."

"Okay," said Sam. "Now things are getting interesting."

***

"Chip! Take a look at this!." Pedro pointed at his monitor and touched a couple of buttons to zoom in. "It looks like another group of campers found our entry gate."

Chip stood behind him to check out the scene. "Yep, it looks like we have some nosey hikers. You better alert security."

Pedro picked up his phone and dialed the perimeter security desk. When they answered, he said, "Three intruders at the north entrance gate." He then hung up and sat back to watch. "This should be fun."

***

Two minutes later, there was a rustle in the wood.

Sam whispered, "Did you hear that?"

"What?" said Paul. "I didn't hear anything."

"Hush. Listen." There was a second rustle—louder this time.

"Something is in here with us, and it doesn't sound friendly."

"It sounds like an animal of some kind. A bear, maybe?"

"Well, whatever it is, we are in no position to defend ourselves," said Paul. "Let's get the hell out of here."

The three men walked quickly back to the highway and headed north. "Let's get back to the van," said Sam. "We need to think about this."

***

"There they go," said Pedro. "It works every time."

Chapter 58

When they got back to the van, they climbed in and sat quietly for a moment. "What just happened?" said Sam.

"I think we just got scared off by some sound effects," said Tylor. "A real animal would have followed us."

"I agree," said Paul. "Something strange is going on in those woods, and we need to find out what it is."

"Should we chuck it in for tonight or continue watching?"

"It's only nine o'clock," said Paul. "I vote we stay on and see if anything else happens."

At that moment, a Triple-B semi-truck passed their viewing spot out on the road. It continued south for about a quarter of a mile and then disappeared around the curve.

***

"It's coming down," said Dr. Gilford. "Are we ready?"

"We are," said Karen. "Let's get it loaded."

A semi-truck entered the chamber from the west and backed up to the loading dock. Sharon and Karen manned pallet jacks, and Dr. Gilford drove a fork truck. They worked as quickly as possible and made sure the modified units were randomly positioned throughout the trailer. They had to stack the pallets two-high to fit them all in.

When they were finished, the truck left the way it had come.

"How did it get down here? Does the tunnel lead out to the road?"

"No, there is an elevator at the end of the tunnel," said Dr. Gilford. "It lifts the trucks to and from the surface."

***

From the viewing spot, Sam saw the Triple-B truck drive past. It was headed toward Red Lodge but had not come from the hidden driveway. It just drove by. *Strange. Where did it come from?* He recorded the time and the trailer number in his notebook.

Nothing of interest happened the rest of the night, and at dawn, they decided to go back to the hotel. When Sam turned on his cell phone, there was a text message waiting.

Chapter 59

Alexander Cooper had been the Coroner in Billings for more than fifteen years—he was sixty-three years old, overweight, and completely bald. When he wasn't at work, he spent as much time as possible with his three grandchildren—two boys and a brand-new baby girl. He adjusted his glasses when Special Agent Lyons walked in.

"Hey Dave, what's going on?" he said.

"Alex, did you get the results from those DNA samples?"

"You mean the ones for the Melvin Richards case?"

"Right."

"Let me check." He rifled through a stack of papers and pulled it out. "Here it is. I meant to call, but I haven't had a chance."

Agent Lyons leaned forward and took the report.

"Why did this take so long?"

"They are pretty swamped in the lab these days. Sorry. We lost a technician last month and haven't been able to replace her yet. Besides, the accident happened in January. Why the rush?"

Agent Lyons scanned the report. "So, it *was* Melvin Richards."

"Yes. There's no doubt about it."

"But why the rush, all of a sudden?"

"It's a rush because the accident was not an accident, and the car was rigged with explosives."

"Really? I was told it was a routine accident." Alex sat back in his chair and stared out the window.

"There was a video of the crash from a home security system. The Waltons. I understand they talked with you about it."

"These local residents, they all think they're detectives. I can't be expected to follow up on every lead. For Christ's sake."

"Alex. What's going on here? You are better than this."

"I used to be. But I am getting old—I am going to retire next year."

"Alex?"

"I can't tell you about it, Dave. They threatened my family and my grandchildren. I can't."

"This is a murder investigation. You have to tell me."

"No. I can't."

"Nobody needs to know where we got the information. But if you know something, I need to hear it."

"Okay," he said. "They told me to gloss over the accident and let it go at that."

"Who told you?"

"I don't know his name. He only gave me his initials, DT. He called me on the phone the day of the accident. He said his boss would destroy my family."

Alex spun his chair around and looked directly at Agent Lyons.

"He threatened to hurt my granddaughter, Dave. And he was not kidding around—I could feel it. I've never been so scared in my life. I will never forget that call. She was only six months old, for Christ's sake. I had no choice."

"Could DT stand for Dan Turner?"

"I don't know. He probably lied about his initials. He could have been anyone. All I know is, I couldn't allow him to hurt my family."

Chapter 60

"We rented an empty warehouse for staging. So, when the drones arrive, we will have a place to stage them. It's on the east side of town—the team will arrive on Thursday."

"Good," said Jicard. "Mr. Fu wants it done on Friday night."

"You know," said Forgue. "I'll do anything if the money is right. Hell, I'd sell my own sister—but I have to ask you. What does he have against this guy?"

"That's none of your business."

"Maybe not. But last week, we destroyed his pipeline, and now we are planning to hit his cornfields. Fu Tong must seriously hate this guy."

"Well, I do not know the whole story, but I understand it's some family honor bullshit."

"Family honor?"

"Fu Tong was born in China, and his parents moved to South Korea when he was a kid. I think he said he was eight or nine years old, something like that. Anyway, his dad was very wealthy, oil money, I guess, and he bought an island off the coast at Ulsan."

"A whole island?"

"That's what he told me—it was called Haengun-do, I think. Anyway, the Kentala Family, Mr. Kentala's dad and grandfather, built a processing plant on the other end of the island, and when Fu Tong was nineteen years old, it all blew up. The explosion leveled the entire island and wiped out his family. So, now he's duty-bound to destroy Kentala."

"But the current Mr. Kentala isn't responsible for things his father did. And from what I hear, he's a stand-up guy."

"It doesn't matter. His family hurt Fu Tong's family, so now it's a revenge thing."

"Okay. That's bullshit, sure enough," said Forgue. "But from my point of view, his money is still good as the next guy's. So, when do the drones arrive?"

Chapter 61

"Okay, ladies, we have a lot of work to do. We have less than two weeks to make sixteen drums of the gelator."

"I thought it was fifteen," said Sharon. "And in any case, I only see six drums over there."

"I know. I told Jicard we're short. He'll have the rest of the drums delivered on Saturday, along with the additional chemicals that we need."

Karen and Sharon munched on rosemary crackers and brie that Maurice had sent down.

"The formula is simple, but the reaction time is long. It will take almost twenty hours to make each batch. And the most we can make is one hundred gallons at a time."

"So, about eight batches should do the job," said Karen. "We should have plenty of time."

"We should," he said. "As long as nothing goes wrong."

Sharon pushed the tray of snacks closer so he could reach them. "The instruction sheet says one hundred ninety-two kilograms per drum. That seems like an odd quantity to shoot for," she said.

He continued, "Jicard wants the drums labeled as vegetable oil, and a drum of vegetable oil weighs about one hundred ninety-two kilograms. So that's how much gelator can be in each drum."

"I see."

"But the gelator is about fifty percent denser than vegetable oil, so the drums will only be about two-thirds full. The stuff may slosh around a bit during shipment."

"So the drums will weigh the same as vegetable oil, but they will only be about two-thirds full," said Sharon.

"Right."

"I know Karen is familiar with this stuff, but I'm a newbie. What is it exactly?"

"It's called a deep eutectic solvent."

"You lost me already."

"That's okay—they aren't very common. They are solvents made from two or more crystalline components. The interesting part is that the melting point of the solvent is lower than the individual components."

"Again?"

"Basically, you mix two powers together in the right proportion, and the result is a liquid solvent. It is quite remarkable."

"Hmm. So, when do we start?"

"How about now?" He led them into the chamber and stood next to the one-hundred-gallon mixing tank. "I thought we'd make the first batch together so we are all on the same page, and then we'll take turns watching it. We can label the drums while we wait."

Chapter 62

Forgue and Cyrus arrived at one o'clock. The warehouse was larger than they needed, but it was the only available space in town. It had four dock doors, some office space at one end, and a break room for employee lunches.

"Boy, this place is a ghost town," said Cyrus. "I saw one pickup truck on the way over here. That's it—one. How do people live like this?"

"Quietly, I would guess."

"So this is the place, then. When do the boys arrive?"

"The drones and the herbicide arrive this afternoon, and the team will be here in the morning. We'll use that fork truck over there."

"Are there really seven hundred of them? How can we fly that many at the same time?"

"Well, the controllers have been configured to handle up to forty each, so we'll have eighteen operators. The rest of the team will be filling tanks and changing batteries."

"How many are coming?"

"Forty-four."

"Wow."

The rental agent had promised a large meeting area, Forgue and Cyrus went into the break room to make sure. It was indeed spacious. There was a kitchen counter on the left, with a sink, a microwave, and a refrigerator. The rest of the room was occupied by banquette tables and a long rolling rack filled with folding chairs.

"This will do nicely," said Forgue. "Let's set the chairs up while we wait for the trucks. They should be here any time now."

Forty-five minutes later, they arrived. Forgue opened the first dock door for the drones and the second for the herbicide. Cyrus climbed onto the fork truck and began offloading pallets—it took less than an hour.

After the trucks left, he looked at the pallets lined up on the floor. There were two long row of pallets and third of herbicide drums. "That's a lot of drones—I can see why we need so many people."

"Yep, and there are a lot of batteries as well," he said. "So, let's get them plugged in. We need to be ready for tomorrow."

***

At ten o'clock the following day, the team arrived. It was a caravan of three minivans and eighteen rental trucks. They drove single file through the center of town and then east on 4th Street. For the people of Quinter, it was an unusual sight indeed.

When they turned in, four trucks backed up to the loading docks, and the balance found space along the fence line. Everyone was eager to see the drones.

The team members had been meeting online for the past two weeks, but this was the first time in person. They made a beeline for the equipment pallets.

"Wow, so that's what seven hundred drones looks like," said Basel Homset, the team leader.

Forgue walked over and shook his hand. "It's nice to see you again, Basel. Are they ready for this?"

"They are chomping at the bit. It's going to be quite a site."

Forgue started for the breakroom. "The room is ready. Ask everyone to come in."

***

The group was an odd assortment; young and middle-aged, clean-shaven and bearded, tattoos, tee-shirts, and headbands... but Cyrus seemed right at home. He put some slides up describing the drones, their navigation units, and the modified control units. There were several questions, but everyone seemed pretty much on the same page.

He then put up a map of Gove County, showing the area to be sprayed. It encompassed about twelve square miles of farmland north of Gove Bb and west of Gove 78. There was a collective gasp.

One of the team members piped up. "I have the same map on my computer back home. It's about seventy-five hundred acres, or about eleven acres per drone. We should be done in about ninety minutes if all goes well."

"That is exactly what I calculated," said Cyrus. Another gasp filtered across the room.

He had the map pre-marked to highlight the drone truck stations and the battery-refill areas. He pointed them out as he spoke. When he was finished, he sent copies to everyone.

"Okay," he said. "If there are no more questions, then let's get started. The equipment is identified with associated drone truck and controller numbers, so find your set and dive in."

"Pardon me, Cyrus, I do have one question."

Cyrus nodded to the second man in the front row. "Certainly."

"Is the corn even growing yet? It is only the third week of April."

"The weather in Quinter has been warm this spring, and they completed planting about ten days ago. Right now, the corn is about six inches tall and especially vulnerable to the herbicide. So it is an ideal time for the attack."

***

Out in the warehouse, the group swarmed the pallets and began unpacking equipment. Before long, the floor was abuzz with activity. Drones were unfolded, rotors were tested, controllers were switched on, comm addresses were checked, and GPS coordinates were verified.

Cyrus stepped aside. "I think it's a good group," he said. "They seem to know what they're doing."

"Basel has been a friend for many years," said Forgue. "We have done dozens of projects together, and he has never failed me."

After about an hour, the activity shifted toward the dock doors. They loaded eight drums of herbicide, forty drones, and a master controller into each truck, except for the last. It was loaded with twenty drones, a master controller, four drums of herbicide, and spare batteries. As soon as one group of trucks was loaded, it was replaced by another until all were complete. It took nearly three hours.

"That's the lot," said Basel. "Everyone's excited to go."

"Great," said Forgue. "They've done an excellent job, but I need them to keep a low profile this evening. This is a very small town, and we don't want to attract more attention than necessary."

Basel nodded while Forgue continued.

"So, we want everyone to hang here in the warehouse until it's time. They can brush up on the owner's manuals, and we'll order some pizza and beer for dinner. Then about ten-thirty, or so, they can leave for their attack stations. But make sure they go in small groups, one or two trucks at a time. We don't want all eighteen rolling through town in the middle of the night."

"Sounds right," he said. "We'll keep a low profile."

"When they reach their stations, they will have at least a half-hour to set up, and then at midnight, we will launch."

"Got it. And when we're finished, we collect the drones and proceed to our rendezvous points."

"Correct," he said. "No one should come back here tonight. We'll shut everything down as soon as the last truck leaves."

Satisfied with the situation, Forgue walked outside and sent a short text message to Jicard:

Everything is set for midnight.
Inform FT

***

Thirty minutes later, a loud motorcycle sped away from the Kentalas' front door. When Angela went to investigate, she found a second white envelope lying on the porch. She picked it up and carried it to Declan's office.

"We got another one," she said as she handed it to her husband. "I wonder what this one's all about."

Declan cautiously opened the envelope and extracted the note with a pair of tweezers. He placed it on the desk, so they could read it together.

Mr. Kentala:

This note will alert you to the next phase of our mission. It will happen tonight.

I imagine you are still reeling from the pipeline attack, but you might find the next experience even more distressing.

*By the way, I do regret the death of Mr. Hankin. It was unintentional;
I never wanted anyone to die. However, accidents do happen, as you well
know.*

*And to that point, you might wish to review the 'accident' that occurred
about twenty-five years ago on Haengun-do. When your father's terminal
blew up, it took the rest of the island with it. Everything was destroyed,
including my home and my entire family. Had I not been in Ulsan that day,
I would not be alive to avenge them now.*

*Family honor is paramount, in my view. And for the crimes that your
father committed, you will surely pay.*

"Who is this guy?" said Angela. "He's insane!"

"Certifiable."

"You are not responsible for your father's actions. You had nothing to
do with them. It's ridiculous."

"Clearly, this guy disagrees with you," he said. "And I wonder what he
means by more distressing? The pipeline outage will affect the lives of more
than two thousand families, from the oil fields all the way to the refinery.
Not to mention our vendors and the dozens of service companies that work
for us. The repair cost will be close to a billion, and gasoline prices will
skyrocket for months. What more does he plan to do?"

"This is all so horrible. Are we going to be okay?"

"I think so, but it is going to hurt a lot," he said. "I'll forward this to
Floyd, so he knows what's going on, but I doubt if he can do very much.
Our operation covers more than eight hundred miles of territory, and this
guy could hit us anywhere—oil fields, truck terminals, tank farms, maybe
even the refinery. We could have an army at our disposal, and it still
wouldn't be enough." He stared out the window, shoulders slumped. "It's
impossible."

Chapter 63

"So, he died that same day," said Robin. "In a car accident." She dropped her head and shook it slowly. "That is so sad."

"We are sorry for your loss, ma'am," said Special Agent Stanton. "But we don't believe it was an accident. We have evidence that the car he was driving had been rigged with explosives."

"Dan Turner did it, I'd bet ya," she proclaimed. "I'm right. Aren't I?"

"We don't know yet. But why would you say that?"

"Dan comes across all jolly and fun. You know, with that red mustache and his big toothy grin. But underneath, there's a darker side. He never shares much information with anyone, and it seems like he always has something going on the side."

"Is that right?"

"Yeah," she continued. "He and Melvin were in here a lot during the construction. It was the best place to meet, off-campus, if you know what I mean. Dan drove him like a slave, but he never complained. Melvin just soldiered on. For him, it was all about the work. He loved what he did, you could tell. He was one of the good guys."

"So you liked him a lot, then."

She took a sip of her tea.

"Of course I did," she said. "He was one of the most caring and genuinely good people I've ever known, and I miss him a lot. And I never believed the story that Dan was spreading around. There is just no way that Melvin would have taken off like that. Not him, no way." She shook her head.

"And since Dan was the last one to see him. Yeah, it wouldn't surprise me at all—he's probably up to his neck in it."

***

Dr. Nugent had been on the phone with Jicard for more than twenty minutes, and he was seething. "So, I sent Dan out there—he left a few minutes ago."

"What do you mean 'you sent him'? We need him in Broadview."

"Well, as I said, Betson disappeared a week and a half ago. The best engineer you could find for us, just up and left. Imagine that. We need someone onsite now."

"I'll talk with Dan," he said. "Between us, we'll find a replacement."

"That doesn't solve the immediate problem. The contractor is going nuts out there. He's been calling me every day, sometimes every hour. Dan will cover the job until you find someone else. He'll arrive late tonight and be in the trailer first thing tomorrow."

"But I don't think…"

"Shut the hell up, Jicard. None of this would have happened if you had done your job in the first place. I am fed up with your excuses!"

"Well," he said. "We've been busy."

"We need to do everything at once," he said. "We can't afford to let anything slip through the cracks. You have more than two hundred people in the Cave—make it work."

"Yes, sir."

"I don't want any more slip-ups, Mr. Jicard. Goodbye." He hung up the phone.

***

It took a few moments for him to decompress. *Jicard is such an asshole! Why did we ever hire him?* Then his phone rang again. *Jicard, what do you want this time?*

His hand shot toward the receiver. But when he looked at the caller ID, it read 'Reception'. He picked up the receiver and half-shouted into the phone. "Yes, Millie. What do you want?"

"Sir?" she said. "Are you all right?"

He realized how he must have sounded. "I'm fine, Millie. I'm sorry I snapped that way." He paused again. "I just got off a difficult phone call, that's all." He took a deep breath and shook his head. "Really, I'm okay. What can I do for you?"

"Those two agents from the FBI are back. They say they have a few more questions."

"Not today," he said. "I have far too much to do. Ask them to come back on Monday morning." He glanced at his calendar, "Give them an appointment for nine-thirty—that should be good."

She looked at the agents for a second and then continued with Dr. Nugent, "Sir, they seem pretty insistent. I think you better see them today."

"But I can't, Millie. I don't have the time."

"Sir, I think you better make the time."

What can they want? Can I find no peace? "Okay, Millie, if I must," he said. "Go ahead, and send them up. They know the way."

Dr. Nugent opened the door to his office and waited for the agents. As they approached from the elevator, he extended his hand.

"Gentlemen," he said. "What can I do for you today? I thought we covered everything during your last visit."

Special Agent Lyons shook his hand. "We have a few more questions," he said. "May we come in?"

He stepped back and motioned toward the conference table.

Special Agent Stanton began. "Dr. Nugent, how well do you know Daniel Turner?"

"How well do I know him?" he said. "He works for me and manages this plant."

"We are aware of that," said agent Stanton. "But outside of work, how well do you know him?"

"Not well at all, I would have to say. Ours is strictly a workplace relationship. I think he's single—I don't remember him mentioning a wife or a family. He hasn't offered that kind of information, and I've never asked." He shifted in his seat. "Why do you want to know?"

"We are just trying to build a complete picture."

"I see. I guess."

"How much latitude do you give him?"

"Latitude. Do you mean in his job?"

"Yes."

"Well, let's see," he said. "He consults with me on capital projects and major expenditures, of course, and we discuss personnel issues when we need to. But otherwise, he is free to run the plant. We have five plants in three states. So I don't have time to micromanage."

"So, while you're away, he runs the plant."

"He runs the plant while I'm here. I spend the majority of my time in Broadview, that's true, but I have offices in the other four plants as well. I imagine he feels a little less pressure when I'm away."

"So you travel a lot."

"Quite a bit. I try to visit each plant at least once a month. We do a lot of video conferencing."

"I understand," said Agent Stanton. "And where is Mr. Turner today?"

"Right now, he is on his way to Owanka."

"I don't know that town. Where is it, exactly?"

"It's in South Dakota. We're building a new plant there," he said. "It's about forty miles east of Rapid City."

"A new plant? So, there will soon be six."

"That's right. We will put Owanka back on the map. Right now, only a handful of people live there."

"Will Mr. Tuner be running that plant as well?"

"No. This assignment is only temporary. Our project engineer left us a week ago, and Dan will be managing things until we find a replacement."

The agents made some notes and then put their pads in their jackets. They looked at each other and nodded.

"We thank you for your cooperation," said Agent Lyons. "But I am afraid there are many more questions to ask. So we would like you to come to our office in Billings and make a formal statement."

"Are you arresting me?"

"We can if you wish, but we would prefer that you come voluntarily. It would save a lot of paperwork."

"Right now?"

"Yes. If you wouldn't mind."

He looked around his office and thought about all of the things he had to do. Then, he looked at the agents.

"Well, I guess I would rather go voluntarily. I am not sure what you want to know. But I've done nothing wrong that I'm aware of. So, okay, let's go. The sooner we get there, the sooner I can get back." He closed up his desk, turned off his computer monitor, and held the door. "Gentlemen."

On the way out, he stopped at Millie's desk. "I am going down to Billings this afternoon," he said. "And I'll be gone for the rest of the day."

She knitted her brow. "Sir?"

"Now, there is no need to worry, my dear. Everything will be fine," he said. "They just want me to make a statement. I'll be back on Monday morning."

"Okay, then," she said with a smile. "I'll see you on Monday." She sat down and went back to work.

The agents escorted him to their car and helped him into the back seat. Special Agent Lyons sat next to him. It was a long ride to Billings.

Chapter 64

It was ten-thirty in Quinter when the drone trucks began leaving the warehouse. The route was north on Long Street across the tracks, west on Gove Aa, and then north on Castle Park Road. From there, the first six found their stations on Gove Bb, the next six on Gove Cc, and the last six on Gove Dd. The minivans left separately and headed further north to Gove Ee. They established supply and recovery stations to take care of any drones that might experience problems. Truck number eighteen met them on Gove Ee and offloaded the necessary supplies.

After the last truck departed, Forgue and Cyrus closed up the warehouse. They shut off the lights, locked the doors, and walked to their car. "So, where do we go next?"

"Back to Louisiana, my boy," said Forgue. "Our job in Quinter is done—Basel will handle it from here."

***

Basel Homset had planned the attack well. The eighteen trucks would be spaced on three parallel roads about a mile apart. The drones would fly north to the next road, shift eighteen feet to the east and then fly back to the south. Each round trip would cover about five point six acres. The drones would then be resupplied with herbicide and fresh batteries for a second-round trip. Launches would be in groups of ten from each truck. And would be staggered ten minutes apart to allow time for resupply on their return.

Weather conditions were perfect for flying. The sky was clear, temperatures were in the low forties, and the wind was still. Unfortunately, the moon was only a thin crescent, but abundant starlight made up the deficit.

By eleven p.m., all eighteen trucks were in position. Then, one by one, the drones were unloaded and positioned on the pavement. Rotors were locked in place, and power switches and navigation lights were turned on. When activated, the drones flew automatically to their starting positions, landed, and waited for the launch signal.

When midnight came, the first one hundred eighty drones lifted off and turned to the north—they were all but invisible in the darkness. The hundreds of low-wattage navigation lights looked like so many fireflies, and the buzz of a thousand mosquitos was unnerving. Then, ten minutes later, the second wave took to the air.

The round trip flying time for each drone was about twelve minutes, so the first group landed for resupply before the third group took off. But by twelve-thirty, all seven hundred drones had been launched.

As they completed their second trips, they were systemically collected and loaded back in the trucks. The operation was very efficient, and by one-thirty, it was complete.

As planned, each drone delivered forty liters of herbicide, and collectively, the operation destroyed over seven thousand acres of newly planted corn.

Operationally, only one drone had a problem—the eighth from truck number sixteen. It lost its communication signal on a return leg and crashed to the ground. However the damage was minimal, and a minivan team found it in minutes.

By one-forty-five in the morning, the empty herbicide drums had been picked up, and all seven hundred drones were back on the trucks. They left no trace.

Forgue and Cyrus were halfway to Wichita when Basel's text arrived:
Quinter complete.
Undetected. No Trace.
As Forgue read the message, he thought of the large deposit that would soon be made to his account. He smiled.

Chapter 65

"Thank you for calling so quickly. I can't believe it either," said Declan into the telephone. "Did anyone get hurt?" He paused to listen. "Good. At least that's something. Well, do the best you can, and I'll get back to you." He hung up the handset and turned to his wife—his face was drawn.

"That was the plant manager in Quinter. They hit our cornfields during the night. Over seven thousand acres of new plantings are gone. Why the cornfields? I don't understand."

"My God, Declan. This guy will stop at nothing. There was no way to prepare. Did anyone get hurt?"

"No. Nobody was hurt, thank goodness. They attacked around midnight. No one was anywhere near the fields at that hour."

"So, what can we do about it? The employees must be worried sick."

"I don't know yet, and I certainly don't want to lay anyone off. But if there is no feedstock, then I am not sure what can be done."

"Maybe we can purchase enough corn to keep the plant running. We could operate at half-capacity or something. That way, we could keep it open and not lay off the people. What do you think?"

"If we can get it cheap enough, it might be possible, I guess. We'll give it some thought."

As they discussed the magnitude of the attack, Angela heard a noise in the driveway. "Oh my God," she said. "Did you hear that? Not another one!"

They both rushed to the door, but the motorcycle was gone by the time they got there. And lying on the porch, was a third envelope.

"I'll get this one," said Declan as he scooped it up. "This is getting tiresome." He carried it to his office, extracted the note with tweezers, and then laid it flat between them.

Mr. Kentala:

By now, you have heard about the attack at Quinter. It went well from our perspective, and we expect your ethanol production to be seriously affected.

We used a particularly nasty herbicide. It kills all the way to the root and persists for several months. So, you won't be replanting, at least not this year.

On a brighter note, we have no additional attacks planned at this time, at least not in the states. Instead, we will focus our efforts on your holdings in southeast Asia. Assets like offshore drilling platforms, undersea pipelines, and the like are on the list. We might even visit Haengun-do. Your plant on the north end of the island is of particular interest.

By the way, did you know that half of the island is now underwater due to global warming? That is another small problem to which your family's business has contributed.

No, we are not yet finished with Kentala Petroleum. The next attack will be truly devastating. It may break your back.

"We have to stop this nut job," said Angela. "Has the FBI made any progress at all?"

"They are working on it," he said. "They are in touch with South Korean officials to find out who lived on the island back then, but progress is slow. Most of the public records were destroyed in the explosion. They are also working leads here in the states. They'll find him."

"I hope they do it soon."

Chapter 66

"What are we doing here?" said Sam. "Karen is out there under a mountain. We need to be out there looking."

"I agree," said Tylor. "But according to her text message, they have cameras everywhere, so we will need a few things to deal with that."

"From a camping store?"

"Exactly," he said. "From a camping store. And we might need to visit the army surplus store as well." He motioned for them to follow.

"But since we're here. Let's amble over to the hunting and fishing department. We are looking for high-power night vision binoculars, a dozen or so remote-control lasers, battery packs, and six tripods. Oh, and three extra-large camouflaged ponchos."

***

Special Agent Stanton was sitting at his desk on Saturday morning when a message appeared on his Sentinel Screen. It was from the Salt Lake City office:

We are two hundred scientists kidnapped and held by North States Renewables. I don't know our exact location, but we are inside a mountain-cave system south of Red Lodge, MT, about twelve miles north of the Wyoming border. The entrances to the system are camouflaged and hidden. People in charge of the 'Cave' are Dr. Emil Nugent, Mr. Louis Jicard, and Mr. Daniel Turner. Please help us. Caution: security is very tight. There are camera systems inside and outside and many armed guards. Please hurry. Our lives are in danger. Dr. Arthur Gilford.

"Dave. Did you see this?"

"Did I see what?"

"On the Sentinel this morning from Salt Lake."

Agent Dave Lyons read the drone message and then sat back in his chair. "What is south of Red Lodge?" He opened a map program and zoomed in. "I don't see much, and the terrain looks pretty rugged. I think it's part of the Custer Gallatin National Forest."

"Federal Land."

"Yes. I think so," he said. "I'll call the ranger in Red Lodge first— maybe he can shed some light on the situation. And then, I'll re-read Dr. Nugent's statement from yesterday. Especially that part about Mr. Jicard."

"I'll get the warrants," said Agent Stanton. "And I'll ask Rapid City to send a couple of agents to Owanka."

"Fine. And get some background on this, Dr. Arthur Gilford." He paused and thought for a moment. "Okay, Let's get to it. There may be lives at stake."

Chapter 67

"Yes, Dan, what do you need?"

"I need to get out."

"What do you mean, 'out'?"

"I mean, out of the country. I think I'll spend some time in Canada—a year or so, perhaps. And then maybe I'll go to the South Pacific. I always wanted to visit the islands."

"You'll have to give me a little more than that."

"Millie said the FBI is looking for me, and that's all I need to know," he said. "I'm leaving."

"Where are you now? I'm at home, but not for long. My bags are packed."

"Nugent said you went to Owanka."

"That's what he thinks. No. I'm not going anywhere near an airport. That's the first place they'll look."

"Are there any ticking time bombs that I need to worry about?"

"None. I'm going to stop by the plant to pick up my laptop and a couple of thumb drives." He glanced at his watch. "And then it's straight north to Canada. I'll be in Medicine Hat before midnight."

"Just don't leave anything behind that the FBI can use," said Jicard. "They'll take your office apart, piece by piece, and then hunt you down."

"They'll never catch me. And if they do find anything in my office. Well, that will be your problem," he said. "Say, if you're ever in Tahiti, look me up—I'm gone."

***

Twenty minutes later, as he was going through his office desk, he heard a noise in the hallway—a soft footstep followed by a scuffing sound. *This is Saturday. Nobody should be here.*

He called out, "Who's there?" No one answered. He walked to the door and peeked out, but the hall was empty. *Get a grip, man. Now you're hearing things!*

He returned to his desk and resumed working. Then he heard it again. That's it. I am out of here. He stuffed the thumb drives in his pocket, slipped the laptop into its satchel, and sprinted down the hall.

"Mr. Turner. Stop. We're the FBI." Special Agents Lyons and Stanton ran after him. "We have a warrant for your arrest."

By the time the agents reached the door, Dan was well inside the processing plant. They stepped through and then stopped to listen. Dan saw them from his hiding place and said nothing.

"Mr. Turner, please come quietly. There is nowhere to go. You can't escape."

Dan held his breath.

After a few moments, the agents advanced slowly into the plant. The building was enormous, at least a hundred yards wide and more than five hundred long, and filled with equipment.

The left side of the building housed cane preparation and diffusion equipment. The right side was lined with fermentation tanks, and the far end was used for alcohol distillation and purification. The floor was polished concrete, and a network of steel catwalks hung overhead.

The agents crept past the cane shredders and the diffusion tanks and then angled toward the fermentation section.

"Mr. Turner. Give yourself up."

Dan watched their progress from his hiding place behind a large filtration unit. And when they were passed, he sprinted for the opposite side. The agents heard him and took up the chase.

Dan ran up a set of stairs to the top of the fermentation tank, and Agent Stanton went after him. Agent Lyons followed their progress from the floor.

He then took a series of catwalks to arrive at the distillation tower. It was taller than the other equipment, about forty feet, and the roof had a raised section to accommodate it.

When he reached the ladder, he started climbing. His computer satchel felt heavy on his shoulder and swung randomly against his leg. The upper part of the tower was much warmer than the bottom, and he was sweating heavily when he reached the top.

"Mr. Turner. There is nowhere to go. Please come down."

"I can't do that, Agent Stanton." He took a deep breath and wiped his forehead. "I don't want to go to prison."

He stepped to the backside of the tower and across a short bridge. The sign on the door read 'Roof Access'. When he opened the door, it was caught by a gust of wind, and he nearly fell off. He closed it quickly and locked it.

"Where did he go? I can't see him."

"I don't know," said Agent Stanton. "He was on the top platform a minute ago."

"Get up there and check, dammit."

Agent Stanton climbed the ladder to the top, but Dan was nowhere to be seen. The door to the roof was locked from the outside.

"He's gone, Dave. He's out on the roof."

Agent Lyons sprinted back to the office, through the hallways and the reception area, and out to the parking lot. But Dan's car was gone. Agent Stanton joined him a few minutes later, sweating heavily.

"Are you okay?" said Agent Lyons.

"I'll give him one thing," he said between breaths. "He's in pretty good shape. That climb nearly killed me." He braced himself on the hood of the car and took several deep breaths. "And he still got away... dammit!"

"Not for long, I think. I have his license number."

***

Dan was racing north on State Route 3, toward Lavina. His left ankle was throbbing with pain, there was blood dripping from his right forearm, and his shirt was soaked red. *Shit! That was close. Now, what? I can't go to the border—they'll be watching for me. Maybe the Cave? No, they'll catch me for sure if I try to go through Billings. The only direction is north. I'll go to Fu Tong's. He has a plane.*

He glanced at his speedometer. *Slow down, you idiot. This is no time to get pulled over for speeding.* He eased his foot off the accelerator. He then noticed his shirt and the dripping blood. *Damn! This is not going well. I need to get cleaned up and put on some clean clothes.*

He felt light-headed, and Lavina was still ten miles away.

***

Dan's race across the rooftops had not been without incident. From the roof-access door, he climbed down a long vertical ladder to reach the main level. His satchel kept swinging in the wind, and at one point, it got caught on a steel bracket. When he reached down to free it, a jagged piece of metal sliced through his sleeve. The cut was deep, and within seconds, the entire right side of his shirt was soaked with blood. He gripped the wound to staunch the flow and kept moving.

When he reached the edge of the roof, he paused for a couple of seconds. He looked down to judge the distance and then jumped off. He hoped that the storage pile of sugarcane would break his fall, and for the most part, it did. But when he landed, his left ankle got caught in a hole and twisted beneath him. He nearly passed out from the pain.

A searing bolt of lightning shot up his leg, and instinctively, he grabbed for his ankle. He rubbed it gingerly for a few seconds to ease the throbbing, but it did little good. And he was running out of time.

He pushed himself to a sitting position, gritted his teeth, and slid the rest of the way to the ground. When he stood up, he tried to put weight on his ankle, but it was no use. He limped to the car, tossed his satchel inside, and sped off. He cleared the parking lot mere seconds before Agent Lyons' arrival.

Chapter 68

Dan was almost to Route 12 but was feeling weaker by the minute. His ankle was screaming, and his arm was still bleeding. *I need to do something now!*

He spied a convenience store on the right and whipped into the parking lot. He opened his trunk, grabbed his suitcase, and limped inside. "Where are your first aid supplies?" he said hurriedly.

The clerk behind the counter was shocked at Dan's appearance. His hands and shirt were soaked in blood, and he was covered from head to toe with dirt from the sugarcane pile. His face was contorted in pain.

"It's in the third aisle next to the snacks," he said. "Hey, buddy, can I call someone for you? You look like you need help."

"Shut up, kid, and mind your own business," replied Dan. "I need to use your men's room."

He pointed toward the back of the store. "It's back there. But hey, man, don't mess it up. I just got done cleaning it."

Dan grabbed a box of gauze, some ace bandages, a tube of disinfectant, and a roll of adhesive tape and then limped to the men's room.

Five minutes later, the clerk was still trying to make sense of it when another customer walked in. "Excuse me, do you have any brake fluid?"

"Yessir. Of course, we do," he replied. "You'll find it in the first aisle, next to the windshield wipers."

"Thanks." The customer stepped to the aisle and held up a can. "Is this the right one for my pickup truck?"

"How would I know, man," he said. "Don't you have your owner's manual?" He stepped from behind the cash register and walked toward the customer.

Moments later, Dan emerged from the men's room wearing a clean set of clothes and a long-sleeve shirt.

The clerk returned to the cash register. "Tell me the items you selected, and I'll ring you up, sir."

Dan ignored the clerk and walked toward the customer. He saw his pickup truck parked outside. "Excuse me, sir," he said. "Is that your truck?"

"Yeah, it's mine. Why do you ask?"

"I want to borrow it for a while."

"What? I don't think so," he answered. "I don't even know you. What makes you think I would lend you my truck?"

"I need it."

"Go away. I am not in the mood for jokes."

"This is no joke, sir. I need your truck."

"I told you to go away." He turned back to the brake fluid display. His pulse was racing. "Just go away."

Dan pulled out a hunting knife and pointed at the man's stomach. "Give me your keys right now. Don't make me use this."

The man looked at the knife, and his eyes went wide. He stumbled back a few steps. "You're crazy, man! Leave me alone!"

Dan stepped closer and placed the tip of the serrated steel blade against the man's shirt. "Now, sir. I really don't have time to discuss it."

He backed up two more steps and found himself wedged against the beverage case.

Dan pressed the tip of the blade into his shirt until it drew blood. And then pulled it back. "Now!"

The man winced and grabbed his stomach. "You cut me. You bastard! You son of a bitch!"

"Now, sir."

"Okay. Okay, you win." He retrieved the keys from his pocket. "You can have it. Just leave me alone."

Dan grabbed the keys and limped out the door. He stopped at his car to get his satchel and then sped off in the truck.

Inside the store, the clerk dialed 911 while the man went to the first aid section for some band-aids.

"That son of a bitch stole my truck," he said. "The bastard!"

"Yessir, that's right, in a white pickup truck. He stole it from one of my customers at knifepoint."

The clerk listened while the man unbuttoned his shirt and applied the band-aid. Fortunately, the cut was not serious.

"I would say he was about forty years old, five feet eight inches tall, stocky build. Oh, and he had short red hair with a bushy red mustache. He turned west on Route 12 and took off like a bat. He was really moving."

He hung up and turned to his customer. "The 911 operator says a cruiser will be here in about ten minutes."

***

A half-hour later, Dan was speeding west on Route 12—he had just passed through Shawmut. *This old pickup is a beast.* The accelerator was all the way to the floor, and the speedometer read eighty-five miles per hour. *I guess I made a good choice.*

It was a two-lane highway, so he was constantly passing other cars. Occasionally he would have to slow down a bit until the oncoming lane was clear but then wasted no time getting back to speed. He glanced at his navigation app. *Fu Tong's Estate is still three hours away. I need to keep moving.* He stood on the accelerator pedal.

Fifteen miles ahead, on the outskirts of Harlowton, the Montana Highway Patrol set up a roadblock—three cruisers sat crossways on the highway. All eastbound traffic was blocked, and westbound traffic was filtered through.

For Dan, the absence of eastbound traffic made passing all the easier. So he picked up the pace. Then, from about a mile away, he saw the flashing lights. *Shit! A roadblock! I'll pull into the gas station and make a U-turn.*

He took his foot off the accelerator and touched the brakes to slow down. They felt spongy. He swerved right to enter the station and touched them again, but they didn't work. He stomped on the pedal—nothing. He was going seventy-two miles per hour at the time.

One hundred twenty feet ahead on the west side of the station sat a gasoline tanker truck. An operator was filling the underground tanks and was about to move the hose when he spotted the pickup. Instantly, he dropped the hose and ran for cover.

Dan searched for a way out, a path to safety, but saw none. A row of pine trees blocked him to the left, and the filling station and gas pumps were on the right. The tanker was dead ahead.

He angled to the right slightly to miss the tanker and struck a concrete curb in the process—his right front wheel launched into the air, and the pickup flipped on its side. A tenth of a second later, it slid into the tanker—the result was cataclysmic.

The force of the impact split the tanker wide open, pushed it almost twenty feet to the west, and sheared off the base of a utility pole. Two thousand gallons of gasoline spilled onto the asphalt.

Dan tried to crawl out when the pickup stopped moving, but his leg was trapped in the wreckage. Blood flowed from an open gash in his forehead, and there was no feeling in his left arm. The smell of gasoline was nauseating.

Then, a gust of wind caught the damaged pole, and live power lines fell across the tanker. The explosion that followed rocked the station and shattered windows a mile away.

The tanker operator and the staff stood inside the station and watched in horror as the fireball ensued. For nearly ten minutes, Dan shrieked in agony. His dying screams would haunt them for years.

Chapter 69

"I am hoping they haven't," said Tylor. He raised the binoculars to his face. "And with a little luck..." He scanned the side of the mountain. "There! I found one."

Sam and Paul used their glasses to look at the same area. "You're right. I can see them too. They are like little specs of light," said Sam. "This is going to be easy."

"As soon as you zero in on one, lock the laser in place and turn it off. Don't tag them for more than a second or two."

Sam and Paul looked at the lasers mounted on the tripod and nodded.

"And remember, what you are seeing are the infrared emitters. If they have any thermal imaging cameras, we won't be able to spot those."

"Right."

"But their cameras can see our lasers. So don't leave them on. And for that matter, make sure your binoculars are in passive mode."

"Got it," said Sam. "No more than a second or two."

Paul set up his gear at the previous viewing site, Sam found a spot about a quarter mile up the road, and Tylor found some cover around the bend. They had radio gear for group communication, night vision binoculars, remote control lasers, and enough supplies to last them through the night. Their camouflaged ponchos helped keep them warm and made them nearly invisible against the foliage.

Hours passed. "Checking in," said Paul. "I have found three cameras, but nothing is happening."

"Be patient," said Tylor. "I have two, so far. Sam?"

"Four."

Two more hours passed, and Paul whispered into his microphone. "Heads up, guys. A car is coming."

Out on the highway, a black SUV approached from the north. It passed the hidden sliding gate and then slowed down. Its headlights were blinding through the night-vision gear.

A moment later, a second gate slid open, and the SUV turned in. Tylor could see nothing from his location, but Sam and Paul followed the action with their glasses.

As the gate closed, the SUV continued into the wood, wound its way through the trees, and stopped at the cliff's base. Then, a large opening appeared in the wall, and the SUV drove inside. Five seconds after that, the opening was gone.

"My God. Did you see that?" whispered Sam. "There is a hidden tunnel!" Sam trained one of his lasers on the spot and then switched it off.

"I lost sight of the SUV when it went into the trees. Can you tag it?"

"Already done."

"What's happening?" said Tylor. "I can't see."

Sam responded, "A black SUV drove through a second camouflaged gate and then into a hidden tunnel. I marked the entrance with one of my lasers."

"Great," said Tylor. "Keep watching."

Nothing more happened until just before dawn, when Paul piped up again. "Gentlemen, we have a Triple-B truck approaching from the north."

The truck drove past the first gate and the second, and then proceeded around the curve.

"Heads up, Tylor, it's coming your way."

"I see it."

The truck passed Tylor and slowed down. In moments, a third gate slid open, and it turned in.

The sun was not yet up, but there was too much light for the infrared emitters to work well. So, he made a decision.

"I'm going to follow it."

"What? No way. Stay where you are," said Paul. "We'll call the FBI."

"That will take too long." He slipped on his backpack. "I only have a few seconds."

He leaped from his viewing hide, slid down the hill, and jogged across the pavement. As he entered the woods, he spotted the truck moving slowly toward the mountain. He sprinted toward it.

"Gentlemen," he said as he ran. "This is the right place, I am sure of it." He swerved to the right to miss a tree. "Call Agent Lyons and tell him what's going on. My lasers are locked in position and labeled. I'm going to follow the truck."

"Are you crazy?" said Paul. "You don't know where it's going."

"Hopefully, it is going inside." He reached the back of the trailer and tucked behind it so the driver couldn't see him.

"You have lost your mind."

"If I manage to get inside, I will probably lose signal, so listen up."

The truck angled right onto a circle drive.

"Ask Agent Lyons to send help." He stepped closer to the back of the trailer to hide from the cameras. "The gate is about twenty yards south of my surveillance hide. The road runs about twenty yards straight in and then curves to the north."

"Tylor! Are you sure you want to do this?"

"Shut up, Paul, and listen," he said. "Okay, the truck has stopped." He stood quietly. "I hear mechanical noises. Wait, a section of the pavement is rising straight up in front of the truck. It's some kind of elevator, I think. Okay, we're moving again, creeping ahead, very slowly."

The truck drove onto a long concrete slab and then stopped. There was a steel roof overhead, supported by four I-beams, on either side.

"It's an elevator, all right. I'm going to crawl under the rear of the trailer and go down with it. Call Agent Lyons as soon as you can."

The elevator descended, and the radio signal went dead.

***

"Chip. Did you see that?"

"What?"

"On camera fourteen," he said. "Something moved in the trees."

Chip selected number fourteen and looked closely. "I don't see anything."

"Well, it is gone now. But I saw something move. I am sure of it."

"Pedro. How many animals do you think are roaming around out there?" He studied his monitor again. "Something is always moving in the trees. Just forget it."

Chapter 70

"He did what?" said Special Agent Lyons. "I told him to let us handle it."

"What can I say?" said Paul. "When he gets something in his head, there is no changing it. Besides, I think he's sort of smitten with Miss Wagoner."

"Great. That's all we need. He's risking his life, and he's emotionally compromised at the same time." He paused. "Exactly where did you say you are?"

"Twelve and a half miles south of Red Lodge on the west side of route 212. We're set up at the edge of the forest, so give me a call when you get close. But remember, they have cameras everywhere, so keep a low profile."

"Fine," said Special Agent Lyons. "Clifton Yang, the district ranger from Red Lodge, will get there first. He has jurisdiction but knows almost nothing about the case, so bring him up to speed. Then, about three hours later, Special Agent Stanton and I will show up with additional help. And for God's sake, keep your distance until we get there."

***

"Did anyone follow you?"

"I don't think so," said Christi. "Red Lodge was a ghost town, and it was three in the morning when we drove in. So we're good."

"So, why did you want us to come in?" said BJ. "The Kentala job went as planned, and since then, it's been nothing but quiet."

"It didn't quite go as planned, you idiot. Tiny killed a security guard. I gave strict instructions that nobody be killed, and he did it anyway."

"But sir, that wasn't our fault. It wasn't even Tiny's fault. He didn't mean to kill the guy."

"Maybe not," said Jicard. "But you've been screwing up a lot recently. And I thought it would be better to have you inside, where I could keep an eye on you."

"What the hell? I'm not going to stay in here. I'm not some kind of bat."

"You'll stay where I tell you to stay. I've got enough on you to put you away for life."

"Now you're threatening me? You're a fool, and you're crazy!"

The vein in Jicard's neck pulsed rapidly. "Crazy? I am not crazy—I am serious. And you have jeopardized my plans for the last time." He raised his left hand.

Instantly, Max appeared from nowhere and grasped BJ by the collar. "Sir?"

"Put him in chamber ten. I'll decide what to do with him later."

"Yes, sir. It will be my pleasure."

***

Christi watched as Max escorted BJ to the elevator. "Was that really necessary? He had nothing to do with the guard's death."

"I know, but he needs to understand that failure has consequences. Besides, his work of late has not been exactly stellar. The lab fire in Ft. Collins was a fiasco, he screwed up the garage attack, and he failed to stop Miss Wagoner."

"I thought you said she was nothing more than a distraction."

"She was until she recruited help."

"How do you mean?"

"This Tylor York guy—he is quite the pain in the ass. And his friend Sam Wilson—we need to get rid of them both."

"But Sam is… "

She was interrupted by Jicard's phone. She sat back and said nothing.

"Yes, sir," said Jicard. Fu Tong was talking fast on the other end of the line.

"I am not sure that's a good idea, sir." He gripped the receiver tight and listened.

"But sir, I don't think we can do it that soon. Dr. Gilford is swamped as it is."

A bead of sweat broke out on his forehead while Fu Tong continued.

"Yes, sir. Of course, sir. I'll get started on it right away. Thank you, sir."

He replaced the handset on the hook, stared at Christi, and picked up his scotch bottle. "Well, that was unexpected. Care for a drink?"

Christi nodded. "Sure," she said. "But what's unexpected?"

"Let's have several," he said. "Talk about crazy. I think Fu Tong has lost it."

"Why?"

"He wants us to make up ten drums of Gelator-T and ship them to his new company in the Philippines. He bought an old chemical plant east of Manilla, and he plans to make the stuff there. And then, get this—he wants me to destroy everything in the lower chambers and seal them off permanently." He took a slug and handed her a glass. "Unbelievable. We were just getting things ramped up."

"What about Gilford?"

"Gilford will go with the shipment, and Tong wants me to go as well. He plans to put Dr. Wells in charge of the Cave."

"So you'll be in the Philippines, permanently? When is all of this supposed to happen?"

"He wants to ship the gelator next week, and I would follow the week after. It's insane!"

Chapter 71

When the truck finished its delivery, it turned around and drove back toward the elevator. Tylor crouched behind some crates at the end of the tunnel.

The driver centered the truck between the steel columns and drove slowly onto the slab. He stopped at precisely the right spot, leaned out of the cab, and punched a number into a keypad. A few moments later, the elevator began to move. It rose quietly to the street level, stopped while the truck drove off, and then returned to its starting position. The whole cycle took less than five minutes. *Impressive!*

Tylor picked up his backpack, passed the elevator, and inched his way forward. The lights on the roof of the tunnel were dim compared to the truck's headlights, and he blinked a few times to help his eyes adjust. As he made his way forward, he scanned the walls and the ceiling. There were no security cameras. *I guess they don't need them down here.*

When he reached the chamber entrance, he was awestruck. *It's enormous! What is this place?* The overhead lights were intense, and the polished white floor magnified the effect. The smell was somehow industrial and damp at the same time.

And it was huge. At least one hundred yards across, the chamber was circular in shape, with a truck dock to the right, a grouping of stainless steel process equipment in the middle, and stacks of empty packing crates everywhere. At the far side was a small office suite attached to some prefabricated modular units. But there were no people—it seemed deserted. *Someone must have unloaded the truck. Where is everyone?* He knelt down and waited.

Soon, he heard the whining sound of a hydraulic lift, and a fork truck rolled into view. The driver, an elderly black gentleman wearing a white lab coat, was moving a pallet of drums toward the process equipment.

Then two women appeared next to one of the tanks. One was Sharon, and he didn't know the other. He was so relieved to see her—he almost called out but then caught himself. *Wait a minute! Karen's message talked about armed guards. Where are they? Where are the guards?*

Sharon and the other woman started applying labels to the drums while the fork truck went back for another load. They were speaking to each other, but he was too far away to make it out. *I need to get closer.*

The fork truck arrived with the second load, and he watched as the ladies approached. Then, from the right, somewhere beyond the fork truck, he sensed movement. He concentrated his attention on the office module, and after a few seconds, he spotted him.

The guard was a middle-aged man wearing military fatigues. He looked threatening enough with his polished boots, beret, and epaulets, but he was an obvious hack. He was reclined on a metal chair with his feet on a small crate, reading a paperback. His weapon was leaning against the wall, at least four feet away. *I guess they don't need their best people down here, either.*

Tylor continued to scan the chamber but saw no other guards, and thankfully, no cameras. *I don't understand—her text said they would be everywhere.*

The fork truck was between him and the guard, so he used it as a shield the next time it moved toward the dock. Eventually, he was behind a stack of crates, no more than six feet from the driver.

"Sir," he whispered. "Over here."

The driver looked in his direction and almost cried out, but Tylor put his index finger on his lips and opened his eyes wide.

The driver glanced at the guard and then back at Tylor. "Who are you?" he said in a low voice.

"My name is Tylor York. I am here to help get you out of this place."

His eyes lit up like it was Christmas. "This is incredible! I am Dr. Gilford, and boy, am I happy to see you!" he said. "My God, you are actually here. I never really thought it would work, but it did! I can hardly believe it."

"What worked?"

"Oh, I have so much to tell you. But we can't talk here." He twisted in his seat to glance at the guard, the office suite, and then the ladies at the mixing tank.

"Okay, I know what to do," he said. "But you'll have to trust me."

Tylor looked at him expectantly.

"We need to get you out of sight. So, stay behind these crates while I move them toward the lunchroom. When we get there, duck inside and hide in the first room on the right. I'll get the girls and join you in a few minutes."

Tylor nodded and followed along as the fork truck moved toward the other side of the chamber. The floor was spotless, and the rubber tires rolled smoothly on the highly polished surface.

Despite his excitement, Dr. Gilford kept his cool—he drove slowly, but not too slowly, and kept a constant eye on the guard as they went. Thirty seconds later, Tylor was hunkered down behind the lunchroom refrigerator.

Outside he heard the fork truck drive away, and then there was silence for about five minutes. He nervously glanced around the room. *Shit, How do I get myself into these spots? If that guard walks in, I've had it. There is nowhere to run.*

Then, he heard voices approach. The guard was talking with Dr. Gilford. "What do you think you're doing? You are supposed to be working."

"We've been busting our buts all morning, and we need a break," he said. "But don't worry. We'll be back at it in twenty minutes or so."

"I don't know about this. I am not supposed to…"

"Nobody is going to know. Besides, the reaction will be running for six more hours, and there isn't a whole lot to do at the moment."

"Well, okay, I guess. But don't take too long. I'll be right over here, watching." He returned to his chair and picked up his paperback.

"Thank you."

Then, the door swung open, and Sharon walked in. She took one look in his direction and ran to his arms. "Oh, Tylor," she said. "I can't believe it. I'm so glad to see you. They told me you were dead." She held him tight for several seconds. "I thought I would never see you again. How did you get in here?"

"It's great to see you too. Are you all right? We were all so worried."

"I'm okay," she said. "Thanks to these wonderful people."

"Oh, and excuse me. I have a couple of new friends for you to meet." She stepped back and gestured toward Karen. "Allow me to introduce Dr. Karen Wells, not so dead after all, and this is Dr. Gilford. He saved us both."

319

Karen stepped forward and shook his hand. "I am delighted to meet you, Tylor. Sharon has told me a lot about you." She smiled.

"It's nice to meet you both," he said. "But is it safe to talk in here?" He didn't ask about her bruises.

"It's okay, at least for a while," said Dr. Gilford. "The guard has been here a long time and sort of trusts us, you might say. But we can't stay long."

"Before we get started," said Karen. "I understand you know Sam Wilson." She looked at Sharon.

"Yes, he and I have been looking for you."

"And my mother?"

"She is safe in Ft. Collins, and Sam is outside with the FBI."

"The FBI?"

"Yes. Just a few agents. You know, in case we need them."

She smiled.

"But they could use our help to get in. So, can we operate the truck elevator from down here?" He looked at Dr. Gilford.

He shook his head. "No, I've tried it many times, but there is just no way. It's interlocked with central control." He sat down at the lunch table and invited the others to join.

"You see," he continued. "The driver punches in a code number, but the motors don't start until it's acknowledged by the central control room. They monitor the entire operation."

"I see," said Tylor. "Can we bypass the system?"

He shook his head. "I am afraid not."

"How many ways are there to get into this place?"

"We call it the Cave, Mr. York."

"Fine," he said. "How many ways are there to get into the Cave?"

"Only three that I know of—the truck elevator, the west entrance, and the north entrance," he said. "The west entrance is smaller and meant for passenger vehicles. The north entrance is for big trucks and semis. They are both on the upper level."

"Upper level? How many levels are there?"

"Just two. There are two chambers down here and eight upstairs."

"Eight chambers like this one?" said Tylor. "This place must be huge!"

"Over thirteen acres, they tell me," he said. "But there are only three entrances."

"Wow. Okay, then. The other two entrances. How are they guarded? Which is the easiest to access?"

"The two upstairs are used frequently and are heavily guarded. I guess the truck elevator *would* be the easiest."

"Can it be operated from the control room directly? I mean, with no truck on the elevator."

"I think so."

"Good. Then that's what we'll do," said Tylor. "How do we get to the central control room?"

"We have a plan for that, but first we need to alert M."

Chapter 72

Ranger Clifton Yang arrived at nine-thirty—he was driving a dark green van with 'US Forest Service' painted on the door. Paul spotted him and stepped out to wave him in.

"You must be Ranger Yang," he said. "Agent Lyons told us to expect you."

"I am. Are you Tylor York?"

"No, I'm his partner, Paul Betson."

"Great to meet you. I need a place to set up the drone. Is there a clearing nearby?"

"About fifty yards ahead," he said. "If you give me a lift, I'll show you the way."

"Absolutely."

Ranger Yang hit a button to unlock the doors, and Paul walked around to the passenger side. When he sat down, he leaned over to shake hands.

"I am glad to meet you, Ranger Yang—we can sure use your help." He pointed through the windshield. "The clearing is on the other side of that rocky outcrop. Just bear to the left after that group of trees."

A couple of minutes later, they were parked and standing behind his van. Ranger Yang started to unpack the drone.

"So," he said. "Can you bring me up to speed a little? Agent Lyons just gave me the highlights."

"Sure," he said, "but I think we should wait until Sam Wilson gets here. He actually knows more about the case than I do."

"Fine. Then, if you could help me set this up, we'll have time to chat when Mr. Wilson arrives. Oh, and if it's okay with you, I would prefer a less formal conversation. So, please, call me Clifton."

"I would be happy to, and you can call me Paul."

Clifton nodded and started to unload the equipment. He removed the drone from its case, attached the landing gear, and set it on the ground behind the van. Next, he installed the rotors and mounted two cameras.

The case had special foam compartments for batteries—there were ten in all. "How many batteries will you need?" he asked.

"Just two," he said. "But they need to be a matched pair. So hand me the ones with 'A' stuck on the side."

Paul handed them over, and Clifton installed them in the drone. He then switched the power on, and they both climbed inside.

The interior of the van had been modified for field surveillance missions. A long workstation with three swivel chairs was installed against the left side of the cargo space. There were computers, recorders, communications gear, and a few gadgets he didn't recognize. Two large monitors occupied the center.

"Wow, I see you came prepared."

"We love this van," he said. "We've had it for almost two years now. It has everything we need."

"I've used drones before, but they always came with hand-held controllers," he said. "I've only seen rigs like this in the movies. I had no idea they actually existed."

"Well, we don't go out of our way to advertise. That's for sure. The less people who know about our tools, the better. Please take a seat."

Paul sat in the chair, nearest the front. "So, why are there two cameras?" he asked.

The rear doors of the van were open, so Clifton turned in that direction. "The camera on the right is for high-definition video, and the one on the left is for thermal imaging. The onboard processor can stitch them together in real-time—it's a very handy feature. We use it to track animals in the forest and to spot unauthorized campfires. But it will also show minute amounts of heat where it shouldn't be, like cracks around a door frame, for example."

"So you think it might show the entrances to the underground tunnels."

"It might," he said. "But it will also help us find hidden cameras and other security devices." He switched on the controller to check the cameras. "Do you think he will be here soon? The drone is ready to go." He touched the power button to test the rotors.

A few minutes later, Sam knocked on the outside of the van and stuck his head inside. "Gentlemen, I came as soon as I could. There was some traffic out on the highway that I needed to document."

Paul responded, "No problem, we've been busy getting the drone set up. And Sam, I would like you to meet District Ranger Clifton Yang with the US Forest Service. He prefers to be called Clifton. And Clifton, this is Mr. Sam Wilson, my other partner in crime," he smiled.

They shook hands. "It is nice to meet you, Clifton, and please call me Sam," he said. "Say, this is quite the rig you have here."

"We like it," he said. "Step inside, and I'll give you the tour. Paul was about to bring me up to speed."

The three of them spent the next fifteen minutes discussing the case. Sam did most of the talking, and Paul filled in the gaps.

"So you've only been working on this for a month?"

"About that, yes," said Paul.

"Well, you've done an amazing job," he said. "Maybe you should come work for me. We are always looking for good investigators."

"Thanks, but I don't think so," said Paul. "I like my weekends off."

Clifton smiled. "Well, okay then. Let's see what the mountain looks like from a thousand feet up."

Paul and Sam watched the drone lift off and then turned to the monitors.

"Right now, I have the video image on the left screen and the thermal image on the right. We can swap them if we want or overlay one on top of the other if we find something of interest."

Outside, the drone rose one twelve hundred feet straight up and then turned east above the forest. It was virtually silent.

"The resolution is amazing," said Sam. "Very impressive. Will the breeze be a problem?"

"No. It's a very stable platform. I've flown it in twenty-mile-per-hour winds several times. So today's breeze will be a piece of cake."

"How long will the batteries last?"

"About thirty minutes," he said. "And if they run low, the drone will automatically return to its launch point for a fresh set."

Sam touched Paul's arm. "Check it out. You can see our surveillance hides." He pointed at the monitors. "You can even make out Tylor's further to the south. It's amazing."

"Yep, it's great," answered Paul. "Too bad they didn't have one of these at the army surplus store."

"Fly a little more to the east," said Sam. "Let's check out the access driveways."

Clifton moved his joystick forward, and the drone responded. "They are hidden pretty well by the trees, but I can make out two driveways to the north and one further south. I guess that's the one Tylor saw." He veered to the right and hovered over the circle drive.

"Look at the thermal image," said Paul. "The outline of the elevator slab is clearly visible. It's incredible."

Clifton took note of the coordinates and then moved the joystick left. "Now, let's see if we can find the hidden tunnels."

Chapter 73

"How was your nap?" asked Jicard.

"A little short," she said. "What's on our agenda today?"

"I would like to talk for a while about security. Could you come to my office?"

"Sure," said Christi. "Would twenty minutes be okay?"

"Twenty minutes would be fine," he said. "I'll have Maurice set up a little lunch for us."

"Great, I'll see you then."

Christi had a permanent apartment in the security module. She hadn't been there for quite some time, but her wardrobe was just as she had left it. She selected a clean jumpsuit, washed her face, and headed out.

Downstairs, she found an idle 'Cave Security' golf cart and drove through the petroleum and staff living chambers on the way. When she reached Jicard's office, she knocked twice, and he opened the door.

"Welcome, my dear. You're right on time. Please, have a seat at the table." He followed her and pulled out a chair. "If you please," he said. "I'm afraid we will have to serve ourselves today. Maurice has other duties."

"No problem," she said. "What delicacies did he prepare for us?"

Christi had been looking forward to this lunch. Not only was she famished from the night's travels, but in her view, Maurice was the best thing that ever happened to the Cave. He was a true master of his craft.

"Well, let's see," he said. "From his menu card, it looks like we'll be having a Mediterranean lunch—Fattoush salad and chicken shawarma on pita bread with yogurt, herb cheese, and his special tzatziki sauce. There is a selection of fresh fruit and baklava for dessert. The beverage is lemonade."

"It sounds amazing. That Maurice, he is a force of nature."

Jicard nodded. "He *is* excellent."

He took a seat across from Christi and sampled the lemonade.

"So, what do you want to talk about?"

"First, I want to say how delighted I am to see you. It's been a long time, and I am happy that you're back."

"It's great to be back," she said. His bottle of Macallan was sitting on the credenza. "Maybe I'll stop by later this evening... I could help you polish off that bottle..."

"Yes. We *do* have some catching up to do. And when that one is empty, I'm sure I have another. Say about eight-thirty?"

"Done," she said. "But first, you wanted to talk about security. Did you have a specific topic in mind?"

"Yes. I think we should start with Dan Turner," he said. "At the moment, he is at the top of my list."

"I haven't talked to Dan in days. How is he doing?" She took a bite of her sandwich. "This is really amazing!"

"Well, I'm not sure how he's doing, or where he is, for that matter. He called yesterday in a panic. He said he's out."

"What do you mean, 'he's out'?"

"He said the FBI was looking for him, and he had no intention of going to prison." He took a forkful of salad. "The pantywaist... he is so weak."

"Does he have some kind of a plan? The FBI is pretty good at what they do."

"He said he was thinking about going to Canada for a while, and then maybe the South Pacific."

"I hope he makes it. The FBI would have a field day if they ever caught him."

"I agree. He could ruin everything."

"So, what are our options?"

"I don't see any reason to panic just yet," he said. "As long as we're in here, we're safe. The Cave is impregnable."

"Nothing is impregnable," she said. "If the FBI wants in, they will find a way."

"Maybe, but first, they have to find us. It's not like we have a neon sign out front. And even if they do manage to get inside, we always have the chute."

"I assume there will be room for two?"

"Absolutely," he said. "I wouldn't think of going without you." He took another sip of lemonade.

"But for now. I'm quite sure we're safe. And anyway, I need to hang around until I get the second payment."

"Three-point-six," she said. "That is quite a haul."

"It will be when it comes in," he said. "And there will be a lot more in the future. This order is just the beginning." He skewered a chunk of melon.

"That all sounds great, but what do you have in mind for me today?"

"I want you to take charge of security and make sure both entrances are buttoned-up tight. And I will talk with Dr. Gilford. Maybe we can improve the delivery schedule a bit."

***

Chip was sitting at his monitor when a text message popped up.

Chip:

The selection for today is egg salad. I know you'll enjoy it. Meet me in the dining area at twelve-thirty.

M

He read the message two more times and then deleted it. *Egg salad! It's actually happening!* He glanced a the time on his monitor, it read 12:18 p.m. *I have to go now!*

"Pedro," he said. "I am going to take my lunch now. I'll be back in an hour or so."

He nodded his head. "Sure thing. I'll keep an eye on things."

Chip left the control room and walked as calmly as he could toward the dining area. When he got there, he took his usual seat and picked up a menu to browse. He could barely contain his excitement.

A couple of minutes later, Maurice showed up carrying a sandwich on a serving tray. He placed it gently in front of Chip and said in a low voice, "I know you have been looking forward to this, my friend. Enjoy! And I suggest you finish it before five-thirty this afternoon." He straightened his back, turned, and casually walked toward the kitchen.

"Thanks, Maurice, it looks incredible."

The sandwich came with a small salad, some potato chips, and an ice-cold diet cola. It was delicious, and he savored every morsel. When he was finished, he removed a small note from the bottom of the plate, tossed his napkin in the trash, and left.

On the way back to work, he made a short stop in the men's room. He checked each stall to make sure he was alone and then retrieved the note from his pocket. He read it several times, memorized it, and then flushed it down the toilet. Ten minutes later, he was back at his workstation.

"How was lunch?" asked Pedro.

"It was fantastic. Maurice makes one hell of an egg salad sandwich."

"Yuck. I hate egg salad. Give me a ham and Swiss any day."

"To each his own, my friend," said Chip. "Did anything interesting happen while I was gone?"

"No, not a thing. Same old, same old," he said as he pushed his chair back. "But it's my turn now, and I think a ham and cheese sandwich sounds perfect."

Enjoy it, my friend. But today, I am loving the egg salad! He grinned and resumed his surveillance duties. The time on his monitor read 1:12 p.m.

Chapter 74

"Yes, Mr. Jicard. We are right on track. We have eight drums ready to go."

"Do you have enough materials to complete the order?"

"Yes."

"Then I need you to finish it by Wednesday."

"But sir!"

"No buts, Dr. Gilford. I don't care if you need to work around the clock. I need it Wednesday." He hung up the phone.

With the call finished, Dr. Gilford returned to the mixing tank. The girls were busy weighing components for the next batch.

"What does he want now, Gil?" asked Karen. "I'll bet he increased the order again."

"No. But he wants us to finish this one by Wednesday."

She turned to make sure the guard couldn't see her smile. "Well, it looks like he's going to be disappointed." She tilted her head toward the lunchroom.

Dr. Gilford responded with a smile of his own. "It does look that way."

***

Across the road, Special Agent Lyons was inside the van with Paul, Sam, and Clifton.

"That's right, Agent Lyons—we made a thorough search with the drone and pinpointed each of the entrances. We also verified the camera locations that York's team found."

"Any motion sensors?"

"None that we saw," he said. "But they tend to be quite small and are not easy to spot with a drone.

"Okay, then. When the team arrives, we'll blind one of the cameras with the laser and disable it. Then, when they send someone to fix it, we'll make our move."

"When do you expect the team?"

"A little after two," he said. "And in the meantime, I'd like to take another look at the drone video. Especially the truck elevator."

***

The SWAT team arrived at two-thirty in a Bearcat G3 armored vehicle. There were twelve agents in the group—six from Billings and six from Helena.

They wore black tactical body armor, bulletproof vests, and polished boots. Each agent was equipped with a standard issue Glock M17 semiautomatic pistol and an M4 carbine submachine gun. They also carried communication gear, and an array of tactical aids, including flashbangs, stinger grenades, and tear gas.

Special Agent Lyons briefed the commander on the situation and asked him to deploy the team along the edge of the wood on the west side of the highway. He asked Paul and Sam to remain in the van and help Ranger Yang with the drone.

Ten minutes later, Special Agent Lyons turned on the laser and signaled the commander. Immediately, three special agents sprinted across the road, made their way through trees, and climbed up behind the camera. They cut the video feed and took up positions to wait.

Inside the van, Clifton, Sam, and Paul watched the action on their monitors. "How long do you think it will take?" said Sam.

"I have no idea," replied Clifton.

***

A red light on Pedro's console flashed, and he automatically touched the corresponding camera button. Nothing happened.

"Damn," he said. "We lost camera twenty-eight."

"Another one?" said Chip. "That makes three this month."

"I know. How many have to die before they decide to upgrade?"

331

"Beats me," he said. "But I'll make the call."

As he punched in the number for maintenance, he felt a grin starting to form. He turned away from Pedro and straightened his face. The time on his monitor read 3:05 p.m.

"That's right, camera twenty-eight." He paused for a couple of seconds. "Thanks. I'll tell him."

"They said they'd get right on it. I'll cancel the alarm."

He rose from his console, strolled into the server room, and pressed the 'Acknowledge' button on the video camera rack—it stopped blinking. He then found the controls for the tunnel entrance door, flipped a rocker switch from 'Auto' to 'Manual', and returned to his station.

"I acknowledged the alarm."

"Thanks, man." The light on Pedro's console was off.

***

Karen caught her foot on the leg of the mixing tank and tumbled to the floor. "Damn," she said as she lay sprawled on the polished concrete.

Sharon ran to help her. "Are you okay?"

"I think so." She took Sharon's hand and then fell back to the floor. "Son of bitch, I may have broken my ankle!"

The guard looked up from his book and yelled, "Hey! What's going on out there?"

Sharon yelled back, "Dr. Wells hurt herself. I need some help to pick her up."

The guard jogged over, and Dr. Gilford walked out from the lunchroom.

"Are you okay?" he said. He stooped over and grasped her arm. "Just take it easy. I'll get you into the lunchroom, and then we'll call for help."

"Okay," she said. "But it really hurts. I think I may have broken it." She staggered to her feet and hung heavily on the guard's shoulder.

As they turned, Dr. Gilford injected a sedative in the back of his neck. Three seconds later, he was on the floor.

Tylor had been watching from the lunchroom and ran out to help. Together they dragged the guard inside, where they bound and gagged him.

"Well," said Dr. Gilford. "We're committed now! If we fail, we're dead." He grabbed the key from the guard's pocket and headed for the door. "I hope your friends are out there."

Karen and Sharon followed immediately. Tylor stopped at the guard's chair, picked up his carbine, and sprinted after them.

Karen looked at him suspiciously.

"Just in case," he said.

***

Twenty-eight minutes had passed since the agents cut the video cable. "Agent Lyons? What do you think?"

He glanced at this watch. "Patience," he answered. "Let's give it a little more time."

"Roger."

Eight more minutes ticked by—and still nothing. Then, suddenly, the door began to move. It was virtually silent.

"Heads up, team."

The agents crouched to the side, and when the maintenance man stepped out, they grabbed him. One of them spoke into his headset, "Target is secure, all clear."

They found a medium-sized boulder, wedged it into the doorway, and then stepped inside. The agent spoke again, "The tunnel is at least thirty feet wide and about twenty feet high. It is well-lit and smells of diesel exhaust. The floor is asphalt, and there are surveillance cameras." He screwed a silencer onto the barrel of his pistol. "We blocked the door open to maintain radio signal."

They walked past the maintenance golf cart, stayed close to the wall, and shot out the cameras as they went. When they reached the entrance to the main chamber—they crouched low.

"We have reached a large round chamber. It's brilliantly lit and very large, at least five hundred feet in diameter. There is a security barracks to the left, a truck dock to the right, and a farm patch in the center. So far, we are undetected, but there is no cover. We need the Bearcat." Then, he grabbed his left shoulder and pitched over backward. Blood soaked through his shirt and seeped between his fingers. "Shit, I'm hit," he said. "Send in the cat!"

The second agent pulled out his first aid kit to work on the wound and spoke into his headset, "Shots fired, agent down, send back up." The third agent raised his weapon.

Outside, Agent Lyons nodded, and two more agents ran into the tunnel.

***

"Where is Douglas?"

"What?"

"Douglas. He went out to work on the camera, but he hasn't returned. And look, all of the cameras in the north tunnel are out. I better call security."

Chip picked up a paperweight and struck the back of his head. "I am afraid I can't let you do that, my friend." He slumped to the floor.

Pedro no sooner hit the floor than Jicard walked into the room.

"Mr. Jicard!" said Chip. "What can I do for you?" he fidgeted with the mouse on his workstation.

"What's going on, Chip? It seems we have a breach in the north tunnel." He looked down. "And what happened to Pedro?"

He let go of his mouse, looked at Jicard, and took a deep breath. "Well, sir, I noticed the cameras were out in the north tunnel. And when I said something to Pedro, he told me that maintenance was working on them. But I knew they weren't. When I asked him again, he got angry and started for me. I picked up the paperweight and hit him. I thought he was going to punch me."

Jicard looked at him lying on the floor. "That was quick thinking, Chip." He crouched down and felt his pulse.

"Honest, Mr. Jicard. I didn't mean to hurt him. He was just acting crazy."

"He'll be okay. We'll have the doctor check him out. Did he do anything else?"

Chip paused for a moment and then pointed toward the server room. "He was in the server room a few minutes ago. I don't know what he was doing."

Jicard walked in, checked the cameras for the north tunnel, and then looked at the entrance door controls. "It looks like he switched the door to manual."

"Really?" he said. "Why would he do that?"

He flipped it back to automatic, returned to Pedro's workstation, and then punched in a speed dial number.

Christi answered, "Security."

"How's it going?" he said. "We lost the cameras in the north tunnel, and Pedro had the door set on manual."

"Yes, I know. There are FBI agents in the tunnel. I think we hit one of them, but I don't know how many there are," she said. "We're on it."

"Good. Round them up and put them in the storage chamber cells. I'll be out later." He looked at Pedro again. "And send Max to the control room."

"Will do," she said. "It looks like we'll have to postpone our little drinking party."

"Yea, it's a shame. I was looking forward to it," he said. "But the scotch isn't going anywhere—we can do it another time."

***

Sam and Paul had their headsets on and were glued to the monitors. Ranger Yang was controlling the drone.

"Clifton, look at that," said Sam. He pointed to the monitor. "Zoom in on the entrance. I think it's closing."

"It sure is." He zoomed in close, and they watched as the massive door slid shut. When it hit the boulder, it didn't even slow down. "Wow," he said. "That is one powerful door. It crushed that boulder like it was nothing."

Inside, the five agents surrendered as thirty armed guards entered the tunnel.

"Good afternoon," said Christi. "I think you may be in the wrong place. I don't remember inviting the FBI."

The second agent replied, "I am Special Agent Peter Stanton," he said. "We have a wounded man here, and he needs medical attention."

Christi lowered her pistol and put two rounds into the agent's head. "He doesn't need medical attention any more."

"You bitch!" One of the agents raised his weapon and stepped toward her. He was killed immediately.

"Now, just settle down, gentlemen," she said. "There is no need for more bloodshed." She took a couple of steps backward. "If you'll be kind enough to drop your weapons, my men will escort you to your quarters."

***

The steel bolt slid closed with a metal clang. And a voice outside the cell said, "Relax for a while, Pedro, and think about what you've done. I'll be back later to chat."

Max! That son of a bitch! BJ rose from his bed and walked to the peephole in his door. "Hey buddy, my name is BJ. Who are you?"

"I am Pedro," came the reply. "What is this place?"

"This, my friend, is chamber ten. It's where they put you when they don't want to see you any more."

"The Cave only has eight chambers."

"We are one level below the Cave—chambers nine and ten are down here. What did you do?"

Pedro touched the back of his head gingerly. "I don't actually know," he said. "I was sitting at my workstation watching my monitors when I saw something odd—I work in the central control room. And when I picked up the phone to call security, my best friend, Chip, hit me with something." A large goose egg was forming and it hurt like hell. "Now I'm here, and I don't understand. Why would he do that?"

"Who is Chip?"

"Chip Woodsen. He and I work in surveillance. We watch the monitors and keep track of what's going on in the Cave."

"Wow, no kidding. So, what did you see?"

***

Tylor, Karen, Sharon, and Dr. Gilford were listening from the end of the cell row. Karen was standing closest to the door.

"Who is that? I hear someone talking," she said. "Max left a while ago, but I still hear voices." She opened the moved slowly. "Come on, let's check it out." The four of them crept along the passageway.

"I think they're in the first two cells," she whispered. She looked at the others and placed her index finger on her lips. "Quiet." She tiptoed forward and peeked into cell number two. "Hello, in there?" she said softly.

He walked to the peephole to look, but Karen had stepped to the side. "My name is Pedro. Who are you?"

"I'll ask the questions," she said. "How did you get here, Pedro?"

"Mr. Jicard, I mean Max, put me in here."

"So, you work in the Cave. Where exactly?"

Dr. Gilford pushed Karen to the side. "Did you say your name is Pedro? Are you Chip's friend?"

"Yes, my name is Pedro Sanchez. Chip knocked me out in the control room, and the next thing I knew, I was in here."

He used the guard's key to let him out. "I am sorry this happened to you, Pedro. Please forgive him. He was acting under orders."

"Orders? Whose orders? What's going on?"

"Please." He held up his hand. "I'll explain everything, but first tell me, who is in the other cell?"

Pedro turned his head toward cell number one. "He said his name's BJ."

BJ! Let me at him! Sharon grabbed the key from Dr. Gilford and unlocked cell number one. She then took the carbine from Tylor and stood in the door.

"What are you doing, Sharon?"

"Relax, Tylor. I've got this."

She looked at BJ. "Well, isn't this an interesting situation?" she said. She pointed the carbine at him, chambered a round, and released the safety. "You're the bastard that attacked me in the parking garage."

She slid her right foot back a few inches to improve her stance and pointed the carbine directly at his head. "And you are also the son of a bitch that killed Melvin. Aren't you? And poor Molly Greene, too."

"I don't know what you're talking about, lady. I've never seen you before in my life."

"You lying bastard!" Tears ran down her face, and her body trembled with anger. "I'll shoot you dead, right here. I swear I will!" She pulled the trigger.

Chapter 75

"I am Special Agent Peter Stanton, with the FBI, and we have a warrant for your arrest. I suggest you release us at once and surrender."

"Well-rehearsed, Agent Stanton, it sounded very official. But since you and your comrades are in my detention cells, I don't think your position is very strong."

"Mr. Jicard, I urge you to reconsider. Things will go much better for you if you surrender."

"I doubt that."

"I say again, surrender now or face the consequences."

"I'll take the consequences if you please. I haven't worked for all these years and built what I have, to give it up now."

"Mr. Jicard, what you have done is kidnap two hundred people, and conspire to murder at least three more, now five, and perhaps more."

"I didn't murder anyone. And what I have built is the best biogenetic research facility in the country, maybe the world. We have made breakthroughs here that you can't even imagine. The scientists working at this facility are not kidnapped, they are employed, and paid handsomely, I might add."

"Your time has run out," Mr. Jicard said. "We have a force of agents outside right now, and more are on the way. Your position is not sustainable."

"And you, sir, are deluded. The Cave is impregnable. We are self-contained and have had sufficient supplies for several years. Had it not been for a misguided maintenance man, you would still be outside scratching your head. And if it comes down to it, I do have two hundred scientists to bargain with."

"So, you admit to kidnapping."

"No."

"What about the murders?"

"Our research is top secret and critical to our nation's security. It will literally change the world. We have the best people in the country working here."

"And that justifies murder?"

"Of course it does," he said. "What do a few ordinary lives mean, against a chance to change the world?"

"So you admit to murder?"

"No. I certainly don't," he said. "Dan Turner was responsible for all of that."

"So it was just you and Dan Turner, then."

"No. Mr. Fu Tong set the overall objectives, I broke them down into individual goals, and Dan Turner decided how to meet them. I understand he's on his way to Canada right now."

"Are you telling me that Fu Tong financed all of this?"

"Of course," he said. "What did you think?"

Agent Stanton looked down and shook his head. "You're a psychopath," he said. "You're completely mad."

Christi had been standing nearby. He stepped back from the peephole and turned toward her. "Button everything up. I want maximum security."

"Yes, sir," she said.

***

The round hit the wall two inches from BJ's head.

"What the hell? You crazy bitch! You almost killed me."

"I will," she said. "If you don't tell me the truth." Her jaw was clenched.

"Okay, okay." BJ took a deep breath. "I'll tell you."

"Start with Melvin Richards," she said. "What did he ever do to you?"

"Nothing. I didn't even know him. It was just a job."

"A job?"

"Right." He moved closer to the wall and a little further from the loaded carbine. "Dan ordered the hit, and I rigged the car... it was just a job."

"And..." She stepped closer.

"I don't know why. I promise I don't. I just did the job." A bead of sweat appeared on his forehead. "But later, I heard him say that Richards was nothing but a boy scout, and couldn't be trusted to keep his mouth shut. I guess he was afraid he might go to the cops."

"Okay, I can believe that," she said. "And what about the homeless ladies?"

"I don't know anything about no homeless ladies."

A second round hit the wall on the other side of BJ's head. "The next one will be in the middle."

"Oh, the homeless ladies! You mean Linda and Molly?"

"Yes, Linda and Molly."

"Well, that was another Dan Turner job. He wanted me to find a ringer for Dr. Wells and then make it look like an accident."

"And why did Linda have to die?"

"She was Molly's best friend—we had to silence her. But Tiny was very gentle—she never felt a thing."

"Okay, Mr. BJ, I won't kill you right now. But I'm sure the FBI will have a lot more questions. And you will answer them. Right?"

"Yes, ma'am," he said. "I will answer them."

"I'll let them know where you are." She locked the door and handed the weapon back to Tylor. "Thanks," she said. "Let's get going."

As they made their way past the pit, Max appeared.

"Stop right where you are, all of you!" he said. "Where do you think you're going?"

Tylor stepped from behind Dr. Gilford and pointed the carbine at his stomach. "I don't know who you are, mister, but I suggest you get out of the way."

Max picked up a piece of a packing crate and hurled it at Tylor. It hit the side of the carbine and knocked it from his hands. Then he grabbed Karen by the neck and stepped back a few feet. "Down here, nobody tells me what to do. I am the boss— I'll snap her neck like a twig and then toss her in."

Tylor held up his hands. "Okay, okay, mister. I don't know who you are, but maybe we can talk about this."

"This is bullshit," said Dr. Gilford. "And I am not going put up with it any more." He picked up the piece of packaging crate and struck Max on the side of his head. "You unbelievable bastard! You are not going to hurt anyone ever again."

Stunned by the sudden attack, he released his grip on Karen—she dropped to the floor. But an enraged Dr. Gilford was not about to stop, and he hit him again—much harder.

Max's eyes grew wide. He staggered back, off balance. Dr. Gilford charged and drove his right shoulder into Max's gut—he lost his footing entirely and stumbled backward. Dr. Gilford dropped to the floor, arms outstretched.

As Max fell, he twisted his body in mid-air and tried to land on one of the small ledges. He reached for a handhold but missed, and the sharp granite sliced through his forearm like a razor. His eyes went wide when he saw the exposed bone, and the scream that followed was bloodcurdling.

From the edge, the group watched as his body tumbled its way down. When it finally hit bottom, his arms and legs were broken, there was a long gash in his back, and his neck was gushing blood—but he was still conscious.

Then the Scutigera appeared, dozens of them. They went for the blood first and then attacked his body. In minutes they were everywhere.

"It looked like an accident to me," said Tylor. "He simply lost his footing."

The rest of the group nodded as they walked north in the tunnel. There was no emotion or regret, and they could still hear his screams as they climbed the concrete steps.

***

Chip was at his station, keeping an eye on things and wondering what would happen next. *Boy, we really put our foot in it. If Gil's plan fails, we're cooked.* Just, then a light blinked on his console, and he hit the acknowledge button. It was Pedro.

"Chip! It's me. Can you see me?" He was using a two-way monitor.

"How can you be on the monitor? I mean, where did you come from?"

"Calm down, buddy. Dr. Gilford told me everything, and I am totally on board."

"I am sorry about hitting you," he said. "I didn't know what else to do."

"Don't worry about it. We'll sort it out later."

"Thanks."

"Okay, so, we just came up the stairs at the petroleum research lab."

"I know. Is that Dr. Wells with you?"

"Yes. I'll explain everything later. But right now, we need to know where Jicard is."

"I've been watching him. Right now, he's standing next to the detention cells. They have three FBI agents in there."

"They captured some agents?"

"Yes. They came in through the north tunnel when I disabled the door. You noticed them shooting out the cameras in the north tunnel, and that's when I had to hit you. I am so sorry about that."

"Forget it, Chip."

"Okay," he said. "Anyway, when they got to the main chamber, the security guards shot two of them and captured the rest."

"Damn," he said.

"I know. What are we going to do?"

Dr. Gilbert stepped into the frame. "Chip, we can't stop now. There are more agents outside, and we need to get the door open again. Can you do it from the control room?"

"I can, but if Jicard finds out, he'll kill me."

"Okay, we'll be there as soon as we can," he said. "Don't flip the switch until we get there."

"You got it. I'll wait until you get here. But hurry. He just finished talking with that Christi woman, and she's on her way to the main chamber. It looks bad, my friend."

***

"Please let me back inside," he said. "Mr. Jicard will hurt my family."

"No," said Agent Lyons. "I am sorry, Mr. Spencer, but we can't do that."

"Well, then, you have to help me. If he finds out you have me, he will track me down, and then he'll kill my family."

"We will protect your family, Mr. Spencer, I promise." He handed him a notepad and pencil. "If you write down your home address, we will have an agent at your house in twenty minutes."

He took the pad and looked at him over his glasses. "Do you promise?"

"Yes."

"Well, then, okay, I guess." He wrote down his home address and handed the pad back to the agent. "I'll answer any questions I can."

"Good," said agent Lyons. "Now, is there any way to open the tunnel door from the outside?"

"No. It's not possible. It was built to keep people out. It is a foot and a half thick and weighs more than two hundred tons."

"Hmm. Is there some way to keep it from closing once it's open?"

"Oh, sure," he said. "We have to block it open when we work on it."

"And how do you do that?"

"Well, there are two ways." He sat back in his chair. "You can lock it out electrically from the control room, or you can use the maintenance panel in the tunnel wall."

"Do we need any special tools to open the maintenance panel?"

"No, just a screwdriver. But first, you have to unlock it, and the security department has the key."

"What kind of lock is it?"

"Just a padlock, but it has a special round key."

"Can it be cut off?"

"I suppose so," he said. "You would need a large set of bolt cutters, or maybe an acetylene torch."

"Great, we have a pair of bolt cutters with us," he said. "So, you and I will camp out by the door, and when it opens, you can go inside and disable it for us."

"But won't they see us waiting outside?"

"No. We knocked out the rest of the cameras. They're blind—at least on this side of the mountain."

"And if I do that, disable the door for you, you'll make sure that Jicard leaves my family alone. Is that right?"

"Absolutely. I guarantee it."

"Okay then. You have a deal."

He made a call to arrange for the agent. "The agent is on his way, don't worry."

Now, all we need is to get the damn door open. Where are you, Peter?

***

344

"Where did you learn to handle a weapon like that?" said Tylor. "You're amazing."

"My father taught me when I was a girl," she said. "He used to be in the army."

"You're just full of surprises. Aren't you?"

"Oh, you have no idea," she said.

Karen stopped the cart around the corner from the control room, walked up, and took a peek. "There is a guard at the door," she said. "What do we do now?"

"You mean apart from just killing the guy?"

"Yes, apart from that."

"I could shoot off his left earlobe," said Sharon. "It would hurt like hell, but it wouldn't kill him."

"We don't want to disfigure anybody either."

"Could you just shoot him in the leg?" said Tylor. "Enough to take him down, but no permanent damage."

"Nothing to it." She picked up the carbine and joined Karen at the corner. "I will put a round through his right calf muscle. He'll drop like a sack of potatoes." She pushed against the corner to steady her aim. "Get ready."

At ten yards, her aim was flawless. She squeezed the trigger once, and the bullet hit his calf, dead center. He dropped immediately and clutched his leg with both hands.

"Son of bitch," he said. "Somebody shot me!" He reached for his radio, but Tylor got there first.

"I don't think you'll be needing that." He kicked it away and picked up his weapon.

Sharon arrived and knocked out the guard with the butt of the carbine. She then tore a strip of cloth from her jumpsuit and bound his leg. "He'll be out for a while, but he'll be fine," she said. "Now, let's get that door open."

"I think I love you," said Tylor.

She touched his arm and smiled. "I know."

Chip stuck his head out and scanned left and right. "It took you long enough," he said. "Say, what happened to the guard?"

Dr. Gilford pointed to the unconscious body. "Hold the door open, so we can get him out of sight."

He stepped back while Pedro and Tylor dragged him inside. Sharon and Karen followed, and Chip froze as they entered.

"Dr. Wells," he gasped.

She looked up. "It's Chip, right?"

"Yes, ma'am. It's such a privilege to meet you."

Pedro piped up. "Chip! Snap out of it and open the north entrance."

He looked at Pedro, not quite understanding.

"Chip! The door!"

It took a couple of seconds, but he finally realized where he was. "Oh, right, the door!"

He walked into the server room and headed straight to the tunnel entrance control rack. He flipped the mode switch to 'Manual' and the operating switch to 'Open'.

"Okay," he said. "That should do it. It's going to be quite a show."

He returned to the control room and looked at Pedro. "This may be the last time we get to work together, my friend. So, man your workstation."

***

Using a map provided by Mr. Spencer, the FBI entered the tunnel in the Bearcat. When they reached the main chamber, they blanketed the area with tear gas and used flash bangs to disorient the guards. It took only minutes to overpower them.

From there, they drove through the cane research chamber to equipment stores and opened the detention cells.

Christi was watching from a distance and decided it was time to go. She swung her cart around and drove to Jicard's office. When he answered the door, she said, "They're inside now and moving from chamber to chamber. We should surrender."

"Not me," he said. "I have too much to lose."

"But they'll be here in minutes. We are outgunned, and there are too many of them."

"Then we will use the chute. I have a car standing by to take us to the airstrip. We can fly to Fu Tong's and then to the Philippines."

"It will never work," she said. "They'll catch us."

"Not if they don't know where to look."

He escorted her through his office and down his private elevator. From there, they ran east to tunnel N-7 and jogged past the petroleum research stairway.

"Are you sure you know where you are going?"

"Absolutely," he said.

They continued north. The ceiling sloped down, and the tunnel lights were off, so they used flashlights. It felt cold and damp and smelled musty.

"This is creepy," she said. "And I hear water dripping somewhere. Are you sure?"

"Of course," he said. "And don't worry. I test it at least once a year. It will be fine."

"Well, okay, if you say so."

They ran another fifty yards, and then she stopped. Jicard stopped too.

"What is that noise?" she said. "It's a clicking sound. It's all around us."

"Oh, it's nothing," he said. "It's just a few of our slithering friends." He panned his light on the wall, and dozens of troglobites scurried away. "They're everywhere down here. But they're harmless." He took her hand in his. "Come on. It is just ahead."

When they reached the door, Jicard pulled it open. The screech of its metal hinges sent shivers up her spine.

"I think it needs some oil," she said.

They stepped inside, and he flipped on the lights. The stench was worse. It was stale and damp, and the sound of dripping water was more noticeable.

"What is that stench? I think we should go back," she said. "I have a bad feeling."

"I tested it last fall. It's fine," he said. "And it always smells like this." He bolted the door behind them.

Five feet away sat a small metal car on a steel track, and it looked like it belonged on a roller coaster. It was bright blue with a white stripe down the side. Jicard led her toward it—she hesitated.

"It's safe, I promise."

She stepped in first and slid to the far side of the bench—Jicard squeezed in beside her. The dripping sound seemed louder. "How far is it?"

"The track is about eight hundred yards long, and the ride takes less than a minute," he said. "It comes out on the west side of Greenough Lake."

"Let's not," she said. "I don't like this. Let's go back."

He pulled a lever to release the car, and it started to roll.

"Where are the brakes? Can we stop if we need to?"

"There are no brakes. The end of the track slopes up, and the car will stop on its own. Just hang on," he said. "It will be over before you know it."

They continued to move forward and picked up speed as the slope increased.

"How fast are we going? It feels really fast."

"Relax, we're already halfway there."

The sound of dripping water grew louder as they descended, and rivulets of water streamed down the walls. Ahead, the tracks leveled out for a bit and were partially submerged.

"What is going on?" said Christi. "Is this normal?"

"No," he said. "This is not normal." He grabbed her hand and started to stand up. "Hurry, let's jump." But he was too late.

The tracks ramped up slightly and then disappeared entirely. The overhead lights were out, and Christi screamed as they launched into the darkness. Jicard gripped the handrail.

They fell twenty feet, hit the opposite wall, and splashed into a pool of icy water. The impact crushed the front left side of the car and pitched them both forward. Christi's legs were trapped in the wreckage, and Jicard's were broken. He was on top of her.

"Son of a bitch," she said. She tried to move but could not. "It's pitch black in here. I can't see a thing. What just happened?"

"I'm not sure," he said. "I guess water from the lake seeped into the tunnel and created a sinkhole."

"No shit," she said. "How do we get out?"

Just then, a boulder, dislodged by the impact, slid down on top of them. It crushed Jicard's left arm and then rolled into the water. He screamed in agony, and the car settled deeper. It was up to Christi's chin.

"It's freezing! Do something!" she screamed. "My life is not going to end like this."

"I'm trying. But I think my legs are broken."

"I don't care if they're cut off!" she said. "Just get us the hell out of here!"

He reached up with his right hand, pulled himself out of the car, and slid into the water. His legs were twisted at odd angles, and the pain was unbelievable. But he gritted his teeth and turned on his light.

"If you can reach your flashlight, switch it on," he said.

She felt around under the water and found it wedged in the seat cushion.

"Shine it over there," he said.

They panned their lights around the sinkhole, but there was no way out.

"You've killed me! You stupid, arrogant bastard." She was livid. "You unbelievably stupid son of a bitch. You have killed us both. I told you to go back. But no, not you!" Her legs were almost numb. "Why did I ever believe you?"

The end of the missing tracks was far above, and the walls were wet and smooth. There were no handholds for climbing. He looked back at Christi.

"I am so sorry, my dear," he said. "But I don't think we're going to make it. There is no way to climb out."

"Shit. And nobody knows we're down here."

"I am deeply sorry. I had such hopes for us. You know you're the only one I ever really cared about."

She tried to respond, but the car shifted, and she went with it. When it stopped again, she was at least two feet below the surface—bubbles rose from her mouth as she struggled.

Jicard tried to reach for her, but he could only watch as she fought for her life. She flailed her arms violently and pushed on the handrail with all her might, but it was no use. Finally, the bubbles stopped, and her arms were still. Her death stare was clearly visible in the beam of her flashlight.

He looked away and hung his head in despair. "My dearest Christi. You were the one," he muttered. "Why didn't I tell you? You were the only one." He found a large flat rock sticking out of the water and dragged his mangled body from the water. He exhaled in exhaustion.

"So, this is it," he said aloud. "This is where I die." He panned his light down and saw something white sticking out of his leg—a piece of his shin bone. Blood spurted with each beat of his heart. *It's a good thing that the water is ice cold... It shouldn't be long now...* He laid perfectly still, ignored the pain, and waited for death—he was prepared.

But then, in the darkness, he heard soft tapping noises—at first only a few but then, many more. He used his flashlight to investigate and saw giant centipedes slithering down the wall—they were inches from his head.

Their pale white bodies were more than a foot long and at least three inches in diameter. They had dozens of legs, bulging eyes, huge mandibles, and sweeping antennae.

Adrenaline flooded his body. His eyes went wide, and he shrieked in terror. "Noooo!"

Moments later, the first group found his bleeding leg, and a second targeted his face and neck. Soon, hundreds were slithering and surging all over his body—each one seeking its share of the bounty.

As parts of his body were chewed off and devoured, he screamed and writhed in pain. He tried to swat them away, but there were simply too many.

Scutigera! God, help me!

Chapter 76

Special Agent Harris flew to Helena to join in the arrest. Including her, there were a total of eleven agents on the team. They arrived at the Fu Tong Estate at about five o'clock in the afternoon and immediately split up. Two agents proceeded directly to the airstrip, one detained the guard at the main gate, and the balance drove up the main driveway.

The unauthorized entry tripped a silent alarm, and Fu Tong switched on his security monitors. "So, they've arrived," he said aloud. "Well, I'm not surprised. I should never have trusted that idiot, Jicard. He is a rude and arrogant man. What an amateur."

He finished what he had been working on and put it safely in the top drawer of his desk.

Outside, the team reached the upper helipad and had it surrounded. There would be no escape by chopper.

He darted to the French doors and peeked out. *Good, the veranda is still clear.*

Special Agent Harris looked at the team and raised her arm. "We need a man on the side entrance and one in the back. Agent Baker and I will go in the front. The rest of you cover the gondola. She pressed the doorbell, and a few seconds later, it opened.

"May I help you?" said Drysdale.

The agents flashed their identification, and she said, "I am Special Agent Harris, and this is Special Agent Baker. We have an arrest warrant for Mr. Fu Tong. Please take us to him."

"I am sorry, ma'am, but he is currently on a conference call with some business associates, and I cannot disturb him. If you would care to wait, I am sure he will be finished shortly."

"That won't be happening," she said. "Please step aside."

The agents pushed past Drysdale and proceeded into the foyer. She turned to him, "Take us to Fu Tong, now."

As they made their way down the hallway, Fu Tong stepped onto the veranda. It had rained heavily during the night, and small puddles dotted the stone surface.

The smooth soles of his patent leather shoes were not designed for off-road use, so he ran a zig-zag pattern to avoid the puddles. But the extra few seconds were sufficient for the agent at the rear of the house to spot him. He sprinted across the veranda.

"Stop! FBI!"

The seat of his golf cart was wet, but he ignored it. *Armani will never know.* He jumped on, flipped the switch to 'Forward', and it took off like a shot.

Agent Harris ran through Fu Tong's office and stepped onto the veranda just as the agent arrived.

He pointed north. "He is on a golf cart. I think he's headed for the gondola."

She spoke into the radio. "All agents converge on the gondola. Now!"

As Fu Tong sped down the driveway, he noticed the agents running through the trees. He snapped the wheel left at the first footpath and pressed the accelerator again. Far below and nearly a mile away, the crest road came into view—it was deserted. *If the plane is ready, I just might make it.*

He called the airstrip, and his pilot answered immediately, "Mr. Fu?"

"Yes. It's me," he said. "Warm up the engines. I will be there in a few minutes."

"Will do, sir."

The agents arrived at the upper end of the gondola, but Fu Tong was already halfway down the mountain. So two of them grabbed a golf cart shuttle, picked up Agent Harris, and took off in pursuit.

The main gate is blocked. He must be headed for the dam. She used the radio again, "We think he is headed for the airstrip. Cover the south end of the dam."

Two agents standing guard at the airstrip commandeered a shuttle and sped off.

Fu Tong raced down the mountain. He drove as fast as he could, but the winding path was treacherous. At one point, the switchbacks were so tight; he nearly rolled the cart. *Be careful, you fool. You have to get there in one piece!*

Finally, he reached the top of the dam. The crest road was smooth and flat and only thirteen hundred feet long. He floored it.

He was across in less than a minute, but the agents from the airstrip were there to meet him. He made a U-turn to go back, but the agents from the mansion had reached the north end by that time.

This is a most unfortunate development, but I can't allow them to take me. I have but one card to play. He drove to the center, stopped his cart, and moved toward the handrail. There was a strong breeze blowing across the lake. It was icy on his face.

"Mr. Fu Tong. I am Special Agent Evelyn Harris with the FBI, and I have a warrant for your arrest. Please come with us quietly." She stopped about twelve feet away.

"No, Agent Harris. I am sorry, but I don't think I will be doing that." He stepped closer to the handrail. "Are you aware that the road we're standing on is one hundred twenty feet above the river?" He inched closer.

"No, Mr. Fu. I didn't know that."

"Well, it is," he said. "And it will be more than adequate for the task at hand." He peeked over the side.

Excess water from the previous night's rain was surging across the spillway, and far below, the river was a torrent.

"Don't even think about it," she said. "You don't have to die."

"Stay where you are, Agent Harris. I have very little to lose at this point, and I will dishonor my family no longer."

She stood motionless. "Okay," she said. She held up her hands, palms out. "I won't approach. But before you go, please tell us why you did all of this."

"Why?" he said. "You must be kidding. I did it because nobody else would. I had to do it."

"You had to do it? You had to kill two homeless ladies from Denver? They were no threat to you. Why I ask you, did you have to do that?"

She shifted her weight to her left leg, and her arms were crossed in front of her body.

"And what about your engineer, Melvin Richards?"

"I had nothing to do with the killings," he said. "They were all Jicard. I was livid when I found out. He told me Richards was a boy scout and couldn't be trusted."

"And the guard at the pipeline terminal? Why did he have to die?"

"Actually, that was an accident. Tiny just hit him too hard—he never meant to kill him. But regardless, he was acting under Jicard's direction. In fact, I gave strict orders that there be no casualties during the attack."

"I guess you just can't trust twisted psychopaths and murderers."

He shook his head. "No, it would appear not."

"And what about Dr. Nugent? What was his role in all of this?"

"Amil? Oh, he had nothing to do with any of it. He is a brilliant biochemist running a successful alternate energy company, and that's all. His work with sugarcane will change the world. But as far as the Kentala project was concerned, we told him nothing. He was utterly oblivious."

He put both hands on the handrail.

"Oh, and please tell him not to worry about capital for the expansion. I left him my entire fortune—money, property, businesses, everything. There is a letter in my office for him—it explains everything. He will be a very wealthy man, indeed."

He then climbed over the top and clung to the outside of the railing. Agent Harris rushed to stop him, but he was gone before she took two steps.

At that point, the face of the dam sloped toward the river at a very steep angle. And when Fu Tong jumped, he did so with resolve. He flew out so far that he dropped nearly eighty feet before he touched the concrete. His head hit first, followed by his upper back and tailbone. The force of the impact snapped three vertebrae in his neck and split his skull wide open—blood and brain matter spewed out and soaked into the porous surface.

His then lifeless body tumbled the rest of the way down and plunged into the surging Missouri River. It was two and a half miles downstream before the agents found it.

Chapter 77

Mordecai and Tylor arrived in Dusty Fork with a truckload of equipment and twenty drums of the acetone/DMSO solvent.

Jack had the pipeline open when they arrived, and together, they rigged up a delivery system. They used a modified cleaning pig with injection nozzles to mount the ultraviolet lamp and used pressurized solvent as the propellant.

As the pig moved forward, ultraviolet radiation softened the polymer, and the solvent dissolved it away. The resulting sludge was then pumped into an empty tank truck for disposal. Progress was slow in the beginning but improved as the pig advanced.

When the pipeline was cleared, they focused their attention on Tank 101. It was half-full of the gray crystalline material, but the piping was too small to use the pig approach. So, they came up with an alternate method.

They hung the ultraviolet lamp through the inspection hatch and used hoses to pump in the solvent. Twenty-four hours later, the entire mass had turned to sludge, and they transferred it to waiting for tanker trucks for disposal.

The following week, they drove to Alliance and applied the cleaning pig method to the Kentala pipeline. It was a much bigger job, so they used four separate rigs. The Kentala Company supplied the labor and relied on Tylor and Mo for supervision. Sixteen men worked around the clock for two solid weeks. But in the end, the pipeline was cleared, and it was back in operation three days later. More than fifty truckloads of sludge were removed from the pipeline.

Chapter 78

During his brief time on this planet, Melvin Richards touched the lives of countless people. And as Robin James said, 'He was one of the most caring and genuinely good people she'd ever known'. Over two hundred fifty people were in attendance at his memorial service.

Everywhere he went, he'd made friends. They came from southeast Texas, where he grew up, and from Austin, where he went to college. There was a large contingent from the Denver area, and at least a dozen people flew in from Broadview and Billings. He was universally loved.

For Sharon, it was a heart-wrenching and soul-crushing event. She cried pitifully for most of the day and sometimes could barely speak. Of course, Tylor, Paul, Sam, and Karen were there for her, but the impression was indelible. It was a day that would live forever in her memory.

***

For Fu Tong, there was far less sympathy. In his will, he requested that his body be laid to rest with those of his family on Haengun-do. And Dr. Nugent carried out that wish to the letter. It was buried in an unmarked grave at the southern edge of the cemetery and quickly forgotten. The only people in attendance were the grave diggers.

Two years later, that part of the cemetery was flooded by rising water levels and later destroyed by a raging typhoon. His casket was washed out to sea and was never seen again.

***

The remains of Linda Johnson and Molly Greene were released to the care of their loving families. For them, it was a confusing time of sorrow and relief.

Nobody knew where Linda and Molly had gone while on the streets, and their families worried constantly. So, when the authorities contacted them, they were devasted. For days, there was much anger and resentment, but in the end, they came together and gave them a heartfelt farewell. Their bodies were placed in a small cemetery on the north side of Denver.

***

His loving wife and two children mourned Norris Hankin's passing. The service was held on a Saturday afternoon in Alliance, Nebraska, and was well attended. At least thirty people from the Kentala Company were there, along with an equal number of family members. Declan Kentala gave the eulogy.

During the following week, he met with Terra to set up trusts for Martin and Charise. He gave her a check to cover their college expenses and promised to match Norris' life insurance payout.

***

A search and rescue team recovered the bodies of Dr. Jacobs and Max from the pit, along with the skeletal remains of seven other people.

Dr. Jacobs' body was returned to his family, but no one came forward to claim Max. DNA samples were collected from the others, but their identities remain a mystery.

When the team ventured into the chute, they found the bodies of Christi and Jicard, but before they could be recovered, there was a massive cave-in. They remain there still, buried forever under a thousand tons of granite.

***

The families of the FBI agents that Christi killed in the Cave sued North States Recovery jointly for twenty million dollars. In arbitration, it was determined that the company was not liable for the independent and unauthorized actions of its employee, so the suit was dropped. Dr. Nugent, however, felt that the company should be held responsible, so he paid the claim in full.

***

The remains of Dan Turner were recovered from the tanker truck fire and returned to the Billings coroner. Nobody came forward, and they were eventually interred in a numbered grave.

Epilogue

Six months later…

The weather north of Helena was unusually chilly for November. Temperatures were in the teens, and it was snowing heavily. Downstream of Holter Dam and far above the river, the gondola swung violently in the wind.

"Whoa," said Tylor. "That was a strong one!"

Sharon gripped the handrail with one hand and Tylor's forearm with the other. "I'm glad it's only a four-minute ride."

Tylor looked ahead. "Hold on. We're almost there."

"Are we the last to arrive?"

"I think so."

The gondola reached the upper station and came to a smooth stop. A golf cart shuttle was waiting for them—Sharon climbed in first, and Tylor followed.

"Welcome the Nugent Estate," said the driver. "It's good to have you with us."

"It's good to be here," said Sharon. "How've you been, Chip?"

"It's a lot better than staring at security monitors all day. I can tell you that," he said. "It's great to see the sky again, and the mountains here are so beautiful."

"And how is Pedro doing?"

"He's working in the maintenance department—he always enjoyed tinkering with things. Dr. Nugent is a great boss, and Pedro and I are having a great time."

"I'm glad to hear it," she said. "Have they all arrived?"

"Yes. Most of them flew in yesterday afternoon before it started snowing, and Sam and Karen, that is, Dr. Wells, got here this morning. You two are the last."

She turned to Tylor. "This is so exciting. It will be great to see everyone again."

***

Moments later, they were greeted by Maurice at the front door. "It's nice to see you again." He smiled. "Please, come this way. Dinner will be served in the gallery."

Sharon gave him a quick hug and followed him down the hall. When they entered, she was awe-struck.

The room was magnificent, with a high arched ceiling and delicate chandeliers. Doors and columns were trimmed with hand-sculptured woodwork imported from Brazil, and sliding glass doors offered a sweeping view of the veranda.

Tasteful displays of seasonal cornstalks, gourds, and fall greenery were positioned strategically, and the table was exquisite. It was white linen with a black centerpiece topper. The topper was decorated with small white pumpkins, colorful gourds, and occasional bits of lush greenery. White pillar candles in clear glass hurricanes were added to complete the look.

Individual place settings featured the finest china from Stoke-On-Trent, lead crystal glassware, and polished sterling silverware. Name cards and menus were printed in a sophisticated black script.

"It's stunning," she said. "Will you be our chef this afternoon?"

"No. Actually, I will be at the table with the rest of you for a change. I have a kitchen staff now, so these days I spend my time planning and supervising. But I assure you the quality has not diminished."

"I am sure it hasn't. It will be a delight to have you with us. I've been looking forward to it."

"You are too kind, Miss Wagoner."

She circled the table to check out the place cards. Dr. Nugent was across from the sliding glass with Dr. Gilford, Dr. Thomas (Bud) Xavier, Dr. Stephan Coleman, and Maurice on his right. Her place was on his left between Tylor and Sam, and Karen's and Paul's were further down on Sam's left.

"Is that you, Sharon?" It was Sam, and he was standing close to the glass with Karen. "Come over here, so we can get a look at you!"

She gave him a quick hug and then noticed a conspicuous sparkle on Karen's left hand. She stepped back. "Do you two have some news to share?"

Karen grinned. "In fact, we do." She held out her hand so she could get a better look. "The wedding will be in March, and we want you and Tylor to be there."

"We wouldn't miss it," she said. "And your ring is gorgeous. Sam is one lucky guy."

"I certainly am," he said. "I just couldn't stand being apart any longer, so I popped the question." He was beaming. "She and her mother moved to Mowata last month, and our new house should be ready in time for the wedding."

"Fabulous," she said. "You certainly deserve some happiness."

"Well, it doesn't stop there," said Karen. "We're also setting up a new laboratory in Crowley. I will have both my work and my love at the same time. And my mom will finally be able to retire."

***

Paul was standing next to the bar, nursing a glass of scotch.

"Hey man, it's good to see you."

"It's great to see you too." They shook hands. "I saw you come in with Sharon. Are you two, like an item now?"

Tylor blushed slightly. "I don't know if you'd call us an item, exactly. She's still working through some stuff. But it's getting better, and I'll be there when she's ready."

"You know, I'll always have a soft spot in my heart for her. After all, I did see her first." He grinned.

Tylor smiled, too, and stepped closer to the bar. "Do they have any imported rum?"

***

At five minutes to four, Dr. Nugent stood up and loudly cleared his throat. "Excuse me, folks! May I please have your attention?"

Everyone stopped what they were doing a turned his way.

"Maurice has informed me that dinner will be out in a few minutes, so please find your places."

When they were all assembled, he continued.

"First, I would like to thank you all for being here today. Thanksgiving is next week, and we have a great many things to be thankful for. Please raise your glasses."

There was a slight pause.

"I am fortunate, indeed, to call you my friends. Here's to a healthy and prosperous future.."

"Here, here," said Tylor.

There was clinking all around, and he paused for a moment while they enjoyed their champagne.

"Please have a seat. I have a few quick remarks and a couple of announcements."

Everyone relaxed as he continued.

"It has been a tough year. We've been through a lot. And if it hadn't been for the dogged determination of Tylor, Sam, and Paul, we certainly would not be standing here today. We owe them a lot."

Everyone applauded.

"Thank you," he said. "I've just a couple more things...

As you know, the Cave is closed. It took three long months, but it has now been completely decommissioned. All entrances to the system were sealed with explosives.

The Gelator-T production was stopped, and the formula was destroyed. The FBI filled the drums with real vegetable oil and alerted the German authorities. Three weeks later, Mr. Fazal al-Latif and seven of his associates from Baghdad were arrested in Munich.

Everyone in the Cave has been fully compensated and offered a position in our new Billings facility. I am pleased to say that only six people declined. Bud accepted the position of director, and Drs. Gilford and Coleman will be his advisors.

The Owanka facility will come online early next year, and the Stillwater-Yellowstone expansion is going forward. So farnesene production will soon be a reality.

And finally, we have one deep regret. We are losing one of our brightest colleagues to a new life in Louisiana. Yes, Karen is leaving us.

She and Sam have started a new lab in Crowley and will be getting married in March. I, for one, intend to be there."

There was another round of applause.

"And of course, we hope to be one of their biggest clients in the future."

Maurice held up his hand and nodded. "Sir? It's time."

"Oh, it seems that dinner has arrived. Please enjoy…"

***

After dinner, while they were laughing and enjoying a few cocktails, Tylor received a text message. He stepped close to the glass doors to read it.

Sharon joined him and peered over his shoulder. The snow had stopped, and the veranda was blanketed with a thick layer of fresh powder. It sparkled like diamonds in the moonlight.

"What's up, Tylor? Why are you over here all alone?"

"Oh, I was just reading a text message," he said. "It looks like my next project may be in the New England area."

"Really?" She took a sip of chardonnay.

"Yeah. It should get started after the first of the year."

"You know, my folks live in Vermont, and I'll be with them over the holidays. Maybe you could come for a visit."

Printed in the USA
CPSIA information can be obtained
at www.ICGtesting.com
LVHW021818280624
784154LV00005B/741

9 781800 1677